The
ECSTASY
of
OWEN MUIR

The ECSTASY of OWEN MUIR

a novel by

RING LARDNER, Jr

Cameron & Kahn · New York

Copyright 1954, by Ring Lardner, Jr

All Rights Reserved. No part of this book in excess of five hundred words may be reproduced in any form without permission in writing from the publisher.

SECOND EDITION

PRINTED IN GREAT BRITAIN

PART ONE

The
MILK
of
PARADISE

CHAPTER I

At the age of twelve Owen Muir was elected president of the student body at the East Point, Long Island, Progressive School. It was one of those reversals of form which sustain the sporting character of popular rule.

Mr. Mollison, the headmaster, had decreed that the office, with its responsibility of leading the Pledge of Allegiance at morning assembly, must automatically fall to the class president of the eighth and highest grade. Since the school was new and it had been easier to recruit children at the lower age levels, the eighth was also the smallest group numerically, consisting, at the term commencing in February 1935, of five girls and three boys. Mr. Mollison himself served as its supervising instructor and it was he who suggested that only the boys be considered for the presidency, implying that it would be undignified to have a female in so important a post. The girls accepted this proposal less readily than the boys but there was too much disaffection among them to permit organized resistance.

Of the three possibilities left in the field, Owen, who was the youngest, shortest and fattest child in the class, was ignored until after six deadlocked ballots between the two older boys, and even then his name was not entered in nomination by a member of the electorate. Rather it was Mr. Mollison, concerned lest their restless young minds become impatient with the democratic process, who pointed out that a third candidate might serve to break the tie.

Owen's classmates quickly recognized the merit of the idea. It did not matter how unqualified the new nominee was, since his only function was to vote for himself and thus reduce the significant ballots to an odd number. But this, Owen, sharing the general estimate of his inadequacy, failed to do. Twice more the vote was counted at four to four.

Mr. Mollison had not anticipated the fresh impasse but he rose to it in full awareness of the contribution Owen's parents were making to his potentially profitable enterprise. The traditional American solution to such a dilemma, he advised his pupils, was for the two deadlocked candidates to retire in favour of the one around whom a new unity could be forged, free from the festering memories of past factionalism. He cited to advantage the precedents of James K. Polk in 1844 and Abraham Lincoln in 1860, omitting the controversial analogy of Warren G. Harding.

There was no ninth ballot. Owen was elected by unenthusiastic but unanimous acclamation.

The news was communicated to Willis Muir in an effusively congratulatory note from Mr. Mollison and so startled the financier that he managed to remember it during the nightly hour set aside for children and cocktails. Owen sought to acquaint his father with the actual circumstances of his election, concerning which he felt only shame and depression. Though he was fearful of the anger he expected in response to his confession, it was temperamentally impossible for him not to correct a false impression of such magnitude. He was bewildered when his father cut him short, dismissing the painful details as totally irrelevant.

'What are you telling me all that nonsense for? Look, Ownie, you're a bright fellow in your own peculiar way, skipping grades and getting those marks. You ought to be beginning to think about things in grown-up terms, realistically. One of the basic rules of life, and don't you ever forget it, is results count, nothing else does. If a man's got a million dollars, you don't take it away from him by proving it was just luck he made it. Or in a war, the hero is the man whose idea worked. Period. Only small minds quibble about whether it was a good idea or not.'

'Isn't that kind of a broad statement, Willis?' Owen's mother said. Although she was still in her thirties, overweight had impaired her original decorative function and she was beginning to make occasional forays into the realm of thought. Her gaze, however, remained discreetly on the olive which she was trying to pluck, as decorously as she could, from her Martini. 'I mean, aren't you saying the end justifies . . . ?'

'Small minds and women,' Mr. Muir broke in by way of

amendment. Having thus brought the subject to a conclusion, he turned to nine-year-old Phyllis and strove with his most coquettish smile to win her attention away from the sports pages of the *New York Daily Mirror*. 'What do you say, sweetheart? Want to sit on Daddy's lap for a while?'

Phyllis read to the end of a paragraph and rose. 'Sure,' she said amiably. 'If Ownie and me can go to the movies tonight.'

No such eminence as that achieved in grammar school came to Owen during the remaining seven years of his scholastic career. These were passed in New England institutions which so treasured the revolutionary tradition in which they had been conceived that they doled it parsimoniously among young men whose higher education could be budgeted at more than ten thousand dollars.

His only distinction during this period was that he continued to be very fat. In defiance of normal adolescent procedure, his girth rose relentlessly with his height, and his sporadic experiments in diet and exercise were so consistently discouraging that he had abandoned them entirely by the time he matriculated from a colonial brick preparatory school to an arch-Gothic university. His nickname — Buffalo, more often rendered Buff — was a successful invention of his own, thoughtfully contrived to forestall less kindly alternatives.

In college as in school his unorthodox appearance was held against him and the fact that his attitudes were also nonconformist made him even more of an outcast. Barred from some undergraduate pursuits by ineptitude and from others by popular demand, he was compelled to the solace of his own devices. He listened to Sibelius in the hours devoted to football practice, read Schopenhauer during proms, and absorbed facts while his classmates were exchanging gossip. His academic standing was never distinguished, except at an occasional coincidence of the curriculum with his own researches, but in spite of all the obstacles to education with which the campus was so lavishly equipped, he was on his way to acquiring one when he was called upon to register under the Selective Service Act.

This event, occurring in the spring of 1942 and near the end of his junior year, found him drastically at odds with the main stream of American opinion. After a promiscuous procession of allegiances to the most divergent philosophies, he had been pursuing for a whole year an almost sequential line of thought from Gandhi back to Antisthenes, returning, by way of Rousseau and Thoreau, to Tolstoy. He was so engrossed in *My Religion* on the afternoon of Pearl Harbour that it took the raucous distraction of a dozen radios to bring him out of his room. His mind wholly given to the brotherhood of man, he did not stop to determine what was so exciting the commentators before he made a typically mild inquiry about the unusual amount of noise.

His gentle manner was not matched in the response he got. 'Where you been, you stupid prick bastard? Japan's bombed the American fleet!'

Owen absorbed the news for two seconds, then reacted. 'We mustn't fire back,' he said urgently.

The polemical arguments of the great Russian swayed his reason with their logic and passion, but their most compelling effect on him was to revive and justify his repressed impulse toward religion. This had been strong in him from his initial pre-school enravishment with the idea of an all-knowing God and through his encounter, at the age of eight, with *The Christ Story Retold for Young Readers*. But then his faith had been shaken and all formal religious sentiment dispelled by the shocking spectacle that confronted him on a chance intrusion of his parents' bedroom. His father, alone, was kneeling at his bedside in prayer. Owen had fled before his presence was discovered, and refused, without explanation and against considerable pressure, to attend church or Sunday school again. Some facet of his abnormally sensitive nature made it impossible to embrace a deity with whom Willis Muir could also find communion, but he was quite unable to explain his determination in terms of a logical cause and effect. As in all the important decisions of his later life, it was the emotion and not the reasoning behind it which was dominant and utterly compelling.

Tolstoy's presentation of Jesus as the prophet of scorn for state authority dissipated the effects of this traumatic memory. The God of gentleness and loving forgiveness and anarchy could not be the same as his father's God. He had been right, he now realized, in his opposition to orthodox, organized religion; wrong only in his sense of guilt about it. He became a devout, fervent non-churchgoer instead of a morbid, troubled one. He pledged his mind and body and soul to the service of the pre-Constantine Christ and the principle that evil must not be resisted with evil. Although his intense youthful appetite led him to compromise in the matter of meat-eating, he was, in the broader application of the doctrine, a more consistent Tolstoyan than Tolstoy. His temperament was so much less fierce than the founder's that he was able to devote far more of his time to the practice and contemplation of brotherly love than to indignation and anger toward the property system which subverted it. Despite the fact that he actually suffered emotional wounds of much greater acuteness than ordinary people would from the same blows, he assumed that others were at least as sensitive as he was, and concerned himself more with protecting them than himself, applying this transference even to individual representatives of groups he despised. But when an issue was directly joined, as between his draft board and himself, he summoned a resistance which was resolute to the ultimate degree of non-violence.

Still several months short of his twentieth birthday, he was not threatened with immediate induction. The requirement was simply that he register so as to be on the books when he reached service age or when the age limit was lowered to include him. But even this step called for submission to a power with which his conscience told him he must be inflexibly unco-operative. His first impulse was to ignore the obligation entirely; then he heard that many such cases of failure to register went unnoticed for months. A more significant contribution to the cause in which he believed would be a public declaration of his position, setting an example for other unregimented minds to follow. Accordingly he addressed a letter to his draft board: 'Gentlemen: I do not intend to comply with the instruction that I register for military service. Such a course is in obvious conflict with divine law and I must in all conscience continue to abide by the latter. My decision on the subject is final, and any communication from you will be returned unopened.'

It occurred to him that by using the mails he was collaborating with the processes of a government which had no moral right to exist, but the alternative of sending a private courier the two hundred and fourteen miles to East Point seemed a trifle ostentatious.

The chairman of the local board, a patriotic textile manufacturer with a small but advantageous army contract, was outraged by the body of the letter but restrained his indignation when he observed the signature. His profits had provoked yearnings for a timely investment of a more rewarding character than war bonds, and Willis Muir was the obvious man from whom to seek advice. This consideration led him to the theory that Owen's missive might be no more than a boyish prank and instead of referring it to the FBI, he called on the youth's father for clarification.

Muir was furious at what he also assumed to be Owen's inconsiderate levity, and summoned his son home by telegram. It was only when he mentioned the affair to his wife and daughter at dinner that he got the first intimation the problem might be serious.

'I bet he really means it,' said sixteen-year-old Phyllis. 'He's a pacifist, didn't you know? What gets me, though, is why the army would want him. The Japs must be praying for targets like Ownie.'

'Why can't they leave him alone?' Mrs. Muir complained. 'Why, with all the people in the country they could make soldiers of, do they have to pick on a boy who's just getting started in life? Willis, can't you do something?'

'I intend to,' said Mr. Muir grimly. 'I intend to set our little honey-lamb straight on his obligations to his family and his country. A stunt like this could kill a job I've got lined up in Washington.' Their looks requested a further explanation. 'It's one of those dollar-a-year things that if I played it right I could make enough to retire on.'

'If you need Ownie's co-operation, you might as well forget it,'

Phyllis said. 'The way I heard it from Bert Sayre, the big slob's so Christ-bitten the Notre Dame backfield couldn't get through to him.'

Phyllis's information turned out to be accurate. Mr. Muir began with a frontal sally against Owen's position and found it could not be taken by storm. He regrouped his arguments for a flanking attack. Though he disagreed sharply with the boy's views, he told him, he nonetheless respected his right to hold them. It was unthinkable, in the birthplace and citadel of democracy, that a man with sincere religious scruples against violence would be compelled to act counter to his principles. On the other hand, and there were always two sides to every issue, he mustn't blind himself to the fact that his stand was likely to be misinterpreted as cowardice, and that this kind of unfortunate impression could create unnecessary shame and distress for his innocent sister, his sainted mother and, yes, even his not invulnerable father.

'Luckily,' he concluded, 'there's a way out which can take care of everybody's sensibilities all round. Just looking at you, it's obvious you weren't meant to be a soldier and the chances are they'd put you in 4-F anyway, in the normal course of events. But in your case there doesn't have to be any risk; we can make sure of it. I've talked to Masterman, the chairman of your board, and he's agreed you're a physical washout sight unseen.'

Owen began his answer with a sigh. He had no filial feeling for his father but he didn't exclude him from a compassionate attitude toward humanity in general. 'I wish I could do it your way, Dad, really I do, but I can't. I'm not just a passive pacifist. The thing I want to accomplish, the main thing any one individual can accomplish, is to make his opposition known, to add his voice to the others on the same side and persuade as many people as we can that this isn't their war.'

'It's too late for that. Has been ever since the dummy election with that damn stooge Willkie. No matter who got us into the war, we've got to fight our way out of it. It's a question of survival.'

'Survival of whom?' Owen demanded. 'The people or the

government? Do you really believe that if a hundred and forty million people refused to fight back, they'd be massacred?'

'They'd be enslaved anyway.'

'How do you enslave a slave? What greater authority could anyone exert over me than what a handful of men in Washington claim: the power of life and death, the right to order me to kill in violation of God's express commandment? I don't see why I should lift a finger to help that handful of men stay in authority.'

'I can understand that feeling, Ownie.' Muir leaned closer to his firstborn, resting a hand on his knee. 'But first things first. When we finish the job overseas, we'll bring Doug MacArthur back and knock that whole crew out of there.'

'I'm not talking about any particular people who happen to be in power at the moment. I'm talking about government in general.'

'Oh, you mean there's too much of it? Well, you're perfectly right. Been growing piece by piece till it's way out of hand.' His manner became positively intimate. 'And I'll tell you something, Son, it's all part of a plan. They don't need this much power in Washington for what government was originally supposed to be about — I mean just keeping things in order.'

'Of course they don't!' Owen was stirred by a sudden startling hope. The last thing he had expected from this interview of obligation was any kind of meeting of minds and yet, incredibly, they seemed to be nearing agreement. He began to feel more warmly toward his father than he had since before the dimly remembered occasion when Mr. Muir had taken an arbitrary hand in his toilet training. 'The idea of the state as simply a central co-ordinating agency for the general good of society is a mask to keep people from seeing its real function.'

'That's a very shrewd observation. What would you say that real function was?'

'The protection of private property. That's the beginning and end of all evil, Dad!' He spoke with growing emotion, dazzled by the prospect of such an improbable convert. 'Laws, police, jails, armies — they all serve only one purpose, to keep property in the hands of the owners and out of the hands of everybody else.

That's why Jesus told his disciples to dispose of their worldly goods and ...' He broke off, aware of a drastic change in Muir's expression. Their moment of harmony had ended with alarming abruptness.

'You know what kind of talk that is, don't you?' His father regarded him with cold and menacing eyes. 'You know what it means to oppose your government in time of war, to defy the express orders of the Commander-in-Chief? Treason, my boy. An extremely ugly word.'

Owen felt the painful sadness that anger from anyone always created in him. The actual words meant little to him; treason had if anything a favourable connotation in his mind. But his distress at the unchristian emotion in his father's tone was the more intense because of his previous hope for accord between them. He said listlessly, without bitterness: 'I didn't think you felt too warmly toward the Commander-in-Chief yourself.'

'I don't. Toward him as an individual, that is. But I'm phoning the White House in the morning, to place my services at his disposal for the duration.' His rage had departed and there was an unfamiliar note of humility in his voice, born of the realization that his son was as strong-minded as he was. 'Why can't you do the same sort of thing, Ownie? Hang on to all your reservations about the government and the property system and so on, but just put them aside until this war is over with. Then there will be plenty of room again in America for different kinds of ideas. And even if there isn't, you're bound to have outgrown yours by then.'

'I'm sorry,' Owen said with sincere regret. 'It won't be easy for you, will it, in Washington, with a son like me? I wish I didn't have to complicate things for you but there just isn't anything I can do about it. Maybe you can make them understand you're not responsible for the way I am.'

'But I am responsible. In the eyes of God anyway. I should have read Freud while you were still a baby.'

This, to Owen, was the most surprising turn in the whole conversation. 'I didn't know you ever had read him.'

'Not read, exactly. But a fellow gave a talk a few years ago at the

Bulls and Bears, and I've never forgotten it. Made me see what I could have done with you if I'd known about the Oedipus complex.'

'What? What could you have done?'

'Made it clear to you there was no reason to be jealous of me. You could have had your mother full time for all I cared. Then this whole rebellion impulse would never have come up.' He grew thoughtful, brooding over his past errors. 'And even without that, there's another thing I could have done later on, when these tendencies first started showing up. Put you in a good military school.'

It was the first time Owen had ever seen his father in such a self-critical mood.

He had to draw on his full reserve of stubbornness to withstand the efforts to keep him out of jail which now commenced. His draft board tried to give him a more acceptable status as a member of a recognized religious group with conscientious scruples against war, but Owen denounced all organized forms of Christianity as perverters of the apostolic creed. The War Department, which had availed itself of Willis Muir's services on the theory that his former connections with German cartels made his appointment a gesture of broad national unity, sent an informal representative to see Owen. This functionary sought to persuade him that enrolment in the Medical Corps would involve him in exclusively humanitarian work, but he replied that he could not bind the wound of any man who intended to fight again. Even after he was finally convicted of violating the Selective Service Act, the judge spoke enticingly of the civilian public service agencies into which he might go with a suspended sentence, but Owen maintained that they all contributed to the prosecution of the war.

The judge, who had once been the pride of his high school debating team and whose mind had not deteriorated noticeably since, probed for a flaw in this reasoning. 'The court finds your thinking very superficial, young man, like that of all extremists. If you carried your contention to its logical conclusion, the only solution would be a life of absolute indolence. Any job you take in these times releases someone else for war work.'

Owen always paid careful attention to other people's arguments, even to the point of sometimes undervaluing his own, but this was an area he had worked over thoroughly in his mind. 'I don't see it that way, Your Honour. It's like saying — well, you probably disapprove of prostitution...'

'Of course. Few men on the federal bench have devoted so much of...'

'You'd have scruples, wouldn't you, about being an attorney on a retainer for a brothel? But it would be quite a different thing to refuse to take any job because some girl might conceivably be encouraged to become a whore because you got it instead of her. You couldn't even be a judge according to that line of reasoning. The only consistent way to oppose prostitution would be by a life of absolute indolence. I don't mean any disrespect, I hope you realize. I'm just trying to make clear to you why I can't accept a proposal which I'm sure Your Honour meant very kindly.'

'The only thing you make clear,' said the judge, 'is that you are an arrogant egomaniac with a large yellow streak running down your spine. I wouldn't be surprised to find out that you are an enemy agent besides, but that's outside the purview of this proceeding. Still, your attitude is something I'm obliged to take into consideration in pronouncing sentence, as well as the importance of the precedent in this kind of case at this time.'

He finished by giving Owen a sentence of two years, making him eligible for parole in eight months and for conditional release, assuming good behaviour, in nineteen and a half.

Because of the nature of his crime Owen was sent, not to a penitentiary, but to a Federal Correctional Institution in the lumbering country of northern Wisconsin, near the Michigan border. Other jails of this type, closer to the area of his residence and conviction, were filled beyond normal capacity by new wartime crimes, and this one, named for the nearby village of Moose Head, was absorbing such of the overflow as could be entrusted to its relatively mild custodial restraints. Newly built and designed to suit the most modern techniques of reform, Moose Head was founded on two harmonious theories. One was that hard, outdoor physical labour had a benign effect on the criminal mind. The other, emphasized in the Congressional debate preceding its authorization, was that it could provide inexpensive lumber for a variety of federal projects.

Here again Owen was compelled to invoke the distinctions, so clear to him and so annoyingly subtle to the undedicated, which his conscience imposed on him. The issue arose during his classification interview with Mr. Blankenship, the associate warden, whose responsibility it was to find a job for each inmate in keeping with his needs and those of the institution.

Blankenship was a scholar as well as an administrator, and adhered to the advanced school of penology. As he could seldom be restrained from pointing out, his background was a blending of the academic and the worldly. After winning his master's degree in psychology with a thesis entitled *Comparative Responses to Clinical Improvisations in Pseudohysterical Introversion*, he had gone to work for one of the large advertising agencies which were beginning to enliven the drab greens and browns of the American landscape with brilliant highway displays. By 1929 he had been able to compute that another year of shrewd speculation would furnish him the capital to start his own agency, and by 1932 he was desperately taking civil service examinations in search of a post that promised modest security and eventual retirement on pension. Despite the intense competition of that period, he had qualified as an assistant supervisor of education with the Bureau of Prisons and risen to his present rank through his stubborn insistence that enlightened confinement could rehabilitate criminals, even in a nation which kept a quarter of its employables out of work.

Surveying Owen's soft, ungainly body, Blankenship said it was lucky the boy's educational background qualified him for one of the few clerical jobs in the place, and that there happened to be a vacancy in the record office. He was taken aback when Owen began to question him about the job, and astounded when the new inmate finally concluded that he would be unable to accept it, explaining that he could not take part in any administrative function.

'There's nothing personal about it,' Owen assured him. 'It's simply that I don't approve of prisons and don't want to help run one.'

'Quite a few of our guests here share your opinion about prisons,' the associate warden said with a smile. 'But I hardly expected to hear that kind of talk from a man of your background. Surely, whatever resentment you may feel about your own case, you must recognize that most of the inmates need a dose of our treatment.'

'I recognize it's commonly believed they do, but I don't happen to believe anything can be accomplished by compulsion. Not to get into any big discussion — I just want you to understand that my principles on the subject were formed long before there was any question of my going to jail myself. I believe no good can come from the use of force in any situation, whether it's what the Allies are trying to do in the war on a large scale or what you're doing here on a small one.'

'You have the virtue of consistency. I wish you could overcome your scruples, though, because this record office spot would give you a chance to see how we work from the inside. Then, whether you changed your mind or not, at least you'd have more firsthand information to go on. Now you must admit that's reasonable, isn't it?'

Owen hated to hurt the feelings of a man so anxious to be persuasive, but there was no way of avoiding a direct answer. 'It would be just as reasonable to say I had to have a try at combat and kill one enemy before I could really be sure that what I'd done was a mortal sin.'

Blankenship decided that more forceful tactics would have to be applied. 'You realize we have the power to assign you to any type of job we want to, and if you refuse to work we can put you in isolation — solitary confinement.'

'Whatever's customary.' Owen said obligingly. 'I won't hold it against you personally.' He gathered his bulk and raised it to a standing position. 'How do I get there?'

'Wait a minute. Don't be so precipitate, man. I'm only speaking of what I could do, according to the regulations. Actually, I suggested an office job primarily because I thought it would be better for you. But I can also assign you to one of the lumberjack details if you think you could stand up under it. What have you ever done in the way of physical work?'

'Literally?' He searched his recollection earnestly, conscious that he ran the risk of sounding facetious. 'Well, I helped another fellow change a tyre once, two — probably three summers ago. Also I've cut flowers with my mother on several occasions, reluctantly, when I couldn't get out of it — sometimes pulled up small weeds the gardener had overlooked.'

'And you feel ready to chop down trees?'

'Not ready, resigned. Where are they?'

After his first three hours on a two-man saw, Owen collapsed so completely that he had to be rolled out of the working area to a safer spot in which to succumb or revive. The two stalwart prisoners who propelled his inert mass were sharply divided as to which of these two possible results was the more probable, and wagered three packs of cigarettes, in violation of institutional regulations, on the question. The proponent of recovery won a qualified victory but the margin was so narrow that the loser volunteered as a stretcher-bearer in the hope of a reversal en route to the prison hospital.

Because of the demands of the armed forces, Moose Head had no doctor during the war. Instead, three medical technical assistants, known as MTA's, from the Public Health Service, whose training would have seen them through the first-aid test required of an air-raid warden, served alternate shifts in charge of the hospital. Among them existed a friendly competition to see who could detect the greatest number of malingerers. A malingerer, according to the rules of this contest, was defined as any inmate who sought medical attention and did not receive it.

The MTA on duty when Owen was borne in cast a suspicious glance at the contents of the stretcher, noting that the eyes were open and the arms apparently capable of autonomous movement. 'Any bones broken?' One of the men who had carried him started to answer but the MTA indicated he wanted to hear from Owen himself.

'I'm all right,' Owen said in a faint, laboured voice. 'Just a little dizzy.'

'Stand up,' commanded the MTA.

Owen obeyed but it took him a full minute to achieve an erect position and when he had, he fainted again and fell headlong, his forehead crashing against the tile floor. Blood streamed from the resulting gash, furnishing the MTA the kind of concrete symptom with which he could cope. 'Head wound,' he wrote on the card in front of him, and ordered Owen put to bed.

On his second attempt at the saw, Owen lasted almost an entire working day before the officer in charge of the detail pronounced him, over the boy's objections, the victim of a technical knockout. By this time the soft flesh of his hands was so thoroughly blended with the shreds of the cotton gloves designed to protect them that the inmate male nurse who treated him had to distinguish between the two substances by Owen's vocal reaction to the pressure of the tweezers. But his convalescence took only half as long as before.

Actually, to his own and everyone else's surprise, it developed that in spite of disuse and external distortion his body was a rather fine and basically sound product. After three months of strenuous and painful adjustment, while the surplus fat was converted into sweat and muscle, it responded much like a truck whose gross tonnage has been cut in half and its missing cylinders restored at the same time.

At the end of six months his work reports marked him as one of the most ruthless destroyers of timber among the inmate population. A tree not wholly lost to fatalism would have shuddered at his approach.

CHAPTER II

Startling as Owen's physical progress was, the prison authorities had to face the fact that this was a mere side-line to their correctional function. As emphasized in frequent mimeographed instructions from Washington, their job was to transform criminals into orthodox citizens, to teach the inmate the futility of unlawful behaviour, to strengthen his character, reshape his values, and win him over to righteousness. These principles applied to young Muir as well as to narcotic-peddlers, counterfeiters and interstate procurers, and there were three main channels through which they were supposed to be inculcated.

One was the education department, which conducted classes to fill the vast gaps in prisoners' formal schooling, ran the library and a vocational training programme, and strove generally to straighten out the mental quirks of the inmates. The supervisor of this department at Moose Head was a man who recognized some, though by no means all, of his limitations, and rigidly refused to attempt any work with a man whose score on the IQ test fell below 75 or above 140, maintaining that he could not communicate adequately with either of these minorities. Owen was one of the two current inmates who were thus excluded at the upper end of the acceptable range. The other was a former America First lecturer named Allan Mulvaney, who had been convicted of giving aid and comfort to the Nazi enemy.

Then there were the three chaplains, Catholic, Protestant and Jewish. Owen made it clear that he was not open to clerical overtures from any sect.

Thirdly there was the parole office, which sought to prepare the prisoner for the hazards of a possible probationary period in what it chose to call 'the normal community'. Every man with a sentence longer than one year was technically eligible for parole and was assigned to one of the two officers whose responsibility it was to compile a progress report on each case for the consideration of the

United States Board of Parole. In most instances parole was granted or denied according to a simple formula. If the criminal was comparatively well off, the board members reasoned, his crime must have been committed through mere avarice. In such cases the discomfort of a short jail sentence and the knowledge that he would be more closely watched in the future were enough to make an upright character of him. Accordingly, most income tax evaders, bank embezzlers, stock swindlers and corrupt public officials were regarded as good parole risks. Petty thieves, who presumably stole from necessity, were not. The personal and family demands which had driven them to crime in the first place were apt to be even more pressing after they had served their time, and it was only logical to class them as potential repeaters.

The Muir case, not conforming to either of these categories, was one of the few which would have required thought. It was a great relief to his parole officer, therefore, when their first discussion ended with Owen's decision that he could not accept the qualifications of parole even if it were granted him. In his case there need be no doubt about whether he would repeat his crime; he was able to state categorically that he would at the first opportunity.

To a less conscientious man than the associate warden, the fact that none of these regular channels could be employed with a particular inmate would have been reason enough to abandon the effort. But Blankenship saw it as an opportunity to use special techniques of rehabilitation not available to his less gifted colleagues. Additionally stimulating was the idea of working simultaneously with Owen and the Nazi sympathizer, Mulvaney. Whatever he could accomplish toward the reformation of either or both of these men would be a patriotic service as well as a contribution to penology.

Blankenship's personal setback in Wall Street had converted him into a political liberal but it had not shattered his faith in the harmonious co-existence of democracy and capitalism. He was confident of his ability to convert other people to his own fragile synthesis of Jefferson, Lincoln and Franklin Roosevelt, provided only that they had the intelligence and sensitivity to follow his arguments. Unfortunately, it appeared that the prisoners with whom he had done special educational work in the past had been almost totally lacking in these attributes; the man who had responded most satisfactorily to his exposition of New Deal principles, and whose parole he had helped to secure, had subsequently graduated to Alcatraz by way of Atlanta. Such previous frustrations made him the more eager to tackle the cases of Muir and Mulvaney.

Allan Mulvaney was a physically and intellectually graceful man of forty-two. Educated to within a few cubic centimetres of capacity at Princeton and Oxford, he had been a successful young career man in the State Department, filling a responsible post in Manchuria at the time of the Japanese invasion in 1931. After returning to Washington by way of Tokyo, he had been on the verge of an important promotion when he became involved in an acrimonious divorce action, during which his wife demanded an accounting of secret payments made to him by the Japanese government for services performed in connection with the surrender of Mukden. She also accused him of adultery with an Oriental and, after three days of tabloid publicity, the head of his branch reluctantly demanded his resignation, explaining that the interracial indiscretion was a permanent diplomatic liability.

Later, after an apprenticeship on Father Coughlin's *Social Justice*, he had gone to Germany for a quantitatively great Chicago newspaper, returning to lecture on the spiritual significance of the Munich Pact and to aid in the organization of America First when the outbreak of European hostilities made that the slogan of the hour. During the course of speaking and writing in the isolationist cause, he called for mass desertions from the armed forces, accused President Roosevelt of being the paid agent of an international Jewish cabal, proposed the assassination of three Cabinet members, and was elevated into the pages of *Who's Who in America*. Six months after Pearl Harbour, he was apprehended while escorting five enemy aliens across the Mexican border, and charged with sedition. The court before which he was convicted took judicial notice of the fact that he had no previous criminal record and gave him a minimum sentence of a year and a day.

Blankenship reasoned that since both prisoners had been involved in ideological crimes related to the war, he could effect their regeneration jointly. Inmates Muir and Mulvaney were requested to join him in his office after supper once a week for a series of discussions. In accordance with the prevailing etiquette toward such official invitations, they accepted.

Owen quickly determined on a policy of letting the other two men talk during these sessions, not only because of the deference a youth of twenty owed toward men in their forties and because there was no hope of recruiting such resolute minds to his way of thinking, but also because they interrupted each other with a vehemence that gave a third voice no chance to be heard. The first nineteen weeks were devoted to an analysis of the origins of the war, during which it was clearly established (by Blankenship) that the Axis powers were the aggressors and (by Mulvaney) that they were the victims of a Jewish-Bolshevist conspiracy for world conquest. Owen, who had little faith in disputation, had been sure the debate would have no effect on the convictions of either antagonist. By now he saw the error of this prediction. Actually, the process of marshalling and voicing their arguments made both of them grow more dogmatically attached to their original opinions.

The twentieth session started as usual with Blankenship summing up the previous one. For the sake of brevity and because he found it hard to remember what his opponent had said, he confined these summations to a restatement of his own position. 'We were examining the historic role of democracy in Western culture from the time of the Greek city-states. What emerged as of basic importance was the fact that the extension of democratic methods and the progress of civilization have been, if not synonymous, at least interdependent.' The associate warden's phraseology was always loftier in his introductory remarks than it became in the give and take of impromptu discussion. He reached for one of a stack of books on his desk, arranged for ready reference with strips of paper marking the quotations to be cited. 'In this regard, no modern commentator has surpassed the analysis which Bryce . . .' He committed the tactical error of drawing breath while he opened the volume.

'You're still making the same old mistake, you know,' Mulvaney interposed. 'Confusing democracy, which is the rule of the mob — all power to the soviets — with a republican or representative type of government, which is what we have in this country and what, in a more centralized form, the National Socialists have instituted in Germany. Now, as I've told you many times, I don't give my endorsement to everything Hitler's done, but I do understand the historical necessities behind his programme. I can tell you confidentially . . .'

'Listen to the man!' Blankenship's rhetorical appeal was directed at Owen and momentarily captured his wandering attention. 'If it isn't self-evident that the Nazi way of life and ours are direct opposites, then I don't know what is. In this country individual rights are supreme.' He raised the open book. 'Bryce has a particularly fortuitous . . .'

'What's the most important of all individual rights?' Mulvaney asked. 'The right to hold property, isn't it? Without property rights all the others are as empty as a Roosevelt smile. Or perhaps you don't believe in our free enterprise system?'

Blankenship flushed at the accusation. 'You know perfectly well I do, Mulvaney, and I don't have to take aspersions on my patriotism from you of all people. I have an honourable record of service behind me in a great American industry.'

'Nothing personal, old man. Mr. Blankenship, I mean. I'm simply trying to make clear the fact that we and the Germans believe in the same things. The difference is that the Bolshevist menace was closer to them and they were more alert to it. Basically it's a question of sanitation, like vaccination for smallpox. You have to remember they had millions of workers infected with un-German ideas. When we have the same problem, which we will unless Russia is destroyed in this war, we'll have to take the same kind of drastic measures. Maybe the steps wouldn't come in exactly the same order — I don't subscribe to every single plank in the Nazi platform — but I happen to have information from confidential sources . . .'

'That's precisely where you're so wrong. We wouldn't even use remotely the same methods. We believe in the Jeffersonian principle that the only way to defeat an idea is to counter it with a better idea.

Try to suppress it, pass laws against it, put men in jail for believing in it, and you're only confessing it's stronger than you are. As Bryce put it rather aptly...'

'What if the idea you're fighting happens to coincide with the policies of a foreign government?'

'All the easier to defeat it,' said Blankenship with a superior smile. 'If a group in this country tried to sell a programme that was good for Russia and bad for America, they'd be laughed out of existence. We wouldn't have to impair anyone's civil liberties. We wouldn't try to preserve democracy at the cost of democracy itself.'

'Apparently you're not very familiar with the way the Communist conspiracy functioned in Germany', said Mulvaney. 'They had a whole network of dummy organizations which drew people in with innocent-sounding names like the German League for Women's Rights or German Artists United for World Peace. And the fact is that Hitler didn't interfere with civil liberties, either. The way I understand it — of course I was just a casual observer — a committee was set up to look into these organizations and they only moved against the ones that were declared to be subversive. No one was put in a concentration camp for his ideas unless they were disloyal ideas. Surely you don't believe that a state ought to protect the freedoms of the very people who are conspiring to destroy it?'

'Emphatically and categorically, yes. If anyone wants to overthrow this government, let them stand unmolested as monuments to the safety with which we can tolerate error where reason is free to combat it. That's what Thomas Jefferson said. And Bryce summed it up in his observation...'

'Karl Marx and Nikolai Lenin were great advocates of the triumph of reason, too,' Mulvaney said pointedly. 'I'm a mere inmate here and you're the boss but I think I'm within my rights if I protest against your feeding us Communist propaganda dressed up as old American tradition.'

'I was quoting Thomas Jefferson!' Blankenship tried to bluster but he was on the defensive.

'So does the *Daily Worker*. All the time.'

The barb struck home. There was a silence, finally broken by

Owen. 'Excuse me.' The infrequency of his contributions had given them a priority rating and both men turned to him as he addressed Mulvaney. 'What you were saying about people only being put in concentration camps for disloyal ideas. I know of quite a few cases, one of them a Nobel Prize winner, whose only crime was being for peace. They didn't even break any laws the way I did — Germany wasn't at war at the time.'

'You're quite mistaken, dear boy,' Mulvaney said. 'It was never a crime to be for peace and the proof of that is that Hitler himself called for world peace in every speech he made. You never heard of him being jailed for it, did you? No, the men you're talking about were trying to sabotage a defence programme designed to protect Western civilization against Red Russian aggression. They even questioned the necessity of Germany having bases in Czechoslovakia and Poland as a part of preparation against Soviet attack. Under the circumstances their talk of "peace" was a direct invitation to the enemy, and that, my boy, is subversion in any language.'

'That may be so,' said Blankenship, conceding the point in Owen's behalf. 'But what about the Jews? They were imprisoned more or less en masse and there are even rumours that some of them have been put to death.'

'Same principle,' Mulvaney said. 'They all owed their loyalty either to Russia or Palestine.'

'You state that definitively, as a proven fact?' The associate warden's voice was incredulous.

'It stands to reason. Any Jew who knew Hitler's attitude toward them would have been insane not to be against him. You could pick them out at random and be sure you had either a hopeless imbecile or an enemy of the state. And whichever it turned out to be, you couldn't let them run around loose.'

'Well . . .' Blankenship hesitated in the face of this unfamiliar argument, 'I couldn't call myself a liberal if I closed my mind to any sincere point of view. But it seems to me you're admitting that the Nazis' anti-Semitism was itself the cause of . . .'

'They had a right to their beliefs, didn't they?' Mulvaney broke in. 'Anti-Semitism isn't a crime.'

'I'm not so sure of that.'

'You're not? That's very interesting. Muir, I hope you're paying close attention to what's being said here. Because it so happens that Mr. Blankenship is making a very significant confession. It's quite true — I shouldn't have stated it so positively — that there is one place in the world where anti-Semitism *is* a crime, by law. Not in the Third Reich, certainly, not in the United States of America. The doctrine to which you're expressing your allegiance is contained in Article 123 of the Constitution of the Union of Soviet Socialist Republics!'

'I didn't express allegiance to anything!' Blankenship countered indignantly.

'You said anti-Semitism was a crime. I'm simply pointing out for the record . . .'

'No, I didn't. I said I wasn't sure it shouldn't be considered as such. And I didn't really mean even that — I hadn't thought it out. Now, with the help of the arguments you bring up on the subject, I have, and I can see that it's a very dangerous principle, a two-edged weapon. What I mean is, it cuts both ways.'

'I still find it very interesting,' Mulvaney said, 'that, for all your talk about American history, your first, instinctive frame of reference is not the great charter of liberty we all learned to cherish in the cradle, but rather an evil, foreign, blood-stained . . .'

'That's enough!' Blankenship finally managed to summon an element of authority to his tone. 'I don't want to hear any more about it.'

'What are you going to do?' Mulvaney asked blandly. 'Write me up for insubordination?' They looked at each other, the one challenging, the other thoughtful. 'Or wouldn't you care to have a public hearing on the subject?'

Blankenship closed the volume of Lord Bryce and replaced it on top of his other reference books. 'I'm not going to do anything except admit to you that I've been guilty of an error in judgment. I thought it might be possible to make some headway with these discussions but I don't believe now there would be any point in continuing them. You may return to quarters.'

Owen rose to leave along with his fellow inmate but the associate warden restrained him. 'I'd like you to stay a minute, Muir. There's a matter I should take up with you.'

When the other prisoner had gone, Blankenship's manner took on an intimacy appropriate to men of more or less like mind liberated from an alien presence. 'I carry patience too far. That's my greatest weakness. A man who has something to contribute must be ruthless in the apportionment of his time, else he isn't making efficient use of himself.' He paused out of respect for the profundity of what he had said.

Owen let fifteen seconds go by, then inquired politely: 'You said there was a matter you wanted to talk to me about?'

'That was for Mulvaney's benefit. I didn't think it was discreet to let him know we were going to continue these conversations without him.'

'Are we?' Owen succeeded in keeping most of the disappointment out of his voice but he thought wistfully of his cot in the dormitory and the books awaiting him there. All day as he laboured with axe and saw, the precious hours of horizontal comfort loomed in his consciousness as a goal and a palliative.

'Of course it's entirely up to you,' Blankenship said in a tone indicating no doubt of Owen's acquiescence. 'But I've had the feeling you've been responding very well to the ideas we've been examining here.'

'Responding? I've hardly opened my mouth.'

'You've listened, though. You're a good listener. And I've sensed you weren't reacting favourably to anything our Hitler-loving friend had to say.'

'Certainly not.'

'I thought as much. I also flatter myself I've given you some new food for thought in regard to what this war is about and why we're fighting it. Haven't I?'

'Is that an official question? Is an answer required, I mean?'

'Absolutely,' Blankenship said with a broad smile. 'Under penalty of severe disciplinary measures.'

'Then I'm afraid it's no. I can't think of anything you've said that's had any influence on me whatsoever.' The hurt in Blankenship's eyes was so great that Owen was instantly remorseful. 'It's only that I've heard all that stuff before,' he explained. 'You express it very well and it's always interesting to hear an articulate man discuss his beliefs but . . .'

'Never mind,' the associate warden broke in curtly. 'I should have known better than to try to cure a case of cowardice with logic.' He made a gesture of peremptory dismissal and Owen, at a loss how to console him, went out.

He crossed the open yard to his dormitory at a brisk pace. A biting wind had brought the temperature down to far below freezing. Ordinarily Blankenship would have telephoned the control room for a guard to let Owen into his quarters, but such courtesies were of the past and he had to wait for the officer on yard duty to arrive in the course of his regular rounds. Through the windows he could see his housemates in warm, cozy groups around the radio and the game table in the recreation room. A couple of them noticed him and shivered sympathetically but the door was locked from the outside and there was nothing they could do to hasten his entrance. Snow began to lash his face, borne almost horizontally by the wind, reaching blizzard strength within a matter of seconds. He paced the length of the building, pausing at each end to look out toward the wire fence which marked the prison-yard boundary. Spotlights from the rear walls of the dormitory buildings usually kept the fence clearly lit at night, but now the intervening gusts of driving snow made it all but invisible. The realization crossed his mind that it would be easy to get over the barrier unobserved; it was not a pleasant prospect however, weighed against his impatience to be locked into the warmth and security of the concrete barracks.

'Want to come in?' The guard had approached without Owen's hearing him over the sound of the wind. It was Mr. Meglin, one of the older and mellower custodial officers. He was dressed more warmly than Owen but he had been exposed to the cold for a longer period and the resistance in his ageing body was not as great. Owen could see the pain and fatigue that lay behind the pleasant surface of his manner. The man's hands trembled as he found the key on the heavy ring which hung from his belt, and unlocked the metal door.

'You don't have to stay out there all night, do you?' Owen asked.

'Just till lights-out,' Mr. Meglin told him. 'Another hour. From then on I take thirty minutes inside for every thirty out.'

'Doesn't it ever get to be spring in this part of the country?'

'It always has,' the guard conceded. 'But along about this time every year, I begin to doubt it.' He was holding the door open and there were indignant shouts of protest from the men inside. 'Good night, Muir.'

'Good night, Mr. Meglin.'

Owen stood at the window for a while, watching the guard struggle to make progress against the storm. He himself had only one more winter to look forward to at Moose Head but Mr. Meglin, he knew, had nine years ahead of him before he reached retirement age. It could easily turn out to be a life sentence for the poor man, Owen thought sadly.

Two days later the snow still lay on the ground but the sunshine had such an encouraging trace of warmth in it that the men on Owen's work detail were able to function in shirts and sweaters. The group was a newly formed one, the result of a re-organization designed to spread some of the more experienced hands among the recent arrivals. Owen was supposed to be the spark-plug igniting its morale, but he had an uneasy feeling about the prospects for unified effort from this particular aggregation. One of its seven members was a morose, taciturn Negro youth serving two years for a seventeen-dollar mail theft, and Owen had noted that racial feeling was much tenser among confined criminals, even of Northern extraction, than in a normal American cross-section. Another cause for misgiving was the officer in charge of the group, a former detective in the Chicago Police Department named Matt Clark. There were a variety of conflicting stories as to what had reduced him to the ignominy of his present job, but his customary expression was that of a man who considers himself a victim of persecution. It was also rumoured that he drank heavily from the moment he went off duty.

Additionally disturbing on this particular day was the presence of Allan Mulvaney, who had promoted himself to a vaguely defined sinecure which involved his moving from one work detail to another and reporting on their comparative efficiency. It was a tribute to his charm and his knack of scaling his conversation up or down to the level of his immediate environment that most of the other inmates admired rather than resented his idleness.

The trouble started when they broke for lunch. Even though the meal was eaten most informally on the job, there was an unofficial segregation policy requiring that Calder, the young Negro, be separated from the rest of the men. On this occasion the youth refused to go along with the routine, seating himself on the ground in what seemed to him the warmest available spot, regardless of its location between two white men. The most belligerent defender of white supremacy in the group, a black-market tyre entrepreneur named Ragsdale, was instantly ready for physical action in spite of the fact that the guard Clark was sitting only a few yards away. Mulvaney, however, gestured him to be patient while a subtler approach was tried.

'We have a rare opportunity today, boys,' said Mulvaney. 'We get a close-range look at the eating habits of primitive man. Genus Dingus Africanus. Observe how both front paws are used to clutch a sandwich which we can easily manage with one hand.' He threw a sharp glance at Ragsdale, who hastily dropped one hand from his own sandwich.

Calder, barely listening to what was being said, only became aware that he was the subject of discussion when the laughter started. But by that time Owen had thrown himself into the breach.

'Say, Mulvaney,' he said conversationally, 'you mentioned the other night what this country would be like if we won the war. What I'm even more curious about is what if the Nazis won?'

'We'd win, too, if we were smart. As soon as Russia's wiped out, the real patriots in this country will toss old No-legs Rosenfeldt out on his ear and make a deal.'

'We ought to make a deal right now,' Ragsdale said. 'Before any more of our boys get knocked off over there.'

'Not with them Japs,' a cheque-forger protested. 'I don't trust them little yellow bastards.'

'Neither does Hitler,' Mulvaney assured him. 'He knows if a man isn't white outside, he can't be white inside.'

The Negro looked across at him but said nothing.

'In other words,' Owen said, still trying to avert an explosion, 'you feel that we'd be better off if we made a negotiated peace?'

'Better is an understatement. Why, do you know that with a scientific government under strong leadership, we could practically abolish mongrelization in a generation?'

'Abolish what?' inquired the former sales manager of a heroin-distributing outfit.

'Polluting the race. The coon over there knows what I mean, don't you, coon? All it would take is a simple law limiting the right of reproduction to people of pure white, Gentile stock. Sterilization. You wouldn't have to kill them, except the ones who were Commies. Just let them die off.'

Calder rose to his feet with a six-syllable epithet which, while it suggested that Mulvaney had sexual relations with his unmarried mother, was no more than a mild reproach in ordinary prison parlance. Owen looked quickly over at Clark and observed with relief that the guard was facing them and in range to hear everything that was said. His presence was sure to have a restraining influence since any kind of fight meant immediate isolation for all participants.

'You shouldn't ought to let him talk to you like that, Al,' Ragsdale said. 'You got the dignity of the whole race to think about.'

'Oh, why don't you lay off, both of you?' said an interstate auto-thief, also getting to his feet. 'The kid didn't start it. You did.'

'We sure as hell didn't ask him to lunch,' Ragsdale said virtuously. 'The goddam judge give me eighteen months but he didn't say anything about I had to eat with a puking nigger-smell under my nose.'

He started to stand up in order to be better prepared against possible attack but before he had quite made it, Calder, successfully goaded to fury, was on him. They went down with the Negro on top, but two of the other white men grabbed Calder and pulled him off before he could accomplish much damage.

'Hold him right there,' Ragsdale instructed, sitting up and striving to regain his breath. 'I just need one good, clear swing at him.'

They all looked over at the guard. Owen was suddenly and sharply aware of the contradiction in his own feeling. A resolute opponent of all man-made authority over man, he was now depending on it, anxiously, to take over the situation.

'Back to work in a few minutes, boys,' Clark called to them. 'Have fun.' He turned away and walked off.

Because experience had inured him to betrayal, the Negro was the first to realize that the guard was deliberately abandoning him. He made a violent effort to free himself and probably would have succeeded if Mulvaney hadn't sprung to the assistance of the two prisoners who were holding him. Gripping him around the waist from behind, the former diplomat used his free hand to unfasten Calder's belt, letting his pants drop to the ground. Then he produced from his pocket a knife, possession of which was one of the most serious violations of prison rules, and tossed it over to Ragsdale.

'Your privilege, Rags,' he said. 'We don't need a sterilization law for this one. Unprovoked attack on a white man. What's the matter? You know how to do it, don't you?'

'I done pigs,' Ragsdale said uncertainly. 'My old man used to let me when I was a kid.'

'So what's the problem, one kind of animal or another?'

'Better not come no closer, man,' Calder said to Ragsdale. 'You touch me with that knife and I'll tear your eyes out. I got friends on the street'll rip your old lady apart and fry your kids in gasoline. Sweet bleeding Christ is my judge, they will.'

'The hell with it,' one of the men holding him said suddenly. He was a boy of twenty who had been in institutions of one kind or another almost continuously since the age of eleven. 'You want to take a poke at him for stepping out of line, okay, but the worst son-of-a-bitching cop in Milwaukee wouldn't go for slicing a man's private business, black or white.'

He relaxed his grip on Calder and once again the Negro almost wrested himself loose, but Mulvaney brought his knee up from behind between the youth's thighs and pulled him down on to his lap with a full nelson. The cheque-writer took care of the legs and Ragsdale seated himself astride the stomach, his back to Mulvaney, the knife poised for its function.

Of the six white men on the scene besides Owen, three were now taking a passive attitude, counting the narcotics executive, whose eager eyes indicated partisanship but who took no direct hand in the proceedings. The other two non-participants were obviously in moral opposition, but it was just as apparent that they weren't going to risk their accumulated good time or social standing in the inmate population by actively preventing the proposed mutilation. Clearly, if force were going to be resisted with force, it would have to be applied by Owen, who hadn't struck another human being since he was nine years old, nor even intentionally injured an insect during the preceding year and a half.

'He hit me,' Ragsdale said, addressing himself especially to the neutral faction. 'He would have killed me if he could of. You all saw that.'

'Sure,' Mulvaney said. 'Anyway, this is just a matter of crime prevention, which J. Edgar Hoover says is every citizen's job. You're preventing rape.'

Owen grabbed Ragsdale's wrist, twisting it so that he would drop the knife. To his surprise he succeeded not only in this purpose but in turning the man over backwards, against Mulvaney, whose hold on Calder was loosened enough for the Negro to break away from it. The cheque-writer, who was the nearest of the group to Owen's size and strength, sought to retrieve the situation, but Owen, swinging at his jaw in order to discourage his effort, sent him sprawling. Ragsdale and Mulvaney tried to tackle him simultaneously but Owen, who had never even watched a football game in his life, sidestepped the one and fended the other off with an instinctive straight-arm technique. By this time Calder was on his feet and ready to fight alongside his deliverer; the opposition, however, had lost its ardour and the two forces were no longer in contact when Clark reappeared on the scene.

It was impossible to tell from the guard's face how much he knew or was able to guess of what had been taking place. All he said was: 'Okay, come on. Siesta's over. Put your pants on, black boy. What do you think this is, a burlesque show?'

That night was almost sleepless for Owen and the fitful slumber which did finally overcome him was broken by a disturbing dream. He was in the army against his will and his unit was fighting its way into a ruined town. An old man lay dead at his feet, with a gaping hole through the left cheek. It was no one whom he knew personally but Owen felt a great sense of personal loss; he wanted to bury the man or else find his family and see that the body was properly taken care of. Then suddenly there were three men standing near him, laughing at him. Before he saw them he knew that they were responsible for the old man's death and that they wanted to kill him too. When he looked up at them he could make out neither their uniforms nor their faces but he knew one was the guard Clark and another either Ragsdale or Mulvaney.

Instead of waiting passively for them to shoot him, which had been his first impulse, he raised his gun and began to fire at them, not to protect himself but because he wanted them to suffer as the old man had suffered. The feeling he had toward them was an unfamiliar one but he recognized it as hate.

In the morning he filled out a request slip for an interview with Blankenship.

The associate warden saw him through the glass partition and considered how he should treat the boy. The interview he was conducting with a newly admitted parcel post embezzler was nearly over, but Blankenship prolonged it with unnecessary questions about the man's grade school truancies and chaotic home life. While paying just enough attention to the responses to keep them going with new queries, he reviewed his painful experience with young Muir. Had he himself been at fault? Had he taken the wrong approach with the boy? From his advertising career he recalled the precept that the product and the consumer must be regarded as constants, with the particular sales campaign as the fallible variant between them. It had taken creative imagination and resourcefulness, he remembered with pride, to rechristen a harmless skin cream a 'deodorant' and sell it with portraits of beautiful American brides on their wedding nights.

By the time he waved Owen into his presence, he had worked out a new appeal directed to the youth's emotions rather than his intellect. Without waiting to hear what had prompted the visit, he handed Owen a clipping of an Ernie Pyle dispatch from the Salerno beachhead and instructed him to read it. The story described an upstate New York boy's identification of an Italian dawn with sunrise over Schenectady, his rhapsodic recollections of which had been cut short by the explosion of an anti-personnel mine directly underfoot.

'Sears a hole right through your guts, a story like that, doesn't it?' Blankenship said.

'What?' Owen stared at him blankly for a moment. 'Oh, I didn't quite follow you at first. Yes, it is rather tragic, isn't it? Thanks for letting me read it.'

'I guess a lot of the kids you grew up with are over there.'

'A few. The fact is, most of the men I know turned out to have just the right qualifications for commissions in Special Services.'

'Well, it takes all kinds of functions to fight a modern war. Wherever they're serving, their mothers are no less proud of them.'

'I suppose so. I've kind of lost touch with them and their mothers lately.' In despair about ever getting around to the subject that had brought him here, he decided the only way was to plunge right into it. 'I don't know if you know, Mr. Blankenship — I let my parole date go by last month, signed a waiver. I thought maybe you could tell me, or be willing to look into it for me — would they consider my case now if I agreed to go into active combat service?'

Blankenship's astonishment momentarily exceeded his gratification. 'Are you serious?'

'I've heard of cases where fellows have been able to swing something of the sort,' Owen continued diffidently. 'I won't try to argue I wasn't guilty of a very serious crime, because I was, only it just seems I could show my remorse in a more practical way if I...'

'Of course you could!' Tears filled the associate warden's eyes. '*Can* you get a parole on those terms! It can be arranged in two minutes over the telephone.' Blankenship's self-confidence rose to a height unmatched since the debacle of 1929. Never had a new tactic in salesmanship paid off so quickly and effectively.

Now he could write a piece on the technique of political rehabilitation for the *Penal Review*.

CHAPTER III

'There's a kind of nice one,' Phyllis said, 'with the red hair and creamy skin. See him smile. I could have told you he had good teeth.'

She and her mother were watching the soldiers descend from the train. Owen, who had gone directly into the army from prison, was supposed to be arriving for a pre-embarkation furlough and it worried Mrs. Muir that the cars had nearly emptied without his appearing. Phyllis was less interested in seeing her brother after a fifteen months' absence than she was in the opportunity to survey a crop of young males and to bask in their reciprocal appraisal of her. She was beginning to think it might be a good idea to come down here some afternoon without her mother.

'Do you see him that way?' Mrs. Muir asked anxiously.

'No — yes!' The disinterested negative became an excited affirmative. 'It's him, look, it really is! Only he's beautiful! Our little butter-ball has grown up to be a swan.'

'Who are you talking about?' Mrs. Muir spoke in a querulous voice as she squinted through her glasses. 'That's not your brother, you scatterbrained . . .' Then she realized it was and started toward him, breaking into a penguinlike trot before she fell against the massive rampart of sinew and muscle that jutted out between his neck and waist.

Phyllis waited impatiently for a break in the embrace, wedging her way in the first time her mother drew back slightly to apply a handkerchief to her eyes.

'Hi, Phyl.' Owen extended one arm and touched her awkwardly behind the shoulder as he bent to kiss her cheek.

'No, I want the works,' Phyllis said. 'Head on, face to face, young body against young body. You ought to see some of the specimens a girl has to get her fondling from these days.'

With her help and after a diffident glance toward Mrs. Muir, Owen complied. This occasion with his pretty seventeen-year-old sister was the first time he had ever held a young woman in his arms or kissed anyone on the lips.

After a while Phyllis stepped back and inspected him in more detail. Even granting that the prison camp and army basic training had wrought a phenomenal change, she couldn't understand how she had overlooked the basic beauty of his features. They had been grossly overladen with fat but they must have had the same perfection of form that was now so strikingly apparent. Nor had she remembered him as being tall, yet she had to stretch as much to meet his lips as she had the previous weekend with a left tackle from Cornell who was listed in the official statistics as six feet one and three-quarters.

Willis Muir, who had organized his dollar-a-year job so as to be in Washington four days a week and East Point three, had a major-general up with him for the weekend, but on the night of Owen's arrival he made a point of speaking to his son alone while the general and Phyllis were analysing big league baseball prospects for 1944. 'Can't tell you how much it's meant to me, your finally seeing the light. I was even going to write you a letter about it, only it's been such a madhouse down there getting all these contracts assigned. But it's made me very happy, knowing you've straightened yourself out. Mentally and physically,' he added with a laugh.

'Yes, I was mixed up,' Owen admitted. 'I don't know how long it would have taken me to get to the heart of the problem if I hadn't happened to come into contact with a man who helped make it clear for me.'

'In jail, you mean? Who was it, the warden out there or one of his . . . ?'

'No, another prisoner, an American fascist.'

'Really?' There was the same disapproval in his voice that an unnecessary piece of profanity would have provoked. 'You know, Owen, I wouldn't use that word if I were you. It gives people a lot of wrong ideas nowadays. So if what you mean is that this fellow was a rugged individualist who saw the menace in all this union coddling . . .'

'No, I mean a fascist. Complete with regimentation of thought, anti-Semitism and . . .'

'The Jewish problem isn't confined to Germany.'

'That's what this man believed. Matter of fact, he thinks the whole Hitler programme is just what we need over here.'

'I hope he doesn't talk about it in those terms. Some very worthwhile concepts can be hurt by being smeared with the wrong label. But I imagine your friend must be a pretty persuasive character to have convinced a tough case like you. You were certainly a long way away from those ideas when we talked last year.'

'So were you.'

'I was?' Mr. Muir looked surprised. 'I hardly think so.'

'You said we had to fight the Nazis for survival. You said they'd enslave us.'

'Of course: they would have. But that doesn't mean I object to all their internal policies.'

'Oh.' Owen paused to consider this. 'What it comes down to, I guess, is that you want to use their methods but fix it so we enslave them instead of the other way around.'

Mr. Muir frowned despairingly. 'You have a habit of making things sound very crude. Now that you're beginning to develop a mature understanding of the world, you should learn to express yourself in a mature way. But at least it's very gratifying to know we're closer to unanimity in this family.'

'I'm afraid we aren't close at all. You see, I was going to tell you, about this man in the prison and a situation he was the cause of . . .'

'You're over all that pacifist stuff, aren't you? You decided to go into the army, didn't you?'

'Yes, but for just the opposite . . .'

'You're ready to fight for your country like the rest of us?'

'That's true. Pure pacifism is a blind alley. I've come to see that now.'

'Then what in the name of Christ are we quibbling about? Congratulations, boy, and congratulations to the patriot who helped you see the light. There's too much fancy sounding-off on what this war's about.' He turned toward his guest. 'It's really a very simple matter, isn't it, General? What the war's about?'

'Nothing to it,' agreed the general, looking up from the business of mixing a fresh highball. He smiled foolishly as he realized he was still squirting water from the siphon several seconds after removing his glass from the spigot. 'Always manage to mess a place up somehow. Never fails.'

Mrs. Muir, to whom this apology was presumably directed, opened her mouth to reassure him as she came forward to repair the damage. But he had already risen above the calamity and joined the other men.

'How's the army treating you, boy? Where you stationed?'

'In transit right now, sir. Outfit's going overseas.'

'Oh.' At first he seemed to view this project as a breach of form, but the whisky prevailed to produce a more tolerant reaction. 'Well, there's lots to be done over there, too. I was flying back and forth to London twice a month for a while last year. Remember, Willis, when there was that big crisis about standardizing abbreviations on requisition forms?'

Owen's father laughed at the recollection. 'Yes, that was a real test of international relations. I was just an observer,' he explained to Owen, 'but there were days there wasn't anything else talked about around the Pentagon.'

'You've heard about the new impasse, haven't you?' asked the general. 'Churchill's ordered the Combined Forces in Italy to rewrite all their dispatches spelling the word theater with an "r-e".'

Owen was incredulous. 'Are men in responsible positions really concerned about things like that?'

'They have to be,' Mr. Muir said.

'You could hardly leave it to a bunch of colonels,' the general explained. 'Not where there's a matter of basic principle involved. You give some of those bastards an inch and they want to go back and fight the American Revolution all over again.'

'I guess it must be easier getting along with the Russians,' Owen said. 'No spelling issues.'

'Oh, the Russians.' The general's tone indicated that this was a problem which he personally had under control. 'They're no trouble if you talk straight to them and let them know they haven't got the only damn army in the world. Like Jake Murrhardt and that little Bolshie major, remember, Willis? Jake's one of our generals, works out of Somervell's office, a hell of a poker player and an all-round guy, but he really knows about strategy and tactics and that kind of stuff. Reads Fielding Eliot and Hanson Baldwin and the *Army and Navy Journal* and Christ knows what else. I honestly think if they suddenly shipped him to the front and gave him a division, he'd be able to bluff his way along with it somehow. Anyway, that's the kind of guy he is. Well, at this cocktail party this Russian major starts spouting a big military analysis full of historical comparisons, only all from European history. And he keeps mentioning this one Russian general as if everybody should know all about him. I ought to remember the name — he said it often enough.'

'Suvorov,' Mr. Muir supplied.

'That's right. Well, I could see Jake Murrhardt was burning same as everyone else, except Jake was the man to take him on in the military history field. Finally he got his opening, looking him right in the eye. "That's very interesting, Major," he says in a nice friendly tone. "I wonder if you'd care to comment on the application of those same basic cavalry principles by Jeb Stuart in the Southern Pennsylvania campaign".' The general began to laugh so hard he was barely able to gasp out the end of his story. 'So of course Ivan had to own up he didn't have an idea in hell who Jeb Stuart was.'

'What happened after that?' Owen asked. 'I mean, you were making a point about Americans and Russians getting along.'

'That did it,' said the general. 'The little Russhki was stopped. Somebody brought up the question who was the better actress, Dorothy Lamour or Betty Grable, and there wasn't another peep out of him.'

Her parents and the general were on their second cups of coffee when Phyllis came down to breakfast next morning. Plunging directly into the sports section of the *Daily News*, she found a scare story based on the rumour that the army was going to add another inch to its maximum height limitation, a move that threatened almost fatal consequences to the coming basketball season. Phyllis expressed her outrage and the general promised to take it up with General Hershey as the first order of business on his return to Washington.

After a while Mrs. Muir asked Phyllis whether she had heard her brother stirring yet.

'Oh, he's gone; I was supposed to tell you! I saw him for a minute before I went to bed last night and he told me he was leaving at five o'clock in the morning and I should say goodbye to everybody for him.'

'How could he?' her mother asked in dismay.

'He didn't make much sense on the subject. Just said if he didn't get away from here immediately, he'd end up right back in jail.'

'I don't understand. Why would he say that, Willis?'

'You've got me,' the head of the family said. 'Unless he didn't have proper leave. That must be what it was. The poor kid wanted to see us before he sailed and he went AWOL to do it.'

'Maybe,' said Phyllis. 'But I didn't get the feeling that was what he meant.'

It was in the United Kingdom, during the preparation of his division for the Overlord invasion, that Owen discovered the value of his new-found beauty in the exchange of sexual pleasures. Having reached his twenty-first birthday, which occurred on shipboard, without having had as much as a social engagement alone with a girl, he learned in Northern Ireland that it was possible for an eager student to master the preliminary curriculum in a single lesson. Not even his first instructress, the daintily aggressive daughter of a Queen's University theologian, suspected his inexperience; she mistook his diffident approach for an unwonted fastidiousness and accepted his final capitulation as a high tribute to her charms.

This initial relationship was the longest and, toward the end, the most troublesome of his amatory adventures on foreign soil. Confusing novelty with uniqueness, he was heavily committed by the time the reaction against premature monogyny set in. Fortunately, in the course of an ominously formal visit to the young lady's home, he was able to stimulate a current of doctrinal dispute with her father regarding the function of the Holy Ghost in the Trinity. It was not an issue on which Owen had any profound conviction but he chose to disagree so doggedly that the theologian ordered him from the house.

Word of a sudden transfer to England impelled him further toward a clean, sharp break. He told the girl it was in her own interest to forget a man between whom and her family there was such an unbridgeable gap.

The colleen demurred. 'What do the likes of us care about the Paraclete?' In moments calling for maximum emotional conviction she favoured a Celtic turn of speech. 'It's you and me counts, lad, and the songs we make together.'

'I don't know. The subordination of the Holy Ghost undermines the whole Triune idea. It's the kind of difference that's likely to grow bigger rather than . . .'

'And if it does? Keep your eyes on the sweet light, man, and don't be giving up to the gloom. What does it do to the soul of you when I put my hand on you there?'

'I'm just trying to think of the practical considerations.'

'And my lips, lad? And my breasts you said were like twin doves in flight? Ah, Ownie, it's belly to belly we should be once more, and banish the dark thoughts!'

'That wasn't really my line about your breasts. I think I mentioned at the time I was quoting a Latin poet. Look, sweetheart, I'm leaving the country tonight. Some day soon we'll be invading the Continent. I may not be able to come back. I may be killed.'

'And if you're not?'

There was no evasion possible; he disdained the refuge of a promise he would not keep. 'Then I won't be back either.' The vicarious pain he suffered from his own brutality was far greater than the actual wound to her. The girl moped for a fortnight; it took Owen months to recover from the effect of his cruelty. He became more aware than ever that it was easier for him to receive a hurt than to give one.

In England, largely owing to the war and its dislocations, further erotic opportunities came his way but he was careful not to become too seriously involved in them. They served to break the tedium of military life and especially to relieve, every once in a while, the tension of the fundamental problem that lay ahead of him.

That was the question which had not been finally resolved by his transformation at Moose Head. Did the fact that he had used force successfully on one occasion mean he could go on applying his altered convictions in practice? Sometimes they didn't seem very much altered. As far as it was possible in retrospect to reduce his decision to a rational equation, it was simply that at one moment a delicate preponderance of logic had seemed to support the first of two opposing courses, and at the next, just enough weight had shifted to favour the second.

The difference in programme, however, was revolutionary. Resisting evil with evil meant a wholehearted absorption in the techniques of evil, a mastery of the means by which the end which justified them was to be attained. From his basic training in the States through his painstaking instruction in the details of beach-head barbarity, he had devoted an alert mind, a fine body and a resolute will to the manly arts of treachery, stealth, intimidation, dismemberment and murder. Would these newly acquired skills be at his disposal when the crisis called for them? Would his divinely bestowed soul remain subordinate to the refinements which his company commander, platoon leader and non-commissioned officers had striven to superimpose upon it?

The inlet was known locally as the Cove of the Sorrowful Fishermen. Neither Rollo the Bold nor Edward the Black Prince, both of whom had landed troops there without the aid of area maps, had found it necessary to rechristen it in the process. But in Eisenhower's headquarters one afternoon during the planning of the June invasion, a major from Duluth who had never seen the Norman coastline and knew its topographical details more intimately than any citizen of the province, had changed its name to Sector K-4, Utah Beach.

Offshore, the lieutenant peered cautiously over the side of the landing craft and announced that the visibility stank. In the midst of his own alarm over what lay ahead of them, he was seized with a misguided urge to steel the characters of the men under his command. 'We don't know what it's like on that beach,' he told them, 'except that some of our boys have gone in ahead of us. There may not be any of them left alive by now. By noon there may not be any of us left alive.'

'That's a hell of a thing to say,' a boy sitting near Owen protested. 'I had my heart set on eating lunch in one of them frog restaurants.'

'Excuse me, sir,' said a bazooka man from New Jersey, pausing till the lieutenant authorized him, with a crisp monosyllable, to continue, 'who takes over if you get your silly head blown off?'

Owen envied these men the release they seemed to find in jokes and insults, but he remained part of the tense and silent majority. When they hit the beach and scattered according to rehearsed procedure, he was relieved to discover that he was functioning at maximum efficiency. Thinking about this moment in advance, he had given much favourable consideration to a policy of caution, but now something impelled him to outrun his comrades and he was one of the first to start up the steep slope which led from the narrow stretch of sand to the fog-shrouded and potentially perilous plateau. The first figure he saw on the height above him was so dimly outlined it could have been friend or foe, and he was grateful to hear it shout in the familiar voice of the communications sergeant of his company, who assumed various alternate functions as occasion required.

'Hurry it up, boys! I need six men right away. Jernegan, Faragelli, Muir, Boehm, Katsman and Reardon.' The urgency was apparently too great for him to be selective; he was simply calling the names of the first six new arrivals he recognized. 'Follow me. We got a spot all picked out for a latrine. Just needs to be dug.'

The spirit of anti-climax was steadily compounded for forty-eight days. Events of great consequence, glorious and shameful, planned and chaotic, encouraging and appalling, took place all over the Norman Peninsula, but Owen's division had never known such dreary idleness since its formation. Its carefully built-up morale was subjected to a series of indignities culminating, through the courtesy of the USO, in its exposure to a pair of superficially male tap-dancers and a 'Hollywood starlet' whose career had been justly confined to still photography.

But despite the widespread delusion among men and officers that they had been mislaid, the division had actually been assigned a leading role in General Bradley's projected assault on the gates of Brittany. After seven weeks of stagnation, it was propelled into forward motion with suddenness and speed. Its route had theoretically been evacuated by the outflanked enemy but this did not mean progress was unimpeded, especially for those units, Owen's company among them, which followed just behind the armoured spearheads. The Germans had left various obstacles, mechanical and human, to slow the advance. It fell to Owen's lot to discover one of the more formidable of these under circumstances which provoked him to bravery.

They were making their way through 'bocage' country, broken up by innumerable hedgerows, each segment of which hid a possible ambush. Owen was one of four scouts sent out an hour before sunrise to explore the first portion of that day's scheduled journey. It was dull work since the odds were hugely against finding enemy remnants in any given small section of terrain, yet the function had to be carried out as if they were lurking everywhere. The four men started out together but during the last part of their investigation they proceeded along separate routes and on their bellies.

Crawling, Owen thought as he inched his way toward the next hedge barrier, has some of the ugliest connotations of any word in the human vocabulary. From our erect position we have an often affectionate superiority toward beings that still go on four feet, but only scorn and hatred for those that creep. And a way of expressing our contempt for a man who has debased himself and dishonoured his species is to say that he has crawled. Whatever their origin, Owen strongly endorsed these judgments of his present method of locomotion. It was particularly inappropriate, he felt, for those of His creatures whom the Lord had equipped with knees, elbows and prominent genitalia.

When he finally reached his objective, the sky was beginning to lighten. He made his way with infinite caution to a gap in the hedge, and froze at the sound of a voice only a few feet away. After a moment he pressed forward just enough to see without being seen. Lying in wait behind the hedge were two German tanks. Technically speaking, they would have been described as medium, but these classifications, Owen realized, were relative. From where he lay, the word was enormous. Both were unbuttoned but the more distant one was distinctly on the alert, the helmeted soldier who stood in its open turret covering the surrounding country for the nearer tank as well. The latter was apparently empty, its two crew members on the ground between their vehicle and Owen. One was replacing a greasy bandage on his leg with a piece of his tattered and almost equally soiled shirt. The other, less than ten feet from Owen, was emptying his bowels and expressing a strong opinion on a subject which Owen's school German was unable to fathom, though he isolated the words 'Cigaretten' and 'Gefrorenes'.

Since there was no chance of retracing his path across the open field behind him in the growing daylight, Owen was faced with two possible courses of action. The first and immeasurably the more conservative was to stay exactly where he was for the hour or so that was due to elapse before the main body of his outfit approached this spot and presented the kind of target the Germans were waiting for. At that point it was reasonable to expect that the tanks would go into action and probably be a safe distance away from him before the guns or planes were brought up which would eventually destroy or disperse them. It was also likely that there would be a rather high casualty rate among the forward ranks of his comrades.

The second alternative was an attempt on his part to prevent such an ambush from taking place, if only by creating enough disturbance, in the process of getting himself killed, to reveal the presence of the Germans to the other members of his patrol, who could then pass the news on either in person or via the walkie-talkie one of them carried.

It was an aggravating dilemma, and if there had been time to examine all its aspects, he might have found the weight of arguments and counter-arguments too unwieldy for confident resolution. But before he had more than begun to explore them, he was forced to a precipitate decision. The nearest and most vulnerable German had completed his function and was about to stand up. It was improbable that there would be another such opportunity for offensive action.

Owen raised himself to a crouch and sprang, hooking an arm around the squatting man's neck. Before the other two visible Germans reacted by turning a pistol and a fifty-calibre machine gun on him, he had dragged his prisoner most of the way back to his former hiding-place, keeping the man squarely in front of him as a shield. 'Nicht schiessen!' he yelled. 'Ich will sprechen mit Ihnen. I mean, ich will mit Ihnen sprechen.'

The Germans began a quick and emotional consultation among themselves, in which Owen's prisoner took a vehement stand in favour of listening to what the American had to say. A fourth soldier stuck his head out of the turret of the further tank and revealed a knowledge of English which, though there was much to criticize in his grammar, considerably raised the level of the ensuing bilateral discussion.

Owen based his case on the ultimate helplessness of their situation. American armoured columns, he pointed out, had already closed the gap behind them, and there was a whole army corps moving up the way he had come. By continuing to fight they ran a great risk of being killed, whereas surrender now would ensure their physical safety and the comforts which America offered its prisoners.

'So habe ich gesagt,' said Owen's prisoner in ardent support. 'Gefrorenes, gute Cigaretten.'

The man with the leg wound was unconvinced. A German

counter-offensive was probably under way by now; Rommel would throw the Allies back and hold them at bay until the inevitable split between the Anglo-Americans and the Russians brought about a negotiated peace and joint victory against the universal enemy to the east.

Owen heaped scorn on this theory. The Americans and the Russians were growing closer every day, he told them. General Eisenhower loved the Russians. So did General Bradley. General MacArthur in the Pacific had called them the hope of civilization. Stalin loved Roosevelt. Churchill loved Stalin. The three leaders had met in Persia for a big love feast and they were going to get together again as soon as they had found costly enough presents for each other. In America everyone spoke of Stalin as Uncle Joe, and that was the highest term of affection and respect in the language. Like Uncle Sam.

The man with the leg wound was impressed with the translation of this argument. But the helmeted man was disinterested in higher strategy. What he wanted to know was whether it was true about the ice cream. Was that really a part of the prison camp diet?

Owen assured them that it was. And the cigarettes were the finest quality produced in America. He gave one of his own to his prisoner as a sample and threw the rest of the package to the others. They tried them and reacted approvingly. Then it occurred to him that they might be hungry and he tossed them a D-Ration chocolate bar. This turned out to be a mistake. The man with the leg wound made a grimace of distaste and the English-speaking man spat his portion out. 'No damn good,' he announced. 'Ist better by us.'

Owen summoned his latent powers of persuasion to overcome this setback. If they would excuse a personal comment, he told them, none of them looked to him as if he were in the best of health. There might be drawbacks to the prisoner-of-war camps in America but he was reasonably certain they would find the living conditions and medical care superior to what they were now experiencing.

The English-speaking German displayed interest and mentioned that he had heard most of the big camps were in the West. Wasn't that where all the cattle was raised? And wasn't it also true that America suffered from a perennial surplus of beef?

Owen acknowledged the last question with a non-committal nod. 'I spent some time out there when I was a boy. Texas. People served steak for breakfast.' He omitted to add that his hosts had been millionaire friends of the family.

After this astonishing piece of information had been translated, the Germans continued to talk in their own language for a while. Then they had a few questions to put to Owen, all dealing with his specific proposals for the method of their surrender and the safeguards with which it might be accomplished. At the end of another quarter-hour of negotiation they yielded him their arms and formal custody of the two tanks. The plan finally reached by agreement of all five men was to move the tanks, unbuttoned, out into the open, with all of them except the two drivers sitting on top in order to create as non-belligerent an effect as possible. The moment American troops came in sight, Owen would raise a flag of truce, jump to the ground and advance towards them. His prisoners would follow behind him, leaving the tanks unmanned.

It was a sound scheme, Owen thought to himself as he mounted one of the tanks after the helmeted man and the man with the leg wound had perched themselves on top of the other. He tried to recall whether he had read of any other soldier in the war to date who had made a capture of equal value. There were plenty of instances of men who had knocked out a tank single-handed with a grenade or a Molotov cocktail or a bazooka. But for a lone infantryman to bring in even one tank, much less two, intact with crew and undamaged — he was sure it was unprecedented. It would mean the Distinguished Service Cross at the very least. Then he thought of what the newspapers would do with his past record as a conscientious objector and the obvious parallel with Sergeant York in the last war. He vividly recalled the image of York, or rather Gary Cooper, being awarded the Medal of Honour. Perhaps. . . .

The plane came in at close to ground level and they were barely aware of its approach before machine gun fire blended with the whine of its motor. Owen felt himself hit on the right buttock and then again high up on his back. Before consciousness left him he heard a curse in German and an agonized scream that could have been any language.

There was no way he could be sure whether the hospital was in France or in England. It was apparently a converted private dwelling and had suffered some bomb damage, but these indications could have supported either hypothesis. There was a picture hanging across the room that might provide a clue; he squinted to make it out but it was too far away. In the end he had to ask the nurse.

Instead of answering she let out a little gasp and scurried off, returning a moment later with a major who wore Medical Corps insignia and a professional smile.

'Good boy,' said the major. 'Listen to me but don't try to talk any more for another day or so. You're going to be all right. Matter of fact, you've got the perfect combination, no permanent injury but enough to keep you out for a nice long time. Till this bloody circus is over probably.'

'Where is this? What country?'

'France. Don't talk. What about his medal, Nurse? Do you have it for him?'

The nurse opened the drawer of a table by the bed, took out a piece of metal suspended on a ribbon and set it down with a flourish on Owen's chest.

He had been awarded the Purple Heart.

CHAPTER IV

His convalescence was extended and pleasurable, progressing in leisurely instalments from France to England to an army-administered health resort in Florida, and finally to his parents' home on Long Island. It was a time for reading and thinking and orienting himself to the world of practical affairs in which he would soon have to find a place.

It was the imminence of this prospect which broke the calm detachment of his recuperation. It bothered him somewhat that he had no specific inclination toward a career for himself. But this, he knew, was a common failing among young men of the dominant class, and it was reassuring to note that all but a few hopeless misfits were soon absorbed into a comfortable and rewarding way of life. What unsettled him more was the lack of a positive faith or set of standards by which to guide himself. In spite of the fact that he had recently acquired a measure of social grace and superficial confidence, there were still insecurity in him and a restless craving for the certainties of a fixed belief.

Formerly that need had been filled by the philosophy of Tolstoy, and later by the urgent and temporarily cohesive cause of the United Nations in the war. But with the approach of military victory and the emergence of repressed conflicts among the allied powers, he again felt the lack of a comprehensive ideology.

He continued to be profoundly religious in an unorthodox way. His gentle spirit could not endure the world's ugliness without the solace of prayer and the promise of immortality. And while he no longer felt that the teachings of Jesus were suitable for literal application, he believed devoutly in a God Whose Son and Alter Ego had redeemed mankind on a hillock in Jerusalem. But none of the organized variations of Christianity was so thoroughly convincing to him as to win his devotion.

His physical removal from the war freed him to observe it, and he became increasingly impressed with the decisive part the Soviet

Union was playing in bringing it to a conclusion. That in turn led him to favourable speculation about the merits of socialism. Judged by its results in industrial production, adaptability and resiliency, and especially by the heroic individuality it seemed to generate in the human spirit, the system had far more to recommend it than had appeared from his first exposure at college to the complex writings of Marx and Lenin. But the concrete evidence in its favour was counterbalanced in his mind by the materialist rationale which lay inevitably behind it. A state which glorified atheism and merely tolerated religion must have the seeds of evil in it no matter how fine and beautiful its outward manifestations. His own government, for all its shortcomings, had at least invoked the protection of God in its Declaration of Independence and, even though the Constitution was unforgivably remiss in this respect, the nation's chief executives had consistently affirmed its divine auspices.

The ideal state of affairs, he began to think, was some sort of synthesis of the ingredients which had made America and Russia the most powerful nations in the world. The Russians should pay more attention to the spiritual needs of the individual, along with their concentration on his economic rights, while what America mainly needed was greater centralization of economic planning to eliminate recurrent depressions and chaotic fluctuations in employment.

This conclusion reversed the one point of agreement he had previously had with his father: their common opposition to the spread of government. It was noticeable, however, following the death of Franklin Roosevelt and the resulting upsurge in Republican hopes, that the elder Muir had also relaxed his views on the subject.

Owen's father, it developed, had a greater sense of urgency about the details of his son's future than Owen himself had. In June 1945 he began to make pointed inquiries about the boy's health; late in July he wondered out loud whether continued indolence was really good for a young man; in mid-August he took to citing instances of sons of friends of his who were getting established in civilian life. Then, one Sunday about two weeks after V-J Day, Phyllis, whose operator's licence had been revoked, commandeered her mother to drive her to a tennis date, and the two male members of the family were left alone together at the breakfast table.

'I gather you've definitely decided not to finish college,' Mr. Muir said.

'Well, I could go back there, I guess,' Owen began apologetically, 'but I really don't care for either winter sports or bridge, and it's inconvenient to be so far away from a decent library. . . .'

'Don't bother to explain — I agree with you. No sense letting a lot of other fellows get ahead of you in life. I was wondering though, as long as you're through being educated, don't you think it's time you got started doing whatever it is you're going to do?'

'I suppose so. Trouble is, I'm not at all sure . . .'

'Not that the first thing you try will necessarily be what you end up in. I spent three years in cotton textiles when I was your age. And a friend of mine, W. L. Koenig — you've met him, the one who knows all the limericks — he started in Diesel engines, quit that to make women's bathing suits, and now they've given him a hotel to run.'

'I'm not even sure I want to go into business,' Owen said.

'What else could you do?'

'I don't know. There's no scientific field I'd be any good at and I haven't any artistic talent except possibly for writing.'

'Everybody thinks they can write. Even your mother did once.' He laughed at the recollection, then grew serious again as he probed to the crux of the issue. 'Anyway there's no money in it, only at the very top.'

Owen was amused by his father's automatic estimate of his capabilities. 'You sound as if you took it for granted I wouldn't ever make that category — the very top.'

'I do. You haven't got the push for it, the kind of personality that sells itself. All the big writers — Hemingway and Steinbeck and this Winsor girl — they're aggressive, they're showmen basically. You'd better stick to business.'

'We haven't quite ruled out all the alternate possibilities, have we?'

'Practically. You couldn't go into law or medicine if you're quitting school. What other kinds of work are there?'

'A few. Somebody has to grow the wheat and bake the bread and mine the coal . . .'

'I'm speaking seriously. You belong to a class and you have the additional advantage of having somebody ready to put up the capital for you . . .'

'I do?' He was an extremely surprised young man. 'Who?'

'Me. I'll discuss the terms with you when you have a specific proposition lined up. But the point is you have a moral obligation to start a business of your own rather than to work for someone else. You owe it to the economy, to your country. If you go on another man's payroll, you're just taking a job away from somebody else. But when you put capital to work, you're creating jobs, not only for yourself but for however many employees you hire. You're adding a new quantity to the national wealth.'

'That's a very interesting way to look at it. Are all capitalists inspired by the same unselfish idea, do you think?'

'Of course. Not exclusively, though. It's a combination of public service and the profit motive. Where you have both incentives working at once, you have the most complete application to success and, therefore, the maximum benefit to society.'

'What would your motive be in giving me this money?'

'Not giving, lending,' Mr. Muir corrected him. 'What kind of a question is that to ask a father? You and your sister are my stake in the future, Ownie; what else do I have to care about? I'll charge you as much for the use of the money as it would normally be earning elsewhere, but that's only because it's better for your character that way.'

'There's just one thing bothers me,' Owen said uncertainly. 'You said I'd be creating jobs, hiring other people. I don't mind that as long as I'm not making a profit on them. I mean I think a man ought to get just as much in wages as the result of his work sells for. I don't believe a boss ought to take a piece of that away from him.'

'Holy Mother of Sorrow!' Mr. Muir's paternal sentiment yielded momentarily to his horror at this heresy. 'What do you think I meant just now about the profit motive? Why would anyone want the headaches of being a boss if he wasn't getting something out of it?'

Owen was confused. He was not very sure of himself anyway and he rarely gained ground in the course of an argument. 'Oh, sure, he ought to get paid for his work like anyone else and certainly in a case like this where you're putting up the money, I'd have to set some aside to pay you the interest, and I guess that comes under the heading of profit. But I wouldn't want to get rich off of other people's labour.'

'You concede that an investor is entitled to some return on his money? Otherwise he wouldn't have any reason to invest it. Well, it logically follows that the higher the rate of profit is, the more capital comes out of hiding. That means more jobs, more spending, more prosperity for everyone. So it's just the opposite of what you're trying to say. It's a fallacy to figure what you should pay a man in terms of what his work is worth to you. What happens in real life is you pay him the smallest sum he's willing to do the job for. That not only benefits you but in the long run it benefits him too. So getting rich turns out to be the most socially useful thing you can do.' He stood up and smiled. 'It also happens to be a very pleasant experience.'

'I'm afraid it's going to take me quite a while to adjust to your way of thinking,' Owen said. But his tone indicated that he was willing to try.

Mr. Muir stopped behind his son's chair and put a hand on the boy's shoulder. 'Not as long as you imagine,' he said confidently. 'You've got a lot of Yankee trader blood in your veins. Did you know that your great-great-grandfather collected himself a cargo of slaves and delivered them to the Charleston market at a total cost of twelve thousand five hundred dollars, and sold the lot for a hundred and seventy-five thousand in cash?'

Owen shuddered. 'It's incredible now to think that a man could do that.'

'Isn't it?' his father agreed. 'The more so when you remember what money was worth in those days.'

It is not enough, in a free enterprise system, to have one's hands on the capital necessary for a new business. One must also think of a product or a service to sell. As the months passed without his finding a satisfactory way to place his money profitably, Owen envied the captains of industry who had faced the same problem in the less refined economy of the nineteenth century. The investors who put their capital into railroads after the Civil War had had to determine, he conceded, whether that method of transportation had greater potentialities than the bicycle or the free balloon. But at least they had a selection of broad new vistas opening up ahead of them. That no longer held true in a culture so highly developed as to contain dog-sitters and ecclesiastical press agents.

Private inquiries and discreet newspaper advertisements did, however, bring him some response. He was offered a chance to manufacture a combination ball-point pen and pocket barometer; to corner the uranium resources of the West Bronx; to found a 'One World Airline' with daily transpolar flights between Chicago and Moscow; and to publish a magazine called *Lure*, which was designed to instruct convent-school graduates in the techniques of home-making. But none of these projects captured his imagination.

His problem was still unresolved when he received a visit from Arnold Blankenship, the associate warden at Moose Head, who by a happy coincidence had come for the express purpose of interesting Owen in a business venture. 'I thought of you right away when I saw the possibilities in this idea.' He took out what appeared to be an ordinary pocket cigarette lighter and passed it to Owen. 'One of our inmates made it, in our machine shop. Extremely bright boy — did some plates for counterfeit war bonds that got by the banks. If we could put this item on the market, it would start him on the road back. Go ahead, try it.'

Owen held up the lighter and pressed the activating lever. Instead of a flame, there emerged from the wick aperture a sliver of wood. Startled, he gazed at it blankly till the other man reached over and withdrew the tiny stick with his thumb and forefinger.

'It's a match,' Blankenship explained unnecessarily as he struck it across the crossribbed metal undersurface of the gadget. 'You can get fifty of them in there, using a specially thin but strong kind we located.'

'It's unexpected,' Owen conceded, not wishing to express too much enthusiasm before he had fully appraised all the possibilities.

'Do one yourself,' said Blankenship encouragingly, returning the device to him. Owen pressed the spring again and couldn't resist a smile of delight at the way the match sprang into position between his waiting fingers. It was all part of the same motion to flick the match across the bottom and bring its flame on up to the cigarette between his lips.

Phyllis Muir appeared briefly in the doorway of the room in which they were talking and started away again when she saw it was only her brother and an unpromising companion. But in his excitement Owen called to her to come and see what they had.

Although it was not in her nature to display her emotions actively, Phyllis was duly astonished at the trick and pronounced it a cute idea. Owen was still not quite convinced. When she had gone he raised the question of whether the gadget's success was unchallengeable.

'You demonstrated its greatest virtue yourself by your anxiety to show it to your sister,' Blankenship said. 'That's an essential part of product appeal — the desire to exhibit it to someone else. It's an established tenet in the advertising world that people don't choose a car or a refrigerator, say, half as much in terms of their own use as they do according to what they'd like to show off to the neighbours. And that's especially true of an inexpensive item like this that a salesman, for instance, can carry around with him. It helps him break ground when he's making contact with contacts.'

Owen required no more persuasion. The rest of their discussion was devoted to production and merchandizing details, settling the royalty percentage to the inventor and deciding that Blankenship himself should leave the service of his country to take over as advertising director of the new enterprise.

It was still necessary to gain Mr. Muir's blessing for the idea before the capital was actually at their disposal, but this turned out to be an easy matter. 'It's a good project for this kind of market,' he agreed. 'Of course, the one product by itself doesn't give you a permanent business — it's much more a quick turnover thing. But maybe you can make enough out of it to start your next item out of your profits.' He looked from Owen to Blankenship as if trying to gauge whether they were worthy of the challenge. 'All depends on knowing right from the beginning exactly what you've got and what you're trying to do with it, and then never letting your eye off that ball. Like Fulton with his steamboat or Henry J. Heinz with his pickles.'

The first step in launching his career as a manufacturer was to find a physical location for the business. With an eye to economy and the convenience of continuing to live at home, he chose a building in Long Island City which provided them with a good-sized shop and four small offices. The name Jet Manufacturing and Sales Company, designed to cover a variety of future products, was painted on the door, and the enterprise moved in.

Owen's second step was to hire a secretary. Though he did not foresee quite how momentous it was to be in his life, he attached considerable importance to the event and felt uneasy about his capacity to handle it. He discovered how hard and unpleasant it was to refuse a living to someone who wanted and needed it, and two such denials left him so shattered and self-reproachful that he might well have succumbed to the third applicant even if she hadn't turned out to be April Wykoff and thus made all further consideration superfluous.

Her appearance alone as she came through the doorway to his office was enough to make him covet her continued presence on the premises. At twenty-three, which was also Owen's age, April had the kind of open-faced, wholesome beauty that made her every thought seem open for public inspection. A model or a movie star the same height, which was average for her generation, might have weighed six or eight pounds less, but April was not at all heavy for the broad, full design of her body. Her two most striking features were the wide grey eyes, ingenuous yet provocative, and the glow in the cheeks beneath them, vermilion against skin like rich cream faintly diluted with coffee. The effect of her colouring was enormously increased by the fact that one admired it from a distance as a technical achievement and then realized at close range it was natural: that some abnormality of the circulatory system kept the area of her cheekbones in a permanent flush. The hair which framed the contrasting colours of her face was an unqualified black. Her legs and arms, Owen noted, were strong and graceful, her hips properly parabolic, her breasts youthful and prominent.

He had decided to hire her before they got around to the question of her technical qualifications, but it turned out that she could type and take shorthand adequately and had enough experience with office routine to compensate somewhat for his ignorance of it.

'I don't like work,' she told him, 'so I try to get through it as quick as possible and that makes me more efficient than most girls in this kind of job.'

'What do you like?'

'Just living, being with other people, men mostly. Music, pictures, books — movies if they don't take themselves too seriously. More than anything else, I guess I like to talk.'

'I'm afraid you won't get much of a chance to talk to anyone around here. Except me. And I've always been rated a better listener than a conversationalist.'

'That's lucky,' April told him, 'because I can carry on a conversation practically singlehanded. As long as a man nods occasionally and looks like he's paying attention, that's all the incentive I need.'

Happily, there was very little work for either of them to do. At first Owen felt obliged to make himself available to the production and advertising departments for consultation and guidance; then, discovering that they preferred to make their decisions without him, he retreated to the principle that executive genius is the infinite capacity for delegating authority. Beyond some correspondence with likely retail outlets and interviews with promoters of possible new products, his only function during the first two months was to reduce Blankenship's proposed advertising budget by twenty-five per cent. This pleased Holtzmann, the shop foreman, because it left him with more to spend on materials. It also pleased Blankenship, who had anticipated a cut of fifty per cent.

It was April who inaugurated the three-hour lunch period for Owen and herself. 'It's not good business for the head man to be around all the time and ready to see anybody who drops in. And it's not good for the two of us either, with so little to do. First thing you know, one of us will be making a pass at the other.'

'Why would that be such a calamity?' asked Owen, who had already given the subject some thought.

'Too obvious. Proximity's such a trite motive, unless you're on a desert island or somewhere, where there's no other alternative. Then any member of the opposite sex is better than none.'

Some days they drove into Manhattan or Brooklyn or out on Long Island to try a particular restaurant; on others they ate quickly and went to a movie or an exhibition or a museum. He enjoyed her company so much and found her comments so stimulating that there were often long stretches of time when he was hardly conscious of his desire to touch and hold her.

Since April also had a preference for the four-day work week, it was more than a month before one of their lunches occurred on a Friday. A few days earlier she had mentioned an interest in *coq au vin* and Owen, without advance notice, now brought her to a pleasant place that featured it. He was distressed when she declined the specialty and ordered brook trout *meunière*. Ordinarily he wouldn't have pressed her since she generally had a pretty firm idea of what she wanted, but he was anxious for his surprise to go the way he had planned it.

'It's Friday and I have to eat fish,' she explained. 'Couldn't we come here again at the beginning of the week?' Taking his compliance for granted, she turned her attention back to the waiter and seduced him into a major departure from the table d'hôte salad.

'It never occurred to me you were a Catholic,' Owen said after the waiter had gone.

'Naturally I don't reveal my darkest secrets right off, especially when I'm trying to make a good impression. Are you an implacable foe of Popery?'

'I don't know enough about it to be a foe or a friend. But I've never quite liked the authoritarian side of it — the having to believe in a doctrine because the hierarchy decides it's so.'

April laughed at him. 'That only goes on with theology. It doesn't have anything to do with what ordinary people are concerned about, just priests. Do you suppose I'm interested one way or the other in the Albigensian heresy or the scriptural authority for the Immaculate Conception?'

'You accept authority about not eating meat on Friday.'

'You accept authority about how to brush your teeth, don't you, or how often to have your car lubricated? Anyway, I like fish about once a week.'

'It tastes just as good on Tuesdays.'

'That would really be ridiculous — to do something on Tuesday simply because the church I was born into tells me to do it on Friday. Why? Just for the satisfaction of committing a venial sin?'

'What about movies? Do you study the lists to see what it's all right for you to go to?'

'Once in a while, only in reverse. If the Legion of Decency's really down on a picture, it's usually a pretty good sign there's something about it I'll like.'

'I thought the censorship was binding on all Catholics.'

'Sure, within the limits of common sense. I'm too mature or corrupt or however you want to put it to ever be corrupted by anything in a movie, so I'm not fulfilling the purpose behind the rule by staying away from it. With children and susceptible adults it's a different matter and I've never thought about it much but I'm inclined to think it's probably a very good thing not to expose them to something they aren't intellectually or emotionally capable of evaluating.'

'That's fine, but it's your individual judgment. I thought the church took a dim view of individual judgment.'

'You've got one thing mixed up,' April told him. 'I didn't say I was a good Catholic. Just a Catholic.'

It seemed to be part of a plan or a code to which April felt bound for their intimacy never to extend beyond the close of the working day. Once or twice she stretched the rule far enough to include a couple of drinks on the way to the subway she took into Manhattan, but she steadfastly denied his appeals to join him in evening or weekend activity. She never expressly stated that such an event couldn't occur, putting off each invitation with a specific excuse that she had a date or felt tired or had to visit her mother, who, Owen gathered, was sporadically bedridden with one complaint or another. But Owen became aware of a firm though intangible barrier, and it grew increasingly frustrating to him as April came to be the focal point of most of his thinking.

In some ways he felt he knew her as well as he had ever known another person. She was so definitive in her attitudes, casually condemning or dismissing the most sacrosanct names in the arts or public life, and usually managing to come up with a refreshing angle of her own on even the most belaboured topics, so unaffected in exposing the areas of her ignorance, so willing to allow her emotions to the surface without apparent censorship, that her personality seemed to have no shaded regions requiring further exploration.

Yet his knowledge of her biography, domestic life and friends was very small. He gathered that while she saw a good deal of her mother, both lived alone in separate one-room apartments. April described her own, on Morton Street in the Village, as unique in that its greatest dimension was height. 'It's the perfect functional design for an aviary,' she said, 'but not very practical for people. Unless you wanted to practise basketball shots.' She was given, she confessed, to small economies and large luxuries. 'I come from distressed proletarian stock and I was taught to pinch pennies almost from the minute I was born. But I never learned how to pinch a ten dollar bill because I never saw one. Then when I grew up, I found out how much less red tape there is in charging expensive clothes than cheap ones. So I dress well.' He also discovered from incidental references that she had graduated from high school and supported herself through a year of business college by working as an artist's model; that she was allergic to cats; and that she had once been placed third in a motor cycle hill climb open to both sexes. This was virtually the sum of his information concerning her.

The first occasion on which he saw her in contact with anyone known to her outside the office occurred just before he finally broke through her resistance toward afterhour dates. They were walking past the Dutch Consulate after a mid-day film showing at the Museum of Modern Art, and found themselves abreast a small picket line marching under the hostile surveillance of an almost equal number of police. One of the pickets, a rather tall middle-aged woman with a youthful figure, greeted April by her first name.

'Hi, Tessie!' April responded warmly. 'What's the beef?'

The older woman turned the sign she was carrying so that they could read its message: *Free Indonesia!* 'Some people have to be reminded what the war was about,' she said, halting for a moment at one end of her prescribed course. 'How is the new job working out, dear?'

'Keep moving,' a policeman said. 'Not you,' he added apologetically to Owen and April; then conversationally, nodding towards the pickets: 'Got to watch these characters pretty close. They're mostly all pros, this bunch.'

'Pros?' Owen asked. 'You mean they get paid for picketing?'

'Sure. That dame just now, I've spotted her three or four times before. Two strikes and one stink they got up about wanting to change the government in Spain or somewhere.'

'Did she tell you she was being paid?' Owen asked. 'Or did you find out from the people who were paying her?'

'Who has to tell me? Stands to reason she don't have any stake of her own in all them different things.'

'She could have,' Owen persisted. 'You don't have any right to . . .'

April cut him off. 'We'll be late. Thank you, officer. See you soon, Tessie.' She waved to her friend, who was approaching them again.

As they crossed the street, Owen entered a mild protest against her having interrupted him. 'I think maybe it could do a little bit of good, making a man like that realize there's something else besides money.'

'You can't argue a man out of his basic principles. And if you did, you'd have ruined his career. You'd have made an idealist of him and he'd be no more use as a cop.'

'How do you know that isn't my purpose, to gradually corrupt the Police Department, man by man, till it falls apart of its own idealism?'

She laughed. 'That's even more revolutionary than Tessie Couto. Isn't she an amazing-looking woman though? I mean, would you believe she's fifty-seven years old?'

'I certainly wouldn't. I thought she was still in her forties.'

'She says it's the picketing does it, more than anything. And then every election time she's out ringing doorbells day and night. Claims there isn't anything like it for keeping your figure.'

'That's an idea I never heard before.'

'I wouldn't take it too seriously. I think it's just her come-on to get other women interested in progressive activities. What really keeps someone like Tessie looking young outside is the fact that she is young, inside, in her spirit and her response to new ideas.'

They walked close together in silence until they reached his parked car. It was trapped between a sedan which had moved in bumper to bumper behind it and a truck parked at right angles in front with its contents being unloaded on to the side walk. While April got into the car, Owen walked over to the truck driver and extracted a promise that he would try to hasten the operation. But the man's sympathy was limited by his critical view of Owen's part in creating the impasse.

'You shouldn't of squeezed so close to the job behind you,' he pointed out.

'There wasn't any car there. He moved in while we were gone.'

The truck driver brushed aside this flimsy excuse. 'You shouldn't of let him.'

Owen went back to his car and got in beside April.

'Did you persuade him to move?' she asked.

'I certainly did. The minute they're through with what he came for in the first place.'

'That ought to give me time for a quick siesta.' She leaned close to him, settled her head against his outstretched arm and closed her eyes. He rearranged himself to give her more support, then looked down at her to see what further improvements he could make. The impulse to kiss her was even more compelling than usual and he yielded to it.

April's eyes remained closed but her lips showed awareness and approval, and when he drew away they invited him back. During the second kiss she opened her eyes and looked into his. 'Tell them not to hurry,' she said.

'I love you,' Owen said. 'That's how it is and there isn't any other way to say it.'

'Your eyelashes are lovely when you really get close to them. I don't think I've ever seen a man with such long lashes.'

'I wasn't going to ask you again for a while but now I have to know. I want you to set a definite night you'll let me take you out and it's got to be soon. I think we should, April.'

'So do I. I can't today or tomorrow but Saturday would be fine if it's good for you.'

Owen sat at the bar in the Hungarian restaurant he had chosen for the occasion and studied himself in the mirror while he waited for April. He tried to judge his charms from her standpoint. The head, he felt, was rather good with its neat brown hair, bright blue eyes and long, straight nose. His height and wide shoulders gave an impression of strength which was borne out in the rest of his body.

Then it occurred to him that she was too superior a girl to be greatly influenced by mere physical attraction, and his self-content faded rapidly. Now it seemed to him that he looked, and in fact was, much too young for her. It didn't matter that she was the same age; she was more mature than he was in every important respect and it would be only natural for her to prefer an older, wiser and more experienced man.

He was not stupid, he knew; by the mechanical measure of an IQ test, his rating was quite high. But he was uncomfortably aware that his thinking, while generally sound, was rarely quick. His temperament, too, tended to be on a plateau, without valleys or peaks. Tolerance, which he had lacked until the last couple of years, and a sensitivity to other people's reactions were to his credit, but these qualities, he suspected, were apt to be less glamorous than mercurial extremes of emotion.

When April came in, the smile she gave him did much to restore his self-esteem. He was startled and stimulated by the extra margin of beauty which he hadn't realized a semi-formal dress and an evening hair-do could provide. At first they spoke little and what they said were the banal words of choosing a drink for her and remarking on the décor of the room. But there was a new sense of closeness between them, a delight in each other that insulated them from the world around them. They lingered at the bar, studying the menu in an elaborate effort to arrive at the ideal combination of its promises, and then ordering a meal that would take enough time in preparation for two more unhurried cocktails. And when they finally moved on to their table, it was not to a dinner of food alone, but one complete with wine, conversation, laughter and slightly subnormal reflexes.

Actually they didn't get nearly as drunk as might have been expected. April was puzzled about this in relation to herself. 'Usually four Manhattans and I'm reeling. But there's something tonight — I guess you must have a sobering influence on me.'

'That's a hell of a thing to say to the man you're getting this expensive spread off. You could tell me I dazzle you, overwhelm you, intoxicate you, excite you, inspire you — anything. But to accuse me of sobering you, that's definitely a deflationary trend.'

She reached her hand across the table to put on his, and held it there for a moment even after she realized her elbow was resting in her salad. 'I don't need dazzling or exciting. I run on too high a voltage as it is; you ought to know that about me if you want to try and understand me. I need calming and soothing and pampering and deceleration, and that's part of what you do for me. Not all of it but part of it.'

'I don't know,' Owen said. 'I always had kind of a vision of myself like Robert Browning in *The Barretts of Wimpole Street*, taking some beautiful creature by storm with the sheer force of my personality.'

'You just try it on the next beautiful creature you run across and you'll catch the point of a dainty evening slipper where it hurts. I thought it was a very unconvincing play anyway.'

'Nevertheless . . .'

'Forget it,' she said. 'Abandon the whole notion immediately. You're practically the kind of a man I want you to be right now, except for a few rough edges here and there we can smooth off as we go along. I'll let you know when I think any improvements are called for.'

'Who's being dominating now? You say I shouldn't try to impose my will on you and in the same breath you're talking about how you can have me done over to suit your taste. Is that consistent?'

'I hope not. The difference is, I'm spoiled and egocentric and you aren't. Fortunately, I do have a few redeeming qualities. Not consistency, though.'

One result, not unconsidered, of their leisurely pace through dinner was that when they left, after coffee and brandy, it was late enough to make it natural that he drive her directly home.

'I want to come up,' he said when they stopped outside her building.

'We'd better leave the car around the corner,' she told him. 'They let you park it there as late as you want to.'

The shape of April's apartment was close enough to her description to justify the exaggeration. Apparently it was a partitioned section of what had once been a loft, in proportion to the original area of which the high ceiling would have looked all right. The room had two outside walls, a third ran along the corridor, and the fourth was broken up into a bathroom, a kitchenette and a closet. A large day-bed was the dominant piece of furniture and there was only one properly qualified easy chair. Nothing marked it as a particularly attractive or unattractive place to live; April had evidently faced the fact that the basic defect of excess altitude presented an insurmountable obstacle to charm, and had settled for an uncluttered effect which was reasonably comfortable and easy to keep in order.

Owen followed her into the kitchen area, which was designed for single occupancy, and put his arms around her from behind while she made them a drink.

'I suppose a girl entertaining her boss ought to have a choice of fancy refreshments on hand,' she said, 'and conversational gambits worked out in advance. But I didn't make any preparations.'

'This'll do fine.' He drew her backwards against him. 'Just let's have your face around at a little better angle.' She obliged and he moved his hands up to her breasts while he kissed her.

When they took their drinks back into the room, April gestured toward the bed. 'I recommend it as the only place you can relax.' He stretched out against the bolster, took her hand and pulled her down beside him. Sitting, April lifted his hand to her thigh and let it rest there. They took a couple of sips of their highballs without speaking or moving, and then quite abruptly their bodies came together in passionate intensity. Before long they undressed, drew back the covers and lay together on the sheet.

Holding her naked body to his for the first time, Owen felt anew that the excitement a man and a woman could furnish each other was the highest and holiest sensation possible to humankind. As had happened before during the best of his sexual experience, he found the period of anticipation and preparation so deeply satisfying in itself that the desire to sustain it balanced for a considerable length of time the impulse to proceed. Also familiar, and therefore to be regarded sceptically, was the sense that he and the other half of the physical unit into which he was now blended were ideal counterparts of each other. And yet, despite previous disenchantment, it was so important and urgent to assure the future that he paused to say the words after their bodies were fully joined in the penultimate stage of ecstasy. 'Will you marry me?'

He felt her press even more closely against every part of him till it seemed there could be no greater degree of tension, and her eyes as she looked up into his were soft and grateful. 'You have lovely ideas. You're a lovely man altogether.'

And they knew one another.

To his astonished delight, the utterly new, the unique phenomenon was yet to come. It lay in the absence of any letdown. There was a change in his feeling toward her, but it was only that passion subsided in favour of a kind of loving tenderness he had never felt before. And when excitement again overcame them and they had indulged it, the unfamiliar bliss was there once more to replace it. His last conscious thought, before he fell asleep with his body against hers, was an expression of pure faith. He knew at last that there was such a thing as absolute conviction in human love, and that he was convinced.

His eyes opened to daylight and the sight of April, in a short, thin nightgown, moving about in the kitchenette. When she turned and entered the room with a cup of coffee and a couple of doughnuts on a plate, he was enraptured all over again with the beauty of her body and the graceful assurance of its movements. Seeing that he was awake, she paused for a moment, answering his need to absorb the details of her loveliness. Then she came forward and served him his breakfast.

'Have you had yours already?' he asked.

She shook her head. 'I'm due for communion today — I should have done it during Lent and didn't — and that means I fast till afterwards.' She smiled. 'I've got enough on my conscience without that.'

He took only a sip or two of his coffee before he set it on the bedside table and drew her down to lie on top of him.

'Is it too soon to insist on a formal answer to my proposal?'

'There's a problem,' April said. 'You see, I have a guy who lives here with me most of the time. He's out in Ohio this week doing some organizational work. He's a Communist.'

CHAPTER V

BECAUSE his own feeling for her was so uncomplicated, it was hard for Owen to be sympathetic toward April's problem. It was easy enough to understand that she might find it embarrassing or painful to break off an established emotional relationship in favour of a new one, but harder to accept an actual and continuing uncertainty as to which of the two promised her the fuller measure of happiness. A further effort was required to overcome his prejudice, conceived before he had ever seen him, against her lover, Gene Couto, who turned out to be the son of the woman they had encountered on the picket line for Indonesia.

He managed, however, to suppress both these attitudes sufficiently to agree to the three-way conference requested by Couto as the proper method to settle an issue of this kind. The conference took a little time to arrange since, while April and Owen were almost constantly available, Couto was heavily involved in political work for several days following his return to New York. The delay was oppressive to Owen and even April's assurance that Couto was busy with meetings far into the night, and that statistically she was spending a much larger proportion of her time with Owen, was not enough to satisfy him. He offered to stake the other man to a hotel room, but April felt the proposal was in dubious taste and gently declined to relay it.

The meeting was finally scheduled for ten o'clock on a Sunday morning, a week after April and Owen had given themselves to each other, at a cafeteria on Sheridan Square. Owen arrived fifteen minutes before the others and paced the sidewalk outside until they arrived. April took his hand and apologized for making him wait. 'I'm supposed to go to noon Mass with my mother and I thought it would give us more time if I got myself all ready first.'

Gene Couto was about thirty, of medium height and sturdy muscular build. In repose his face was unimpressively pleasant, its boyish cast accentuated by the casual disarray of his hair, but when he spoke he gained attention by the authority and conviction in his voice and the practised lucidity of his speech. He had considerable charm but occasionally his self-assurance bordered on patronage, and antagonized people not easily persuaded to his opinions.

When they had settled themselves at a table with cups of coffee, he led off the conversation with a general comment about the leading news item of the day. 'Kind of a tight situation in Iran.'

'I haven't been following it too closely,' Owen said. 'I gather it all hinges on whether the rebels in — I forget the name of the district — are a genuine, domestically controlled outfit.'

'They're about the only group in the country that is,' Couto said. 'England's always owned the place, and we hold the mortgage on England.'

'Hadn't we better come to the point?' April suggested. 'If there is any.' She turned to Owen. 'Gene is a great believer in the constructive value of organized discussion. I'm not at all sure it applies to this kind of a situation but I didn't have any better plan to offer.'

'There's always one advantage to a frank, open consideration of a question among all the parties involved,' Couto said. 'People are more apt to say what they really feel. For April particularly, since her feelings are the main issue here, there's a temptation with either one of us alone, to distort the picture so as not to hurt the person she happens to be talking to.'

'Well,' April began, 'if my feelings are what we're here to talk about . . .'

'I'd like to say one thing first,' Couto broke in. 'The fact that we all have the patience and understanding to meet together like this is an indication that we'll be able to talk the thing out on a mature level. That's important.'

'Yes, I agree,' Owen said.

'We have to rise above our emotions,' continued Couto, 'and discuss the situation on an objective, dispassionate basis. I want you to know, Muir, that I don't feel any animosity toward you whatsoever. If anything, the fact that you're smart enough to appreciate April starts you off very high in my estimation.'

'I'm glad you feel that way,' said Owen. 'Naturally, I couldn't possibly have any animosity toward you. On the contrary, I seem to have messed up your life without meaning to, and I could understand your being a little annoyed with me.'

'I'm the only one anybody has grounds for being annoyed with,' April said. 'I wonder both of you don't tell me to go to hell.'

Neither of the men seemed to hear her. 'Not at all,' Couto replied to Owen's last remark. 'The fact that two men in love with the same woman no longer feel compelled to fight it out like a couple of stags is just one more proof of how human nature is constantly changing. I find it very easy to see why April was attracted to you. It's only frank to say that.'

'We have to be frank,' Owen said. 'All of us, all down the line. For instance, while as I said I have nothing against you, I'm selfish enough to put my happiness ahead of yours. I'm going to try to convince April she ought to marry me and I can't let myself be too concerned with how that might hurt you.'

'Perfectly reasonable,' said Couto. 'One thing I like is when a man is honest, with himself and other people. I feel that what you said just now was very honest, and very fair.'

A trace of impatience crossed April's face. 'If you're through exchanging preliminary tributes, maybe I ought to say this about what I feel. I'm not exactly on the fence, half-way between two opposite choices. I have a fairly good idea which direction I'm headed in, but that doesn't mean there isn't a pull the other way too. Also, so I get credit for my share of honesty, I've been straight with each of you separately about how things stand between me and the other one and what's gone on up to this point. I mean Owen knows about you and me, Gene — and I've told Gene about what happened between us last Saturday night.'

'Yes,' said Couto, looking at Owen. 'I'll be frank to say that's the only objection I have to your behaviour. The fact that you went to bed with my girl while I was out of town.'

Owen started to refute this implication of misconduct on his part but cut himself short when he realized he would be ungallantly transferring the blame to April.

It turned out that she was quite willing to accept it. 'He didn't even know you existed,' she told Couto. 'I didn't tell him I was committed in any way.'

'That was an interesting omission. Is it too curious of me to ask why you didn't tell him?'

'Because I wanted to go to bed with him, I guess. And I figured he'd be less apt to if he knew.'

'Very thoughtful. Do you still have the same urge toward him? I'm not asking for a clinical account of your little episode together, but it does seem pertinent to the matter at hand to know whether the impulse is stronger or weaker at this point.'

Though himself interested in April's response to this query, Owen resented the other man's cross-examination of her, and felt the discussion was becoming indelicately explicit. 'April's not on the witness stand. I think we ought to listen to what she started off to say before.'

'I asked a perfectly reasonable question,' Couto insisted. 'Do you still have the urge to go to bed with him?'

'Yes, I do,' she said. 'But I won't, with either of you, until I'm sure which it's going to be from now on. I may have the makings of a loose woman but one thing I'm not prepared for, yet anyway, is carrying on with two men at the same time.'

'One more point,' Couto said. 'How do you feel about me as a sexual partner?'

'The same as ever. You're two very different kinds of men and I love you each for quite different reasons, but if you can measure a thing like sex attraction, I'd say you rate about equal.'

'You see,' Couto said triumphantly to Owen. 'We've got one major element out of the way already.'

'Yes,' Owen conceded, 'but there are other equally important factors. To begin with . . .'

'You want to get around to economics?' Couto said helpfully. His smile suggested an ability to lay bare his rival's hidden motives.

'No,' Owen said. His bias against the man was developing into a settled antipathy, but he succeeded in displaying less indignation than he felt. 'If you could bring yourself to abandon the Socratic method for a moment and let April talk about her feelings toward us...'

'That's right,' April said. 'And what I feel, or what any woman feels toward any man, has a lot more to it than just sex. Not that I want to belittle sex — it's my favourite activity...'

'Excuse me, baby,' Couto said, 'but I think we ought to be precise as hell about just what our frame of reference is. I can't agree that it's entirely a question of what you feel. Reason has to enter into it too. For instance, as I understand it, young Owen here wants to marry you. So, as you know, do I. I've been proposing to her three times a week for the last two years,' he explained parenthetically to Owen. 'No sensible person, especially a woman in this damn chauvinist society of ours, goes into a marriage completely on the basis of her emotions. You also have to consider the kind of future a guy's offering you. Somebody ought to point out, and maybe it's more tactful for me to do it, that as far as what are conventionally known as a man's prospects are concerned, Mr. Muir has a considerable edge on me.'

Owen had a vague sense that he had been somehow outflanked by this argument in his behalf. 'If you're talking about the fact that I probably have more money than you do, I don't think April's apt to be influenced by that.'

'She has to be. It's not just a question of money either. I happen to be part of a movement that's getting increasingly unpopular in this country, even though its stock is going up all over the world. My future is a pretty hazardous proposition compared to that of a man who's running a capitalist enterprise during a period when the rate of exploitation is higher than it's ever been. You also have a wealthy father behind you, while all I've got is a mother I've had to raise bail for three times in the last year.'

'I envy you on that score,' Owen said. 'Having a parent you can share something with, who has the same outlook you do. That's a very valuable possession, as both you and your mother probably know.'

'Tessie thinks Gene is the most wonderful person in the world,' April said. 'Except possibly Stalin.'

'I gave her something to live for,' Couto admitted. 'She was the most apolitical kind of middle-class housewife till I conned her into going to a League against War and Fascism meeting, and then started slipping her the *Daily Worker* in small doses.'

'You ought to see her with some of her old friends now,' April said with an affectionate smile. 'She doesn't care what it is they decide to go in for — rent control, nursery schools, the United Nations, or what — but she won't let them just sit back and vegetate.'

The digression led to a pause, which Owen ended by addressing April. 'One thing I'd like to know. Mr. Couto says he's proposed to you many times. Why haven't you married him?'

'I've been close to it,' April said, 'on more than one occasion. The main thing that's stopped me, I guess, has been the difference in our ideologies. I don't have any scruples about marrying outside the church — most of the Catholic men I know are hideous bores with guilt complexes that probably come out in bed — but the combination of a Catholic and a Communist does seem a little extreme at this stage of history.'

'Not if they respect each other's beliefs,' Couto argued.

'You don't though, really,' she said. 'I respect yours but you barely tolerate mine. I've heard your friend Ambrose on the subject: "You can't equate a rational philosophical system with a patchwork jumble of superstition and class oppression."'

'I didn't say that. Ambrose did.'

'You sat there nodding your head.'

Couto looked toward Owen for sympathy. 'It's amazing, the number of ways a man can suffer for his convictions.'

'What did you join the party for?' Owen inquired, allowing the malice he felt to enter his voice. 'To improve your social standing?'

'Coming from a top-drawer, born-to-the-manner plutocrat,' Couto said, 'that's the kind of a snide remark a guy could work up a good solid resentment against.'

'I can't say what you choose to resent is a matter of any great concern to me.' Owen hated himself for taking part in this kind of personal exchange, but the impulse toward it was too strong to resist.

'Cut it out, both of you,' April said. 'There's no reason to act like a couple of adolescents just because we've gotten ourselves into an emotional mix-up.'

'*We* haven't gotten ourselves into anything,' Couto pointed out. 'You're the only one that's mixed up.'

'Yes.' Owen felt obliged to agree with the man about something. 'It's an academic point really, but neither Mr. Couto nor I can be held responsible for whatever confusion exists.'

April reacted with bitter defensiveness to this two-front attack. 'In other words there's only one person to blame for anything and that's me!' Tears gathered in her eyes. 'I'm a lascivious bitch who's screwing up the lives of two virtuous fellows with her wanton ways.'

Her hurt tone and her tears provoked Owen to instant and sharp remorse. He leaned toward her and placed a loving hand on her shoulder. 'I didn't mean I had any criticism of you, sweetheart! I haven't at all; it's not your fault you've got a problem.'

'Don't touch her!' Couto said sternly. 'If my girl needs any comforting while I'm around, I'll take care of it. I can't control what you do at your office, though I have my own opinion of employers who take liberties with girls who depend on them for a living.'

Owen withdrew his hand from April and turned to face his rival belligerently. 'That's an uncalled-for crack if I ever heard one.'

'Would you like to do something about it?' Couto inquired in a menacing voice as he pushed back his chair.

'I don't mind,' Owen said. 'I'm younger than you are and a lot bigger and I don't mind at all.'

Couto's answering smile seemed to say he had advantages which would more than compensate for size and youth. Both men were in the act of getting to their feet when they were stopped by the sound of April's unexpected laughter. They sank back down into their chairs and looked at her.

'You ought to have antlers,' she giggled, 'and then you'd really look like a couple of stags.'

They looked at each other, abashed, and a moment later were competing in their contrition. 'We're acting like goons,' Owen said. 'After all our talk about mature, dispassionate discussion.'

'I let my feelings get the better of me,' Couto admitted. 'Which I shouldn't have done even though the provocation was pretty offensive.'

April joined the chorus of self-criticism. 'It's really all my fault. I should have faced the fact it was my decision and there wasn't anything to be gained from this kind of a session. The trouble is of course that you're both such desirable fellows I hate to give up either one of you. But I know I have to and I keep thinking maybe something will come up to make it easier.'

'Like finding out one of us has an incurable disease,' Owen suggested. 'Or a wife and six children in Jersey City.'

'That would help,' she agreed, 'but I guess it's unrealistic to hope for anything that decisive.'

Couto had turned away from their levity. His own expression was intensely serious as he conducted an internal struggle of apparently heroic proportions and, resolving it, faced April. 'I have something that ought to be quite decisive. Only I'd prefer to discuss it with you privately.'

'Hey,' Owen protested. 'No. Absolutely not.'

'He's right, Gene,' April said. 'You were the one who asked for a frank discussion with everything out in the open.'

'Well — let me put it this way,' Couto said. 'You said a while ago that my being a Communist is my main drawback in your eyes, and I've always let you think of me as a very orthodox and inflexible one.'

'Not inflexible in any bad sense,' April said tenderly. 'You have very positive convictions and you stick to them very consistently. I admire you for that.'

'But you find the convictions themselves distasteful.'

'No, I wouldn't say that. Sometimes I think if I had a better character I'd be a Communist myself.'

'You'd rather I wasn't one though. Wouldn't it make a considerable difference to you if you learned I was a lot further to the right in some of my ideas than I seemed to be on the surface?'

'Don't talk like that,' April said. 'It isn't a subject to be funny about and I get a shivery feeling inside even though I know you're not serious.'

'What makes you think I'm not? Everything is subject to change, including a man's political beliefs. I'm asking a serious question and I want a serious answer. Wouldn't it make a lot of difference to you if you knew that some people thought of me as anything but orthodox?'

'It would make a difference, yes,' April said slowly. 'I wouldn't have nearly as much respect for you as I do now.'

'What kind of sense does that make?' he demanded furiously. 'You disagree with Marxism yourself; you've said so plenty of times.'

'That's right. It's a little too mechanical for my taste.'

'Then how could you hold it against me if I felt some of it was mechanical too?'

'I don't know how exactly, but I could,' she said, trying to work it out in her mind as she spoke. 'I guess it's because being a Communist is part of the you I know, the you I've been in love with. If that's changed, then you're a different person, a stranger.'

'I didn't say anything had changed. I simply asked you a hypothetical question.'

'No.' She wouldn't let him reverse his field now. 'You meant something. I'm not sure exactly what, but I don't like it. As a matter of fact there isn't even any need for us to talk about it any more. I'm clear all of a sudden about how I feel and what I want to do.' She turned to Owen. 'How would you like to take my mother and me to Mass?'

The love and warmth in her eyes as she looked at him left no doubt as to what she meant. He had won the prize he valued above all other earthly rewards and for a few seconds he was numb with happiness, unable to move or speak. Then the realization of what Couto must be feeling descended on him and he was overcome with sadness at the thought of the other man's loss. It was distressing to reflect how often a law of compensation seemed to operate in human affairs, exacting a measure of woe somewhere in payment for each award of joy.

April, too, was concerned with the effect of her decision on her rejected lover. 'We'll be going along now, Gene, so why don't you just take it easy for a while? If you get your stuff out of the apartment by mid-afternoon, that'll be fine.'

Ilsa Wykoff was nineteen years older than April but lacked her daughter's mental and emotional maturity. Widowed eight years previously by the combined ravages of tuberculosis and her own personality, she now invested her husband's memory with the love and respect she had steadfastly withheld from him in life. At forty-two she still attracted occasional aspirants to her hand but she was so volubly pessimistic about her health that they were all discouraged in the end by the prospect of imminent medical and funeral expenses. Thus, since she was deeply pious and resolutely chaste, religious activity served as her only outlet for the considerable physical and sexual energy which belied her self-appraisal. Not only did she function in several Catholic organizations within her own parish but she also spoke guardedly of mysterious connections with the arch diocese itself, creating, by her refusal to confirm or deny it, the impression that she was an important figure in the lay apostolate of the New York area.

Owen was anxious to like her and found an immediate basis for doing so in her physical resemblance to April. Though she had never had her daughter's beauty, Mrs. Wykoff was well-formed in a slightly overfed way and her face included less spectacular versions of several of April's features. The fact that she was obviously captivated by his charms and social standing also made it easier for Owen to discount her limitations.

He approached his first Catholic service with similar tolerance. To avoid being conspicuous he made a perfunctory obeisance on entering the pew and descended to his knees or rose to his feet along with the congregation, but otherwise confined himself to listening and watching rather than trying to share in an experience that was alien to him. He wished that he were better acquainted with the sacrifice and its accompanying ritual; some of it baffled him but he also found much of it moving, particularly the sense he gained from the people around him that they were participating in an act of genuine reverence. April was somehow able to be absorbed in the contact with her Saviour and in Owen's reactions at the same time; and Mrs. Wykoff, who was one of those to go up and receive the Eucharist, looked positively exalted by the sacrament.

The appearance and manner of the officiating priest also made a favourable impression on him. Tall and spare with a thick head of snow-white hair, Father Duchesne performed his functions with the assurance of a man in close and constant communion with his Maker. He was at least sixty-five, April told Owen, but so vigorous that his curates dreaded the long walks on which he would take them to expound their duties. He was also noted for the extreme brevity of his sermons and the mildness of the penances he imposed at confession, which were said to run from forty to fifty per cent below the diocesan averages for equivalent sins.

From the church they proceeded in haste to the nearest restaurant in order to save Mrs. Wykoff from possible starvation. Her need for sustenance after a fast of fourteen hours was urgent, she explained, owing to a delicate internal condition which prevented her from consuming more than a sparrow's portion of food at one sitting. She thereupon demonstrated that she permitted herself a certain elasticity in this dosage by ordering a large bowl of soup and a steak with baked potato and salad.

April waited till her mother's strength was sufficiently restored and then revealed that she and Owen were engaged. The precaution was probably unnecessary, for Mrs. Wykoff responded to the announcement as if she had been prepared to hear it and had already weighed the considerations for and against.

'If you can make my child happy,' she told Owen, 'that's the only thing that matters to me. She was all I was left with when the Lord in His infinite wisdom took my sainted husband to his eternal reward at the very moment when job opportunities were finally beginning to open up in his field. Somehow I found the strength to go out and work for the food she needed to fill out her weak, wasted little body.'

'Really, Mother,' April said, 'you ought to wait till I've got him landed before you start knocking my body.'

'Oh, you're fine and healthy to look at now,' her mother said. 'But there were plenty of times we didn't know whether to send for the doctor or the priest.'

'I remember one anyway,' April told Owen. 'I had a tough siege of pneumonia when I was about twelve and this parish we were in then, in Brooklyn, they had the services on the radio every Sunday. I was lying in bed listening when the father came to special prayers for the sick members of our congregation, and there was one all for me. You know what it was? I can give you the exact quote: "O Lord God, Father of mercy, we pray to Thee for the speedy recovery or happy death of April Wykoff." He didn't express a preference one way or the other, which I, looking at it subjectively, found rather depressing.'

'That's horrible!' Owen voiced his immediate reaction without stopping to consider that it might be taken as a criticism of their faith.

'It certainly struck me that way,' April admitted.

'Why?' Mrs. Wykoff demanded righteously. 'If there was any danger of the poor child dying, and believe me there was, could anything be more important than what was going to happen to her little soul? I can tell you a very sad story about some friends of ours who were in such a blind hurry to have their girl operated on, they let her be put under the anaesthetic without anybody even telling her there was a good chance she'd never come out of it. So the unfortunate creature died on the table without having made her peace with God, and then they found out she'd been playing around with the boys in the neighbourhood and there was every reason to believe she'd died in mortal sin. Two minutes with a priest or even a nurse or anybody, and she could have been spared the rest of eternity in torture.'

'She may have been genuinely contrite anyway,' April pointed out, 'even if she didn't know she was going to die.'

'May have been!' Mrs. Wykoff scoffed at the inadequacy of the words. 'That's a great consolation to offer two people faced with the thought that they've brought an immortal soul into the world and then sent it to damnation.'

'My mother is quite an ardent theologian,' April said. 'Practically a one-woman chapter of the Society for the Propagation of the Faith.'

'I don't give my opinions without having something to back them up,' Mrs. Wykoff retorted. 'I've talked about this particular case to Monsignor Frasso and anybody will tell you there aren't many days go by the cardinal doesn't ask his advice about one thing or another.' She turned to Owen. 'If you think I'm wrong, speak to Father Duchesne about it when you go to see him.

Bewildered, Owen started to explain that he had no appointment with the priest, but April, hastily swallowing a mouthful of food, interrupted him. 'Mother's assuming we're further along with our arrangements than we really are.' To her mother she said, 'We haven't gotten around to talking about religion yet at all.'

Owen smiled ingratiatingly at Mrs. Wykoff. 'I promise you I'll keep my mind open and listen in case April ever decides to try and convert me.'

'Decides to try! It isn't up to her to choose. She has a spiritual duty to start now and never stop trying.'

'Okay,' he said genially. 'And if I ever go to work on her to change her faith, I promise I won't use any pressure except logical persuasion.'

Mrs. Wykoff emitted a shocked gasp. 'My dear young man, you don't understand. The only way you could ever possibly get permission to marry her is if you made a sacred promise never to say one word against the true religion. There are other conditions, too, of course, but that's essential.'

'Whose permission?' he asked. 'Oh, you mean if we wanted to get married by a priest? That's one of the things we haven't gone into yet.'

It was apparent that Mrs. Wykoff had a vigorous comment to make on this, but her daughter spoke first. 'We will very soon though, Mother.' She arranged her knife and fork on the plate and applied her napkin to her lips. 'Why don't you ask for the check, darling, and then we can drop Mother at her place?'

While he settled the bill he made one more attempt to appease Mrs. Wykoff. 'I'm sure April and I will be able to work everything out as long as you give me a break and don't be too rigid in the terms you insist on.'

'You can hardly call me rigid,' she told him. 'God's law through His church is no mixed marriages at all — except by a special dispensation on account of unusual circumstances.'

'Like knowing someone in the bishop's office,' April said, 'or making a nice contribution to chancery expenses.'

'Don't say things like that!' Ilsa was in the act of getting to her feet but the sacrilege so shook her that she slumped back into her chair for support. Her voice trembled and so, by way of added emphasis, did her body. 'You've been told a thousand times that my heart can't take your jokes. I've been living on borrowed time,' she explained to Owen, 'ever since I had a seizure in July 1943, the night before the Feast of the Visitation.' She turned back to April. 'When I think of the way I've worked my fingers to the bone for you, the sleepless nights, the special Masses we couldn't afford, the novena I ran a temperature all through — the very least I hoped for was that you'd grow up to be a decent, devout girl with some respect for God and her mother. Don't you know what it does to my heart when you talk like a pagan?'

'I ought to,' April admitted. 'You've mentioned it often enough.' She took her mother's arm and helped her up. 'Come on, we'll take you home and you can put your poor, weak, wasted heart to bed.'

The older woman accepted her daughter's support readily and as they walked out of the restaurant together ahead of Owen, he had the sense that there was a firm emotional bond between them.

He and April went to a hotel that night to consummate their betrothal. They had no reason to assume Couto would not accept his notice of dispossession but even the possibility was enough to make them seek greater assurance of privacy.

It was an undistinguished room, decorated in the neutral taste of a large metropolitan commercial hotel, but the occasion gave it an enchantment they would long remember. After one session of leisurely love making they had supper sent up and then returned to their basic preoccupation with each other. Only now by comparison did he realize that she had yielded but a part of herself before; tonight she was committing body and mind to him without reservation and the difference was measurable in degrees of exquisiteness. They were both so entranced by the thought that what they were finding in each other now they would go on having for the rest of their lives that they couldn't stop voicing it. Objectively considered, their variations on this theme were monotonous in the extreme, but the night was unimpaired by objective consideration.

It wasn't until they were finally ready for sleep that they descended to the consideration of a practical matter and, for a fleeting moment, to the threshold of disharmony. Unwilling to relinquish physical contact, they were lying together in one of the twin beds with his arm under her shoulders, when Owen raised the question of whether her mother's feeling about a Catholic ceremony would be a continuing problem. 'It wouldn't bother me very much where or how we did it, but I'd like to avoid any unnecessary trouble with my family. They were pretty upset last year when my sister was going around with a Catholic boy and I think my mother really believes there's something sinister about a wedding or any kind of goings-on in a Catholic church. I don't know what exactly — burnt offerings to the Antichrist.'

'They'll be safe from contamination. We won't get married in a church.'

He was relieved by this indication of co-operation on her part, and said so.

'I mean we couldn't be, without special permission,' she explained. 'When somebody's allowed to marry outside the faith, a priest has to perform the ceremony or it isn't lawful, but you don't get the nuptial Mass or blessing. And you can't be married at all until the non-Catholic has signed the papers about not interfering with the Catholic's religion and bringing the children up in the church.'

'I'll go along with the part about not interfering with you. And I'll also agree not to try to impose any other beliefs on our children — they can certainly be Catholics if they want to. Will that satisfy you?'

April told him patiently that it wasn't a question of satisfying her. The church made the rules and they had to abide by them absolutely or they couldn't be married at all. As for a civil ceremony, even outside of the fact that it would be a cruel and possibly fatal blow to her mother, she herself wouldn't feel properly married without the sacrament and it would certainly be ridiculous to subject herself to excommunication just in order to cater to a meaningless principle of his. 'A child of ours would decide his own religion in the end anyway. All you'd be committing yourself to is that he'd be educated as a Catholic until he was old enough to make up his mind for himself.'

'But why try to influence them at all?' he asked. 'It seems to me insisting on the right to control children's education is the church's greatest confession of weakness. The whole idea that people belong to a religion because they were born into it is silly. Christ put the obligation up to the individual to choose his path for himself, but Catholics have so little faith in their own doctrines they're afraid to put them up in free competition with other religions. Wouldn't it be a greater glory for the church if, instead of ninety-nine per cent of its followers being Catholics because their parents were, they won over the same number of people from all the different backgrounds in the country?'

'You know perfectly well what would happen,' April said. 'The church would practically die out in a couple of generations. If you believe in leaving everything up to children to find out for themselves, you wouldn't teach them anything at all; you wouldn't give them the benefit of your own experience. Instead of telling a baby a fire would burn him, you'd let him find out for himself.'

'Fire is a fact; religion is an idea. It isn't good to have a whole separate school system tied to one religion. When a child is exposed to only one set of ideas, his mind doesn't develop the way it should.'

'Thank you.'

'What?'

'For the tribute to my mind. I'm a product of parochial schools.' He felt her stiffen in the darkness and turn on to her side away from him.

'I didn't mean it applied to you at all,' he said. 'I think your mind came out just perfect.' He turned toward her back, curving his body around hers. 'You came out perfect all over.' He felt her relax against him and the uneasy moment was over. 'The only thing is, you're such an exceptional person it isn't really fair to judge by you.'

'Don't you think we'll have exceptional children?' She turned her head enough to meet him in a kiss and whatever answer he may have had to the question lost its importance. When their lips parted she spoke again. 'Why don't you talk to Father Duchesne about it? He can give you the reasoning much better than I can and answer any points that bother you. Why don't you at least do that for me, my dearest love?'

He embraced her and the proposal in one ardent movement.

In the morning they took a taxi from the hotel to the plant in Long Island City, where Owen was confronted with an alarming industrial crisis. It had been in the making for some days, he learned, but the desire of his associates to spare him anxiety, combined with his own absorption in personal matters, had kept it from his attention. The gist of the situation as it was explained to him was that they had brought Trulite, which was the name they had given their product, to the market with a very narrow margin of working capital allotted to its continued manufacture, and it was not selling nearly quickly enough to keep them solvent. Boal, the company accountant, presented Owen with figures to show that they would be unable to meet the payroll and other current obligations by the middle of the following week. The rest of their capital was all assigned to advertising contracts.

Probing to the heart of the matter, Owen asked Blankenship how many of the latter could still be cancelled. When the advertising director reluctantly conceded that it amounted to some seven thousand dollars worth, the president ordered him to terminate them all immediately. That would keep them in business for approximately another two months, which should be ample to determine whether Trulite was going to catch on the way they had all expected. If it turned out they had been wrong, then it would be an honourable failure with all employees and bills fully paid.

Although he had no doubts about the merit of his decision or his authority to make it, he felt an obligation to acquaint his father with the danger threatening their investment. This coincided with his desire to break the news of his engagement and, after ascertaining that it was not one of the days when Willis Muir's presence was required on Wall Street, he went home for lunch. He asked April if she would like to go with him but was inclined to agree with her opinion that he would do better alone.

There was one advantage he could see to having a valid business reverse to report, which was that it fitted in with the excuse he had given over the telephone for not returning home the previous day and night. It developed, however, that he didn't have to press this point; his parents were too concerned over his sister's recent conduct to worry about his own. Phyllis was in Los Angeles, where she had gone for the ostensible purpose of visiting a school friend, but it now appeared from an investigation her father had launched, after a few distressing references in the gossip columns, that she was actually there to be with a movie director named Bert Drucker. This man had so many drawbacks in the Muirs' eyes that they took turns listing them. Mrs. Muir covered the points that he was Jewish, foreign-born and Phyllis's senior by twenty years; while her husband supplied the added charges that he was a graduate of City College of New York, had once been associated with the Federal Theatre Project, and was now about to have his option dropped by his studio because his last two pictures had lost money. There was also an unconfirmed rumour that he wore neckerchiefs and buckskin moccasins.

While all of these items were to be scored against him, it emerged from further discussion that the two main counts in the indictment were his Jewishness and his lack of the commercial touch. 'We haven't heard a word directly from Phyl herself,' Mr. Muir complained. 'She won't take our calls or answer wires. But the information I get is that she's thinking of marrying him. How do you like that for Jew nerve? Out of a job, washed up in Hollywood from what I hear, and he wants to marry a dizzy child who treats a roll of twenty-dollar bills like they were Kleenex. No wonder the English are starting to get tough with the bastards in Palestine. We just got through one war on their account and now they're trying to start a new one with their damn refugee ships!'

'Who is?' Owen asked. 'Bert Drucker?'

'Your father's excited,' Mrs. Muir said. 'He knows as well as we do that there are good Jews and bad Jews, just like anyone else. You should have heard the sermon yesterday, Willis. It was all about intolerance and how that's what starts wars. No, for all I know, Mr. Drucker may be a perfectly charming man and I don't have a thing against him as long as he leaves my girl alone.'

'Why should he? I mean, if he's a fine man and Phyl loves him, how do you know it mightn't be the best thing for her?'

'Because he's Jewish and she isn't,' Mrs. Muir said. 'People ought to leave other kinds of people alone, just like Father Paley was saying in this sermon. If we're going to be tolerant, they have to, too.'

'That's right.' Willis Muir was pleased that he and his wife were in such splendid accord. 'The only thing is we do have something additional to go on in this particular case. I asked a member of the board of directors of the company he works for for a report on his character, and he told me they'd given him a chance with a million dollar investment and he turned it into an art picture with all sorts of deeper meanings that laid a great big egg at the box office. He could have had a new contract at a much higher figure than he was getting and he sold out for some fancy phrases from the critics. I say if a man isn't loyal to his employers, you certainly can't trust him as a husband or a father.'

Owen considered the possibility of debating these points with his parents but abandoned it as a futile gesture. In any case he had absolute confidence in his sister's ability to do, not necessarily the right thing but the thing she wanted to do, regardless of any interference from her family. The soundest policy for him in this situation, he concluded, was the opportunistic one of exploiting it to his own advantage.

'At least there's one consolation,' he said. 'This new thing of Phyl's must mean she's through with that man, what's-his-name, that owns the football team, Dennis Carpenter. Remember how worried you were about him last summer?'

'Who was worried?' his mother wanted to know. 'I'm very fond of Dennis.'

'You didn't particularly like his having had all those wives. And you were even more upset about his being a Catholic.'

'I only wish he were still around,' Willis Muir said. 'Say, do you think it might be an idea to speak to him about making a trip out there and having a talk with Phyl?'

'He may be there already,' Mrs. Muir said. 'I think I read he was dating some movie actress since his last annulment. I must say it seems much pleasanter to think about him and Phyllis now than it did last year.'

'Maybe it would help if you let him know that,' Owen suggested. 'There's no telling how much he was put off by the thought that we were prejudiced against Catholics.'

'He was quite wrong if he got any such idea about me,' Owen's father declared righteously. 'I'm on record a dozen different ways that this is the time for all Christians to unite. It's the last, best hope of hanging on to what we've got.'

'Is that what you believe now, Mother? I seem to remember some fairly strong sentiments you had.'

'Never against Catholic people, only their leaders, all those bishops and cardinals pretending to be Americans and taking orders from Rome.'

'There's one thing to be said for the hierarchy, though,' Mr. Muir said. 'They never got fooled about who the real enemy was when a lot of our Protestant statesmen were only worrying about Hitler and Mussolini. Now we're beginning to wake up to the fact that that Pope over there in his silly-looking skirts is probably the smartest international politician in the world.' He invoked his patriarchal right to close this phase of the discussion and go back to practical matters. 'I'll sound out Carpenter through Tiny Buchanan, who handles his legal affairs.' He glanced at his watch and saw that he was nearly due for a game of large-scale croquet on a neighbour's broad green acres. 'Now what about you, Ownie? I gathered you had some problem.'

Owen told him of the crisis that beset the Jet Manufacturing and Sales Company, and of the step he had taken to retrieve the situation. His account began coherently enough but it suffered increasingly from the look of exasperation that grew on his father's face. Before he was through, Mr. Muir was interrupting with questions about the costs of materials and manufacture in relation to the sales price, and he never did get a chance to complete his own analysis of the problem. His father took over in the wounded tone of a teacher whose precepts have been wantonly disregarded.

'I tried to tell you at the beginning what kind of a proposition you had and how you ought to handle it. I purposely didn't spell it out for you because I wanted to give you the satisfaction of working out the details yourself. But I told you it was a quick turnover item, didn't I? So what did you do but go ahead and treat it like a product that people wanted, that had some use to them without it being sold down their throats? Your kind of gadget calls for a set-up like the ball-point pen people, where you only spend a tiny fraction of your retail price on actually making the thing and put the bulk of your capital where it's needed, in advertising, in creating a demand where none could possibly exist because your product doesn't have any conceivable value to anybody. Then you can start off charging every nickel the traffic will bear and begin cutting your price when the novelty wears off. A dollar ninety-eight is a reasonable starting price for your Trulite, but only provided you can still make a profit when you have to unload it for nineteen cents and the only reason people will buy it is because it used to sell for so much more they think they're getting a tremendous bargain.

'All this money and effort you've spent trying to get the best possible materials and workmanship is so much waste, and waste is what we've got to cut out or our free competitive economy can't survive. You get right back there this afternoon and figure out what's the absolute bottom unit cost you can slap the thing together for.'

'I'm afraid it's too late for that,' Owen said. 'We just haven't got the cash for the kind of big advertising campaign you're talking about.'

'Borrow it. I'll back you up. But I mean a real splurge — don't try to be cheap about it. Newspapers, radio, magazines, store displays, whatever it needs. Stinting on selling cost is the most dangerous false economy there is. Look at Coca Cola or the big name cigarettes. You don't think people are born with a craving for a smoke or a pause that refreshes, do you?'

'Maybe what we need is a habit-forming drug,' Owen said, smiling.

'It helps. You find a way to put opium in bubble gum and make it legal, and I'll get you a billion dollars worth of financing. But seriously, that's the exact point you overlooked — you haven't got any sustained product appeal. You've got something nobody wants now and something they're going to want even less after they've bought it. That's why you have to concentrate on the one job of creating an illusion that they want it at the exact moment when they're standing in front of a counter fingering their wallet.'

'I don't know,' Owen said. 'Isn't it possibly sounder, if our product is as useless as you say it is, to just abandon it now and take the loss? I mean I'm worried about the money I've cost you already but I'd also hate for you to lose any more.'

'If you understand what I've told you, there won't be any losses. Ninety per cent of the businesses that go under in this country fail because the people behind them can't or won't raise enough capital to overcome consumer resistance. Listen, I'll give you an example I just heard the other day. Remember, I told you I was talking to a director of the movie company this Drucker works for. He showed me, and he had the figures to prove it, that if you put enough money into selling a picture, no matter how bad it is, it will gross enough to make a big profit over and above the original cost plus the sales campaign. The normal studio figure for promotion and distribution is one-third over what they call the negative cost, but every time some independent outfit with enough money behind it comes along and makes an expensive stinker for, say, three million dollars, and then, after they try it out on preview audiences and it flops, instead of just laying out a million to sell it, they put in another two and a half or three million, why, it ends up one of the biggest grossers of all time — eight or ten million or more. But whenever they get scared of what they've got, or run out of money, and start cutting down on the promotion campaign, they're left with nothing to go on but the unassisted public reaction to their turkey, and they're sunk.'

'Why don't they use the same system on every picture that's made? If an independent group can do it, why can't the big studios which have even more capital to work with?'

'They do occasionally, when they've got a particularly expensive flop on their hands. But the principle only works when it's applied to three or four pictures a year. If you did it with all five hundred, or however many they make out there, there obviously aren't enough customers to make them all smash hits. Even just within one studio they'd be competing against the rest of their product.'

'That makes sense,' Owen agreed. 'But getting back to our particular enterprise, the one aspect we haven't considered yet is the ethics involved. Don't I have a responsibility, as the head of a manufacturing . . . ?'

'Of course you have!' his father broke in. 'We wouldn't be the greatest industrial nation in the world if the men who control capital didn't have a sense of their responsibility to the welfare of the country as a whole.'

'Yes, I remember your mentioning that angle last year, before I got started. And it does bother me — the fact that if I quit now I'd be putting people out of jobs. Still . . .'

'That's only part of it, the handful of people on your payroll.

Every time one of your products is sold in a retail outlet, some of the profit stays in the store and helps keep it going. The money you put into advertising supports advertising agencies, newspapers, radio stations and so on. The particular item you're manufacturing may be useless in the sense that no one in his right mind would buy it of his own accord, and anybody who does buy it will feel afterwards that he's been had. But the way our economy works, no occasion when money changes hands is useless. That's why those of us who have the initiative, and the means, to stimulate new enterprise — a tiny minority really, compared to the vast numbers involved in merely making and growing things — that's why we can be so proud of our contribution.' He paused, then remembered to add: 'At the same time, of course, we feel humble in the realization that we are only playing an assigned part in some higher purpose.'

Owen was overwhelmed rather than convinced. He did not and could not subscribe to his father's morality but he had no other satisfactory solution to offer. The idea that he was participating in a fraud on the public filled him with dismay and guilt, but he realized there was not the slightest chance of persuading Mr. Muir to abandon his investment because of such a consideration. All the objections Owen had to the proposed new programme for his company would have applied just as well to the original venture, and it was then that he should have raised them. That he would have to find a way out of the dilemma, he knew, but to accomplish it now, in a verbal duel with his father, was out of the question.

Taking the boy's silence for compliance, Mr. Muir dropped the stern, reproving manner of his lecture and shifted into a tone of paternal solicitude. 'What's happening with you otherwise, Son? Your mother and I have been feeling kind of out of touch with you lately. Haven't we, Ruth?'

Mrs. Muir had so mastered the knack of shutting off her attention while her husband held forth on one of his theories, that she had to have the question repeated. Then she added her voice to his sentiments.

Owen decided to let the one problem go for the moment and

see what he could achieve on the other and more promising front. 'There's only one thing of any consequence that's happened to me. I've fallen in love and I'm going to be married. She's so wonderful in so many ways I can't wait till you meet her, but there's one rather fortunate coincidence maybe I ought to mention now because it might help in your operation with Phyllis. She's a Catholic.'

'Oh?' his mother said, and there was a good deal of reservation in the monosyllable. 'Well, I suppose it's true that might have some influence on the Carpenters. . . .'

Willis Muir directed a searching look at his son, recalling that it was Owen who had brought Dennis Carpenter into the earlier discussion. Apparently the boy had more deviousness in his nature than his father had ever dared to hope.

CHAPTER VI

As a veteran of many similar conversations, Father Duchesne had an advantage over Owen, who had scarcely even seen a priest at close range before. But the older man put the younger at his ease with great skill, garnishing the business of the evening with brandy, cigars and preliminary talk on non-controversial topics of common interest. The flavour of the priest's speech, much more typically lower middle class New York than his formal pulpit voice, and the pleasant disorder of the parish house parlour, also helped to restore Owen's normal minimum of self-assurance. By the time they came around to the purpose of his visit, he was ready to accept his host as neither a sinister cabalist nor a holy figure set apart from ordinary men.

'There are three steps we have to go through on a mixed marriage,' Father Duchesne explained. 'First of all I'm supposed to sound you out on the idea of becoming a Catholic yourself.'

'Well, there are several important reservations...'

'That's all right. Next it's my duty to warn you that mixed marriages are a pretty risky proposition. We keep close tabs on...'

'Are you all through trying to convert me?'

The elderly priest looked sharply at his young visitor, a slight frown indicating that he would react adversely to any levity on such a sacrosanct subject. 'Do you want to be converted?'

'I don't believe so. I'd have to know a lot more about it.'

'Of course you would. And you've got too many other things to concentrate on right now. Making that girl of yours happy, for one. She's a lovely creature. I've never had the feeling God meant conversion to be a big part of my special vocation, but I'll be only too glad to talk to you about it later some time, after you're married and settled down, if you get the urge.' He paused for a small sip of brandy and a long puff on his cigar. 'Let's see, I hadn't quite finished giving you the warning. We don't ever really approve of marrying outside the faith. We feel the best way you could show your love for Miss Wykoff would be to give her up.'

'I don't think you could ever persuade me of that.'

'Then I certainly won't try.' The man of God smiled benevolently and, with the air of a man who has completed the perfunctory portion of a ritual to which he is committed, proceeded to the heart of the discussion. This, it developed, was the terms on which a dispensation could be obtained.

Owen said he had already been informed in that regard. As he understood it, the normal requirements were that he should not interfere with his wife's religion and that their children be baptized and educated as Catholics.

'You're jumping the gun a little,' the priest told him. 'I just told you the church doesn't ever actually approve of a mixed marriage in the sense of giving it our blessing. That means there has to be a very serious and special reason in each case where a dispensation is granted — what's known in canon law as a "grave cause" — something important enough to stick against the ordinary rules of God and the church on the subject.'

Owen was appalled by this statement of the problem. While he personally felt that his marriage to April was of transcendent importance and could not fail to be permanently idyllic, he realized that the church would have to dismiss these points as mere opinions without objective merit. How could any reason he might present be regarded as grave and special when it was obvious that every couple would submit the same reasons? He remembered April's cynical insinuation that a contribution of money would help but, whether or not such simony actually existed, it was unthinkable that a man of Father Duchesne's obvious sincerity could be corrupted.

'Important enough to outweigh the rules?' he temporized. 'That would have to be a pretty serious reason if the objections are as serious as you say.'

'Right. The only grounds for the church permitting what's usually a sin is if it looks as if it will head off an even graver sin.'

'Oh,' Owen said blankly. He had the feeling there was an

application of this precept to his situation but he couldn't fix on what it was.

'Sometimes,' continued Father Duchesne, 'what we know of the parishioner in question and the set-up in her case makes it reasonably sure that if the dispensation is not granted, she, or he, may be drawn into an illicit relationship.'

Owen began to see light ahead. Wishing to avail himself of this formula without directly impugning April's virtue, he said: 'Well, as Miss Wykoff may already have told you, we're very deeply in love and it might be more than we could endure to give each other up. I don't mean to say that she would ever consent to be my mistress but it's quite possible, if there were no other alternative, that she would agree to be married in my family's church instead of her own.'

Father Duchesne made the sign of the cross unostentatiously, as a man does to whom it has become an almost instinctive reaction, and murmured a few words of Latin. 'If that's the way it is, I'll certainly recommend a dispensation. You make the bigger sin sound like the smaller one but the truth is it would be a lot worse, her going through a Protestant ceremony, than just living in concubinage. Ipso facto excommunication, reserved to the ordinary.'

'But the danger of either one would constitute a grave cause?'

'Beyond the shadow of a doubt. I don't decide these things myself, you understand, but my recommendations usually stick.' He smiled. 'They ought to, after forty-three years in holy orders.'

'You make me feel very relieved. I guess if that's clear, we can go on to the other points.'

'What else is there?' The priest looked surprised.

'Only one thing really, that bothers me. I don't see how I can make an absolute commitment on bringing up children. Frankly, what I question about parochial schools is they only teach the one point of view.'

'They teach the truth as they see it. Isn't that a teacher's job?'

'It's the old problem,' Owen said. 'What is truth? I must confess I find some of your doctrines hard to accept.'

'Well, I'd hardly expect you to accept them all. If you did you'd be a Catholic.' He laughed. 'Then there wouldn't be anything left for us to talk about.'

'That's just it. It doesn't seem right to me to pledge my children to doctrines I'm not clear on myself.'

'Do you believe in secularism and Marxist atheism? That's what you'd be pledging them to in most of the public schools.' He shrugged, conveying the impression that while he didn't relish a theological discussion, he was nonetheless prepared for one. 'But maybe if we take a few minutes now, we can clear you up on a couple of points. After all, the Saviour Himself said His yoke was easy and His burden light.'

A young priest had appeared in the doorway, waiting till the pastor could favour him with his attention. Father Duchesne acknowledged his presence with a kindly gesture.

'Excuse me, Father,' said the curate, 'but Father Shea is on the phone and wants to know if we can take over a requiem Mass they can't handle tomorrow. The trouble is, you can't possibly do it, you've got such a tough schedule from eight o'clock on solid. And I won't be available because with Father Dolan still sick I was figuring on taking the six o'clock for him tomorrow morning.'

'That's all right,' said Father Duchesne. 'I'll say the six o'clock.'

'You haven't been getting enough sleep,' the young priest pointed out solicitously.

'We haven't been getting enough income,' the pastor replied. 'Any stipends Father Shea sends our way we'll accept with thanks to him and praise to God.'

When the young priest was gone Owen volunteered to leave so that his host could go to bed. But Father Duchesne declined the offer and added a few drops of brandy to his guest's portion. 'Tell me what bothers you particularly and maybe if we haven't time to go into it all, I can give you a couple of books to read.'

'Well, I guess the one big point that worries me most is the whole doctrine of baptism: the idea that you can't go to heaven without it, even little babies who die before somebody's sprinkled them and said the right words over them.'

'Do you believe in the Holy Scriptures? What did Jesus say to Nicodemus? "Unless a man be born again of water and the Spirit, he cannot enter into the kingdom of God." '

'What about Protestant baptism? Take people like Abraham Lincoln or George Washington or Florence Nightingale. I don't know whether they were all baptized or not but say they were. Would they go to heaven?'

'You've got two different questions there,' said the priest. 'Protestant baptism is legal all right, most of the time anyway, but while baptism is something you can't have salvation without, it's a long way from guaranteeing it all by itself. The people you mention would have to have died free from sin, and it's certainly a sin to know the facts about the true church and not join it. You'd have to prove they lived and died in what we call invincible ignorance of the real merits of Catholicism.'

'But Jews and Mohammedans, say, or any unbaptized people, would be automatically excluded from heaven, no matter what kind of lives they led?'

Father Duchesne considered the point. 'No, there could be some exceptions, coming under what we call baptism of desire. They'd have to die in perfect charity and contrition without any knowledge of the Gospels.' Then he added: 'I'm talking about Jews who died since Christ, of course. There are a great number of pre-Christian Jews in heaven — a hundred and forty-four thousand at the very least.' Owen's expression of surprise at this precise figure led him to explain. 'The twelve thousand male virgins from each of the twelve tribes who are in constant attendance on the Lamb of God. And probably a smaller number of women and married men besides — certainly Abraham, Isaac, Moses and so forth, and all the prophets. They waited around in the limbo of the fathers until Jesus opened up heaven to them.'

'That's interesting,' Owen said, 'but what I find it hardest to accept is the idea that babies who happen not to have been baptized should be condemned to hell.'

'They probably aren't. Of course, the only thing we know for sure, as a matter of faith, is they don't go to heaven, but most experts nowadays are pretty sure they end up in a limbo of infants, where Saint Thomas says they enjoy at least a minimum of felicity.'

'I still don't see,' Owen persisted, 'why innocent infants don't have as much right to go to heaven as an adult who dies in the bosom of the church.'

'Because they don't,' answered Father Duchesne emphatically. 'The adult has earned his way by faith and works and genuine repentance. You show how mixed up you are when you call infants innocent. Even if they didn't prove it, right from the start, with the deadly sins of anger, gluttony and envy, we'd still know they had the inheritance of original sin from the first parents. Ever since Eden, every child born, except the Blessed Virgin and her Son, has been born with that load of sin. God's grace, which we get from baptism and later as we come to need more of it, from other sacraments, isn't a natural right as you seem to think. It's a special privilege, an act of divine mercy, and it stands to reason it has to be deserved before it can be granted.

'Naturally the church wants to get as many souls into heaven as she possibly can. We wouldn't be doing our job if we didn't. The church has the same soft spot in her heart for little children that our Lord had. I think I can prove that to you beyond the shadow of a doubt when I tell you the lengths we go to, not just to save the souls of infants but even of embryos and fetuses. When a woman dies carrying a child, we try to do a Caesarian on the body so we can baptize the fetus. Our nurses are taught to baptize miscarriages and babies in danger of dying while they're being born, even if they have to use a syringe to do it. Doesn't matter whether its parents are Christians or not, every time they've got a weak baby on their hands they baptize it, on the q.t. if they can, sometimes risking a big fuss if the parents find out. Even if they're almost sure there's no life left in a miscarriage or an infant, they baptize it conditionally so as not to miss the chance of saving a soul. In freak cases where you can't tell for sure if it's meant to be one person or two, they baptize one absolutely, the other conditionally. I bet you can't think of any other organization in the world with more love and concern than that for the little ones our Saviour cherished.'

'Well,' said Owen, putting considerable uncertainty into the word, 'I guess it all depends on whether the basic theory is sound. I mean all the precautions you mention are only justified if baptism accomplishes what you say it does, and if it was meant to apply to babies. But I don't think the Bible says anything about infant baptism.'

'Not in so many words, no. But you've got to remember we know about what Jesus taught from both Scripture and tradition, and one's as important as the other. If the early fathers did something, we know they got it from the apostles, and they in turn either heard it straight from Jesus or later from the Holy Ghost. So we can be sure infant baptism is necessary because St. Irenaeus said it was, and he was a disciple of St. Polycarp, who was a disciple of St. John the Divine.'

'Suppose,' Owen broke in, 'it turned out that the writings of St. Irenaeus aren't authentic. I'm not trying to be argumentative, because I'd like to believe everything you tell me, but what if somebody proved tomorrow that the particular manuscript was a forgery written centuries later?'

'Wouldn't make a particle of difference,' said the priest. He rose and crossed to a bookshelf as he spoke, returning with a small paperbound volume in which he quickly found the reference he sought. 'The dogma would still be proved beyond the shadow of a doubt by the simple fact that it was made dogma. Cardinal Gibbons, one of our greatest American leaders and thinkers, puts it this way: "In judging between the teachings of apostolical antiquity on the one hand and of the Anabaptists on the other, it is not hard to determine on which side lies the truth; for what becomes of the Christian Church if it has erred on so vital a point as that of baptism during the entire period of its existence?" '

'But look,' Owen protested, 'what you're saying, and Cardinal Gibbons too, is that everything your church says is true because it's the true church.'

'Exactly. Luckily our Lord made it very clear just what He had in mind and it's a cinch to see which church fits His definition. "Thou art Peter and upon this rock I will build my church, and the gates of hell shall not prevail against it. And I will give to thee the keys of the kingdom of heaven". Notice He doesn't say "my churches" but "my church" — "one fold and one shepherd" as He calls it another time. So the first test is unity. What church has unity of government based on the primacy of St. Peter and all the other popes who came after him? The next is permanence. He said the gates of hell couldn't prevail against it and later on He told His apostles He would be with them "all days" to the end of the world. That rules out any church that didn't get started till a thousand or fifteen hundred years afterwards. And it has to be a kingdom because that's how Gabriel described it to the Blessed Virgin — one central authority with absolute power.

'Two more tests He laid down were catholicity and apostolicity. Catholic means worldwide. He told His apostles to carry His message to "the whole world... even to the very ends of the earth". And He gave them the job of interpreting His teachings. So no church can claim to represent Him if it doesn't go on teaching everything they taught. That includes auricular confession and absolution; the laying on of hands in confirmation and ordination; extreme unction for the dying or seriously sick; no divorce whatever under any circumstances; virginity, in both men and women, being a higher state than marriage; the fact that the Holy Eucharist is really and literally the flesh and blood of Jesus; and St. Paul's rule that "it is a shame for a woman to speak in the church" and that they have to be respectful and obedient to their husbands at all times.'

'You make a good argument,' Owen said. 'I'll admit that. But there are arguments against each one of those doctrines and it would take a long time, maybe for ever, to prove each one beyond all reasonable doubt.'

'I don't have to. It's what you said a couple of minutes ago: they're all true because the true church says they are. The Saviour said the gates of hell couldn't prevail against His church. He was making a promise that she would be free from error for ever, infallible. Now I don't know if you know this, but the Holy Catholic Church is the only church that doesn't allow, and never has, any disagreement of any kind. A man or a group of men deny just one article of faith and they're excommunicated. What's more, the Catholic Church has never been wrong or ever changed her mind on even the smallest point in the whole nineteen hundred years she's been operating. No organization of mere men, full of human weakness, could pile up a record like that unless they were guided from on high. When the Protestant reformers accused the church of being in error, they were calling God Himself a liar; they were saying that Jesus Christ was never a God or even a good prophet. He said He was "the way, the truth and the life" and anyone "that receiveth whomsoever I send, receiveth me". He gave a pledge to send the Holy Ghost, the Spirit of truth, to His ministers down here to abide with them for ever and guarantee them against ever departing from the truth.'

Father Duchesne paused, wearied by his monologue. Owen was also silent for some moments, absorbing the significance of the case which had been presented to him. The further he got into this subject, it seemed, the harder it was to find the sort of decent, democratic compromise that would dissipate the obstacle to his marriage. Yet when he thought of April and the possibility of losing her, he knew there was nothing else in life that mattered so much to him.

'You've been very enlightening . . .' he began finally.

The priest, catching himself in a yawn, converted it to a smile.

'. . . but you haven't helped me a bit,' Owen continued. 'Here I am, trying to find some kind of middle ground, and all you've succeeded in proving to me is that the church is either totally right or totally wrong.'

'Well,' said the priest, 'I may have let the ball go way out into left field when it could have been handled in close. You've got to remember most laymen aren't interested in these points we've been talking about. There are plenty of good Catholics even, you start spouting theology at them and their minds go blank. I don't expect you to swallow everything I've said all in one dose. All I want to do is help you see that trusting your children to the church isn't exactly handing them over to Satan. We occasionally turn out some quite decent people.'

'I know that. I'm here because I happen to think one of them is the most wonderful person in the world.'

'Okay then, what more do you need than that? Let me tell you something, my son. I've talked to a great many non-Catholic young men in my time, and some young women too, about the arrangements for a mixed marriage, and very few of them have been as far along the road to faith as you are. But they didn't any of them make as much fuss about it. Ten, fifteen minutes at the most, was all I ever needed to make them see the light.'

'I'm sorry about taking up so much of your time,' Owen said in sincere apology. 'And I won't take any more of it because I know it's late and you have to get to bed. What I have to do is think this thing out for myself.'

'By all means.' Father Duchesne subdued another yawn. 'But you know what the reason was all those other fellows saw the point so quick? They were in love and that counted more to them than anything.'

Owen rose. 'I don't believe anybody could be more in love than I am. That's what makes me able to face the possibility of changing my whole way of thinking.'

'Later on, later on,' said the priest, not wholly suppressing the impatience he felt as he walked his guest into the hall and toward the front door. 'You live another thirty or forty years, you'll learn to take things one step at a time. All the roads leading to Rome weren't built in a day.'

The man of God ushered his young visitor into the obscurity of a moonless night.

'There must be something wrong inside me,' Owen said. 'That's why I asked to see you. Other people come up against these very same problems and seem to solve them without any trouble. But I'm stopped; I can't move in any direction. I can't even think straight any more.'

The psychoanalyst nodded sympathetically. 'That kind of block can easily be an indication of a personality disorder. The main reason we try to cure neuroses is because they stop the individual from moving forward, from making the efficient progress in his life and work of which he is inherently capable.' He was a short, rather stout man of about fifty with a gentle voice and scholarly manner. His name was Dr. Millis and he had the reputation of being thoroughly grounded in Freudian principles without applying them in too doctrinaire a fashion.

'What makes it worse,' Owen went on, 'is that neither of them is a decision I can postpone. I've already had to go ahead with my father's ideas about the business for sheer lack of any other choice, and if I'm going to reverse myself on that, I've got to do it before I get in much deeper. And as far as my marriage is concerned, I can hardly expect my fiancée to wait around indefinitely while I make up my mind about this Catholic issue.'

'Would you say there was a possible relation between the two questions?' inquired the analyst. 'For example, if you concluded that you couldn't conscientiously make a capitalist of yourself, that would presumably change your whole financial future. Might that in turn have an effect on your ability to get married or on the young lady's inclination to wait?'

'I suppose it could. Except that if it ever came to the point where I really thought I was going to lose her, I'd give up everything else to prevent that. I know I'd go to pieces completely without her.'

'Then to sum up,' said Dr. Millis, 'your problem is the somewhat unusual one of a man in danger of becoming a business success and a happy husband. But each of these steps involves a moral decision your conscience won't permit you to accept.'

'That's right. My conscience or my inhibitions or whatever the correct term is. I'd be only too glad to be shown that these scruples of mine have no sensible foundation. For all I know, they spring from some repression or frustration that I'm completely unaware of.'

'Very likely. But what it is we can only uncover by analysis.'

'I realize that,' Owen said. 'That's why I'm consulting you.'

'Yes,' said Dr. Millis. 'The question in my mind, however, is whether you are really prepared for what the process entails. For instance, are you aware of the expense? My ordinary fee is twenty-five dollars per hour and it requires at least three hours a week to get satisfactory results.'

'That is a lot,' Owen said. 'Is there any reduced rate if I took twenty or thirty hours a week? I mean I realize it's usually a long process but it just can't be in my case. I've got to get this whole business straightened out in a matter of weeks or it'll be too late to do any good.'

'You're out of your head!' Dr. Millis exclaimed; then hastily corrected himself: 'That's a figure of speech, not a diagnosis. But I would never think of giving a patient more than an hour a day. You need at least that much time in between sessions. And even on a six-day-a-week basis, two years is about a minimum for a successful analysis.'

'Two years!'

'Three years is actually the average with a severe neurosis.'

'But I thought I told you! My problems are immediate ones.'

'We are rarely able to do anything about the immediate decisions facing a patient when he comes to us,' the analyst told him. 'However you happen to resolve this present crisis of yours, the function of psychoanalytical therapy would be to equip you to face the similar ones which will arise in the future. Fortunately, you are an extremely young man and the major problems of your life lie ahead of you.'

'The hell they do! If I thought that, I wouldn't go on living,' he added disconsolately. 'Well, there's no point in my taking any more of your time.'

'In view of your attitude, I am inclined to agree.'

Owen started to get up but his need for help was too great. 'Unless you have any advice to give me, just on the basis of what I've told you?'

'I don't have any that I would consider to be part of the practice of my profession, and I certainly won't charge you for this consultation. But if you are interested in what I think as a person with some experience of the world . . .'

'I'm very interested.'

'I would advise you to make your fortune and break your

engagement. Like it or not, Mr. Muir, we live under an established economic system and the individual who tries to stand apart from it is simply refusing to adjust to the objective conditions of his environment, setting himself apart from ordinary men. There is no peace to be found on that road.

'As far as your proposed marriage is concerned, I can only say that I have had scores of patients who regretted the choice of mates they made at your age. I have never had one who rejected an opportunity to get married at twenty-three and later felt sorry for that decision. You tell me that the only obstacle to your marriage is this question of the religious upbringing of your children. But I am inclined to suspect, although I certainly cannot prove it without therapy, that that is simply a screen for the real barrier, which probably lies hidden in the history of your infantile sexuality. The complexity of these unconscious drives of ours, deriving for the most part from the oral and anal stages of the libido development, is so staggering . . .'

'Excuse me,' Owen broke in. 'I just remembered I told my fiancée I would telephone her at about this time. So if you'll forgive me for rushing off — she may be worrying.' Here he was permitting himself one of those slight departures from the precise truth which he felt were required by the decencies of social intercouse.

'Of course.' The man of science released him with a gesture. 'But you might do well to give some consideration to the subconscious mechanics which led you to forget the obligation until this very moment. Our study of the psychology of errors and the pleasure-unpleasure principle has made us keenly aware that there is no such thing as an unintentional slip of the mind. When you forget to call the young lady with whom you think you are in love, it is because the act which you have thus banished from your conscious mind would have released such a formidable quantity of unpleasure that you were unable to face it. Mind you, I don't say that the unpleasant association is necessarily with your fiancée herself. It may result from a traumatic experience in a telephone booth or a connection between the digits of this particular telephone number and . . .'

'Yes, that's interesting,' Owen said. He had been on his feet for some time and was now standing in the doorway. 'But I feel I can't trade on your generosity any further. Goodbye and thank you.' He was already in motion as he spoke these last words.

Two days later, Owen had a session with Blankenship which was a direct outcome of the new policy imposed on the company by Willis Muir. The sudden switch from retrenchment to expansion in the advertising programme, along with rigid economies in the process of production, had had diverse effects on the morale of the executive personnel. Holtzmann, the shop foreman, retreated sullenly to the brink of resignation. Boal, the accountant, praised Owen for his imaginative audacity and began making confidential inquiries about openings in other firms. But to Blankenship it was a glorious opportunity to display his virtuosity in the great American art of selling.

Owen was so deeply absorbed in his personal difficulties that it took the sternest self-discipline to pay any sort of attention to the samples of the new campaign which the advertising director presented for his inspection. Fortunately, Blankenship's own enthusiasm for his work gave him so much to say on the subject that he scarcely noticed his employer's preoccupied silence.

His proudest accomplishment was a colour photograph, for magazine use, of a lovely young girl gazing with soulful surrender into the eyes of the all but unseen man in whose embrace she was held. Above her head was the word TRULITE; below, where her image ended in a deep pectoral cleavage, was the simple legend: *The greatest advance in its field since the discovery of fire.* . . .

'I've always felt you can achieve more with symbolism than with a too crassly direct approach,' the advertising director explained. 'We went through all the agency directories before we found the right girl, Madonna-like and still sexy, and then I told the photographer I wanted him to recapture the promise of eternally true fidelity as he'd seen it once in the upturned face of his first nubile sweetheart. He said she happened to have been four inches taller than he was but he knew what I meant, only reversing the angle.'

'It's very effective,' Owen conceded. 'But I wonder if you don't lose some of that virginal fidelity with so much exposed bosom.'

'You're missing the basic theory of the composition. First you're caught by the look in the eyes but then there has to be something to pull your attention down to where the slogan springs out at you. It's a first principle: the ineluctability of the message.' He granted his employer five seconds in which to express any further reservations, and then proceeded to unveil his second exhibit. 'This is newspaper copy and naturally you have to have a more specific, immediate sales appeal, but notice how I still avoid any clear statement of what our product is and how it works.'

The whole process of enticing needed money from innocent fellow-citizens with misrepresentations and irrelevances was distasteful to Owen and added to the burden of his guilt, but he forced his attention to the proof sheet Blankenship had handed him. His first glance at it brought a bewildered frown to his face. 'What's this "fifty-two per cent more efficient" and "eighty-four per cent more satisfying"? More efficient than what?'

'Are you serious? That's the indefinite comparative — probably the only completely new grammatical construction introduced into the language in the last decade. You use the comparative degree without any "than" after it; that's why it's also called the non-odious comparison. You must have seen it in advertisements: "purer", "less irritating", "faster-selling", "more nourishing", "more for your money" . . . No copywriter in his right mind would say less irritating than what. It would just be inviting a lawsuit.'

'Yes, but it sounds even stranger when you throw in a percentage. How can something be fifty-two per cent more efficient than nothing?'

'It can, that's all. You're just old-fashioned. Haven't you ever read about a soap making your clothes "thirty-seven per cent whiter"?'

'It still doesn't make any sense to me.' Then, observing that the older man was prepared to argue the point at length and deprive him of the time he needed for meditation, he gave in at once. 'But I don't want to impose my thinking on you in any way. It's your department.' And when Blankenship mentioned that he had several more layouts to submit, Owen told him he would prefer not to see them until after publication, thus avoiding any inadvertent abuse of his executive authority. What actually lay behind his passivity was the realization that to express his true feelings about the advertising programme would lead to abandoning the whole enterprise. And that was a step for which he still lacked the necessary resolution.

After Blankenship had left him, Owen was free to concentrate on the crisis toward which he felt himself increasingly drawn. In retrospect he found that his evening with Father Duchesne had had more of an effect on him than he had immediately recognized. It was still true that the old priest's presentation of his faith reduced it to a proposition that was either wholly right or wholly wrong. But there was something about that very dogmatism that appealed to Owen's need for a shield against the slings and arrows of a conscienceless world.

Nor was it inconsistent, he felt, that, once accepting the divine inspiration of Scripture, a religion should give literal credence to its entirety and, wherever valid questions of interpretation or translation did arise, find the answers in the equally persuasive authority of the apostolic fathers. The Roman Catholic Church, he was beginning to believe, was either exactly what it claimed to be or the most gigantic and outrageous imposture ever perpetrated. It did not matter that one found some of its separate doctrines repugnant or difficult to accept; if they were actually the reflection of God's will, the repugnance and the difficulty must spring from the falsity of one's own standards.

Now he felt the need for the further discussion with April which he had been evading for several days. Before he had the chance, however, Ilsa Wykoff showed up at the office in order to partake of a salary advance April had negotiated. She reacted with astonishment to the news that it was lunchtime, and with vincible diffidence to Owen's proposal that she join them.

While they ate Owen expounded his dilemma. Essentially it came down to the fact that the more he was exposed to Catholicism, the more convinced he became that it was an issue on which no compromise was possible. Either he accepted it for himself or he could not do so for his children. It might turn out that once April and he were married and he had time to study the subject more thoroughly, he would himself be converted and their difficulties thus solved. But until that happened he couldn't conscientiously make the commitment that was asked of him. Instead he wanted April to rely on the sincerity of his present intention and susceptibility, and waive the requirement of a formal, signed agreement. But if she still felt this was an impossible concession, then the only alternative was to postpone their marriage until he had undergone a course of instruction in her faith.

To both women the salient fact about this presentation was that he had made a distinct advance toward conversion on the basis of a single meeting with Father Duchesne. Both foresaw that with further attention and encouragement he might eventually be brought into the church. Their reactions to the development, however, were sharply dissimilar. Mrs. Wykoff experienced deep joy and an infusion of sanctity because of the humble part she had played in promoting it. April felt annoyed and antagonistic, the more irritatingly so because she found it hard to isolate the reason for her aggravation.

'You're making a big complication out of something that's really simple and not so terribly important,' she said. 'Nobody's asking you to become a Catholic. You said you wanted to find out a little more about it before you agreed to anything definite about any children we might have, though I don't know why it doesn't seem to occur to anybody that maybe we won't have any. So what happens? You say you're favourably impressed with what you've learned and it looks better to you than it ever did before. That ought to make you more willing to agree to something that thousands of people sign every year without quibbling. But no. Instead it turns out you're more difficult about it than ever, handing out ultimatums and God knows what. I thought we were going to get married because we were in love and wanted to live together and have each other. I didn't think it was so we could study the lives of the saints or say our prayers together.'

'Darling.' As always any indication from her of impatience with him made him want to take her in his arms and convince her of the depth of his love. He wished fervently that they were alone so that he could say and do the things to her which would bring her back to him. 'The last thing I want is to make any obstacles or any kind of delay in our . . .'

Mrs. Wykoff, intolerant of his appeasing manner, took over. 'Delay! You've got your whole lives ahead of you and you're worrying about a few weeks which you'll probably need for getting her clothes ready anyway.' She gazed in scathing reproach at her daughter. 'What kind of a monster are you? Don't you have any feelings? You know what Dr. Crusinberry says about how I shouldn't be upset. But do you care what it does to me to hear you answer him in that mean way after he's just given you the sweetest and most wonderful proof of how much he loves you?'

'Look, Mother,' said April in a voice pungent with acrimony, 'we might as well get one point straight right now. If you think he's too good for me, wouldn't the decent thing be to warn him off before it's too late?'

'You've no call to say that. You know I've lived and worked and prayed to the Mother of God for only one thing since your dear father died with all those debts he'd never told me about, and that was to raise you up to be the kind of woman an important man would want to marry: pretty and gay and God-fearing and healthy.' She turned to Owen to supplement this point for his benefit. 'You wouldn't believe what a thin, sickly creature she was at fifteen, and then three years later out racing motor cycles in Jersey, grease from head to foot and so many cuts and bruises it's the Lord's mercy they didn't leave any scars. I ask you, what kind of a crazy sport is that for a young girl?' She turned back to April and her main thesis. 'How can you think I'd want to destroy your happiness now when it's the one goal I was slaving for in that sweatshop till the doctor said I'd drop dead if I didn't quit and even so I wouldn't have if you hadn't been earning your way by then, modelling for those designers?'

'They weren't designers; they were artists,' April said. 'You make it sound so dressed. Anyway, the point I'd like to make, Mother, while you're catching your breath, is that I feel quite strongly about my happiness, too, and I happen to think you're endangering it when you support the idea of postponing my marriage. Suppose Owen goes ahead with this either-or attitude and decides a few weeks from now that he doesn't want to be a Catholic, therefore he has to be an anti-Catholic. Then what shall I do? Call it off, or say the hell with the church and marry him in City Hall?'

'There's no danger of that,' Mrs. Wykoff said firmly, placing her hand on Owen's in token of her faith in him. 'He's too fine and sincere a boy not to see the truth once he's opened his mind to it.'

'That's what you hope and you may be right. But you can't be sure. And I still want to know what happens if it turns out the other way. Which means more to you: your religion or your life-mission of getting me married to an important man? The heavenly security or the earthly?'

'That's an insulting question,' her mother said, 'and I refuse to answer it.'

'Well, I refuse to discuss the matter any further until you do.'

The impasse between mother and daughter persisting, lunch was brought to a hasty conclusion and Mrs. Wykoff deposited at a subway entrance. Since it was always unlikely that there would be anything at the plant to occupy their attention, April and Owen went for a long walk before they returned to work. There was an exhilarating freshness to the May afternoon air that penetrated even to the streets of Long Island City, and the lovers avoided by unspoken agreement any reference to their one subject of controversy. April had it on her mind, however, because after they finally did go back to see if there were any telephone messages worth bothering about, she came into Owen's office to say she had Father Duchesne on the line and wanted Owen to get the benefit of his thinking.

The priest had apparently been brought up to date by April for he told Owen he was gratified that their evening together had stimulated such earnest intentions. But he still wished to renew his advice about waiting till after the wedding before Owen gave any serious thought to the possibility of conversion. 'You naturally want to get married as soon as you can and that would put a lot of pressure on you if you felt you had to make a decision about the church first. You wouldn't be making a free choice from strictly spiritual motives.'

'I don't know about that,' Owen said. 'In my case the decision might turn out to be a very quick one and not hold us up at all. Don't you have some sort of courses for people who think they might be interested in joining?'

The priest admitted that they did. If Owen wanted to take instruction or even start attending Mass as a catechumen, or probationary Catholic, he was welcome to do so. But in order to avoid the slightest danger of taking a spiritual step under the impetus of physical desire, the process shouldn't be related in any way to the timing of his marriage. And it would be only a reasonable gesture of good faith, a token of his present sympathetic interest, to sign immediately the pledge of agreement with the church's mild requirements concerning the education of children.

Owen found it hard to argue with such a plausibly presented programme, especially with April leaning over the back of his chair and diverting him with caresses. Instead of challenging it directly, he hedged. 'Suppose I die during the period of instruction? Wouldn't I be endangering my salvation by taking it so slowly?'

'Not at all. You'd have nothing to worry about. There's an airtight canon law entitling you to full ecclesiastical burial.'

'Well,' Owen said, feeling cornered, 'how long would you guess this instruction would take before I knew where I stood?'

'There's no way of telling. The early fathers insisted on at least two years and I'm old-fashioned enough to think that was pretty sound doctrine, but it's the general thing nowadays to cover it in a good deal less time than that.'

'I'd certainly want to try to,' Owen said. 'I just have an idea it might go very fast with me. When could I start?'

'I'll have to check my schedule,' the priest said. 'I ought to have some free time either next week or the week after. In the meanwhile do you want me to mail the marriage agreement forms to you at your home or at your office?'

Owen said it didn't matter.

The whole conversation left him quite depressed. April, in

apparent remorse for her earlier sharpness toward him, continued to be very loving and solicitous, and he hid his disturbance from her during dinner and a long goodnight before he left her at her apartment. But on his way home, without the stimulus of her presence, his doubts descended on him in full force. The one procedure that seemed to him consistent and reasonable was for him to make up his mind for himself first and then see what commitment he could undertake for his unborn children; yet to both April and Father Duchesne this was apparently a piece of perverse stubbornness. He felt he was faltering in a bog of compromise.

The quandary persisted, oppressive and exitless, until the following morning when he received a special delivery letter at home, just before leaving for the office. It was on the stationery of the Archdiocese of New York and read:

Dear Mr. Muir: A mutual friend, moved only by the desire for the greater glory of God, has acquainted me with your interest in the true Church. I have had the rare and rewarding experience of being able to demonstrate in a few extraordinary cases of intellectual and spiritual maturity that the process of instruction in the Word of God can be expedited to a tempo in keeping with our modern industrial civilization. In yours, I am prepared, once you give the go-ahead signal to my secretary, to return to New York by airplane from my speaking engagements throughout the country in order to keep appointments with you every other day. I have already taken the liberty of saying some prayers in your behalf and I have absolute confidence that the Mother of Grace Divine will help us make it possible for you to undergo the sacrament of matrimony in its fullest and holiest form. It is, I am sure, unnecessary to mention to a man of your understanding that there is no compensation, direct or indirect, for my services in this regard other than the joy of facilitating the journey of another soul to Abraham's bosom. I await your reply by telephone on the succeeding inst. Until then I remain, in humble veneration of the Immaculate Heart, yours truly. . . .

The letter was signed by Monsignor Stephen A. Frasso. To Owen it was a kindly light in the encircling gloom.

CHAPTER VII

'Let us speak of love,' said Monsignor Frasso, rising from his desk and pacing the considerable length of his impressive modern office as he talked. Dressed, without any of the ceremonial adornments of his rank, in the chaste black costume of a simple priest, admirably tailored of a soft, luxuriant cloth, he was even more splendid to watch in motion than in repose. His sleek black hair and pellucid grey eyes glistened under the fluorescent lights and he walked with the lithe assurance of an acrobat. At forty-three he looked no more than thirty-five, and carried himself as if he felt another ten years younger than that. His resonantly virile voice and copious repertory of theatrical gestures conformed with his reputation as the most indefatigable public speaker of his day. The sum of his physical attributes was such that he might have been cast for his sacerdotal role by a film producer alert to the demands of maidenly concupiscence.

It was widely conceded that his success to date would be dwarfed by his eventual eminence. Not only was he a favoured protégé of the cardinal but the contacts he had established in the Vatican itself while still a student at the North American College in Rome had been strengthened during many subsequent pilgrimages to the seat of ecclesiastical authority. His title of apostolic protonotary was a merely honorary one and his actual function seemed closer to that of a sort of vicar without portfolio to the cardinal. But as he himself delighted to point out, no one had ever succeeded in defining the limits of his jurisdiction. While his duties appeared to be extremely varied and arduous enough to consume the full attention of an ordinary man, he somehow contrived to be available for a constant succession of platform appearances and radio broadcasts, and for the private purification of souls whose corporeal hosts were sufficiently noteworthy to merit his consideration.

'As one on the threshold of the blessed state of marriage,' he continued to Owen, 'you know how sweet the love of a man for a woman can be. But that love has no lasting reality if it is separated from the greater love of God for man and man for God. When we forget that, we descend to the animal level of mere sex. The psychoanalysts would have us believe that bestial lust is the controlling force in our lives. They ignore the immortal soul and its highest impulse, which is to please God. The Freudians would have a much better case if they treated dogs instead of people. They might not find as many wealthy neurotics in the dog world but they would be on sounder theoretical ground.

'Lust and gluttony are among the capital sins. When man performs the conjugal act for the pleasure he gets out of it, it is as much a sin as eating solely for the sake of eating. The ancient Romans used to disgorge their food in the middle of a banquet in order to make room for more. It is equally disgusting for a man and woman to seek gratification in the flesh for its own sake. Their thoughts must be on the purpose for which sex was designed. Only then is their love for each other in harmony with their love of God.

'Everything we do is motivated by love. We love because we see goodness or the illusion of goodness in the object of our love. The dope fiend sees goodness in narcotics, the rapist in rape. Even the Communist finds merit and beauty in subversion. But all forms of love except the adoration of the Almighty are destined to wither and grow stale. Every bride is a vision of loveliness on her wedding day. Ten years later she may be a coarse slut, selling her favours to strangers to keep herself in gin. The husband may find it hard to stop from retching at the sight of her. But if he can cherish her then and keep her in his bed, he will be exalted. His love will have reached a higher level than mere desire. He will cherish her because she is one of God's creatures and because our Saviour elevated marriage to a sacrament. He will be tying his love for her to the love of God, in which there is no disillusion but only mounting ecstasy.

'God proved the depth of His love for us by giving us the free will to reject Him. Consider the miracles He performed while on earth, and since His resurrection through the saints and His blessed mother. They are wonderful to contemplate, yet when you think of the infinite power at His command, they are almost elementary.

Obviously He wanted to furnish us proof of His divinity and still not make it overwhelming. He wanted to leave room for love and free will so that when we do dedicate ourselves to His service and praise, we have the satisfaction of an undictated choice.

'He made it possible for us to figure out His existence through reason alone, but He also wanted us to know the higher glory of serving Him through faith. So He provided us with mysteries utterly beyond our comprehension. Who can explain or understand the Trinity, the incarnation or the redemption? Who can reduce to words the meaning of the sacrifice of the Eucharist — the clean oblation, the offering to the eternal Father of His only begotten Son? Obviously He wanted to give our faith a nobler foundation than mere reason — a mystical foundation. He wanted to give us a glimpse of the divine.

'Perhaps the doctrine of the Trinity is the best example of a conception so abstruse that the unaided human mind could never approach it. Without faith the idea of three persons in one nature makes no sense at all. Yet with faith the early fathers were able to circumscribe it with the precision of a geometric postulate. Heretics tried to attack it from every possible angle; but it was the heretics, not the doctrine, who were exterminated.

'I dare say no religion in the history of mankind has ever preached a dogma more difficult for the human brain to fathom. Only a God of love could want to exalt and enrich us with such a mystery. It is an earthly preparation for the beatific vision — for the day when the blessed will see God directly, though with different degrees of intensity according to their merits.'

The prelate paused to consult his watch and settled himself once more in the upholstered leather chair behind his desk. Owen assumed he had either reached the end of his sermon or at least needed to refresh himself before proceeding with it. It turned out, however, that he had more to say and that his energy was not noticeably depleted. The silence lasted only while he took from a drawer a small mirror and a container of Max Factor Pancake Make-up Number 7-N.

'I'm doing a film short today,' he explained, 'a little one-reel special for the Feast of the Assumption, and the local make-up men just don't have the touch the way they do out on the Coast. I've found I always end up doing it myself and the best way to save time and argument is to get set before I go to the studio. So if you'll forgive me, I'll do it now while we're talking.'

Owen gave his formal assent to a process which was already under way and expressed his willingness to forgo the rest of the session if that would help Frasso meet his commitment.

'Oh, I have time,' the prelate assured him. 'I purposely arranged it so that even if the shooting goes an hour over schedule, I can still be in Chicago tonight.' He resumed his discourse on love, dwelling for some minutes on the inspiration to mankind of those sublime physical organs, the Sacred Heart of Jesus and the Immaculate Heart of Our Lady. There was nothing more purifying for one's own love-life, he counselled Owen, than to have representations of one or both of these valvular muscles, executed by an artist with sufficient anatomical and spiritual training, hanging over the marriage bed and available for private devotion whenever the lurking threat of lust impinged upon domestic tranquillity.

This led him to the subject of the special role played by the Mother of God in the lives and salvation of the faithful, particularly in the United States, whose patron saint she was. Recent history demonstrated clearly how she had guided us into a just war on December 8th, 1941, the Feast of the Immaculate Conception, and on to final victory on August 15th, 1945 (Tokyo time), the Feast of her Assumption. This kind of direct participation in human affairs was an expression of the function God had devised for His mother after the successful completion of her mundane assignment. On earth a vessel of communication between the divine and the mortal, she carried on much the same work in heaven as intercessor with God on behalf of man and as the exclusive agency through which grace and sanctity were bestowed by God upon man. There was no more damnable blasphemy in the whole Protestant heresy than the refusal to recognize this development simply because it was not recorded in the Bible.

'We are frequently accused of Mariolatry,' said Monsignor

Frasso, a smile expressing his scorn for such slanders. 'The truth is that we attach very great importance to Mariology, which is quite a different matter. Good Catholics never make the mistake of worshipping the Blessed Virgin as a goddess. They simply venerate her as the Queen of the Angels, the Mirror of Justice, the Tower of David, the House of Gold, the Morning Star, the Mystical Rose, the Gate of Heaven, the Tower of Ivory, the Ark of Salvation, the Palace of Light, the Queen of All Saints, the Holy Mother of God, the Mistress of Creation, the Queen of the Universe. I'm not trying to list all her titles, you understand — there are almost fifty of them in the Litany of Our Lady alone. But I do want to give you an idea of what an extremely significant and varied contribution she makes to the redemption of mankind. It becomes pretty absurd, doesn't it, when you consider all the functions under her jurisdiction, to accept a so-called Christianity in which she has scarcely any active role at all?

'The love that radiates between the Sacred Heart and the Immaculate Heart casts its warmth on us below. In Old Testament days God Himself spoke to the chosen on earth and informed them of His will. In the Christian Era it is almost always through His mother that he sends His messages to us. When the sun halted its course in Fatima, Portugal, on October 13th, 1917, rotated around one point in the sky, and came hurtling down toward the earth before resuming its normal path, the power behind the miracle was obviously His, but the voice that spoke to those three little peasant children was that of the Blessed Virgin. And what better proof could we ask of her love for us than the timely warning she gave us in those six appearances? Before the Bolshevik Revolution had even occurred, she told us of the horrors that would grow out of it. Only now are we beginning to realize how accurate her characterization of Communism was. Watching us from above with loving tenderness, she recognized what we were unable to discern at close range. She saw the forest into which we were heading while we were admiring the individual trees. She realized that Marxist atheism was the abysmal swamp at the end of a downhill road which Western civilization had been following for five hundred years. When we rejected the authority, stability and piety of the Middle Ages for the false gods of individual judgment, mob rule and secularism, we were headed for chaos. The Protestant Revolution, sired by Satan, gave birth to the French Revolution, and the French Revolution to the Communist Revolution. But our only reaction was to congratulate ourselves on the progress of democracy and science. It took the Holy Mother of God to tell us that "democracy" had opened the door to anarchy, and "science" to blasphemous materialism. And thirty years later we're just beginning to understand what she was talking about.'

Frasso's secretary, a plump, smooth-skinned young priest whose slight stammer made him an improbable candidate for the active ministry, knocked and entered to report that everything was in readiness at the film studio for the right reverend star. He carried his superior's briefcase and called the latter's attention to such major items among its contents as his motion picture script, airplane ticket, breviary and Chicago speech.

The prelate directed a searching look into his mirror, added a couple of final touches to his make-up and confirmed his appointment with Owen for the same time Friday morning, three days later. 'It will be your turn to lead the discussion,' he promised. 'I want you to come in with all the questions you can think of.'

Owen dutifully prepared some questions for his next instruction period, but Frasso began to talk before he had a chance to present them. The prelate's topic was the common misconception of the world as a cruel and anarchic environment in which the survival of one species rested on the harassment and destruction of another. Since God, the essence of love and mercy, could not have conceived life as a cruel and brutal struggle, it was a mistake for us to view it as such. What we failed to understand was the divine law of surrender, according to which each order of being in nature must immolate itself so as to taste the reward of participation in the life of a higher order. Thus, he explained, chemicals are ennobled when they are consumed by plants; plants are elevated to the blessings of sentience only after their destruction by animals; animals can share in a life of thought, free will and love provided they are eaten by men; and man in turn must undergo the annihilation of his lower, sinful nature to find a higher level of existence in the bowels of God. The law of the jungle when seen in this light was part of a beautiful celestial plan, and to be consumed an enriching experience.

It was at this point that Owen, striking quickly during a pause that promised to be brief, asked permission to put a question.

'By all means,' Frasso assured him. 'As a matter of fact, the next time we come together, instead of my dominating the discussion this way, it might be a good idea for you to bring in whatever questions you have on your mind.'

Owen's query concerned his sister's friend, Dennis Carpenter. Knowing and approving the Catholic attitude on the indissolubility of marriage, he was unable to understand how Carpenter had been able to marry and discard three women, and still remain an apparently respected member of the church. 'I think I even heard somewhere he was a papal knight.'

'Of the Order of Saint Gregory the Great,' said Frasso. 'That's right. It happens I'm quite familiar with the case. There was a complicated point involved in the recent nullification proceedings and I was called in for an opinion on it. Sometimes the poor clerics on our marriage courts have to make interpretations of law as difficult as any faced by a temporal judge. I can give you the facts in as much detail as you wish. But first let me make a few general truths clear. A case like Mr. Carpenter's is unfortunate because of the publicity it receives, but the church can be guided by no other considerations except those of natural and canon law. The fact that we made a decision which happened to suit his convenience does not mean that we approve of his conduct. However, any sins he may have committed and the degree of his repentance for them are an entirely separate issue from determining the validity of an assumed marriage. His status as a member of the church or with respect to the honours bestowed on him by the Holy Father would be affected only if he committed some flagrant offence against the sanctity of matrimony, such as being the initiating party in a civil divorce action against a valid marriage.'

Monsignor Frasso proceeded to relate the details of the Dennis Carpenter case. As a very young man he had been married to a girl who, though raised a Catholic, had traded in her faith for a substantial settlement, and divorced him in the courts of Nevada. Such a divorce was recognized as legal by American jurisprudence, but that was just one more evidence of the imperfection of our laws. Actually, according to the authority of the church, which was supreme in such matters, the marriage continued to exist. Disregarding that fact, Dennis had undergone a civil ceremony with another young lady. This one was no marriage at all for two reasons. In the first place he was already married. Additionally, and this became pertinent in the light of later developments, the 'wife' in the case was not a baptized Christian and was consequently ineligible, without a papal dispensation, to marry a Catholic, no matter what claim the civil government which had joined the couple made to its right to do so. This second so-called marriage had also been legally terminated a few years later, after producing two unfortunate offspring.

Following that Dennis had entered into an adulterous relationship with a girl, also unbaptized, who had been divorced from a Jew. Then, his first wife having died and he having succeeded in converting his paramour to the faith, they were married in a proper Catholic ceremony. There had been, incidentally, a slight problem in overcoming the obstacle of the new wife's previous marriage. The church had consented in modern times to recognize the legitimacy of civil marriages between unbaptized persons, and consequently did not honour their divorces. For this reason her new marriage would ordinarily have been regarded as bigamous. But as a convert to Catholicism she was able to invoke the Pauline privilege, an apostolic practice according to which her new union with a Catholic automatically dissolved her previous one to the unbeliever. This, the only form of divorce recognized by the church, was permissible because it served the higher purpose of promoting the faith.

It was this third alliance which had recently come up for determination by the ecclesiastical court. Dennis had requested that it be declared null and void. His grounds were that, since he and his wife had before their marriage committed the crime of adultery with intent to marry — if and when he was freed to do so by the death of his first, and only legal, spouse — their later marriage was an offence against public decency and subject to retroactive invalidation because of the diriment impediment of crime.

Usually that would be considered an excellent case for annulment, but the wife in this instance, clinging for reasons of her own to the marriage, had raised certain objections. One was that during the course of their pre-marital relations they had consistently used contraceptives. On the theory that a marriage in which conception was artificially prevented was no marriage but a blasphemous abuse of the sacrament, she reasoned that adultery with similar restraints was not adultery at all, and that they had therefore been, relatively speaking, sinless.

The official verdict on this contention was that it was ingenious but specious. 'It is quite true,' Frasso told Owen, 'that a marriage from which the right to have children is permanently excluded is void. That is because the main purpose of marriage is procreation. The main purpose of adultery, however, is carnal satisfaction. Contraceptive adultery fulfills that purpose and must accordingly be regarded as criminal intercourse within the prohibition of the Mosaic and Christian law.'

The second objection raised by the wife had been more of a problem. She had discovered, in the course of a routine search of Dennis's effects, some letters exchanged between him and his first wife during their courtship. These revealed a pre-marital agreement to resort to divorce in case of incompatibility. Since indissolubility was an essential property of matrimony, that meant his first marriage must now be set aside. In that case, since his second was patently invalid, he had been a bachelor at the time he had seduced his most recent mate, and their offence must be classed as simple fornication rather than adultery. Therefore, she claimed, there was no crime involved of sufficient consequence to nullify their marriage.

'Now that,' said Monsignor Frasso admiringly, 'was a shrewdly reasoned point which did credit to her legal counsel. I was stopped by it myself for a while before I finally realized where the flaw lay. Do you happen to see what it is?'

'No,' Owen confessed. 'I would have said her case was the sounder one, legally and morally. I don't see why he should be allowed to wipe the marriage out and take a fourth wife.'

'Not fourth, first. No one can be married more than once, at least while the first spouse is still living. But if we find that what appears to have been a marriage is actually no such thing, even if the illusion has persisted for thirty years, we have a spiritual obligation to correct the evil at its roots. Now the point here was that if a married person commits adultery with a promise to marry when and if they are free to do so, any later marriage between them is a sacrilege which cannot be countenanced in heaven or on earth.

'She argued that there was no adultery because both his so-called previous marriages were invalid. True, but what about her own status? Since God does not recognize divorce, either among Christians or pagans, she was clearly a married woman at the time. Hence their relations were criminal and the priest who assisted at their marriage would not have done so if he had known of them. We had no choice but to rule that Mr. Carpenter had never been married and was as free as any other single man to find himself a bride.'

'I see.' Owen digested the argument slowly. 'Her first marriage wasn't really terminated in the sight of God until the moment when, according to this Pauline privilege, she married a Catholic.'

'It wasn't even terminated then, as it turned out, since the new marriage was invalid. We had to inform her she was still the wife of the Jew.'

'What if he had married someone else in the meantime?'

'I understand he was under the impression he had. That made it her duty to notify him that, in the light of these new developments, he was actually living in sin. I don't know what success she had but I hope she was able to persuade him to return to her. If not, she still has the right as a convert to use the Pauline privilege and marry a Catholic. Any Catholic, that is, except young Carpenter.'

* * *

A young lover off to meet his beloved on a sunny June day is practically a symbol of happiness. Owen, perversely, was utterly despondent as he joined the Sunday morning trickle of Manhattan-bound cars on the Queensboro Bridge. He and April had arranged to drive into Connecticut to have lunch and swim at a yacht club near Bridgeport, and he was on his way to pick her up.

There was nothing about the prospect of their day together to stir any sentiment but joy in him. What depressed him to the point of hopeless frustration was that he still had not found the solutions to his two great problems. He wanted intensely to lay a double offering at April's feet as a wedding gift: material prosperity and spiritual affinity. There were indications, in the first responses to Blankenship's campaign, that the former might soon be within his grasp, provided only that he could bring himself to accept it. But he cringed every time he saw one of his company's advertisements and his conscience pricked him whenever he recalled the teachings of Jesus on worldly wealth and the treatment of man by man.

As for Catholicism, he had made some progress toward an intellectual acceptance of the faith on the basis of his two instruction sessions and the supplementary reading to which he had devoted most of his recent evenings. True, some of the doctrine was hard to absorb in large doses, but it was reassuring to remind himself that his reactions were conditioned by his heretical background and therefore untrustworthy. They were also irrelevant since he had already determined that it was not the ramifications of interpretation that mattered but the basic validity of their claim to divine inspiration.

A part of him yearned for an end of doubt. The full and ready answers which the church seemed to provide for every conceivable question promised the kind of secure guidance he had sought all his life — the resolute yet compassionate authority which his parents had consistently failed to furnish him. Also it was the simplest way to secure lifelong bliss with April.

With these considerations pushing him in one direction, a less earnest man would probably have hesitated no longer but embraced the church with the sort of minor reservations which some quite respectable Catholics seem to regard as fashionable to assert. Owen's ardent disposition, however, was as incapable of tepid piety as it was of tepid earthly love. He needed an interior conviction that went beyond mere rational persuasion. He needed, he felt, a sign from on high. Without a conscious link between the thought and the act, he stole a glance heavenward. The top was down on his convertible, affording him an expansive view for possible omens. But the radiant blue of the sky, broken by a few gathering clouds, contained no message for him. Lowering his gaze he jammed on his brakes to avoid hitting the car ahead, which had slowed to turn down the exit ramp.

He crossed Park Avenue, on which he usually drove downtown, and turned south on Madison instead. He was unaware of any specific purpose behind this deviation, but as he passed behind St. Patrick's Cathedral he realized simultaneously that he had never been inside it and that he was quite early for his date. On an impulse which seemed spontaneous to him at the time but which he later conceded might have been supernaturally inspired, he found a parking place for his car just below Fiftieth Street and walked over to the main entrance on Fifth Avenue.

Inside the cathedral he dipped his fingers in the stoup of holy water and made the sign of the cross for the first time in his life, rather pleased that he remembered to proceed from left to right across his chest; and then it occurred to him that it would be less conspicuous to sit for a moment. The centre section was roped off but he found a seat at the end of a row, half way down the right-hand aisle.

This second Mass was a far more splendid ceremony than his first. It was not only the setting itself, though its vast magnificence contributed to the effect. The performance was conducted on a grander scale altogether, with a much larger cast and a greater elaboration of ritual, costume and decoration. On a throne to the left of the altar sat a small, squat, richly adorned figure whom Owen assumed to be the cardinal himself. Instead of being concentrated on the altar, the focal point of the drama moved back and forth between it and the throne, to which came a constant stream of supporting players whose roles were obscure to him, bearing objects he could not identify. At one point the cardinal changed hats, and there were various other pieces of business whose obviously symbolic significance was lost on Owen. Much of the action was staged in such a way that the spectators could not see it, and the greater part of the words were sung in tones too faint to be heard. It was apparent that this was a pageant addressed not to the visible audience but to the Supreme Power in Whose honour it was performed. That, to Owen, enhanced the dignity of the occasion and the sense that he was privileged to sit in on an awesome and mysterious rite.

The serene devotion of the holy men around the altar and the earnest piety of the congregation gave added force to his craving for the peace and security of implicit belief. When the Host had finally been consecrated and prepared for the communicants at the altar rail, he found himself wishing that he, too, could share in the sanctifying grace that was supposed to accompany the sacrament. Yet at the same time he was still repelled by the stark implausibility of the eucharistic conversion. Once again he saw before him the free choice between absolutely irreconcilable alternatives. Either the material substance now being distributed had been literally and actually transformed into the flesh and blood of a God Who had decreed that the proof of reverence was in the eating of Him, or he was witnessing a monstrous hoax.

Christ's own church or history's greatest fraud? So momentous a decision was an almost intolerable imposition on a merely mortal mind. But if one had to choose, and one did, the first alternative was more acceptable than the second. The mystery of the bread become flesh was Christ's great promise to mankind, and it was reasonable to seek final answers in the meaning of that mystery. Could one fully accept the Saviour Himself without partaking of the sacraments He had ordained? And wasn't the institution of this particular sacrament at the Last Supper inevitably bound up with the establishment of His true church through the apostolic succession?

These arguments had logical force but he felt there was no refuge for the spirit in a haven built of logic. He rose and started out without waiting for the conclusion of the Mass. Now he became aware of the row of confessional booths lining the sides of the great chamber, each marked with the name of the priest who furnished forgiveness there, or of the particular order to which he belonged. He wondered what it would be like to bring one's burdens to an unimpeachable authority and receive the solace and direction expressly delegated by God. He thought of Dr. Millis, the psychoanalyst he had visited, and he realized how inferior that kind of costly comfort was to what the church offered almost free of charge. Confession, and in its own way each of the other six sacraments, provided not only release from inner turmoil but the grace and eternal promise which no secular dispensary could stock.

Emerging from the cathedral, he found that the weather had changed abruptly, the late spring sunshine succumbing to a solid mass of dark clouds. Drops of rain began to fall as he walked toward his car. At the corner of Fiftieth and Madison, he heard his name called from across the avenue and turned to see Monsignor Frasso coming toward him from the headquarters of the archdiocese.

'What are you doing in this part of town?' the prelate inquired with a broad smile. 'Did you forget the stores were closed?'

Owen shyly admitted where he had been. Frasso said he had assumed as much from the expression on the young man's face before he had hailed him. 'This is my beat, you know, and I often stop on a busy morning to watch the faces going by. I flatter myself I can always distinguish the ones which have just come from Mass or a quiet moment of prayer in the cathedral.'

'I guess they are a little different from the shoppers and the bright young advertising executives on their way to work,' Owen said. 'You know, it seems incongruous, almost sacrilegious, to me that the centre of the church should be here, right in the midst of these vulgar selling agencies, appealing to the worst and the most worldly in human nature.'

'We were here first,' Frasso said with another smile. 'But you shouldn't be too quick to condemn our friends in the advertising business. After all, Our Lord Himself was not above calling attention to His wares with His own brand of showmanship.'

'You mean the miracles? I never thought of them that way but I suppose you're right. Still, He was certainly down on rich men and the whole business of making money.'

'Not at all,' said the prelate. 'So-called Christian socialists have made a great deal of His saying that it was easier for a camel to pass through the eye of a needle than for a rich man to enter the kingdom of heaven. They fail to note that two verses later He says that what seems impossible to man is quite possible to God. And if He had been against private ownership, He would hardly have instructed the rich young man to *sell* everything he had; He would have told him to give it away. Nor would He have been so pleased with Zacchaeus for giving only *half* his goods to the poor.'

The rain was coming down harder now but Frasso didn't seem to mind it and Owen was far too interested in these unfamiliar ideas to want to cut them short. 'I hardly think Jesus would have approved of capitalist methods, though,' he said. 'People making money from other people's work and so on.'

'He did approve them. Jesus lived in a time of slavery, when the exploitation of human labour was more extreme than it is now. Yet He made no criticism of existing economic relationships. On the contrary, He specifically accepted and endorsed them in His parables. In the parable of the labourers in the vineyard, He upheld the right of an employer to fix wages according to any standard he chose. In the parable of the vine-dressers, He covered the obligations of a tenant farmer to an absentee landlord. And in the parable of the gold pieces, the virtuous man is the one who put his master's capital to work so that it amounted to ten times its original value within a short period of time. The exact rate of return on the investment is given differently in Matthew than in Luke, but the moral is obviously the same.'

Owen had to admit that the evidence was overwhelming. He began to see how deluded he had been by the partisan interpretations of Tolstoy, Bernard Shaw and other revisionists who professed to find equalitarian ideas in the teachings of Jesus. With this realization, a part of the burden seemed to slip from his shoulders, but there was still an element of lingering doubt to disturb him.

'Then why did so many early Christians feel they had to give up their worldly possessions? And what about the holy men and women who take vows of poverty?'

'They also take vows of celibacy and obedience,' Frasso reminded him. 'Yet one would hardly say that God frowned upon marriage or independent thinking. The truth is that such vows are for the few, not the many. Our Lord expressed His own preference for virginity by adhering to that state while on earth and by choosing a virgin for His mother. But He began His mission at a marriage feast and raised matrimony to a sacrament. Church government and the monastic orders require unflagging obedience to one's superiors; yet in the temporal world we may attribute a measure of human progress to the very men who have challenged established authority, even individuals like Galileo and Copernicus who committed the sin of excessive pride in their own conclusions.

'So it is with the question of poverty and wealth. It is true that many saints demonstrated the extremes of privation they could endure. But it is also true that in later centuries equally holy men, whose piety earned them the rank of bishop, abbot, cardinal and even pope, accumulated large fortunes and rivalled the secular princes of their time. Today the church teaches that it is a natural aspiration of man to acquire private property and to protect it against the depredations of those who refuse to accept their lot with the humility recommended by Jesus. We recognize the rights of employers as well as their obligation to pay a wage sufficient, as Pope Leo XIII defined it, to support the employee "in reasonable and frugal comfort".

'I would say in summation that there is a drawing account in the sacred treasury of merits for both the mendicant friar and the devout millionaire, provided each makes his appropriate contribution to the Lord's work on earth. Have you noticed how wet it is becoming? I think I should go back for an umbrella. Can I offer you shelter?'

The young man replied that he had his car parked down the block, and they parted in haste.

Owen had forgotten that he had left the top of his car down. He got in hastily, turned the switch which controlled the top mechanism and found that it stubbornly refused to operate. He tried to perform its function by hand, spurred by the growing intensity of the rain, but without success. Defeated, he had decided to drive off anyway when he was diverted by a sudden strange illumination. It was not, he realized after the first bewildering instant, an external light but an inner one, reacting on some ultra sense beyond the material range. With it came a warmth and a peace and an affirmation never experienced before; from his earlier dejection he had now been transported to a pinnacle of confident serenity.

It seemed unlikely that this new strength and assurance could have come from his own depleted resources. Some power beyond himself had invaded his being and established itself there, suffusing him with love and glory from an apparently inexhaustible supply.

His tenant, with whom he felt in immediate and perfect communion, was not God in the sense that he could distinguish a specific One of the three Persons, but a sort of general divinity that made him aware of, and close to, God in all His manifestations. Nor was any coherent message bestowed upon him. No new course of action was charted for him; rather were the barriers removed from all courses of action. The rigid confines of his despair dissolved and around him lay a limitless vista of unexplored beauty. Nothing he might choose to attempt seemed unfeasible or even difficult. The only wonder was that there could be pessimism or doubt in a world so close to heaven.

Although the sky had brightened perceptibly, the vigour of the rain was undiminished. The inner layers of his clothing were as saturated as the outer, and served merely to conduct a steady supply of moisture to his skin. He tried once again to raise the top of the car but the regenerative effects of the miracle did not extend to the broken mechanism. Now, however, his situation no longer distressed him; he found it amusing, even rather rewarding. What struck him about the rain was its purity, freshness and stimulating coolness; he thought with gratitude of its marvellous usefulness in a well-ordered world. He had the sense that he was being baptized, by a method close to immersion, with one of God's great blessings to mankind.

April, when he reached her door, took no such sanguine view of his plight. She was dressed in a robe, having abandoned her preparations for their excursion when the rain started. The sight of him filled her with loving concern and, dismissing his protests as typically inane assertions of the masculine ego, she forced him out of his clothes and into a hot bath. After keeping him there for twenty minutes she gave him such a vigorous rub down that he found the pleasure and pain of it about equally balanced, and herded him into her bed to wait out the slow drying of his clothes. Then, still unsatisfied with the course of treatment and paying no more attention to his objections than he hoped she would, she administered an extremely thorough and expert alcohol rub. The tenderly firm pressure of her marvellous hands on every part of his body so stimulated his desire for her that it had reached an almost unendurable stage by the time she finally paused to consider an alternative remedy.

'I read somewhere about some experiments the Nazis made during the war,' she said. 'A couple of their goddam bastard doctors used human guinea pigs to test different treatments for exposure to cold — kept them in ice water for hours at a time and then tried various methods for reviving the ones who still showed signs of life. You know what they found worked better than any standard treatment for restoring circulation and warmth?'

'No,' Owen admitted. 'But I hardly think my condition calls for any drastic measures, if that's what you're leading up to.'

'This one has its pleasant aspects. They found that the quickest and most effective thing they could use was to wrap the victim up in a blanket with another person of the opposite sex, nude.' She loosened her robe. 'If you think it's too drastic, we won't try it.'

He raised the covers while she got into the bed beside him. 'I think I could use the treatment all right, but for quite different symptoms.' He took her in his arms and held her tightly. 'It's the most sensible idea by a long shot that ever came out of Hitler Germany.'

Her sustained attentions to his person had aroused April's passion as much as his own and he felt an intensity in the way she clung to him that clearly made all further preliminary excitation unnecessary. They were proceeding in total absorption to the ultimate expression of their ardour when, unbidden and out of context with any previous mental process of which he was conscious, a thought struck him with the force of revelation. He withdrew his body from hers with a suddenness that left her bewildered.

'This is wrong, baby,' he said earnestly. 'We mustn't.'

'It's all right,' she told him. 'I'm protected.'

'No, no, no. I mean we've got to wait.'

'For what, sweetie?' She moved over to where he now lay rigidly on his back, raising herself on one elbow so that she could search his face for a clue to his strange behaviour. Loving him far beyond the force of her immediate desire, she wanted to understand and share whatever was bothering him. 'You don't still want to drive up there in this weather, do you?'

'Of course not. I'm not just talking about now, this moment. I mean making love like this is something for after we're married.'

'Well, sure. We'll do it much more often then. We'll be together all the time.' The prospect excited her and she snuggled down against him with the full weight of her body. 'Oh, my dearest love, just think of it, being in each other's arms all night every night. It'll be so much better than this routine of catching a moment when we can.'

'That's all over with.' He spoke in as firm a voice as he could muster in the midst of his effort to assert control over his physical reactions. 'It's because of what we'll have later that we don't want to spoil it by indulging ourselves now.'

'You're crazy.' Her affection for him was diluted with a small measure of irritation. 'How can you spoil something that gets better each time, not worse? We've found out things about each other already that will start us off at a much higher level than we had at the beginning. Like when you . . .'

'You don't understand what I'm talking about, my darling.' He extricated himself gently from her embrace and retreated to the edge of the bed. 'Please put something on, will you? We have to discuss this as calmly and unemotionally as we can.'

Smarting under the bitter sting of rejection, she threw the covers aside, got out of bed and put her robe back on. 'It's not my idea of how to spend a rainy Sunday, but go ahead, talk. If you're starting to have doubts already, I might as well hear about it.' She seated herself primly on the opposite edge of the bed from him. 'I didn't think we'd either of us ever get tired of what we had together. Oh maybe after thirty or forty years, but that would just be a matter of our physical energy running out.'

'It's a moral question, not a physical one. I've never wanted you any more than I do at this moment. But going to bed together when we aren't married yet is a sin, a bad one.'

April groaned. 'I might have known it would come to this. The other day, after you'd talked to Father Duchesne, I had a feeling you couldn't take religion in moderation. There are people like that, who just can't be satisfied with a swig of it now and then, and unless they learn they're the type who simply musn't touch it, ever, they end up in the boobyhatch or a monastery.'

'I don't think I'm a likely candidate for either,' he said, smiling. 'What I'm saying isn't very extreme or fanatical. It's pretty basic to the whole idea of Christian marriage. For lovers to exercise some self-control is just a way of showing they love God more than they do their own pleasure.'

'You've got it bad, haven't you? — damn my idiot mother!' Forgetting the wound to her pride, she stretched herself out across the bed toward him so that she could take his hand and raise it against her cheek while she gazed into his eyes at close range. 'Look, Owen, my dearest love, even if you're right about it being wrong for us to have had intercourse — which I don't admit or at least I don't think it's a very important sin — what sense would it make to stop now? Is fifteen times worse than ten or whatever? We can't make ourselves pure and virginal for each other; we weren't either of us that when we first met.'

'Is that what a priest would tell you if you went to him for absolution now? Would he say we might as well go right on the way we are because it's too late to do anything about it now?'

She sat up again, annoyed. 'I don't care what a priest would say. They have to interpret everything literally according to the book and the same for everybody. And one thing every intelligent Catholic realizes is that a man doesn't become better or smarter than anyone else just because he's in orders. There are stupid priests and crooked bishops, even popes.

'When I'm ready to confess about you and me, which I certainly wouldn't get married without doing, it won't be just to *a* priest; it'll be to my priest, Father Duchesne, who understands that some people have different needs than others sexually. But I've always felt it was a ridiculous waste of my time and his to confess anything until the moment when I was ready and willing to give it up. That's why I didn't say anything about Gene and me until we were through, and then I did penance for the whole two years at once. Any other way of going about it seems hypocritical to me.'

This time it was Owen who reached over to establish a physical contact between them. 'It won't be ridiculous or hypocritical if you go to him now, because you are through with this sin. You aren't going to commit fornication ever again, for the rest of your life. That's one thing I feel absolutely definite about, baby. No matter what we have to answer for already and even if we only have to wait another week or two, we'll feel cleaner and stronger afterwards.'

'I feel pretty strong right now, and reasonably clean. But...' She hesitated for a moment, considering whether she was yielding anything more important than a few hours' pleasure. 'All right, if it means so much to you. No fornication. God, what a horrible word.' She transferred his outstretched hand from her shoulder to her breast. 'You don't think it would be just as good to swear off an hour from now, do you?' His hand dropped to a more decorous location. 'I didn't imagine you would.'

'We're going to get a lot of satisfaction and happiness later on out of making this decision today,' he told her.

'Yes,' she said absently, her thoughts already fixed on a more basic matter. 'But now that we're facing our past mistakes, I've got a more important one to own up to. I've been very unfair with you, right from the start, on this whole business of making you sign up on my church's terms, just because it seemed easier to me to go along with the rules and also not make an issue with my mother. I pretended it meant more to me than it really did and I want to say to you now what I should have said in the first place. I love you more than anything else in the world and I'll marry you on any terms you want, before a judge if you like, as soon as we can get the licence.'

'You're a darling,' he said with conviction, 'but I wouldn't think of it. Do you suppose I'd let you be excommunicated, now when I'm finally beginning to understand the beauty and mystery of Catholicism?'

'It wouldn't mean excommunication exactly. I looked it up last night. A civil ceremony isn't nearly as bad as a Protestant one. The church simply regards it as no marriage at all, the same as two people openly living together. You're just barred from the sacraments and sacramentals until you repent. That's something I could face for a while because I'd always be able to make it right eventually.'

'You won't have to face it.' In keeping with the decisiveness of his expression and tone, he swung his feet to the floor and started to stand up. Then he remembered he had no clothes on and stayed where he was. 'I'm going to ask Monsignor Frasso tomorrow how soon I can be baptized.'

'I wish you wouldn't. Rush into it, I mean. I just have this feeling about you — it's hard to explain. I don't want to see you get too serious about anything. You've had so much already, prison and the war, and you're still only twenty-three years old.'

'That's a long time to have run the risk of perdition. Oh, my baby, this is going to mean so much more to us than just being able to get married properly. Now we'll be united in every way, for our whole lives.'

'I don't think I want you to do it,' she said. 'It's too much to ask of you.'

'Don't worry, my love, I'm not making any sacrifice. If you told me tomorrow you didn't love me any more and I found some way to still go on living, I believe I'd be converted just the same.'

'You would?'

'Yes.'

She conceded defeat with a sigh. 'Then I guess there's no sense in my trying to argue with you.' She got up and began to walk around restlessly, conscious of her claim to credit for an accomplishment she now regarded with disfavour. 'Well, what indoor sports do we have left to kill a rainy day with?'

'You can come here and kiss me,' Owen said. 'I don't know what the bounds of behaviour are for engaged couples but I'll go for a broad interpretation till I find out different.'

'I sometimes think the story of creation would be even more wonderful,' said Monsignor Frasso, 'if the sacred writers had had a more accurate conception of the enormous spans of time and distance involved. Every new discovery of science makes the proofs of God's existence more inescapable. On how much grander a scale does His plan emerge when we retell the first chapter of Genesis in the light of our present knowledge.

'The first step, we now realize, was the glorious conception of mass which is also energy. To express it in practice He had to fashion infinite numbers of protons, neutrons, mesotrons, electrons and whatever other particles there are, and distribute them into the number of basic elements He considered desirable, ninety-four or ninety-five or ninety-six or however many it was. Then, for reasons far beyond our capacity to fathom, He created a universe trillions of times as large as man's eventual abode, a universe which, in the course of billions of years, would produce a galaxy which would produce a solar system which would produce a world upon which man, after many more millions of years, would develop. We don't know why such vast expanses of space and time were necessary, but we do know that all the space but ours is subordinate, and all the time before us merely preparatory. The alternative, that Jesus Christ's stay on earth was just one visit on a continuous tour of mankinds which had to be redeemed, is impious and unthinkable.

'The theory of evolution, which seems ever more valid with the passing years, immeasurably increases our awe of God. We knew that every thing, every being, were reflections of an archetypal idea in the divine mind. Now we realize that He conceived not only of a horse but of every type of horse and every previous and future evolutionary stage of horse. It is staggering to contemplate the complexity of the development of life from protoplasm to Pithecanthropus erectus, a being finally capable of standing on his own two feet and worthy of immortality. At that moment, when God gave the man Adam a soul, His original purpose in creation was revealed and history begins.'

The prelate had been gathering energy as he spoke and there was no telling to what lengths he might proceed from the initial impetus of his variations on a theme in Genesis. At the moment, however, when he reached the dawn of human history and was considering the dozen different directions his discourse might take, he glanced at his pupil for the gratifying reaction his outgiving nature so rarely required, and noticed instead a look of concern.

'Something is bothering you, my son. If you have a question, please ask it. It's one of the best ways there is of achieving our purpose.'

'Thank you.' Owen had been growing pessimistic about his chances of being able to press his burning inquiry. 'There is one rather important matter I'd like to . . .' He paused, fearing the effect of his temerity. Would he be considered presumptuous for thinking his conversion already complete?

'By all means,' Frasso assured him. 'It's more than likely, because of my long experience in this work, that I can guess the doctrinal point which you find it most difficult to accept. You probably share some of the traditional rationalist scepticism on the question of theophagy, god-eating. You wonder if perhaps Christianity didn't borrow the Eucharist from all those primitive religions in which the poor barbarians were deluded into thinking they were eating and drinking their gods. You're bothered by the connection with cannibalism and worship of sacred animals.'

'No, that doesn't disturb me particularly,' Owen said. 'When there are so many important differences, you can lay a few similarities to coincidence.'

'Then perhaps it's the matter of relics. You think it's foolish to venerate the bones of saints and you don't see why an altar can't be consecrated unless it contains the relics of a martyr. You may have read about unhappy mistakes like the milk of Our Lady in the grotto at Bethlehem which turned out to be powdered white rock in the water. That leads you to doubts about all the Masses that may have been said over bones that really belonged to uncanonized skeletons.'

'Not at all. I used to worry about things like that but not any more. I just want to serve God and pray to Him for mercy, not set up a whole lot of barriers between us.'

The prelate looked searchingly at the youth in front of him. 'I'm going to say something that will startle you, my son. If that's the way you feel and you're quite clear on the points that confuse most people interested in the true faith, then I think you're probably ready right now. And it isn't just your words that make me say that. Like a doctor who can diagnose almost by instinct, I have acquired over the years the ability to sense the amount of piety emanating from a person. I can feel such an inner glow coming from your soul.'

'You make me very happy, Monsignor, if you really believe I'm worthy of joining the church. I'd be very anxious to do it as soon as I'm permitted.'

Frasso referred to his desk calendar. 'Let's set it down for Wednesday morning. I'll be in Washington all day tomorrow with the apostolic delegate, and also you could use about forty-eight hours steady prayer.' He beamed paternally on his pupil. 'Sometimes I happen to strike just the right chords straight off with a particular catechumen. Not that I should take credit. The celestial temptress is obviously extending herself to lure you into grace.'

'I won't forget to thank her,' Owen said. 'But I also want you to know that these hours with you have meant a lot to me at a very critical period. I'm especially grateful because I realize how pressed you are for time. By the way, I meant to ask you how your movie went last week.'

'Quite a pedestrian affair,' said Monsignor Frasso. 'The director learned his camera angles in army training films, and he had about as much understanding of the Blessed Virgin as a Two-Seed-in-the-Spirit Predestinarian Baptist. But I've asked the Archbishop of Los Angeles to use pressure to get the cutter I want and we may be able to rescue it on film.'

A sense of deep personal privacy about his conversion led Owen to keep it a secret even from April, and to enlist two virtual strangers for his witnesses. The ceremony took place in the cathedral, which was majestically empty except for a few scattered worshippers fortifying themselves for the spiritual rigours of a Manhattan business day. Monsignor Frasso received his profession of faith and solemn abjuration of heresy, and administered the sacrament of baptism. This last rite was performed conditionally, to take effect only if the Episcopal baptism he had received in infancy failed to meet the tests of celestial jurisprudence. Then another priest heard his detailed confession, covering nearly a quarter-century of accumulated sin. Finally Frasso took over again to say Mass, preside at Owen's first communion and deliver the blessing and exhortation.

The only uncertainty Owen felt throughout the process was on the question of whether he would be permitted to make a donation of money in acknowledgment of the privilege bestowed on him. Frasso set his mind at ease, informing him that his cheque should be made out to the Archbishopric of New York.

A half an hour later he was at the plant, exhilarated by a blend of sanctity, romantic love and executive energy. April was at her desk typing obscure answers to an obscurely worded questionnaire from the Senate Small Business Committee. When he told her the news she covered her face with her hands to conceal whatever emotion it was she was feeling.

'I never hoped it could be done as quickly as that,' Owen said. 'Now we can go right ahead and be married.'

April raised her head. 'The hell we can. Now that we're both Catholics, it means the banns have to be put up, three Sundays in a row. In a mixed marriage there aren't any.'

'Nobody told me that.'

'Well, maybe you can claim they took you in under false pretences. Want to apostatize?'

He laughed and kissed her. 'I think we'll get enough blessings out of it to make up for three weeks.' He lifted her to her feet for a thorough embrace. They were tightly locked in each other's arms when Blankenship burst into the office, excitedly exhibiting some letters. His jubilation was too intense to be restrained by the scene which confronted him.

'This is even more important than sex,' he said as they drew apart. 'Macy's, Marshall Field and three other stores that didn't give us a tumble before! We're going to be rolling in the sweet fruits of toil, children.'

The commercial genius of Willis Muir had triumphed again. It was an occasion of joy, the turning point in the history of the Jet Manufacturing and Sales Company. Owen shook his advertising director's hand and April added her tribute in the form of a kiss, which Blankenship sought to convert into a more ardent expression than she had intended. It was while she was disengaging herself from him that she heard her future husband's voice behind her in an earnest mumble. All she could distinguish of what he was saying were the words 'Thank you'.

She turned around and saw with a shudder that he was not addressing anyone visibly present.

PART TWO

No
CROSS
no
CROWN

CHAPTER I

Dennis Carpenter couldn't quite figure out what he was doing at the Stork Club with this girl. He had gone to the party at Owen and April Muir's with his wife, but when the crowd had thinned out and he had looked around for Dellie to see if she was ready to leave, he found that she had already done so without bothering to consult him. This Miss Elliot, who claimed they had met at the Muirs' wedding more than two years before, had been very sympathetic and volunteered to keep him company after Dennis decided that Dellie, no matter what frivolity she was pursuing, would probably end up at the Stork in accordance with normal routine.

Miss Elliot, he gathered, worked in an office somewhere and was a relic of April's plebeian past. In his semi-drunken state the idea of taking her to a bastion of privilege had stirred his philanthropic instinct. Now, however, when they were sitting against the wall together in the room reserved for celebrities of the second rank, her voice seemed a little too loud, her party dress a little too spangly, her enjoyment a little too obvious. He suspected that she had staying powers which would present a problem either way, whether Dellie showed up or not.

He did not know with what man his wife had gone off, nor did he consider it a point of any great significance. Her motive in deserting him, he was certain, had sprung from the presence at the party of Phyllis Muir, with whom he had once had an affair bordering on marriage. Dellie's reaction on meeting Phyllis had been enough to make him regret the excess of conjugal candour in which he had confessed the episode.

For her part, Ann Elliot regarded Dennis as an opportunity to be exploited for whatever advantage might develop. Just as an acquaintance, a name to drop around the office, he would provide her some satisfaction. If the thing with his wife turned out to be serious, he might be a lover who would undoubtedly contribute to her material welfare for the duration of the relationship. Best of all, he was a potential employer or a contact through whom she might secure a more rewarding job. That way he could change her life to a really useful and permanent extent. She liked his freckles and crew-cut, his slight, agile body, his inherited wealth and the stories she had heard of his many marriages and affairs.

The Muirs were their only topic of common interest. Dennis was unsure in his attitude toward Owen. Trained by Phyllis to dismiss him as a hopeless idealist, he had found him, on the basis of a dozen social gatherings during the past year, to be a normal and not unpleasant companion most of the time. But the fact of his conversion was disturbing. 'I don't see why a man would go for a stunt like that.'

'I thought you . . .'

'I'm a Catholic myself, of course, a pretty good Catholic, I think. I even have a papal decoration, for whatever that's worth. But changing what you were born into like Owen did, making a public thing of it, I don't know. It's kind of obscene. And he has a way of bringing religion into a casual conversation when you're least expecting it, where it doesn't belong.'

'Yes, but on him it doesn't sound so bad,' Ann said. 'Owen's different from other people. He's the most absolutely honest man I know. And the sweetest. April told me she's never once seen him lose his temper or raise his voice, even at her. You won't find many men taking it the way he did tonight when that girl, what's-her-name, got sick all over his desk.'

'Marjorie Ainsworth,' Dennis said. 'You don't invite the Ainsworths unless you're prepared to have her puke on something.'

'I never get sick from drinking. If I ever did, you can take my word for it, I'd never touch the stuff again. I get hangovers though, sometimes.'

'The worst hangover I ever had was in San Francisco,' he said. 'I went to a place on the waterfront with some football players of mine, and we got into a deal where each guy paid for a round, only all the others had to have what he was drinking.'

'I've never been in California,' Ann said. 'There's a girl in our office comes from Seattle.'

'I don't know what I had to drink that night,' he continued. 'Zombies on top of gin and whisky and, just to run the gamut, I had three stingers when I got back to the hotel. Couldn't get out of bed the next morning till I had the doctor over to give me a shot of B-one.'

'Vitamins.' She spoke the word with disdain. 'That's the worst racket in the country. The pills I mean; I guess maybe the shots are different.' The tactful amendment was unnecessary because he wasn't listening. He was looking toward the door, watching for Dellie. It was a breach of good manners and he was too well trained in the tradition of aristocratic gallantry not to realize it. By way of compensation for the slight, letting her know he was still aware of her, his hand dropped, behind the protective screen of the tablecloth, to her thigh.

It was an absentminded caress at best but Ann felt it merited some acknowledgment. Unable to catch his eye and reward him with a look, she slipped her hand beneath his extended arm and reached over to his lap in a reciprocal gesture. The directness of the response captured his attention and he turned to face her. Their eyes met, reflecting the stimulus from below.

'Excuse me,' said the captain's voice above their heads. 'The management...'

Guiltily they withdrew their hands from each other. Ann wondered for a fleeting second what it would be like to be ejected from a place like this for lewd behaviour. She looked up timidly to find herself the recipient of a small gift package, elegantly wrapped. She was being favoured with a vial of Mr. Billingsley's next-to-the-finest perfume. In addition, the captain proceeded to assure Dennis, they would honour the establishment by accepting a bottle of champagne.

'Thanks, Emil,' Dennis said, 'but we'll skip it tonight. My wife and I got our signals crossed and I'm beginning to think she must have gone on home.'

Ann admired the shrewdness of this reply. There was no point in their lingering here any longer, and the timely reference to Dellie would help obscure the sinful trail on which they were about to embark. It wasn't till they reached the sidewalk outside that disillusion struck.

'You don't mind if I send you home in a separate cab,' said her escort, 'seeing we live in different directions.' He pressed two dollar bills into her hands, ushered her into the taxi, smiled, flicked a finger across her cheek, and was gone.

Marjorie Ainsworth often said there was one good thing about getting sick: it sobered you up, sometimes enough so you could make a fresh start. By the time she and her husband had reached their winter quarters on Seventy-Ninth Street just east of Park, she was in acute need of a restorative dose of whisky. Otto fixed it for her although he himself took coffee. While some aspects of his wife's alcoholism were displeasing to him, he liked the feeling of superiority it gave him, the sense that he was temporarily more articulate than she and had the right to do most of the talking. Some of his nocturnal dissertations, he felt, were quite profound. Unfortunately their effectiveness was limited by the fact that his only listener retained nothing of them in the morning.

'The Muirs fascinate me more every time I'm exposed to them,' he said. 'They should be subsidized by the State Department, you know, to go on a world tour. The ideal American couple.'

'Not typical,' Marjorie objected. 'Millionaires.'

'I don't mean typical, I mean the best. Owen simply oozes with charm and he's so terribly virile, he's the perfect answer to the cartoon myth they've got of the American capitalist, the fat, bloated type with the silk hat. And April is so refreshing you just know she'd be a sensation anywhere. I'm convinced of that objectively, even though physically she doesn't happen to be my sort of woman.'

'What is your sort of woman physically?' Marjorie inquired. 'That's something I often wonder about.'

Otto Ainsworth refused to be sidetracked. 'It renews my faith in myself, really it does, to remember that I saw possibilities in Owen back in college when practically nobody else did. I have to laugh when I realize that all the boys who were supposed to be big shots, the leaders of their class, they've most of them ended up as doctors or engineers or chemists or something, with no chance of ever getting ahead of themselves. But old Buff — that's what we called him — who all the big-balled heroes thought was a drip is one of the few with a really successful business of his own and there's no telling how far he'll go.'

'I like him,' Marjorie admitted. 'He wants me any time, he just has to wiggle his finger at me. But I don't see he rates so much credit for using his old man's money.'

'You're missing the most important point as usual, my sweet. He may have started off using his father's money but he isn't using it any more. The fact of the matter is Owen's been frightfully enterprising, always branching out into something new. I happen to know all sorts of people tried to discourage him from making television aerials. They said there was no market, too many concerns in the field already. So what did the dear boy do but open up a market no one else had thought of? — the people who couldn't afford sets yet but wanted an aerial on their roof so the neighbours would think they had one. That's going old Mr. Emerson one better, wouldn't you say? You don't have to worry about making a better mousetrap than your neighbour as long as you're aiming at customers who don't have mice.'

'There's one thing wrong with your ideal American couple idea. I just remembered. April saying she'd voted for Wallace. That's hardly the kind of talk the State Department wants spread abroad.'

'It happens that is not what the lady said. If you'd stay sober for an evening, you wouldn't always be misquoting everybody. She said people had a right to vote for Wallace, as much as Truman or Dewey. Now I don't go along with even that myself — it's an absurd contradiction to extend American freedom to people who don't believe in it — but somehow you don't mind it when April says a thing that would be outrageous from anyone else. And the truth is that's exactly the kind of high-sounding nonsense that has a very wide appeal in countries like England and France where the fashionable thing these days is to speak of America as a semi-fascist country.'

Marjorie rose with her glass in her hand and headed for the kitchen. 'I'm going to get a little more medication for my throat. It's still sore.'

Her husband said, 'Your rationalizations are really preposterous. Why have any more now? It will probably just make you sick all over again.'

'Not if I don't eat,' she told him. 'That's the mistake I made at the Muirs', eating all that buffet stuff. You never get sick just drinking.'

Arnold Blankenship and Tessie Couto were a chance combination. They had descended in the elevator together from April and Owen's apartment to find that a light, pre-Christmas snow was falling outside. Learning that Mrs. Couto intended to walk six blocks to a subway entrance and that her route home was not too different from his, Blankenship offered her a ride in his taxi. His chivalry was unmarred by any trace of carnality. Having left his wife and children in the more wholesome surroundings of the Middle West when he moved on to New York and a higher income level, he had found it satisfying to concentrate his attentions on females at least fifteen years younger than himself. A relationship with a woman his own age, which, underestimating her sixty years by a whole decade, he assumed Mrs. Couto to be, was something he could always achieve by responding favourably to one of his wife's persistent letters.

While Mrs. Couto's activities seldom left her free to accept April's invitations, her personal friendship with her son's former mistress had survived the collapse of that alliance. But fond as she was of April, she reacted unfavourably to most of the guests at an affair like the one she had just left.

'Pleasant party,' said Blankenship for lack of a better conversational opening.

'Yes,' she said in polite, unenthusiastic agreement.

'I find it refreshing to be with young people once in a while, don't you? Sort of keeps you in touch.'

'I wonder.' Mrs. Couto had no desire to start an argument but neither could she bring herself to endorse this view. 'I wonder if that group tonight is very typical of our young people. I rather hope not, after some of the things I listened to.'

'You find yourself shocked by them?' There was sympathetic understanding in his voice and at the same time the suggestion that he himself was able to rise above the fragile sensibilities of his generation. 'I know how crass their talk can sound sometimes but don't you think, madam, that our own middle-aged standards are often at fault when we flinch from the radical ideas of our juniors?'

'Radical!' She was incredulous. 'The thing that appals me is to hear boys and girls in their twenties mouthing the stuffy outdated platitudes you'd expect at a bankers-for-Dewey rally.'

Blankenship regarded her with new interest. 'Forgive me for misjudging you. I too am a lifelong liberal who has not lost his faith in the mission of Franklin Roosevelt. His death impoverished us all.'

'Except the Missouri gang,' she agreed, 'and the men who think they can monopolize atomic energy. Those people there tonight, I don't blame April so much for having them; she's not very political and I realize she has to make some concessions to Owen's business connections. I just feel sorry for her, being surrounded by all that decadence night after night. From a simple standpoint of morals they're so distasteful.'

'You shouldn't misjudge Owen,' he said. 'I don't know how well you know him but I can tell you there isn't a finer, purer, more unselfish young man anywhere. He's no genius as far as business is concerned but at least he's shrewd enough to put his affairs in the hands of people who understand those things.'

'I didn't mean I had anything against Owen personally. He's a good, decent boy compared to the others. But he looks out at the world through the fog of his class interest. I was talking to him tonight about the organization I work for, the Council for Permanent Peace...'

'Oh.' He felt obliged to indicate recognition but there was no assurance in his voice. 'Is that the group that fellow Hiss they indicted the other day...?'

'Certainly not. They're just an imperialist front organization, a mouthpiece for John Foster Dulles. Our programme is to reach a real understanding with the Soviet Union, with both countries agreeing to disarm and not make atom bombs — let every nation in the world decide its own political future without outside interference.'

'A very laudable platform, I should say. Did Owen have some criticism of it?'

'He'd been warned against it; in church of all places. He told me there was one thing wrong with it: it was exactly what the Communists were agitating for.'

'So it is,' he said quickly. 'The boy's right. I was about to make the same point myself. Right out of the *Daily Worker*.'

'But isn't that good? I mean don't you think the American Communists very frequently have the same policies as the Russian ones?'

'Frequently! I'd say invariably.'

'Well, then, that's another argument for our programme, isn't it? Not only do we have a policy which is a very laudable one, as you say, from the American point of view, but we can also be pretty sure it will be acceptable to the other side.'

'My dear lady,' Blankenship said earnestly, 'you're falling into the most dangerous kind of pseudo-logical trap. You're forgetting the warning the Trojans failed to heed. "Timeo Danaos et dona ferentes." I fear the Greeks bearing....'

'I fear them too — the kind of Greeks we're supporting under the Truman Doctrine.'

'You must never do what the enemy want you to do,' he continued. 'That's basic military strategy.'

'Perhaps so, but is it sound peace strategy? Seeking an agreement is a different proposition from seeking a favourable battleground.'

'We're in a war, a cold war. Mrs. Couto, you may find it presumptuous but I want to give you a piece of advice. This group you're working with, get out of it right away. I'm convinced, without knowing any more about it than you've told me, that there are Communists in it.'

'So am I. As a matter of fact . . .'

'Don't say it!' he broke in, with an apprehensive glance at the cab-driver. 'I don't want to be a party to your guilty secrets.'

She saw that his distress was genuine, and apologized for having unsettled him. 'I didn't mean to embarrass you. But we have a policy that all people who agree with our general programme should work together, no matter what other differences they may have.'

'It's the same trap,' he told her. 'You see, the Communists aren't for peace as a matter of principle, because they believe in it. They just think it's a better atmosphere to spread their propaganda in.'

'But do you really think their ideas can stand up against ours in a free, peaceful competition?'

'Of course not. I didn't say that. I said they probably thought so.'

'Oh.' She called to the driver: 'Just let me out on the corner, please.' Then she turned back to Blankenship. 'If that's the case, you know what I think? I think we shouldn't let on to them they're wrong.' The cab stopped and she opened the door. 'If we did, we might be driving them to force and violence.'

He watched her start down the sidewalk with the trim vitality of a young woman.

'I shouldn't have come here,' Dellie Carpenter said.

'You're not relaxing,' Phyllis Muir told her sternly. 'I can't loosen you up unless you really let yourself go.' She was standing behind the other girl's chair, kneading with strong fingers the flesh and muscle of her neck and shoulders. 'Why shouldn't you have come?'

'Because I have such a weak character. I'm always being influenced by somebody who's stronger and more forceful than I am.'

It wasn't much of a tribute, Phyllis thought to herself; almost anyone could qualify as more forceful than Dellie. At twenty-two only a year younger than Phyllis, she seemed hardly more than adolescent, and this in spite of two years' service in the ranks of Hollywood starlets. Her vapidity made Dennis's behaviour the more insulting; it was hard to believe that he could have married her at a time when Phyllis herself was again available to him, following the rupture of her affair with Bert Drucker. Outside of her natural impulse to annoy Dennis, one of Phyllis's reasons for enticing Dellie from Owen's apartment to her own had been to probe more closely into the mystery of the girl's charm. The visual part of it was clear enough nor was Phyllis immune to it herself, but she felt she had the right to expect more than mere prettiness.

'Are you afraid of my influence?' she asked. 'It was you who said you were bored at Ownie's, remember, and you had a head-ache. I simply suggested it might make you feel better to listen to some of my records.'

'I'm not blaming you,' Dellie protested. 'Please don't think that. You've been terribly sweet and I can't tell you how wonderful it makes me feel, what you're doing to me. I just meant I should have realized — ever since school I've been getting crushes on girls like you who are smart and sophisticated, and I follow them around like a poodle and make a terrible nuisance of myself.'

Phyllis bent down and kissed her under the ear. 'You won't ever be a nuisance to me.' She came around the chair and sat on the arm of it, taking Dellie's hand in one of her own and continuing to stroke the girl's neck with the other. 'Tell me what you think of my brother.'

'He's wonderful,' Dellie said, 'just wonderful. I think it's wonderful the way he listens to everybody and hardly ever says anything but when he does they all hang on every word and tell it around to people who didn't hear him. I should think he'd make you feel very proud and wonderful.'

'He makes me feel nervous. He's cracked, you know.' She took Dellie's gold chain from the table beside them and refastened it around the girl's neck, pressing the crucifix back into place beneath the tight strapless bodice. 'Some day he'll come apart like a clay pigeon. I think April realizes it too; she's always in there buttering him up whenever he gets that Messiah look in his eye.'

Dumbfounded, Dellie said, 'But they're so wonderful together. I always say to Dennis that's what marriage should really be like. Do you mean he's actually insane?'

'Not actively, at the moment. It's one of those split personality things: half of him wants to be a normal, decent person and a respectable representative of his class in society, but the other half is burning to save the world with whatever screwball remedy he happens to be sold on at the time. It's the sort of thing that can be dangerous even if you don't see it on the surface. That's why I always try to warn people about him.' She took the other girl's chin in her fingers and turned her face up toward her own. 'But what about you and Dennis? Isn't your marriage what you think it should really be like?'

'Oh, it's pretty good, I guess, but Dennis is so spoiled by all the women he's had. You know what he's like. Maybe you know better than I do. I'm terribly jealous about him and you. At least I was when I first met you tonight.'

'I'm the one who should be jealous,' Phyllis said. 'You've got him. But there's something very strange I should tell you. I envy him more for having you than I do you for having him. And I hope what's over and done with in the past won't stop you and me from becoming very good friends.'

Dellie was deeply moved. Nothing, she felt, could give her such a sense of security as to come under the protective friendship of this warm, capable and altogether lovely girl.

The two extra servants had left and their regular couple gone to bed by the time the Muirs' last, dogged guests were herded out of the apartment. April had already transferred most of the mess from the social rooms to the pantry and kitchen, and there were only a few glasses and ashtrays to collect before they were ready to go upstairs. She made Owen go into the bathroom ahead of her and hastened him to bed because she was aware how increasingly difficult it was for him to endure affairs of the sort they had just been through. Although their guests, except for Blankenship, Ann Elliot and Tessie Couto, were all people she had met since and through her marriage, many of them long known to Owen, it was April who had initiated this party and their social life in general.

The difference in their attitudes towards such occasions was one of the two conflicts which marred an otherwise ideally happy marriage. Owen was reasonably gregarious but large gatherings devoted to alcohol and inconsequential gossip depressed his spirits and inflamed his conscience. April shared many of his reservations about the particular set into which they had drifted, but the whole atmosphere of leisure-class living was still new and pleasing to her, and she loved people enough to find an interesting side to even the most unpromising specimens.

When he lit a cigarette in bed and his face took on an earnest expression instead of the admiring one with which he usually watched her undressing, she knew that his revolt had reached a crisis. She completed her preparations hurriedly and slipped into the oversize bed beside him. He put the cigarette out to take her into his arms and they lay in silent intimacy a minute before he spoke.

'Maybe I'd like company a little more if I didn't enjoy being alone with you so much.'

'Well, it's certainly a theory we can test. I'll be just as nasty as I can to you for a week and we'll see what it does to your social attitude.'

He paused to kiss her before he continued in a more serious tone. 'I guess what's really at the basis of it, though, is the waste of time. I mean I wonder if people like us who get so much strength out of loving each other don't have a special obligation to do something useful with their lives.'

'That would apply to me mostly,' she said. 'You have the business to give you a sense of accomplishment. I sometimes wish I hadn't quit working.'

'I don't want you to work. At least not until we find out why you get tired and have those pains in your chest. No, it's the routine we've gotten into that's worrying me — the business of going out or having people in four or five nights a week. And always the same people. Some of them are perfectly all right taken one at a time, but in mass formation...'

'I know exactly what you mean. Everyone in New York thinks alike and talks about the same things. It's kind of incestuous. One trouble with us is we haven't been out of town since — well, it's practically four months since we came back from Easthampton.'

'Yes,' he said without any real feeling of agreement. 'But that's not all that's behind this restlessness of mine. Part of it, I know, is...' He stopped and drew her more closely to him. 'Darling, I hate to bring up the old problem when I know how much it upsets you to even talk about it. But I've got to a state now where I...' He hesitated again before blurting it out. 'I can't take communion again till we've given it up.'

He felt her grow rigid against him. Physically, she was as close to him as before but there was the same intangible distance between them that always arose at a mention of this, the second and more serious source of friction in their life.

'Look,' she said with a tight-voiced and artificial patience, 'can't you get it through your head that it's my sin, not yours? I've never asked *you* to use anything, have I?'

'I've tried to accept that idea but I just can't any more. Whoever does it, the guilt is shared by us both.'

He had no compelling urge toward fatherhood. In fact it was a strange aspect of their disagreement that April was much more receptive to the idea of having a child than he was. What she was firm about was that she did not want to have a succession of annual pregnancies throughout the whole period of her fertility like some of the more literally pious Catholic women she knew. Three children seemed an ideal figure to her, four or five an acceptable maximum. But she was so determined to assert control over their number and frequency that she felt it vitally important to establish the precedent at the beginning and then proceed to voluntary conception in conformity with a fixed principle.

Owen's position was more complex. He wanted to have children eventually but he also had a strong feeling that it was important for them to have several years of independence and discovering each other first, and then to undertake the responsibilities of parenthood in the greater maturity of their late twenties. Also he was more concerned than she herself was by the occasional spells of exhaustion which interrupted the copious flow of her energy. For this combination of reasons it was preferable to him that she should not become pregnant yet. But artificial prevention was a mortal sin he could no longer countenance, and even if his passionate nature and desire for April specifically had not made continence an unthinkable solution, he was aware that it was also an evasion of the primary end for which God had instituted human marriage. The same drawback applied to the 'rhythm' method, in spite of those theologians who maintained that it was unreliable enough to be morally acceptable. In the end the only truly devout attitude was to take the path of procreation and trust that its blessings would not come apace.

April now realized she could no longer depend on his uneasy fluctuation between tacit acceptance and inconclusive rebellion. She needed a new formula to hold him in line. 'You wouldn't share in the guilt if you didn't know about it. That's where the trouble's been.' She was excited by the simple beauty of a solution that should have occurred to her long before. 'I won't tell you now whether I agree with you or not. Then even if I do go on using the thing, you won't know that I am, and your conscience will be clear.'

She saw signs that he was going to raise further objections and she made haste to close the discussion. 'It's much too late to talk it out now. Why don't we both give it some more thought?' She reached over to put out the light and then turned back to him. 'But I think you're right about needing a change from the city. Let's go up to a ski place in New Hampshire or somewhere over Christmas and New Year's. I can call around in the morning and see what's still available.'

He accepted the proposal without fully subscribing to its therapeutic promise. Skiing was something he had deliberately avoided as an overweight college student but when the Ainsworths had persuaded them to try it during the first year of their marriage, both he and April had found the sport and the surroundings invigorating. Whatever the long-range benefits of her plan, it was an appealing prospect for the holidays immediately ahead of them. And perhaps she was right; perhaps the contact with rural American reality was just the antidote for an overdose of false cosmopolitan values.

Lover's Leap Lodge, the latest addition to the cluster of inns and motels around the base of the great slope at Webster Falls, had been designed for quality rather than quantity patronage. The twelve guest units were appointed to suit the tastes of sports-lovers who found indoor comforts a compensating balance for the rigours of their outdoor pursuits; and the dining-room was under the direction of a former head-waiter at the Twenty-One Club. Also in residence was a genuine Tyrolean instructor who had served in all the great skiing resorts from Garmisch-Partenkirchen to Steamboat Springs, moving on after each crack in the thin veneer of discipline which contained his homosexuality. And as the definitive touch to set the lodge apart from the less patrician establishments, it maintained its own separate ski-lift which whisked its light load to the summit so rapidly that a determined guest at Lover's Leap had twice as many daily opportunities for bodily injury as the ordinary enthusiast.

They would have preferred a less fashionable vacation site but they had had no choice when accommodations were so solidly booked for the holiday period. April had been able to secure the reservation at Lover's Leap only because a couple withdrew from the Ainsworths' party in pique over a disputed Canasta score. As it turned out, virtually all of the guests at the lodge when they arrived were acquaintances, among them — in addition to Otto and Marjorie Ainsworth — the Dennis Carpenters, Lilith Herkimer and Josh Pawling, the latter pair in temporary cohabitation to allay the pangs of trial separations from their respective spouses.

A sudden freeze following a thaw made the slopes hazardous

the afternoon before Christmas Day and thus provoked an early observance of the holiday ritual at the bar. The pauses that would have punctuated their drinking in New York as they moved from one party to another were omitted here: even dinner, served to them where they sat, was not a serious interruption. By shortly after ten o'clock the number of active celebrants had appreciably diminished; three of the original group were physically present but unconscious, and two more had been transported to their rooms. One of these latter, the only single girl in the crowd, had been the subject of a coin-matching competition to determine who would carry her inert body to bed, and the victorious male was now likewise numbered among the missing. People were already saying it was the merriest Christmas they could remember.

Neither April nor Owen was a particularly zealous drinker but she was more skilful than he at concealing the fact, her voice and laughter always managing to conform to the prevailing level of intoxication. Owen sat out most of the evening in earnest silence, reacting with warm interest whenever he was directly addressed, then lapsing back into contemplation. April, watching him from across the room, sensed that his present brooding was a continuation of what he had called his restlessness with their way of life. She felt a deep tenderness for him and she resolved that the time had come for them to conceive a child.

Yielding to a strong impulse, she went over to him and bent down to kiss his cheek, then allowed herself to be drawn down on to his lap. Ordinarily they avoided public demonstrations of the sort, but in this particular atmosphere such niceties were out of place.

Dellie Carpenter interrupted their embrace. 'Hey, that's enough of that. I want you to hear the wonderfully funny things Oggie's been telling me. About how they have to write their ads. It's wonderful.'

Oggie — Ogden Rutherford — was the astute and aristocratic proprietor of Lover's Leap Lodge and also of another hotel, much larger and less expensive, a quarter of a mile away. At the Lodge he mingled with his patrons on an equal footing; during his rare appearances in the common rooms of his other establishment, he was actively condescending. 'I've been telling Dellie,' he explained to the Muirs, and others in the immediate vicinity, 'about our little cold war with the Jewish pressure groups. They've got it fixed so the newspapers and magazines we advertise in in New York won't let you say "Gentiles" or "Christians only" any more. And each new way you think up to phrase it, they get after you sooner or later.'

'Can't you simply turn them away when they apply?' Otto Ainsworth asked. 'You can usually tell by the names.'

'Not always,' Josh Pawling said. 'Or by the way they look, either. My father did business with a man for twenty years, had lunch with him every time the fellow was in New York, and then one day this man mentioned he had to catch a train for Philadelphia to be back in time for his grandson's circumcision. Fortunately they'd always operated on trust, without ever a written agreement between them, and Dad was able to cut the business off flat, the moment he found out.'

'Anyway, that isn't quite our problem with the ads,' Rutherford explained. 'We aren't so concerned with keeping the Yids away — they generally stay clear of a place unless they're sure it's open — as we are with letting the white people know it's restricted. That's one of the key words, of course: "restricted". But there are some publications now won't even go for that, and you have to use your ingenuity to get around them. A guy I know in the business uses lines like "ham every Saturday", but I prefer something a little subtler like "near church" or "select clientele".'

' "Ham every Saturday".' Dellie howled with laughter. 'That's wonderful.'

'There's one thing I don't get,' April said. 'What makes you so sure people — Gentiles — really care whether a place is "restricted" or not? I bet if you took a poll of your guests over a year, say, you'd find the majority had no objection to there being Jews here.'

'Oh, the majority, sure,' Rutherford conceded. 'I'm talking about the ten or fifteen per cent or whatever it is to whom it does make a difference. They won't come near a place that does allow

Jews, while your majority, people like yourself maybe, they practically never stay away because there are restrictions.'

'To me...' Otto began. He paused, waiting for the complete silence he felt was warranted by his conclusive pronouncement. 'To me the issue is fundamentally a question of free speech. Our good friend Oggie here is a businessman — considerably more charming and resourceful than most of the breed, but that's beside the point. It ought to be entirely up to him how he wants to run his business and whom he chooses to have here. It's wrong for some pressure group to be able to dictate what he can say in his ads and what he can't. It's un-American.'

'Exactly,' said their host. 'Thank you, Otto, for saying it so well. What I object to is a small group being in a position to tell me how to run my affairs. It's minority rule, that's what it is, and I can't stomach it.'

Owen spoke unexpectedly. 'All in all, it's a hell of a topic for Christmas Eve: keeping Jews out of an inn. Tell me, Mr. Rutherford, when you say you're near a church, what church are you talking about? I'm wondering whether we could get to a midnight Mass.'

Everyone's attention immediately turned to the consideration of this problem. Rutherford explained that the obstacles were rather serious. The nearest Catholic church was an hour away, in normal driving weather. While it was quite common for guests to go there for Sunday morning services when the roads were clear, doing it at night and under the present ice conditions was another question. It was apt to be a dangerous trip and even if they made it safely, he thought it improbable that they could get there in time.

Somehow this negative prognosis only stimulated enthusiasm for the project. Owen, full of self-reproach for not having thought of it earlier, was determined to make the trip if it was at all possible, and April felt the cold night air would be refreshing. Dellie thought it was a wonderful idea and Dennis revived from an alcoholic stupor to suggest that his car was the most suitable for the trip because of its size and the fact that it was equipped with snow tyres. Lilith Herkimer was unwilling to join such a risky expedition while in a state of mortal sin, but the Burgesses, another young Catholic couple, were all for it. Otto Ainsworth felt it would do Marjorie good to get away from the bar for a while and volunteered to take a towel along in case she got sick, provided the others thought it was permissible for them, as non-Catholics, to go. The faithful assured him the doors of the church were always open to misguided souls in need of solace.

Even the Carpenters' Cadillac couldn't seat eight without some crowding. In their varying degrees of drunkenness, ranging from mild to extreme, it seemed more amusing to separate couples. Dennis, who could look fairly sober even when he wasn't, took the wheel, with April alongside him, then Otto Ainsworth with Sally Burgess on his lap. In the back Dellie sat on Owen, Rolf Burgess in the middle, and Marjorie Ainsworth by the window in order to minimize the damage if she were suddenly overcome.

It was an eventful ride. They had a dozen minor skids and four bad ones, two of them on a steep mountain road with a light board fence marking the precipice at the edge of it. As if the ice and his retarded reflexes were not menace enough, Dennis insisted on keeping a supervisory eye on Dellie and Owen through the rear-vision mirror. Marjorie claimed to be in such a panic that she moved to the floor, which she maintained was a safer location for the moment of inevitable disaster. Rolf Burgess joined her there and they soothed themselves with the bottle he had had the forethought to bring along. April observed loudly that this left plenty of room for Dellie on the seat, but Dellie said she felt a continuing obligation to keep Owen warm. Sally Burgess bumped her head during one of the bad skids and blamed it on Otto, who she said was trying to crouch down behind her for protection.

Once a general screaming occasioned by Dennis going off the road briefly was followed by such an abrupt silence that they could hear Marjorie murmuring from the back-seat floor: 'Don't, your hands are too cold.'

Sally snickered in reference to her husband. 'He's always pawing people,' she said as she stretched in front of April to get a look at herself in the mirror. 'I think I'm bleeding.'

The reproach in her voice was directed at Otto but he chose to ignore it. 'Are they usually pretty punctual about these things?' he inquired. 'We've only got about ten minutes.'

'We'll make it,' Dennis said. 'We have to make it.' A woman was standing in the icy road ahead of them, one hand held up to solicit their help, the other indicating a car which had smashed into a tree. Dennis swerved around her, sounding his horn. 'You can't ever really capture the true spirit of Christmas if you don't start off with the midnight Mass.'

They did make it, more or less, entering the little village church during the Kyrie Eleison. Most of the worshippers turned to glimpse the strangers as they stamped their feet to shake off the snow and proceeded to find places for themselves in the pews. But the interest was only momentary, flaring up again when Marjorie, anxious to conform, tried to genuflect along with the others during the Agnus Dei and fell over sideways along the kneeling-rack.

When it came time for those of the faithful who so desired to partake of the holy Eucharist, April was surprised and pleased to see Owen rise and go forward. Since he could hardly have forgotten his ultimatum of the other night, she assumed his willingness to receive the blessed sacrament must mean he had accepted her compromise proposal on the birth control question. Although this development had no immediate value in view of her decision to become pregnant, she regarded it as a most important precedent for the future. Grateful to God for her husband's apparent amenability, she also went up to the communion rail, not noticing that Marjorie was staggering dutifully behind her.

Otto, however, did observe his wife's move and tried unsuccessfully to restrain her from what he feared would amount to a sacrilege. He was unaware, in his heretical ignorance, that the contingency was one long since covered by canon law; and that the non-believer who swallows the body of Our Lord under false pretences does receive Christ but is denied the sanctifying grace bestowed upon those who merit it.

Marjorie, as it turned out, failed to qualify for even the first part of the reward. At the very instant when the Sacred Host was presented to her, a queasy sensation in her stomach reminded her of one of her fundamental precautions. 'No, thank you,' she told the priest politely. 'I never eat when I'm drinking.'

April was right in thinking Owen had taken communion in full awareness of his earlier stand on the subject; she was wrong only in her theory that he was agreeing to her solution of the problem. What he had actually done was to locate the mechanical instrument of their sin and, with the aid of a needle, reduce its efficacy to something like the sporting proposition devised by providence in the first place. The clandestine nature of the act was distasteful to him but he was as morally certain of its virtue as he would have been of the obligation to unload a pistol to which a potential murderer had access. Indeed the analogy grew stronger the more closely he examined it.

Thus on Christmas morning there came out of their divergent rationales an inadvertent harmony of purpose. Awakening at almost the same moment they exchanged the presents which they had hidden under their respective sides of the bed. For him she had a small bedside projector to contain his watch at night and flash the time on the ceiling at the flick of a switch, and an altimeter for the car with a range of fifteen thousand feet. His main gifts to her were a new rosary and a bottle of a perfume called *Prurience,* so exclusive that the manufacturers restricted it to one customer per million population in a given sales area.

After they had examined these acquisitions and established by the altimeter that their present elevation fell a hundred and fifty feet below the management's advertised claim, they turned to each other and the enduring delights of marital love. There was a moment when Owen wondered whether his pious sabotage had been unnecessary, but April finally excused herself in time and departed into the bathroom. There she remained, brushing her hair, for long enough to cover the function she wanted him to think she might or might not be performing, and then returned to the fervour of their embrace.

* * *

Later that day, after several strenuous descents on the main run, April decided she needed a rest and a feet-warming at the little café half way down. Taking her place, Marjorie joined Owen and the instructor, Kurt Mayer, in a session devoted to the technique of the Christiania. At first Owen couldn't fix on what was disturbing him about the behaviour of his two companions, then became uncomfortably aware that they were competing for his attention. It was an open question to which he was the less attracted physically. Twenty-four hours before it would have been clearly the Austrian, but Marjorie's performance at the altar, of which she seemed happily unconscious, had diminished his slight affection for her.

The rivalry came into the open when Marjorie suggested that she and Owen test their new accomplishments alone on an unfrequented secondary slope. Mayer dissented on the grounds that the snow was still too fast and the threat of a new storm too great. It would be more advisable, he said, if he took just Owen down the unfamiliar route today and accorded her the same privilege tomorrow.

'Oh, come off it, Kurt,' Marjorie said. 'You know you really just want to be alone with him.'

'How strange,' Mayer said. 'I was only now thinking about you the same thing.'

'Well, at least that would come under orthodox biology. Look, if you're so sex-starved, I'll tell you what I'll do. I'll give you my husband for the rest of the day, all week if you want him. There you won't be blazing a new trail.'

'Excuse me,' Owen broke in. 'I'm going down to see if April's got her wind back.' He glided off toward the top of the main run without waiting for their reactions.

Marjorie laughed. 'I withdraw my offer,' she told Mayer. 'The exclusive rights anyway. Poor Otto, we'll just have to share him.'

'It doesn't quite do it, does it?' Owen said to April. 'Give us that reinvigorating antidote to decadent city life, I mean. How would you like to start off before dark? Spend the night in Manchester or somewhere.'

'I've had enough,' she admitted. 'The only thing is, I wonder if you won't have the same restless feeling two days after we get back.'

'Maybe I would if I were going back to the same sort of pointless life I've been leading. But I'm not. One value I've gotten out of these couple of days here is I see it isn't a question of where you are but of what your attitude is, your purpose in life. That's what's been building up in me till I finally realize now that what I need is a whole new set of standards to go by.'

He added no further details, nor did April press him to do so. She preferred to have them broken to her gradually.

CHAPTER II

WHAT it had taken Owen two and a half years to realize was that his conversion, despite its supernatural origin, had been in effect a formality, without any revolutionary effect on his life. How significant was a change of religion, he asked himself on the skiing trip, if religion was still practised on a part-time basis?

It was true that in a superficial sense his new faith occupied a good deal of his attention. He was scrupulous about going to Mass and confession, and regularly performed many devotions which the average layman reserved for special occasions. He was an avid reader of periodical Catholic literature and an earnest student of church history and the great theological writers; he even compiled his own list of the contradictions between Saint Augustine and Saint Thomas, and then struck them out one by one as he made his way through the later scholars who had reconciled the two philosophies into a single set of dogmas.

Yet there remained a distinct separation between his spiritual and his worldly life. He no longer had reservations about the merit of capitalistic enterprise, but he could not bring himself to believe that it was actually enriching his soul as well as his bank account. No more than two hours out of every twenty-four, he calculated, were devoted to the proper goal of every immortal spirit: its own salvation. The two traditional roads toward that end were prayer and mortification on the one hand, and good works on the other. His inclination pointed to the former path, his fortunate material circumstances to the latter. A series of conversations with Father Boyle, their present parish priest, confirmed his own fear that his inclination was not to be indulged. His mission lay rather in the vast, variegated field known as Catholic action.

In order to free himself for such activity, he raised Blankenship to the level of a partner and gradually reduced his own participation in the business to a minimum. He also undertook, with the new year of 1949, a regimen of daily communion to bring himself closer to God and clarify the difficult selection ahead of him. For three weeks it brought him nothing but a series of late and inferior breakfasts.

He already belonged, nominally except for his money donations, to the Holy Name Society, Knights of Columbus and Catholic War Veterans, and it seemed reasonable that his first step should be to switch to an active role in one of these. But he hesitated to make an arbitrary choice; he felt the need of inspiration from a divine source. It was precisely this which was bestowed upon him on the twenty-first day of his search. He had just performed the stations of the cross, petitioning for celestial guidance at the fourteenth station where, it is said, no request is ever denied. Before he rose from his knees, he had determined, with a certainty that could hardly have come from within, the painful course he had to follow.

All his life, almost as vehemently since his pacifist phase as during it, he had hated veterans' organizations. Repugnant in theory to begin with, they were, to his mind, revolting in practice. His membership in the Catholic one had come about as the only alternative to an unthinkable repudiation of Father Boyle, who had arranged an evening of social camouflage for the express purpose of his recruitment. He had never attended a meeting and he had occasional misgivings over the uses to which his contributions were being put when he read about the pronouncements and activities of some of the local posts. The present programme of the organization, he noted, had much the same spirit as had moved the Catholic War Veterans of Jersey City a decade earlier, when they rallied around Mayor Frank Hague to defend an open-shop town against organized labour and the American Civil Liberties Union.

Now, reduced by his steady eucharistic dosage to something like proper mortal humility, he saw that the most odious path demanded the greatest sacrifice and was therefore the most pious one to take. Since the hierarchy itself clearly endorsed the work of the veterans, his own distaste for them could only spring from the deadly sin of pride. Functioning as an active member of CWV would help expiate that sin through the suffering it was bound to inflict on his sensitive soul. And if physical self-abuse was traditionally rewarded with divine grace, surely he could expect the same prize for the more grievous wounds of the spirit.

It was to the veterans that he must pledge his talents and his energy.

The day-to-day unpleasantness of the work matched his expectation; what he had not foreseen was his rapid rise in the organization and the immediacy with which he would face a critical test of his adaptive capacity.

Prepared for a cool response to his sudden change of heart, he found himself welcomed effusively by his local post and almost simultaneously by the New York County chapter. He soon realized he had been wrong in thinking they would regard his wealth and family connections as his principal assets. While by no means dismissing these advantages, his new comrades were discerning enough to set a far greater value on his criminal record. In much the same way as reformed drunkards are featured at temperance meetings, Owen was launched on a series of stellar appearances as the zealous pacifist awakened to the virtues of violence.

He learned that in the broadest sense there remained only one enemy against whom the final resort of forceful repression might have to be applied. That one enemy was Communism, whether it revealed itself in the arrogant blasphemy of open party members or in the subversive secularism of liberals and socialists. The message he brought to each meeting at which he spoke was the need for stern vigilance against the foe within; the ways and means of checking his infiltration of schools, films, government, science, art and some of the less rigid Protestant sects.

Drawing on his growing knowledge of Roman Catholic history, he cited the mass slaughters with which the crusaders purged the Holy Land, the extirpation of the Albigensian heretics, the implacable fervour of the Spanish Inquisition, and the painstaking decimation of the Huguenots by Cardinal Richelieu, as precedents for the righteous wrath to which a Christian majority might be provoked in its own defence. But he was always careful to make a firm distinction between the need for more severe discipline at home and what he considered the folly of belligerent moves abroad. Protective steps against domestic treason, provided they were carried out within the spirit and framework of the Constitution, and preparedness against external aggression — these were prudent and salutary measures. But any idea of reforming the pagan world outside by armed persuasion was unthinkable in the era of nuclear weapons.

The mere process of public speaking was repellent to him but what distressed him even more was that at almost every gathering he addressed there was a small group among his listeners who could not see how the nations were to be brought to God and Rome by peaceful means. Enlarging on the very ideas he had presented to them, they arrived at conclusions and proposals for action which could only intensify the danger of another world war. And even when this was pointed out to them, they shrugged it off with the calm assertion that even a great atomic holocaust was not too high a price to pay for winning the survivors to the ideal of Christian brotherhood.

Owen would remind these extremists that Our Lady of Fatima had called for the *conversion*, not the conquest of Russia. That end could not be achieved by military expeditions nor by the councils of the United Nations, which had disqualified itself as a force for good by openly and flagrantly barring God from its proceedings. The Blessed Virgin had specifically said that the way to accomplish it was by prayers and devotions on the part of the faithful.

No matter how hard he stressed this idea, he was left at the end of a meeting with the uneasy sense that most of his audience was unconvinced. They seemed unable to accept the theory, even though authored by the Mother of God, that they could solve the ills of the world by diligent attention to their rosaries.

It was nearly six months before he was freed from this wearying routine by his election as the delegate of his post to a new archiepiscopal group which convened in late July under the name of the Catholic Action Council Against Communism and Creeping Socialism. This title was quickly abbreviated to CACACACS and the organization, without ever achieving any formal status or jurisdiction, expanded nonetheless toward a national scope. In the midst of his confusion about the whole new world to which he had exposed himself, Owen was delighted to find that the spiritual adviser and motive force of the council was Monsignor Stephen A. Frasso. It was hard to tell from the way they embraced at the first meeting whether teacher or pupil was the more enthused by their fortuitous reunion. They went out together for coffee afterwards, conversing in friendly fashion about the new trend in musical comedy and the pressing need for more American saints.

The decisive test of Owen's adjustment to the lay apostolate came two weeks later at the second plenary session of CACACACS. Arriving early at the newly rented quarters of the organization, he found an old acquaintance in confident possession of an outer office. It was Allan Mulvaney, the Nazi partisan with whom he had clashed at the Moose Head prison.

'Dear boy!' There was a warmth in the way Mulvaney spoke and came forward to greet Owen that clearly indicated a willingness on his part to forgive what lay in the past.

'Are you part of this group now?' Owen asked incredulously. 'I didn't even know you were a Catholic.'

'A recent convert, like yourself. No, I'm not a member of the council, simply a humble employee. You probably recall authorizing your publications committee to find an editor for the bulletin. Well, they made a thorough investigation of the best available talent and hired me.' He chuckled to show that the self-tribute was not to be taken seriously.

'It's a remarkable choice. I may have to question their report.'

'That doesn't sound very friendly.'

'I didn't mean it to be.'

He had a chance to talk to Frasso before the meeting began. 'There's been a bad mistake about the bulletin editor. The man's an extremely unsavoury character. I can give the council the facts on his record.'

'I imagine they're pretty well known,' said the prelate. 'Where is your Christian charity, my son? Jesus sought out the greatest sinners, to take them to His bosom.'

'But this man was an outright Nazi. I saw him every day for eleven months, in jail. He was full of the worst kind of racial hatred and lynch-law psychology, even tried to castrate a Negro prisoner. And he hasn't changed; I read an anti-Semitic article by him only a few months ago.'

'That has nothing to do with his work here. Surely you don't believe that an organization pledged to defend American freedom ought to question the private political opinions of its employees? Our task is to expose Communists, wherever they are, and see that they are removed from their jobs, public and private. With that programme Mr. Mulvaney is in full sympathy, and that's all I think we have a right to demand of him.'

Owen was unconvinced. 'But there's still no reason to pick him from all the possible people for this job. I think the worst trap the anti-Communist movement in this country could fall into is to ally itself with all the fascist crackpots and bigots on the right.'

'Spain might not be a Christian country to day if General Franco had had your scruples. If he had refused the help of Hitler and Mussolini because he disagreed with a few of their policies, it might easily have meant a Red victory.'

'I don't know what the answer is on Franco: whether he was right or wrong. But I know what this fellow out there is like and I can't stomach the idea of working with him.'

Monsignor Frasso grew stern. 'I don't like to hear you talk that way, my son. Your words are not spoken from a heart dedicated to God's work: they spring instead from your personal prejudices and pride. Perhaps it is because you do not fully appreciate the enormity of the struggle in which we are engaged. This is in truth the final conflict toward which human history has been building for centuries. Arrayed on one side is the absolute of matter: irrational Communism, which fails to recognize the freedom of the will. On the other is the absolute of metaphysical reason, the supreme exponent of which is necessarily the Roman Catholic Church, which has always glorified the power of human reason and free will. The third camp — agnosticism or Cartesian "scientific reason" — is no longer of consequence.

'For this great battle, which may extend over many decades, we need the widest possible unity of effort, including unity on many issues with heretics and unbelievers. Yet you are questioning the possibility of unity within the church itself.'

'I don't think I am,' Owen began uncertainly. 'As I understand Catholic doctrine . . .'

'One thing we ask particularly of those who are new in the faith is humility. I often think pride is the deadliest of the sins because it is the most common. Debase yourself, be abject before the Lord, consider how unworthy you are of His blessings. An hour of good, earnest prayer would straighten you out on this matter, I'm sure.'

'I'll admit I haven't had time to think it through,' Owen conceded. 'I just saw him outside and rushed right in to talk to you.'

'Take it up with Our Lady,' Frasso recommended. 'She is always ready to lend us a measure of charity toward our fellow-man from her limitless store. Ah, the meeting seems to be getting under way.'

When the chairman called the session to order, it was Frasso who suggested that the report of the publications committee be considered first so that the editor of the proposed bulletin could be admitted and have the benefit of hearing the rest of the proceedings.

Mulvaney was placed on the payroll without a dissenting vote.

'If this is pregnancy,' April thought to herself as they got into the car for the trip back to New York, 'maybe there's something to be said for taking the veil after all.' She felt almost ready to abandon her fond dream of a small troupe of young Muirs, assorted in size and sex but united in the combination of her black hair and Owen's blue eyes.

She had not been enjoying life lately. Owen's new activities had taken him away from her and prevented them from going out of town until well into August. New York had alternated between spells of miserable heat and miserable dampness. During one of the latter she had taken a summer cold out into the rain and contracted a persistent throat infection. Using this and Owen's depressed reaction to the Mulvaney episode as grounds for a change, she had won the concession of two weeks at the beach in Easthampton, where they had fourteen days of almost steady fog and rain in which to regret the move.

The only auspicious note during this period had been the increasing probability that she had finally conceived, and now even that satisfaction was dissolving amid the secondary symptoms which accompanied it. She felt weak and listless and her legs hurt her; on the drive into town she developed a nosebleed and the ache in her lower joints spread to her right elbow. She wished she had paid more attention to the many discussions she had heard about the early signs of pregnancy. There were supposed to be strange variations of appetite, she recalled; hers had simply declined. She couldn't remember any mention of the chills with which she was intermittently seized.

Uncertain whether her discomforts were normal or not, she minimized them for Owen's benefit. But when he put her into a taxi in Long Island City so that he could pay a visit to the plant, she gave the driver Dr. Goldberg's address.

She had selected him as her doctor, on the occasion of a previous, unfounded suspicion of pregnancy, largely because his name made him an unlikely co-religionist. It was while she was living with Gene Couto and she had wanted a diagnosis unmixed with moral judgment. In this respect Dr. Goldberg had proved something of a disappointment. Without imposing any unsolicited advice on her, he had nonetheless made it clear that he had the rigid moral outlook of a pious Jew. In spite of this failing, his pleasant humour, conscientious methods and a genuine modesty rare in his profession had given her a confidence in him she had never felt with another physician, and she had continued to consult him on the rare occasions when she thought she needed medical advice.

Goldberg was a large man, tall and overweight, the impression of awkwardness enhanced by the habitually careless way he dressed. And there was in fact a clumsiness in his physical movements that disqualified him for a society practice; his short, thick fingers were no more suited to polite gynaecology than the ingenuous candour of his speech.

April had discovered that making an appointment with him served no purpose: he saw each patient in turn regardless of prior arrangement and took as much time as he felt the complaint warranted, no matter who was waiting. In April's case he questioned her intensively about her symptoms, studied his records of her former visits and asked for more details about her childhood illnesses. He discovered some manifestations she hadn't yet noticed herself; a slight rash on the chest and small lumps forming under the skin around the knees and the back of the neck. He showed particular interest in her heart, observing it through a fluoroscope as well as listening to it at length. The whole examination, she realized, went far beyond an ordinary pregnancy check.

'You're almost certainly pregnant,' he told her finally. 'We'll get that definitely confirmed at the lab. They'll do some blood tests at the same time: count, sedimentation and Wassermann; and meanwhile I want you to have an electrocardiogram made, right away when you leave here — I'll call the fellow and fix it. As soon as that's over I want you to go home and get into bed; you've got a slight fever and my guess is it may go up in the next day or two.'

'What is it? Do you think there's danger of a miscarriage?'

'No, there's something else. It's in a kind of borderline field where the pathologies of several diseases overlap in the early stages, some serious, some not so. I've got a theory but I've been wrong on it before and my diagnoses aren't as slipshod as most. So I'd rather not say anything till I see you again at home, say tomorrow night after I get through here.'

'I can stand the suspense,' April told him, 'but I'm not sure if my husband can.'

'Just tell him I'm ultra-cautious. It's a pretty accurate statement.'

She lingered in the doorway on her way out. 'It isn't polio, is it? The stiffness in my legs. . . .'

'No, I don't think it's polio.' He refrained from saying that he would be no more anxious for her if it were.

* * *

Owen sat on the side of the bed holding her hand while Dr. Goldberg related his findings. April was definitely pregnant, he told them, probably in the early part of her second month. She also had a rather severe case of rheumatic fever, a recurrence, he thought likely, of an adolescent attack which had gone undiagnosed at the time. It was proof of the inherent strength of her constitution that she had been able to exert herself so much physically in spite of the probable previous damage to her heart, and to go so long without an overt renewal of the infection. But this in no wise lessened the gravity of her present condition.

He told them something of the nature of the disease, admitting frankly that medical science knew neither the cause nor the cure of it. 'We've been using sulfa and penicillin lately, but about the only thing you can say with scientific certainty is that they don't make it any worse. There are some experiments going on with this new drug they've got for arthritis, ACTH, but no results have been published and it isn't available for general use. Aspirin and other specifics to relieve the pain — that's the prescription, along with complete rest in bed and avoidance of any kind of strain on the system, not only in the virulent stage but during the all-important recuperation period afterwards.

'It's a killer, this disease is. I say that because I think you both ought to know how serious a problem you're facing. Children are its main vicitms but I think only tuberculosis outranks it as a cause of death in your age group.'

Owen sat in rigid silence, only his eyes showing the shock. April pressed her fingers tightly against his hand to give him the reassurance of her closeness.

'But I don't think Mrs. Muir is going to die,' Dr. Goldberg continued, 'or even become an invalid — *if* we take the proper steps to minimize the danger to her. The first and most imperative of those is to terminate her pregnancy.'

In the midst of his anguish Owen recalled the twinge of disquiet with which he had read of an address by Pope Pius XII to the International College of Surgeons delivered only a year before. The pontiff had solemnly warned the men of science that their moral duty was to spare unborn infants even at the risk of their mothers' lives. Owen's momentary misgiving had been dispelled by a footnote in the Catholic publication which carried the story, pointing out that such choices were increasingly infrequent.

'Fortunately,' the doctor continued, 'a therapeutic abortion at this stage is a minor affair, surgically speaking.'

'I don't want an abortion,' April said. 'I want to have a baby. I want to have several babies.'

'Then you'd better not have this one, because it could very easily kill you. Even if you survived it, I don't think you could ever carry another. The surest way for you to have a family is to wait a year or however long it takes until your heart is strong enough.'

'It isn't entirely a medical question,' Owen began uncomfortably. 'I mean there's a moral angle to abortion....'

The doctor turned to him indignantly. 'Do you think it's necessary to tell me that? Under no circumstances would I ever be a party, directly or indirectly, to arresting a pregnancy where it wasn't actually a question of life and death. I wouldn't feel at ease with God if I ever had helped in such a case.'

'I'm sorry,' Owen said. 'How quickly do you feel she should have it done?'

April looked at him, her eyes full of love. Persuaded herself by Goldberg's last argument, her greatest worry had been that Owen would make a theological controversy of it.

'Depends on how she comes along in the next few days,' Dr. Goldberg said. 'I'd rather do it when her fever's down but I don't think we should put it off more than two weeks in any case.'

'Good,' said Owen. 'I'd like to have another doctor take a look at her, if you don't mind....'

'Of course not.'

'Why ... ?' April began.

'A doctor of our own faith,' Owen went on. To April he said, 'Dr. Shane. He's a member of my veterans' post. Supposed to be a very good man.'

'I won't see him,' April said. She sat up to add emphasis to her assertion. 'If you want to call in some specialist, okay, though I'm perfectly satisfied with Dr. Goldberg's opinion. But I won't let it be turned into a religious issue!' She started crying suddenly and her defiance rose to a scream. 'I won't see him!'

Dr. Goldberg moved quickly to her side, pushing Owen away as he eased her back into a reclining position. He spoke in an even voice but with authority. 'You will both have to realize that this kind of excitement is the worst thing for Mrs. Muir. She's going to be on her back for a long time. The more complete the rest she gets, especially now, the shorter that time will be.' He moved to where he had left his bag. 'I'll be on my way now. I've told you what I think and that's all I can do. Gestation and delivery in this case could be fatal. At the very least you'd be throwing away the chance of a full recovery and a normal life, including motherhood. It's a hard proposition to put up to anybody but that's it.'

Owen saw him downstairs and then returned to her bedside, tender and devoted and contrite. He nuzzled his face against her shoulder, kissing the hot, feverish skin in a dozen places. 'I love you as much as it's possible for a person to love. You know that, don't you?'

'Oh, I do, I guess, most of the time. It's only once in a while, when you get that fishy pious look in your eye ... Hey, lay off; remember what he said. Isn't it fantastic? Here I am, aching in every part of my body, feeling as ghastly as I've ever felt, nauseated, out of breath, hot and cold at the same time — and you just touch my breast and I start getting excited all over. We're going to have to think up some new rules around here.'

Gathering on the telephone that Owen wanted to consult him about his wife rather than himself, Dr. Shane suggested they meet at a bar in the same block as his office. The cocktail hour, he explained when Owen joined him, was the indispensable respite in his working day; he didn't even mind talking business during it as long as he didn't have to investigate any orifices or listen to the monotonous rhythms of human respiration.

Shane was thirty-five, intelligent without being intellectual, energetic, delighted with himself and his profession. Immune to fear, he had been one of the most decorated officers in the Medical Corps. His parish priest knew him as the most dependable and uncomplaining man to be found in emergency charity cases.

He listened to Owen's story, asked a few questions about April's symptoms, and arrived at a characteristically rapid judgment. 'I don't know anything about this Goldberg but what you tell me sounds like he's on the ball. They make very good doctors, most of them, you know. We've got a man up at St. Anne's — Sol Greenblatt — that's probably the sharpest proctologist in America.'

'I was favourably impressed with Dr. Goldberg,' Owen admitted. 'I certainly have no reason to distrust him, from a purely medical point of view. But I'd still like you to have a look at her and tell me what you think we ought to do. The only problem is we've got to go a little easy on it because at this moment April is convinced Goldberg has the answer. She went as far as to say she wouldn't see you.'

'Mrs. Muir and I have something in common. I don't want to see her either. Professionally.' Owen's expression of hurt bewilderment led the doctor to explain quickly. 'I simply don't take that kind of case. What can I tell a husband who loves his wife and wants her the way she is, alive and whole? Any time I run up against this sort of thing, where the book calls for therapeutic abortion, I pass the case on to a Protestant friend of mine, the same way a Catholic judge is supposed to do with a divorce. And since my damn conscience won't let me take a split fee, my friend is very grateful.'

'Yes, that solves it for you, I can see. But it's not much help to me, is it? I can't shift the responsibility over to a Protestant husband.'

'Maybe not.' Shane felt a keen sympathy for the younger man and his problem. 'But there's one advantage you've got as a layman, especially seeing you're new in the church. You don't have to ever have run across the official word on this particular subject.'

'But I have. The minute Dr. Goldberg said the word "abortion", the whole thing came back to me.'

The doctor winced, swallowed his drink and got to his feet. 'Don't be so literal-minded, pal, or you're cooked. The next thing you'll do is go and talk to a priest about it.'

The next thing Owen did was talk to a priest about it. Father Boyle was one of those clerics who find their vocation only after a trial excursion into the secular world. Applying himself to wholesale lingerie until his thirty-second year, he had returned home unexpectedly from a selling trip to discover his wife sharing the bathroom with his immediate business superior. The man was taking a bath; Mrs. Boyle was brushing her teeth, clad only in a nylon petticoat with a three-tiered pleated lace flounce which Boyle regarded as gaudy and which was in fact the product of a rival firm. Disillusioned simultaneously with sex and commerce, he had turned for comfort to the faith in which he was born and served as sacristan of his local church until the avenging hand of God exterminated Mrs. Boyle in an automobile accident and made him eligible for holy orders. In the priesthood his bent for salesmanship had reasserted itself and he had forged his way to the pastorate of one of the most prosperous parishes in the archdiocese. The souls of the Muirs were among those currently under his husbandry.

Father Boyle had equipped himself for the expeditious disposal of just such problems as Owen's by maintaining, in a handy desk drawer, a conscientious cross-index of papal attitudes. He was thus enabled to answer the distraught young man's question promptly in words of irrefutable infallibility. ' "It is never permitted, above all, to derange the supreme intentions of the Creator in the matter of new human lives...." That gives you the moral basis of the law. Getting down to brass tacks, his Holiness puts it this way. He says it is "illicit — even in order to save the mother — to cause directly the death of the small being that is called, if not for life here below, then at least for the future life, to a high and supreme destiny." I'll be happy to copy these quotes out if you like, so you can show them to your wife.'

'No, thanks. Mrs. Muir doesn't go much for written authorities on a thing like this.'

'That's the way it should be,' said Father Boyle. 'It's your job as the head and ruler of the family to find out what's right and then tell it to her in words she can understand.'

'We don't function quite like that in our household . . .'

'Women in this country are always stepping out of line,' continued the priest, ''specially on things they've got an idea belong in their department. There isn't any subject I have to use my quotes on more often. Leo XIII: "The man is the ruler of the family, and the head of the woman . . ." Pius XI: "This false liberty and unnatural equality with the husband is to the detriment of the woman herself . . ." And the present Pope has. . . .'

'Excuse me, Father. I can't tell my wife she may have to die and that she isn't to put up any argument about it because I'm the head of the family.'

The priest smiled. 'No, hardly. You certainly wouldn't say it in those words. There's such a thing as psychology and it's almost as important as being firm when you're handling a woman.'

'It isn't a question of "handling" anybody!' Owen's anger was augmented by his growing sense of helplessness. 'I care at least as much about saving April's life as she does. I couldn't live without her. I think I'd kill myself if she . . .'

'Muir!' Father Boyle's voice was harsh and imperative. 'There's a limit to what I can allow here. You can't sit there and announce your intention of committing a mortal sin and expect me to . . .'

'All right, I take that back. I just want you to understand that I'm talking about the woman I love more than life . . .' He caught himself up sharply. 'Well, more than any material consideration in the world. You keep making it sound as if the problem were simply persuading my wife to lie down and die.'

'Of course, of course,' said the priest soothingly. 'A husband's love is very often a factor to be considered. We are all slaves of the flesh until we rise above it. But you under-estimate the Holy Father if you think he isn't aware of that. He speaks of "the understandable anguish of husbandly love", making it clear, however, that surgeons must not heed that anguish when faced with a choice between mother and fetus.'

Only the strength of Owen's faith kept him from absolute despair. There must be a way out of this seeming blind alley. He remembered how, in his first discussion with Father Duchesne, the bars against a dispensation for the marriage had seemed inflexible and then suddenly the way had been opened through the doctrine of waiving a lesser sin to forestall a graver one. Surely now, in this even more vital dilemma, there must be an acceptable solution. Invoking divine guidance, he sat in silent concentration for a moment.

Presently there came a glimmer of hope. 'Look,' he said. 'Supposing — I'm not saying this is the case; I'd still have to get further medical opinion — supposing it were scientifically established that the mother would die during the pregnancy, before there was a chance of her having a live baby, that would eliminate all possibility of saving the child, wouldn't it? In that case there'd be nothing wrong with an abortion to save the mother's life.'

'There most certainly would,' declared Father Boyle. 'You'd still be destroying a creation of God, with an immortal soul of its own. You can't bring that life to an end one second earlier than the Lord, in His inscrutable purpose, planned it.'

'Even if . . . let's say you knew absolutely there was something wrong with the embryo, that it couldn't live whether the mother did or not?'

'My son, you don't seem to realize that you're going over ground that's already been covered, down to dotting the last "i", by much brighter and holier men than we are. If you brought me an X-ray showing that your wife was carrying a six-headed idiot monster that couldn't possibly be kept alive, and nine affidavits from doctors saying she would die tomorrow if the thing wasn't removed, the answer would still be the same. You can't oppose the will of God. Now if you'd like to talk about saying some special Masses for Mrs. Muir, I'll be happy to . . .'

'No!' He was almost as shocked himself as the priest was by the way he screamed the word. He summoned his strength to bring himself under control. 'I'd rather not talk about that yet. I'll be going now, Father. Thank you for giving me your time.'

'It's simply part of my humble mission,' Father Boyle assured him. 'My time belongs to God and my flock.'

He didn't expect Monsignor Frasso to be of much help, but the faintest chance of finding a less inflexible attitude in a higher authority was worth pursuing. The prelate had no direct consolation to offer on the problem itself, gently confirming Father Boyle's version of the ecclesiastical law, but he did try to enrich Owen's understanding of the broader implications of the doctrine.

'Either you believe that man is simply another stage in the evolutionary process, with no fixed point at which you can say "This is a brute and this a human being", or you believe in a divinely ordained and revolutionary leap from the animal to the human, occurring at only one place and time and providing all mankind with a single pair of first parents, endowed with souls and free will and earning for themselves and their descendants the awful burden of original sin. There is no compromise between these two conceptions. Rejecting the materialistic and embracing the sublime one, it follows inevitably that every human life is sacred and the injunction "Thou shalt not kill" admits of no qualifications. Except of course in case of war or capital punishment. Once we begin to make distinctions, once we say that this adult is more valuable than this unborn child, the door is opened to a hideous succession of further distinctions based on the same principle, beginning with euthanasia and the right of suicide, and ending with eugenic sterilization and Hitler's ovens.'

'I can see the logic,' Owen admitted. 'My quarrel isn't so much with the basic principle as it is with applying it so rigidly.'

'You mean applying it so personally, don't you?' asked Frasso with a telling smile. 'You don't object to the fact that the way is hard for some as long as you aren't one of them.'

The accusation was valid. It was the bitterest cup he had ever had to swallow but he knew in his heart that once again he had been the creature of his pride, setting himself and his love and his wife on a higher plane than the ordinary level of mortal man.

Quick to sense that the battle was won, Frasso changed to a more sympathetic tone. 'There is a reward in store for you of which you cannot fully conceive yet. What a poor, puny thing our faith is when it is still soft and untried! But when it has been shaped and hardened in the crucible of pain and grief, then it undergoes a qualitative change and becomes indeed a weapon to sustain us against the fiercest blows of Satan.

'But at the same time as you prepare yourself for the worst, never cease to pray to the Blessed Mother of Mercy. After all, as I understand it, there's nothing hopeless about April's condition.'

'No, but the doctor thinks there's a danger, if she does pull through, of her being a heart case the rest of her life.'

'A pity. Such a vibrant girl. Still, invalid life has produced some quite remarkable contemplatives and not a few saints.' He felt it was time to pass on to another topic. 'Have you read about this Peekskill affair?'

'Just headlines. Some hoodlums broke up a Paul Robeson concert, didn't they?'

'Not hoodlums, not all of them by any means. The affair was organized by the Associated Veterans' Council up there, which has the local post of your own organization as one of its three main forces. Of course some aspects of the thing were very crude but I think they may have the makings of a new, bolder technique more in keeping with the times than some of our methods to date. In any case it's of enough importance to merit some attention from CACACACS and I wouldn't be surprised if one of the lay members proposed at tonight's meeting that we send a couple of observers up there. It seems Robeson's sponsors are going to try to stage the whole thing over again this coming Sunday.'

'I didn't know that,' Owen said absently. 'You'll have to forgive me, Monsignor, I'm not really in any frame of mind for . . .'

'Naturally. I hardly expect you to attend the meeting tonight. But at the same time I think some outside activity, beyond your own personal affairs, is very important for you right now. And the opportunity is apt to come up very soon. I have a feeling the two men selected to go to Peekskill on Sunday will be you and Mulvaney.'

Even in his present state, Owen had a sharp reaction. 'I don't think Mr. Mulvaney and I would make a very harmonious team.

'Precisely why I predict that you will be chosen. We will want a synthesis of two widely separated points of view. Believe me, I'm thinking of your own welfare when I urge you to accept the assignment. Providing of course that my prediction is fulfilled about you two being the ones chosen.'

Owen promised that he would not close his mind to the idea.

Ilsa Wykoff was finishing a cup of tea at her daughter's bedside when Owen returned. The fact that April had so abruptly overtaken her in ill health, especially in her own cardiac domain, was a staggering blow to Mrs. Wykoff. Besides her natural maternal interest in April's recovery, she was competitively aware of the threat to her own status lurking in her daughter's potential invalidism. Yet in spite of these considerations, she had reached, through a quite different process of reasoning, the same moral judgment to which Owen had been reluctantly persuaded.

'I've been telling her,' she informed him, 'that she cannot have an abortion. There must be a reason why this has happened to her and I think it's perfectly obvious it's a punishment for her sins, which, heaven knows, the three of us don't need to go into. Well, I say if somebody tries to escape God's punishment, that's just asking for more. But if she accepts it in the spirit of true penance, then she may find herself getting better a whole lot quicker than anybody expects. My guess is He's just trying to throw a scare into her.'

April, who was only waiting till she was alone with her husband to establish a definite date for her operation, was grateful she didn't have to take her mother seriously. 'You'd better watch your own immortal soul, Mother.' She appealed to Owen. 'That's one of the famous heresies, isn't it, darling? Believing that your rewards and punishments come on earth?'

'I didn't say only on earth,' Mrs. Wykoff protested. 'But what about Sodom and Gomorrah and the plagues in Egypt? If those weren't judgments on the living, then I don't know what you'd call them.'

'Well,' April said, 'you're certainly a cheering influence to have in a sickroom.'

'What have I got to be cheerful about? Pain and sorrow all my life. Brought up in poverty and hunger; losing my sainted husband when I'd barely reached my prime; work, work, work till I was ready to drop; sacrificing my health to bring up my only child; and then to cap it all, learning that she's maybe going to be snatched away from me...' She was finding it hard to speak without choking on her emotions.

'That's right,' April said, feigned sympathy in her voice. 'You have had a pretty miserable life, haven't you?'

'Worse than you'll ever know. I've borne a lot of crosses only God and I knew about.'

'All in all, it would be hard to find somebody who's suffered as much as you have, wouldn't it?'

'Well, there aren't many who've had more. I'll tell you that.'

'Then you know what, Mother? I think that must be proof you've been a very sinful woman. You know, like the plagues in Egypt.'

Owen laughed for the first time in a week. It was not only the neatness of April's trap that pleased him, but the fact that she must be feeling better to have conceived it.

Mrs. Wykoff was far more piqued by the rare insult of his amusement at her expense than she was by the daughterly abuse to which she was inured. She bade them a cold farewell and added the pointed request that he should not see her out.

When she was gone April said, 'That's what I love about her, you know. Lots of people have little flashes of inconsistency, but you rarely see a real virtuoso at it.'

He came over to sit on the bed and stroke her hair. 'You're feeling a little more chipper, aren't you?'

'I'm all doped up. Just not feeling any pains for a while is a delightful sensation. Still my temperature is less than it's been any day at this time. I don't know how much that means.'

'It must be to the good.' He turned his most earnest gaze upon her. 'Darling, I know you don't quite see eye to eye with me on the value of prayer...'

'I just can't go along with the idea that every prayer made in good faith is answered, always.'

'That was Christ's promise: that whatever we asked in His name would be granted. Which doesn't necessarily mean we get the exact thing we want. He reserves the right to give us something of greater value instead, because He obviously knows so much better than we do what we need at a given moment to help us toward salvation.'

'Listen, sweetie,' she said, 'if you're just leading up to the idea that we ought to do some praying in the particular spot we're in now, I'm all for it. I've even made a start on my own. I may not go along with your theory the whole way but I certainly don't think a prayer ever did any harm.'

'All right, then. We ought to work out some kind of a schedule, for the two of us together and for us each separately, concentrating, I think, on Our Lady but also picking out those saints who we think would be most inclined to intercede for us. That's something we can go into detail about later. But first there's a whole other aspect that can't be ignored and that you have to undertake mainly by yourself because I can't help you on it directly. You have to start preparing yourself for . . .' He hesitated only a second. 'For the possibility that it isn't just a scare, as your mother would say.'

She looked directly into his eyes. 'Make my peace with God, you mean?'

He nodded. 'It's the one all-important obligation a person has.'

'The old speedy recovery or happy death routine. You're building up to something, aren't you, Owen? So far you've gone down the line with Mother as far as my need for repentance is concerned. Have you also come to her same conclusion about Dr. Goldberg's recommendation? No therapeutic abortion for this mama? Just toss me on to the sacrificial block?'

He poured out everything that had been accumulating in his mind and heart on the subject: the objections he had raised and the answers his reason had forced him to accept; the impiousness of all other alternatives; the superior wisdom of not defying God's will but bowing to it, and then throwing oneself on His mercy.

It was a thorough presentation of the case and it had its effect on her. She was by nature incapable of accepting in good grace the course he urged upon her; she could not actively embrace a decision which ran counter to the strongest force within her, her will to live. But she could accept it in bad grace, in resignation, passively abandoning the will to live. And that she was ready to do in the first devastating shock of her realization that there was something he loved more than herself. All his arguments and papal quotations added up, in her simple view, to one appalling fact. If he valued these abstract ideas more than the concrete reality of their life together, his feeling for her fell short of what she asked and what she had thought she had.

When she finally spoke, it was in a voice drained of emotion. 'Well, you're really going to find yourself in a spot, aren't you, if I go under on the delivery table right in the act of giving birth? A motherless child on your hands in the midst of your grief.'

'It's unthinkable.' He strove to speak in terms that would mask his feelings, lest she be swayed from the path of piety by an obligation to succour his weakness. 'Still I suppose, even though now I can't conceive of such a life, that God would somehow give me the strength to bear it. I'd have to for the child's sake. Poor kid, it would have a pretty grim time of it, born into a house of gloom.'

'I don't think so. I see a much brighter future for my child. For one thing, I'm sure you'd marry again pretty quickly. Your spiritual advisers would convince you you owed it to the baby, and they'd be right.'

'Well,' he said. 'I've thought about that a little . . .'

'That's very enterprising of you. Got someone picked out already?'

His pained look reproached her frivolity. 'I'm inclined to believe it's the one field where the church is inconsistent,' he continued.

'I can think of several.'

'They teach that sex is replaceable but that married love is not. It's a union not just of bodies but of souls, and that's why it seems to me it doesn't come to an end with the death of one body. I think it's a loose, materialistic attitude toward the sacrament of matrimony to permit the remarriage of widows and widowers, and I can't understand why the Vatican does it.'

'You ought to write them about it. I think they'd feel set up to get one letter saying the Catholic attitude on marriage wasn't strict enough.' Laboriously she shifted herself into a new position. Staying in one place for more than a few minutes seemed to intensify the aches in her joints, but the act of moving was a trial in itself; her muscles didn't respond properly to her control. When she had her breath again, she said, 'Would you like to talk about the funeral arrangements? I don't want anything gaudy, just . . .'

'Darling! You mustn't!' The protest in his voice was intense. 'Facing the fact that there's a risk of your dying doesn't mean we have to treat it as though it was going to happen. We mustn't give in to it — you mustn't especially!'

His emotion was genuine; she knew that. And in a detached way she felt sorry for his suffering. But uppermost in her mind was the conviction that their difference of outlook, which she had avoided facing for so long, had reached a stage where it could only be settled by the surrender of one to the other.

CHAPTER III

FINDING herself helplessly indecisive at a time when she needed to be calm and sure of what she wanted to do, April turned to Tessie Couto for guidance. Despite the difference in their ages, there was no friend of whose devotion she was so certain and who had proven herself so dependable in emergencies. Already, since her illness, April had called her, and Mrs. Couto had come immediately, as if she had no other responsibility, full of sympathy, cheering talk and light reading matter.

This time, however, there was a strange quality to her manner on the telephone as if she had something on her mind and were surprised to receive this particular kind of a call at this particular moment. She finally said that of course she would be right over, but April couldn't figure what was wrong until, with her arrival, the explanation came.

She entered the bedroom with a puzzled look. 'I couldn't tell on the phone whether you'd read the papers or not.' When April explained that she hadn't, Mrs. Couto laughed. 'No wonder. I must have sounded just as peculiar to you as you did to me. I had so many calls this morning from people who knew, I just assumed there wasn't anybody who didn't.' April's bewilderment increased. Mrs. Couto explained: 'I made my début on the front pages. I was indicted by a federal grand jury for failure to register as a foreign agent.'

This was such an astonishing development that it won precedence in April's attention over her own problem. Mrs. Couto explained that the law she was accused of violating was the Foreign Agents Registration Act. Because the Council for Permanent Peace had sent two delegates, including her son Gene, to the Paris World Congress for Peace the previous April, and had since publicized a manifesto emerging from that congress, the Department of Justice had concluded that the American organization was operating as a publicity agent for the six hundred million people, largely foreigners, in whose name the manifesto had been issued. Nor could the Department comprehend the stubborn refusal of the council to register as such. Its activities were in no wise threatened; repression of that sort was abhorrent to the government. All that was demanded was that the council label itself, its words and its deeds as being of alien origin. When Mrs. Couto and the other three officers of the organization still declined to do so, their crime had been presented to the grand jury. Arraignment was scheduled for the following week.

'My God!' April said. 'Think what they could do to the church with a law like that. The bishops aren't responsible to anybody except Rome. And we're always publicizing the statements of a Prince of Peace, a foreign agitator who openly instructed His followers to spread His teachings in other countries. Why wasn't Gene indicted too? They'll let you stay out on bail, won't they?'

'Gene's a member of the executive committee but not an officer. I'm not sure about bail; they may hold my criminal record against me and set it pretty high. You know, four arrests for picketing, one suspended sentence. Incidentally, I haven't talked to Gene yet. He was due to come over to my place when you called me, so I asked him to drop by here and pick me up instead. Do you mind? We can have him wait downstairs if you don't feel like seeing him or if what you've got on your mind is something you wouldn't care to talk about in front of him.'

April said she would enjoy seeing Gene again and that while the question she had wanted to take up was one she would just as soon not discuss in his presence, she now felt Mrs. Couto was facing too great a crisis of her own to pay any attention to her problem. Mrs. Couto disagreed and gave instructions in her hostess's name that her son was to be kept waiting below until they told him to come up. Then she arranged April's pillows for her and told her to start from the beginning and get the whole thing off her chest.

Mrs. Couto had observed enough of the Muirs' marriage, along with what April had told her from time to time, to have a pretty good idea of the background leading up to the present situation. She listened attentively to April's account of Owen's attitude and the official Catholic position, of which she was generally aware but did not know the specific details.

'Would there be any doubt in your own mind,' she asked, 'if it weren't for Owen's feelings on the subject? What I'm getting at is, would you have any reservations yourself on religious grounds, if it were entirely up to you?'

'None whatsoever. They just want to keep the Catholic birth-rate up and it's easier to say no abortions at all than to make exceptions which everyone would say applied to their own case. Anyway, I couldn't take seriously what a bunch of dried-up old men who've never been married decide on a question like that.'

'Good,' the older woman said. 'It's always seemed to me that to treat human birth on the animal level, as a kind of relentless cycle the parents themselves have no control over, is an insult to the dignity of man. So I'm with you in theory. As far as the practical side of it is concerned, the only question is whether you tell him first or just go ahead and do it. Ordinarily I'd say you owed it to him to let him know, but there is the problem of how much resistance he would put up and whether you could stand the strain of it in your present condition.'

'He'd never give in. He'd get hold of a bunch of priests to lecture me in shifts. Or just Monsignor Frasso — he could take all the shifts by himself.'

'Then the sensible thing would be not to tell him till after you're strong enough to stand up to him. It's not as if it were a serious piece of surgery at this stage. You can have it done some morning while he's at the office.'

'He hardly ever goes to his office any more. But he'll be away all day Sunday. He's going up to Peekskill.'

Mrs. Couto reacted sharply to this news. 'What for?'

April told her something about the Catholic War Veterans and CACACACS. 'Owen is going as an impartial observer.'

'Impartial?' She made a noise which succeeded in being derisive and ladylike at the same time. 'How can you even start off being impartial toward people who burn crosses on hills and try to kill other people because of their race or their politics?'

They heard the doorbell ringing downstairs. 'If that's Gene,' April said, 'tell him to come up.'

'Sure you don't want to talk a little more first? I'm afraid I haven't been much help to you.'

'Yes, you have. Maybe I didn't need a lot of persuading but you gave me just the right amount.'

When Couto came in, the greetings he and April exchanged were warm but brief. It was the first chance mother and son had had to talk since the news of the indictment, and he had some urgent advice to give her. 'I think you ought to get out of the country. Now while it's still possible. I'll arrange to send you some money wherever you go.'

April was amazed. It was the first time she had seen him since before her marriage and she had responded to his entrance with a glow of affection, recalling the best features of their former intimacy. But his proposal to his mother seemed so outrageous to her that she wondered whether he had suffered a mental decline. 'Gene, you can't really believe there's a chance of her being convicted on a ridiculous charge like that!'

'I certainly can. The government believes it, and never forget the courts are part of the government and the only function of the whole apparatus is to keep the ruling class in power.'

'But if I ran away, it would hurt the case for the others,' Mrs. Couto said. 'Everyone would take it as a confession of guilt.'

'The others are men and they're all a good deal younger than you. You can get five years for this thing; that's practically a life sentence at your age.'

His mother looked at him searchingly. 'Gene, is that the same advice you'd give someone else, who wasn't your mother?'

'Yes,' he answered with a positive immediacy that somehow lacked conviction. 'Provided she was a woman over sixty and all the other circumstances were the same.'

'I don't think it is. I think you're being weak and sentimental and I love you for it. But you're forgetting that the issue of peace is a lot bigger than any of us. I'm going to stay here and stand trial.'

'It will be in Washington,' he warned her. 'That means a jury of mainly government employees who'll be afraid for their jobs in this kind of a case.'

'This is my country and I'm not going to leave it.' She looked at her watch and asked April's permission to use the telephone in order to check on the time and place of a meeting with her alleged co-conspirators and their lawyers.

While Mrs. Couto was making her call, April beckoned Couto to come closer to her bedside. 'I've been curious about something for three years now: what you said that day in the cafeteria with Owen and me. I got the impression you were on the verge of some kind of switch, but apparently I was wrong.'

Couto glanced at his mother, who was winding up her telephone conversation. 'Someday you'll learn I'm a more complicated person than you think.'

'We'll have to start right away, Gene,' Mrs. Couto said. 'Ben thinks it's very important for you to be there.' She bent down over April and kissed her. 'You're going to be all right, sweetheart. Just do what's sensible and don't feel too sorry for yourself and concentrate on getting well.'

'I don't know what you've been talking about,' Couto said, 'but whatever advice you've been getting, you'd better take. Mom knows best.'

Reviewing the newspaper accounts of the previous week's disturbance did not give Owen a very clear idea of what to expect on his trip to Westchester County. The fourth of an annual series of concerts in the Peekskill area featuring the man he regarded as America's most distinguished native-born singer, this one had been scheduled to take place on a private, rented picnic ground some five miles from the town. The proceeds were to go to the Harlem Chapter of the Civil Rights Congress, a group cited as subversive by no less a judicial authority than United States Attorney-General Tom Clark. Inflamed by this fact and by Paul Robeson's reputed Communist sympathies, demonstrators organized by a joint council of local veterans' groups had invaded the area, blockaded the public highway and private entrance leading to the picnic ground, and effectively prevented the concert from taking place. In the course of this action a great many people had been beaten and stoned and their cars damaged; the abuse, both physical and vocal, focusing upon those music-lovers whom the veterans identified, by elementary visual examination, as Negroes; or, by a considerably less scientific process, as Jews; or, by a form of extra-sensory perception, as Communists.

Now Robeson's sponsors had announced another attempt to hold their concert on Sunday afternoon, September 4th, on a rented meadow in the same vicinity. A force of three thousand guards had been recruited, the newspapers announced, from the fur, electrical, furniture, garment and maritime workers, and from other militant New York trade unions. Their function was described by Robeson: 'If the state troopers do not protect us, we shall have forces enough to protect ourselves'. The second concert was expected to be a much larger affair than the first, with a possible attendance of from ten to fifteen thousand people. For their part the veterans had called for another counter-demonstration which might include some thirty thousand men from all over the state. The authorities were reported to have entreated the veterans not to hold their parade in front of the concert site itself, but this plea had been denied.

Chosen, as the prophetic monsignor had foreseen, to observe the proceedings for CACACACS, Owen and Mulvaney had little trouble composing the differences between their approaches to the assignment. Mulvaney thought it prudent to provide themselves with defensive weapons in case they were attacked, but when Owen argued that it was more in keeping with their detached role to go unarmed, his colleague appeared to agree. Unknown to Owen, however, he equipped his car, in which they were both travelling, with a revolver in the glove compartment, a black-jack under the front seat, and some rocks and baseball bats in the trunk.

Owen also advanced the view that they should buy tickets and attend the affair as ordinary spectators. 'We don't want anyone — the veterans, the police or the concert guards — to know who we are or what we're there for. If they do, they may be on good behaviour for our benefit. Whatever happens, we'll get a better picture of it if we simply go as part of the crowd and stick to being just that.'

'Whatever you say, my boy.' Mulvaney could see no harm in the proposal and he was anxious in any case to dispel Owen's mistrust of him. Privately he considered it ludicrous to suppose that two such finely bred Nordics could lose themselves in a sea of brachycephalic inferiority.

They met at St. Patrick's for a late morning Mass. It was while they were renewing their celestial ties there that an ambulance arrived at the Muirs' apartment building to take April to the hospital for the abortion Dr. Goldberg had agreed to perform that day.

Discreetly eschewing controversial topics, the two observers lunched congenially at an Italian roadhouse outside Tarrytown, then proceeded to the Peekskill area. Approaching the concert site, they found that this time police were on hand in great force, with local Westchester County officers outnumbering the state troopers by four or five to one. One of the former stopped Mulvaney's car to inquire politely: 'Concert or parade?' and direct them to the concert grounds where thousands of automobiles and scores of buses were already parked. Paying customers, it was later computed, totalled about twice what the sponsors of the affair had anticipated.

If an attempt had been contemplated to prevent once again the holding of the concert, it had obviously been abandoned as impractical. Instead of the huge turnout the veterans had boasted, there were scarcely more marchers in their parade than there were police, perhaps a thousand men. The concert guards, standing shoulder to shoulder in a protective circle around the entire grove, numbered more than twice that many. In addition to these groups and the vast throng of concert-goers assembling in the meadow, there were a large number of highly partisan spectators outside, behind police lines. It was this element, consisting largely of young adults and teen-agers, that contributed the most menacing sound effects as Mulvaney and Owen made their way into the grounds. The veterans marched under the slogan: *Wake up, America —*

Peekskill did; the crowd around the entrance, with the voices of young women predominating, amplified and clarified this message with such shouts as 'Reds!', 'Jew bastards!', 'Dirty niggers', 'Go back to Jew Town!' and 'Go back to Russia!' To Owen, who knew the district, the inhospitality of these housewives and children was emphasized by the fact that they had travelled miles from their homes to a point well outside their city to convey these greetings, which were addressed indiscriminately to visitors from New York and fellow-residents of the area.

One comely young matron, her bodily charms manifest in spite of the slacks, man's shirt and man's hat she was wearing, favoured Mulvaney and Owen with a prophecy: 'You'll get in but you won't get out!' Her ferocity was so intense as to draw an avuncular smile from the deputy sheriff standing alongside her. He touched her roguishly with his club, letting it roll down over the curve of her buttocks. She rewarded him with an intimate simper.

The concert itself was brief and effective, the amplifying system triumphing easily over the shouts and jeers of the demonstrators outside the grounds. Following the national anthem and an invocation by a Methodist minister came folk music and classical piano selections by the sponsoring organization, People's Artists. Then the famous Negro bass sang two groups of songs, separated by a collection appeal from Howard Fast, the novelist. Robeson concluded his part of the programme with 'Ol' Man River', his listeners theirs with an impressive ovation.

At first it appeared that the crowd was going to be able to disperse unmolested. An ominous note, however, was sounded by the security guards, who moved along the line of outgoing vehicles, cautioning the occupants to keep their windows tightly closed. Cars were proceeding in three directions from the concert grounds: either left or right along the state road, or across it on to the narrow byroad which led to the parkway to New York. Mulvaney took this last route. 'There's one of your boys,' he said as they crossed the state road. A man whose insignia marked him as a member of the Catholic War Veterans was leaning, along with a state trooper, against an automobile with a bright new sticker pasted on a window:

*Communism is treason. Behind Communism stands — the Jew!
Therefore, for my country — Against the Jews.*

The road they had chosen turned out to be lined with men and boys, some out in the open, others hidden behind trees and stone walls. At well-planned intervals were large piles of rocks, some of which were manned by policemen with the apparent function of protecting the rock-throwers from a treacherous counter-attack by their targets. This was an unnecessary precaution, Owen realized; the fact that the victims greatly outnumbered their attackers was of no value to them. Spread out over miles of roads in unbroken lines of cars and buses, they were more helpless than a string of covered wagons crossing a prairie because they were less able to concentrate their forces into a single defensive unit.

They saw rocks hurled against the windows of cars ahead of them; then they had to stop when the car two places in advance of theirs was halted and two coloured men dragged out of it by the crowd. They could hear an exultant scream: 'Kill the niggers!' and for a few moments it looked as if the threat would be carried out. Then a policeman strolled over to the mêlée, told the white men they were interfering with the smooth progress of traffic and ordered the Negroes back into their car. One of them lingered sluggishly on the ground and had to be prompted with an official kick in the groin.

Owen, moved to jump out and try to assist the victims of this assault, was restrained more by the obvious impossibility of getting through the intervening crowd than he was by Mulvaney's stern reminder of their non-partisan status. As they started to inch forward again, he looked back downhill toward the concert site and saw that the guards who were trying to escort the remaining spectators out were under attack, with skirmishes breaking out all around and the police for the most part maintaining an oblivious neutrality.

'There's one thing for our report,' he told Mulvaney. 'I haven't seen a sign yet of the Robeson people starting any trouble.'

'That's a laugh. Don't you see, old man, they started it all? What greater provocation could there be than holding this affair here where they're not wanted, after the warning they got last week? And I've seen a dozen cars with black men and white women together in them. That is an engraved invitation to trouble, I assure you, to the decent burghers of this community.'

'You may think so,' Owen said, 'but remember we're here as the representatives of a Catholic organization. Catholic policy is strongly against any kind of colour prejudice or discrimination. And just as strongly against anti-Semitism.'

'That is simply so much official propaganda, mainly addressed to missionary countries. The tip-off on how the big guns in the church really feel is the way they let Father Coughlin go on for years as the best-known Catholic voice in America, telling the truth about the Jews. You know how quickly they slap down a priest like this Father Feeney up in Boston when he steps out of line on an issue they really think matters. The reason they never did that with Coughlin or Curran...'

A rock smashed against the window next to him, splintering it. A second, smaller rock striking the damaged area sent slivers of glass spraying around their heads.

'Jesus and Mary!' exclaimed Mulvaney. 'I thought this glass was supposed to be shatter-proof!' He touched his left cheek and saw on his fingers the definitive red smear of Aryan blood. By accident or design the traffic was slowed to a virtual stop at this point so that there was no escape from the attack. Between barrages young faces appeared outside their closed windows to curse and threaten them. Owen heard himself addressed as 'Dirty Jew kike!', 'Nigger-loving Red bastard!' and — an epithet completely new to him — 'White nigger!' The words and the expressions of hate on the faces shocked and frightened him far more than the missiles.

'There's a cop,' Mulvaney said. 'For Christ's sake, get his attention!'

Owen lowered his window part-way and shouted to the state trooper, who motioned them to pull over to the side of the road, clearing a space in the crowd so that they could do so. Four county policemen materialized abruptly and they found themselves surrounded by the forces of the law as they emerged through the right-hand door in compliance with instructions.

'We'd like to register a complaint . . .' Owen began respectfully.

Mulvaney, behind him, interrupted. 'Those men don't know who we are! They've been throwing rocks at us!'

'What are you talking about? Who are you?'

'Ordinary citizens,' Owen replied promptly. 'We came to hear Mr. Robeson.'

'The hell we did!' Mulvaney screamed. He appealed over the officers' heads to the crowd. 'We're on your side! I'm a personal friend of Gerald Smith's. I've got papers to prove it.' He reached for his wallet, and a nightstick cracked against his wrist.

'Never mind that,' said a policeman. 'You try'n'a say you ain't Commies?'

'Of course we aren't. We're here as representatives of an anti-Communist organization. My name is Allan Mulvaney and I have a long record of . . .'

'What about you?' The officer turned impatiently to Owen. 'You a Communist?'

'You have no right to ask that question,' said Owen, 'and I therefore decline to answer it.'

'That does it!' said the trooper. 'Search their car.' One officer jerked the keys out of the ignition and went around to the trunk while another began to rummage inside.

'For God's sake, Muir,' Mulvaney said, 'this is serious. Tell them the truth.'

'I am. We're decent law-abiding citizens leaving a peaceful and perfectly legal concert and we're requesting police protection from a criminal mob.'

'Listen to the son of a bitch talk back!' shouted a man in an American Legion cap. 'Let us have them, Hank! We'll give them a little lesson in patriotism and then you can throw them in the jug.'

Simultaneous shouts from the two officers searching the car attracted general attention. Mulvaney's revolver and black-jack were brought out and the contents of the trunk displayed.

'Holy Mother of God!' exclaimed the state trooper in genuine astonishment. 'I think we got the ringleaders!'

'We better take them in and work them over there,' said an officer who hadn't spoken yet. 'Carrying a gun without a permit.'

'I have got a permit . . .' Mulvaney began and reached once more for his wallet. This time he managed to get it out before the stick caught him across the face with such force that he dropped to the ground, the wallet flying out of his hand and its contents scattering. He covered his head with his arms as blows continued to fall on him. 'Tell them who we are!' he yelled desperately to Owen.

'We made an agreement about that,' Owen said virtuously. 'I'm sticking to it.' Something hit him with terrible force on the back of his neck and he lost consciousness briefly as he fell.

'That's what I thought,' said the policeman who had struck him. 'It's a real black-jack all right. You can tell by the sound.'

While one of their number gathered up Mulvaney's wallet and its contents, the other defenders of the law went into a huddle to discuss further procedure and incidentally to permit a group of high school boys to release their emotions by kicking the fallen figures on the grass. One of these youngsters was wearing football shoes, though the formal opening of the season was still weeks ahead, and as Owen felt the cleats grind into his ribs, a strange contentment blended with his pain. It was as if he and Mulvaney were expiating by their suffering the inhuman treatment of the coloured youth at Moose Head and all the brutality now taking place up and down the road. Between kicks he vowed to free himself from any responsibility, even by association or tacit consent, for any fresh outbreak of the unchristian spirit which pervaded Peekskill that afternoon.

Meanwhile the officer who was scrutinizing Mulvaney's effects approached his colleagues with a puzzled frown. 'This guy's name *is* Mulvaney and it looks from these cards of his . . .'

'Let me see them!' The man who snatched the papers authoritatively from his hand was not a police officer but another Legionnaire newly arrived on the scene. The uniformed men waited deferentially while he studied the documents, and one of them even gestured to the teen-agers to restrain their fervour.

'You've pulled a big boner, it looks like,' the Legionnaire said finally. He handed the papers to the state trooper while he went over to Mulvaney and assisted him to his feet. 'If this is the man I think he is, he's got one of the best Americanism records in the country.'

'The other one's full of Commie talk,' a policeman said defensively.

'Are you really Allan Mulvaney?' the Legionnaire asked. 'The man who wrote *MacArthur and Destiny*?'

'Of course I am.' He tried to straighten up, then hunched over holding his side, his face twisted with pain. 'I've got to sit down.' His rescuer helped him over to the car seat. 'These men wouldn't listen to me.'

'Who's your friend?'

Mulvaney had a strong impulse to say that Owen was a Communist gunman who had tried to kidnap him, but his devotion to his salary prevailed over this base temptation. 'We're working together here, as observers. We decided to operate incognito and he simply carried it out a trifle too literally. Actually he's a very prominent member of the Catholic War Veterans. Owen Muir.'

'I *was* a member,' Owen corrected him. He had risen to his feet unaided, finding to his surprise and somewhat to his disappointment that he was unharmed except for a headache and a few spots that felt as if they might be bruised.

'He talks funny,' the trooper said. 'That's how come we made the mistake.'

'I don't blame you too much,' Mulvaney said. 'I think we can forget the whole thing all around.'

'That's real sporting of you, Mr. Mulvaney,' the trooper said.

'It's heroic, that's what it is,' declared the Legionnaire. 'A man who can rise above his personal feelings and see the whole picture, he's a patriot in spades.'

A few more tributes of this character were exchanged and then Mulvaney, conscious of a mounting compulsion to vomit and fearful of the demoralizing effect of such weakness upon the flower of Peekskill youth, insisted that he and Owen must be on their way. His side still bothering him, he assigned the driving chore to Owen and stayed where he was in the right-hand seat. Just as they were starting off a worrisome thought struck him.

'How do we know we won't get more rocks thrown at us further up?'

'Just keep your windows open and nobody'll bother you,' the Legionnaire told him. 'The boys have got the word all down the line it's only the Robeson crowd have their windows rolled up.'

This elementary injunction proved invaluable. They reached the parkway without being struck again. Then Mulvaney broke the antipathetic silence to call for a stop so that he might retch. Another car had parked ahead of them and from it emerged four adults and three children, all streaming from head to foot with such an astonishing amount of blood that it created a large red pool on the roadside. Owen got out and approached the group to see if he could be of any help. He found them dazed and bewildered, not only by their wounds and the violence which had been unleashed against them but also by the disillusioning realization that the protective properties of automobile window glass fell so far short of the advertised claims to which, as patriotic Americans, they had entrusted their simple faith. Indeed this latter betrayal was the dominant note in the halting incoherencies of the temporarily deranged driver. Unable to make any sense out of him, Owen was turning to his wife, who seemed calmer, when a state trooper ran up, brandishing his club menacingly, and called their attention to a sign which forbade parking on the highway. At first Owen felt the warning could hardly be meant seriously under the circumstances, but when the officer drew his revolver he realized it was. Lingering only long enough to assist the bleeding children and their mothers into their car, he returned to the one he was driving and found Mulvaney ready to proceed.

For miles along the parkway each overpass was an ambush with its pile of rocks and little group of men and boys ready to hurl them down on any car they thought, often erroneously, might be coming from the concert. After they passed Harmon the attacks finally ceased but all the rest of the way into New York they saw the cars with dented bodies and shattered glass and the people with bleeding faces and arms. Twice more Mulvaney had to stop to vomit. This process so increased the pain in his ribs that he decided the injury was more serious than he had supposed and, as they moved slowly down the West Side Highway in the late Sunday traffic, he asked Owen to take him to a hospital for emergency treatment. Owen obligingly left the highway at the next exit, pulled up beside the first policeman he saw and asked the location of the nearest Catholic hospital.

'The nearest *hospital*, damn it!' Mulvaney said. 'I need my ribs looked at and I don't care whether the X-ray machine has been blessed or not.'

'I was only thinking of your spiritual comfort,' Owen assured him. 'In case your condition is graver than it seems.'

The policeman resolved the question by pointing out that the nearest hospital was also a Catholic one. When they reached it Mulvaney was taken off by an intern to be examined while Owen was left to handle the practical details with the sister in the admitting office. First, however, he telephoned home in order to explain his lateness to April. The news he received threw him into a state of great agitation and he started for the door at a run.

'Hey, wait!' the sister shouted. 'I need the information about your friend for this form.'

'Get it from him! I have to go to a hospital, right away!' He vanished without further explanation.

The sister raised her eyes heavenward in reaction to this palpable insanity. Then she dialled the X-ray room and demanded that Mulvaney be returned to her forthwith for proper admission.

The shame and depression with which the events of the afternoon had filled him gave way to a terrible foreboding as he raced to the secular institution where April lay, a mystical super-sense told him, in mortal danger. He sprinted down the corridor to her room, asserted forcible control of himself at the door, and entered quietly to find her eating ice cream.

'Hi,' she said. 'Want a bite?' Then, noting his pallor as he collapsed into a chair, she summoned her nurse to restore him with a stimulant. It was a quarter of an hour before they were alone again and he was sufficiently recovered to listen to her carefully edited account of her experience.

'I might as well give you the bad news right off,' she began. 'We're not going to have a child.'

He looked at her stupidly, the joyous significance of what she was saying only penetrating his dulled consciousness as she went on to relate how she had been seized with severe cramps shortly after his departure. On being consulted by telephone, she told him glibly, Dr. Goldberg had ordered her to the hospital immediately and she arrived just in time to have a miscarriage in hygienic surroundings. 'I was a little scared but it turned out to be a big anti-climax, hardly any worse than the curse on one of my bad months. Right now I feel better than I have in weeks but Dr. Goldberg thinks I ought to stay here a day or two because they can watch my heart better and I'm still not over the damn fever. And naturally this doesn't change the fact that I have to stay in bed for six months to a year. But I feel fine, really. Only of course I'm sorry about the baby.' She waited anxiously for his reaction to this last sentiment.

'Don't be,' he said. 'I think it's the most wonderful thing that could have happened.' His words were a direct expression of the surge of happy relief he felt at the news, but the moment he had spoken them, he began to have doubts. Did April and he, in view of their sins, really deserve such a fortunate escape? Had they perhaps caused it to happen by an unconscious and impious wish? If so, should they not now be full of guilt and the fear of God's wrath, rather than joy? These were the questions he had to work out in his mind. When he spoke again, it was with slow deliberation. 'Naturally we always have to look for the divine intention behind any event. All we know for certain is that there is one. I'd like to believe this is an answer to our prayers, though we had no right to expect results so soon.'

'We didn't pray for a miscarriage. We prayed for both me and the baby to come through okay.'

'Remember what I said about every prayer being answered but not always in the exact form we ask. Either the Blessed Virgin changed our request herself or God did it when she passed it on to Him. In either case, it's the most convincing proof of the theory you could ask for, because this solution, which neither you nor I thought of, is better than the one we had in mind. That makes sense to you, doesn't it?' His voice was hesitant, reflecting his fear of a self-serving misinterpretation of God's will.

'I guess so,' April said disinterestedly. 'You know I've always cared more about results than causes.' She would have felt much better about having deceived him if he had confined himself to simple satisfaction over the way things had turned out. Instead, his uncertainty made her dislike herself for the fraud and him for not justifying it with unqualified delight. She preferred not to talk about it any more. 'What was it like at the concert?'

'Horrible.' He told her what he had seen that day of man's inhumanity to man. 'I'm going to write out a full report and submit it to CACACACS and my own organization. If they don't pass official resolutions condemning the veterans' council up there, I'm going to resign from both.'

'Good. I hope you stick to that. You don't belong in that kind of dirty politics, Owen. Neither does the church for that matter, but your friend the monsignor is so far in it, he couldn't climb out if he wanted to. Why not have a look at what's happening to your business for a change? I think Blankenship needs a little watching with this combination divining-rod and Geiger counter of his.'

'I've talked to him about it; I think it has a chance. No, I don't believe I could ever go back to taking a really active part in the business.'

'I heard a bishop say once, when he was announcing some large donations to a new church, that making money could be a very pious function. He said God gave some men the vocation of getting rich so they could support the work of glorifying Him.'

'That's quite possible. Only I just don't happen to think it's my vocation.'

They fell silent, both aware that they had strayed too easily from the topic which should be, and actually was, occupying their main attention. It suddenly occurred to Owen to wonder whether, in the midst of her pain and fright, she had remembered to give instructions for the baptism of the embryonic clot which her body had rejected. Certainly no one else would have thought of it in this profane establishment where, in direct contradiction to the teachings of Jesus, the health of the flesh was elevated above that of the soul.

He restrained himself from asking the question. If the indispensable act had not been performed, it was too late to repair the omission now. One more immortal soul — conceivably the soul of a potential saint — uncleansed of its terrible inheritance of sin, had been denied the sight of God. To call it to April's attention could accomplish nothing except to add to her other sorrows the guilty realization that she had failed in her first obligation as a mother.

There should have been many things for them to say about the new hopes and possibilities opened to them by the timely removal of the threat to her life. Yet they could not speak them across the widening crevice.

Despite considerable pressure, Owen adhered to his resolution and severed his organizational ties. Having already broken with the veterans' group over the issue, he made his plea before CACACACS as an individual, without the support behind him which the other delegates had for their predominantly unsympathetic reactions.

Mulvaney, quickly recovered from the effects of his ordeal, followed up Owen's report with his own version of the affair. Only in passing did he touch on the personal jeopardy to which he had been subjected by Owen's perfidy. The danger he had faced he was willing to accept as incidental to the performance of his duty; what mattered to the higher purpose for which they were joined were the broad outlines of the event, rather than the petty and often unpleasant details on which Owen had so shortsightedly dwelt. There was no necessity, he pointed out, for this council, which had merely sent observers to the scene, to pass any sort of resolution approving or disapproving an occurrence which had provoked so much controversy. It should simply note, privately, the results, which he felt were on the whole constructive. While it was true that the concert had taken place as scheduled, the group which had staged it and like groups all over the country would face increasing difficulty in arranging similar affairs.

Owen might have pressed his case further had Monsignor Frasso not taken an unequivocal stand in opposition to his resolution. Once the prelate had spoken, it was obvious that even the minority which shared some of Owen's misgivings would not go along with a statement of outright condemnation. The only gesture left to him was the one to which he had pledged himself. He walked out of the meeting while it was still in progress.

That evening Frasso visited him at home. April, released from the hospital but still fated to many months of confinement while her heart adjusted to its injuries, was upstairs in bed, and the two men were able to conduct their discussion with uninterrupted concentration.

Before proceeding to the occasion of his visit, the prelate inquired after April, and Owen told him of the providential blessing which had been so graciously bestowed on them. Frasso agreed that it was most gratifying. 'How wise we are,' he commented, 'to entrust to the Immaculate Heart of Mary what the unbeliever would assign to the fallible hands of a mortal surgeon.'

Then, coming directly to the topic which immediately concerned them, he explained that he had intentionally curtailed consideration of the issue at the council session. There were certain deeper significances and higher points of policy involved in the matter than he had cared to go into in open meeting. On the question of the Catholic attitude toward racial discrimination, for instance, he was now willing to concede that Owen was clearly correct and Mulvaney, from a simple theological standpoint, in equally manifest error.

'Here again,' he said, 'we have another of those situations so frequent in the complex modern world in which an intrinsically good cause must be subordinated to a better one.'

Owen was in a comparatively argumentative mood. 'I don't think there could be a much better cause than tolerance and interracial understanding.'

'There is, my son. The cause of world peace. Every step we take today must be judged against the standard of whether it increases or diminishes the danger of war.'

'Sure,' Owen said, 'but you aren't helping start a war by following Christian principles.'

'Could Christian principles survive if the church itself were destroyed? There was a time when many powerful nations fought for supremacy in the world, most of them truly Catholic countries and all of them professing some form of adherence to Christ. The church could stand above such struggles. But today there is only one significant world power in which the church has an important influence and whose policies objectively conform with her interests. As citizens of that one great power, we should be the first to appreciate that whatever weakens the United States is a blow against the rule of Christ on earth.'

'I still don't get the connection with Peekskill.'

'The people who shout the loudest about complete equality for Negroes in this country are the same ones who call for the liberation of Africa and Asia from "foreign imperialists", meaning us. All over the world they are pouring new fuel on the fires of revolutionary nationalism. Without exception these so-called national liberation movements are anti-clerical and anti-God. Even in highly civilized countries like France and Italy, the Communists were on the verge of majority control just a couple of years ago. Only American dollars and our insistence on coalition anti-Communist governments saved them from the fate of Czechoslovakia. Do you begin to see my point?'

'More or less,' said Owen. 'But I don't know if I agree with it. Suppose there's a conflict between our present American foreign policy and French interests, say, or Italian ones? Where does the church stand then? Supposing what they're saying abroad is true — that America is trying to dominate the world, imperialistically?'

'Imperialism is just another word and there's no reason for us to be frightened by it. The church, operating within a purely spiritual jurisdiction, condemns no form of government which respects her rights. Catholicism has lived with monarchies, democracies and empires alike, even with fascism. It was the original Roman Empire which spread Christianity to the world of that day, and the Holy Roman Empire which sustained it in the Middle Ages. Cortez and Pizarro were representatives of Spanish imperialism. They have been criticized for their cruelties and their lust for gold. But the fact remains that Latin America would not be solidly Catholic today without their conquests.'

'Well,' Owen said, 'I can see some resemblance between the Spanish conquistadors and those Westchester County Legionnaires. But I don't think I like the idea that we have to suppress free speech at home, especially on things that do need improvement, like minority rights or legitimate labour demands, just so as not to handicap our efforts abroad.'

'It's a question of seeing where the real danger lies,' Frasso explained. 'Is it from without? Do you really think the Russians, with all their internal problems, would be so insane as to attack us? No, the real danger to our programme is from within this country — from the Reds and the Pinks and the Quaker pacifists, from the soft-headed agnostic liberals and the ostrich-like labour and farm leaders who can't see beyond the demands of their own memberships, from the Negro and Jewish organizations who think you can change a pattern of national thinking overnight, from the isolationists who say "Let the Europeans and the Chinese decide their own fate", from the Protestant ministers who preach that it's morally wrong to stockpile atomic bombs and from the taxpayers' groups who say we can't afford to. They add up to millions of voices and every one of them, whether he realizes it or not, is doing the Communists' work for them. We simply cannot afford that kind of confusion. Civil rights and civil liberties are attractive-sounding theories but you should remember that many great minds have never accepted their validity. You can't equate them with the all-important issue of the survival of Western civilization.'

'I don't know,' Owen said slowly. 'I certainly go along with the idea that peace is worth sacrificing some other values to it. But how do we know this programme of ours will guarantee peace? You told me a few months ago that what we were coming to was the final conflict history had been building up towards. That approach seems to rule out a peaceful solution.'

'Let me remind you that I said peace was the goal. We may have to use many weapons along the road to that goal, including force of arms if we are driven to it. But the peace I'm talking about, lasting peace, can never come into being as long as the evil masters of the Kremlin are in power. We have to take the offensive; we have to undermine their authority in the countries they have brought within their orbit. We have to restore a friendly government in China. We have to surround them with our bases so they don't dare make an aggressive move. These and other necessary steps may involve small wars along the way. We will probably experience some temporary defeats — the loss of some ground in Asia, say, or a European ally paralysed into submission. But if we are willing to make the sacrifice of total mobilization, if we seize the initiative and never let go of it, the ultimate struggle when it does come may be blessedly brief, and it will not be our land or our people that will suffer the main damage. Then and only then will we have realized, with God's help, the dream of the generations: a genuine and enduring peace. Is that not an ideal worthy of your fullest dedication?'

'Not mine,' Owen said. 'You may be right — I can't make a comprehensive argument against what you say — but I also can't resign myself to the idea that we can't have peace without having a war first. I have to hope that a better way can be found or I'd have to stop hoping entirely.'

Frasso devoted another thirty minutes to continued persuasion, leaving himself only a narrow margin of time to reach the hotel banquet room where he was committed to say a few testimonial words at a Tammany district leader's birthday celebration. Unwilling, despite Owen's intransigence, to regard his effort as a failure, he was still talking while his host assisted him with his topcoat. 'I believe you'll come to see the picture when you have given it enough thought and watched the way events will be going. Why don't you talk it over with your father?'

'My father?' He was surprised because it was the first time Frasso had shown any awareness of Willis Muir's existence.

'Yes. I have never had the pleasure of meeting him personally but we have a great many common friends. And I have found that men in his position, probably because of the multiplicity of their interests, tend to have a much broader view of the world scene. Among them you find very little of the confusion I was speaking about earlier — all the special pleaders putting their own interests ahead of the nation's.'

It was disturbing to Owen to find himself in such thorough disagreement with his spiritual mentor and with so many other prominent lay and clerical spokesmen for his church. But his faith was unshaken. He had begun recently to interest himself in Christian mysticism, and it was reassuring to find, in such diverse sources as *The Seven Storey Mountain* and the precepts of Saint John of the Cross, that there was a higher realm of Catholicism which did not concern itself with worldly affairs at all. If there were wars, riots, poverty, suffering and cruelty on earth, these authors maintained, the most pious attitude a man could take was to ignore them. Owen was not quite prepared for such an extreme view himself, and even if he were, his status as a married man and potential father disqualified him for that sort of withdrawal from the world. But it gave him satisfaction to realize there were good Catholics who took no part in the ugly anti-democratic activity he had witnessed, and for his responsibility in which he felt an abiding shame. The knowledge sustained him in his devotion to the church; it also bolstered his determination that he would participate no further in movements which countenanced the forcible overthrow of Constitutional guarantees.

There were, of course, many Catholic groups of a pacific and charitable nature with which he could have allied himself, but the specific urge was lacking toward any one of them, and he thought it prudent this time to await a wholly unambiguous expression of the divine plan for his future. He still felt strongly that he was destined for a special vocation of a spiritual nature, but he thought he needed an infusion of prevenient grace before he could freely will himself in the desired direction. In the course of his hagiological reading he noted the aimless periods into which many saints had from time to time lapsed, and he took comfort in these precedents.

He was unable during this period to bridge the gap between April and himself. The marriage bed, so often the locale of reconciliations both genuine and illusory, was denied them because they continued to assume, without any specific medical instruction one way or the other, that intercourse would be an impediment to the slow return of her strength. Thus their sexual needs became a disuniting rather than a coalescing factor.

The Holy Year of 1950 began amid the tribulations of a water shortage in the metropolitan area. Owen was almost unique among New York residents in welcoming it. Dr. Goldberg's most stringent injunction had been that April avoid any risk of catching cold. She had carelessly omitted the year before to avail herself of the blessing of Saint Blaise, preserver against diseases of the throat, and this negligence, which had undoubtedly contributed to her present condition, could not be repaired until that saint's day came around again some weeks hence. Owen, therefore, had been trying to dissuade her from the frequent baths to which she had long been addicted and which, she now maintained, broke the tedium of a bedridden day. The drought added civic virtue to his other arguments and he kept her from the tub for three successive days in early January. On the fourth morning she grew restless and he made a compromise proposal. A sponge-bath, administered by him while she lay in bed, would have the double advantage of guarding her from exposure and using up a minimum of water. She agreed with more good will than she had shown him in some time, and he made elaborate preparations while she tuned in the eleven o'clock news on her bedside radio.

An incidental result of this experiment, not unforeseen by either of them, was to activate their physical craving for each other. She kissed him a few times while he bent over her; his hands began to take on a function beyond the strictly lavatory. The situation recalled that day in her Village apartment during their betrothal when she had ministered to him in somewhat similar fashion. Perhaps their passion lacked the fine edge of intensity it had possessed then; still a few minutes of such stimulation sufficed to bring them closer than hours of talking out their differences might have done. Only an intrusion of major significance could have broken the mood. April was already reaching over to eliminate the distraction of the radio when the news announcer came to an item which provided such an intrusion:

'... In Washington, meanwhile, the defence at the so-called "peace trial" was thrown into a panic by the appearance of the main government witness against them. The blow fell hardest on Mrs. Theresa Couto, indicted executive secretary of the Council for Permanent Peace. Testifying to the foreign connections which she and other defendants disclaimed was her only son, Eugene Couto, thirty-five, a member of the council's executive committee and its representative at last year's World Peace Congress in Paris, where, the government alleges, the illegal links were forged. In answer to opening questions by Assistant U.S. Attorney Harold Swinnerton, Jr., Couto revealed that he had operated for thirteen years within the Communist Party of the United States as an undercover agent for the FBI.'

CHAPTER IV

THE mother-son angle helped to make the trial a prominent news story throughout the ten days it lasted. Though the government presented a few minor witnesses and a great deal of documentary evidence in the form of European statements on peace, and releases of the American group exhibiting similar content, the essence of its case was the uncorroborated testimony of Gene Couto. He told the court how he, principally, and the officers of the council to a lesser but still guilty extent, had conspired with the leaders of the Paris congress to promote a concept of international affairs so abhorrent to right-thinking people that it could not possibly have originated on American soil.

The defence conceded the authenticity of all the documents, maintaining that it was common and proper for people in different countries to have parallel views and that this could not conceivably constitute 'agency' within the meaning of the Foreign Agents Registration Act of 1938 as amended in 1942. The defence challenged as fictitious, in part or in whole, certain conversations Couto swore he had had with the defendants. Other conversations which he said he had had with the alleged foreign principals, there was no way of proving or disproving. With respect to these, however, defence counsel pointed out that, even if they had taken place, they had not been reported by Couto to his superiors in the organization. All they could possibly establish, therefore, was that he himself had functioned as a foreign agent, endeavouring unsuccessfully to subvert the peace council. To this the prosecution replied righteously and unanswerably that its witness was not on trial and that a free American grand jury, listening to the same testimony now brought before the court, had chosen not to indict him.

Couto was also permitted to testify, over strenuous defence objections, that two of the defendants, one of them his mother, were Communists. Under cross-examination he admitted that he had recruited his mother into the party and that he had been an FBI agent at the time. He had taken this step, he told the court, at the cost of great emotional pain but in conformity with his pledge to act in every respect like a zealous member. In his own opinion and that of his employers it had turned out to be the master stroke in disguising his real affiliation.

In his summation the chief of the prosecuting staff conceded freely that there was no evidence of any financial gain by the defendants from their crime. The government's case rested on the similarity of views expressed by the foreign organization and the domestic one, and on the all-important nexus, or link, between the principal and the agent. That link was its witness, the patriot Couto. The question for the jury to decide was whether, the conduit of agency having been thus established, the defendants were in fact promoting American aims or alien ones. The peace council had charged the United States government with aggressive intentions towards Russia and China. If the jury regarded this as a proper American view of the world situation, it could demonstrate such a belief by bringing in a verdict of acquittal. The peace council had accused President Truman of deliberately provoking the Soviet Union with an atomic bomb control plan which his own advisers had told him would be an unacceptable affront to the Kremlin. The jury had an opportunity, by declaring the defendants innocent, to brand the President guilty of inciting atomic war.

In the course of his presentation the prosecutor made the point that, while it was only reasonable to apply the same verdict to all four defendants, one of them, Mrs. Couto, might be considered to some extent a victim of circumstances, and the jury would be justified in recommending leniency in her case.

The defence argued that the political associations and particular views of the accused were wholly irrelevant. Even if there were an absolute identity of opinion between a group in France and a group in this country, that was in itself no more criminal than an identity of opinion among physicists of different countries regarding the quantum theory. There had been no arrangements between the so-called principal and the so-called agent which fell within the scope of the statute except those which Couto claimed to have concluded. And his story, if accepted at its face value, only proved that the case had been deliberately framed by another wing of the same Department of Justice which was prosecuting it.

The court, in its final instructions to the jury, laid great stress on this accusation by defence counsel. Without any evidence having been presented to show that Couto had been instructed by the FBI to behave as he did in his relations with the international group, the defence was charging no less respected an agency than the Federal Bureau of Investigation with conspiracy to imprison innocent persons. The judge told the jurymen they were free to place such a stigma on one of the bulwarks of free government, but warned them to consider the seriousness of that action. If on the other hand, they felt that Couto had not functioned as a provocateur but merely as the conscientious Communist he was supposed to be impersonating, then the officers of the council must be held responsible for the consequences of permitting a known Communist to represent them. Thus it was up to the jury to determine whether Couto had acted as another Communist might have acted in his place. In this regard, the court added, it was now proper, in view of the recent conviction of eleven Communist leaders in Judge Medina's court, to take judicial notice of the fact that Communists promulgated a foreign ideology, employed Aesopian language and were notoriously devious in their methods.

The defence professed to discern prejudice in these instructions and moved for a mis-trial. The court retired for a half hour of sober self-analysis, and returned to deny the motion.

The jury rendered a prompt and unanimous verdict of guilty, recommending special leniency in the case of defendant Theresa Couto. On the date fixed for the imposition of sentence, the court permitted each defendant to make a statement before he learned his fate, leaving Mrs. Couto till last. The other three made simple reassertions of their innocence and received two-year sentences.

Tessie Couto spoke more forcefully and at greater length. She said that any suggestion of special consideration in her case was an insult to herself personally and to the female sex in general, implying as it did that women were subject to the persuasion of their intellectually superior male relatives. 'I believe in peace and socialism because of what I feel in my own head and my own heart. So my only son has turned out to be an informer and a police spy. That's a hard thing for a person to take but if you think it's going to change what I believe in, you're as mistaken in that as you are in this verdict, or in the whole idea that you can stamp out the peace movement with violence and terror. The people of this country don't want another war and once they know the facts, they won't let you start one. I intend to go on doing my part to bring those facts to the people, whenever I'm at liberty to do so. I think it only fair that the court realize that.'

The chief prosecutor, noting the formidable glint in the judge's eye, rushed up to the bench to make a hasty plea in a low voice. The court cut him short, invoking the independence of the judiciary to repudiate any deals the government might have made with its witness, and sentenced Mrs. Couto to the same two-year term as the male defendants.

The Muirs followed these events with close interest and somewhat disparate reactions. April was outraged by Gene's behaviour, the more so because she realized how, and in what painstaking detail, she herself had been deceived by him. She felt a deep sympathy for Tessie in her disillusionment and was outspoken in her view of what was happening to a country in which such a miscarriage of justice could take place. At the same time she regarded Mrs. Couto's defiance of the court as a foolish and fruitless gesture. There was no justification, to April's way of thinking, for inviting a long prison term when it was obvious she might have received a light or suspended sentence.

Owen saw it differently. Though also revolted at first by Couto's unfilial conduct, he was inclined after more careful consideration to attribute part of this feeling to his long-standing prejudice against the man. Couto, he could see, must have been torn between conflicting loyalties and it was possible that he had suffered grievously in the process. As for the mother, what he admired most about her was the splendid consistency of her statement to the court. Even though directed to a false god, it was an expression of faith and courage in the best tradition of Christian martyrdom.

One aspect on which they found no disagreement was the matter of providing bail for Mrs. Couto pending appeal to the higher courts. While the trial judge saw no grounds for bail in the case, feeling that the legal and Constitutional questions involved had already undergone the most thorough sort of judicial consideration, he was quickly reversed on this point by the appellate court. Owen stood bond for Mrs. Couto, and her co-defendants were similarly assisted by relatives or friends.

This act stimulated an appreciation, addressed to April, from her erstwhile lover:

Dearest April: It was most generous of you and your husband to undertake the obligation which should have been mine for Mom's bond.

I have no doubt you were surprised at my appearance as a prosecution witness. Believe me, it was one of the hardest things I ever had to do in my life. Right up to the last minute I almost couldn't face it. Then, the very night before the trial, something happened that gave me courage. I was in a bar with the prosecuting attorney and a couple of FBI men, working out my testimony, and there was a girl sitting at the bar who seemed to have taken a fancy to me and I found myself looking at her every now and then. Well, she was smiling at me and I couldn't help noticing her teeth. They were pretty nice teeth for a girl who would go into a Washington bar by herself and I don't know how it happened but suddenly the idea came to me that there had to be a plan behind that wonderful arrangement of thirty-two pieces of dentine and enamel.

It wasn't just this one girl's teeth any more, you understand. It was the fact that every human being, the world over, had the same number and the same kinds, each in the right place for its particular function. How could that happen without some Grand Design behind it all?

The more I thought about it, the more everything fell into place. If there was such a design, why, I was part of it and so was what I was called on to do the next day. If that was so, then it wasn't my responsibility what would happen to Mom or anybody else. All I had to do was carry on with my duty the way I had always known I would have to do someday ever since I made a decision years ago which I still think was a right decision or at least the only one I could make under the circumstances.

As far as the bail money is concerned, you know how short I always am in that department, but I'm happy to say it looks as if I will be able to take over this responsibility from you in the near future. As you doubtless remember, I have always had the aspiration to be a writer and now at last I have the opportunity to find out once and for all if that is where my talents lie. My agents have *Life* and the *Saturday Evening Post* bidding against each other for my life story, and *Reader's Digest* in on the deal however it turns out. They are also talking about a book and even a movie sale and maybe I will be up there in your class before I'm through. It will be a very refreshing change to have some real money for once, though of course that can never make up for the dirty deal they gave Mom.

As for what I have been through, I count on your understanding because you are the one person who knows how I tried to save my mother from her own pigheadedness, before the trial, I mean. Then when she wouldn't leave, I got them to promise me she wouldn't get more than a three months' sentence. If the judge had had any sense he never would have let her shoot her mouth off.

Thanks once again. What I said about trying to save Mom might be misinterpreted if it got into the wrong hands, so I'll ask you to destroy this letter.   As always,   GENE

The final suggestion was one which had already occurred to her for quite different reasons. She crumpled the letter contemptuously and dropped it into the waste basket at her bedside.

Because his father had taught him that all publicly circulated business periodicals and financial sections were mere propaganda outlets and therefore unreliable, Owen kept up with economic trends through a private newsletter which had the added virtue of brevity in covering a field he had always found dull. It was through this medium that he noted the disturbing weaknesses in the national economy during the first months of 1950. Inexpert as he was, he could see that the decline in employment and purchasing power threatened most immediately a business such as his with its extreme sensitivity to fluctuations in luxury demand. It was time, he decided one May morning, to look into the state of affairs at the plant. Wishing to inform himself about sales and profit figures before entering a policy discussion with his partner, he first called on Boal, the original accountant for the firm, who had been elevated to the rank of treasurer.

Blankenship, who had moved the start of his working day back to eleven o'clock since assuming partnership status, was told on his arrival that Owen had descended unexpectedly on the premises, was now going over the books with Boal, and had requested a meeting with the junior partner immediately thereafter. The news had a devastating effect on Blankenship. He grew pale and leaned on his secretary's desk for support. Then, recovering a little and insisting that he was perfectly all right, he retired to his inner office where he dialled the number of an overseas airline only to hang up before the connection was completed. Instead, he hurried down the corridor to Boal's office, breaking in on the conference between treasurer and president to say that it was urgently necessary for him to see Owen alone. Boal, who had already ascertained that Owen was not even aware of certain developments to which he had supposedly been a party, diagnosed the nature of the crisis at once. Owen was mystified but obliging.

As soon as they were alone, Blankenship began to speak with great emotional intensity and practically no coherence. 'I don't know how much you know — don't really care — want to make a clean breast of it anyway. It's been the damnedest run of bad luck really — odds were twenty to one I'd make a killing for all of us — I didn't mean to do anything wrong — I want you to believe that. Great consolation, isn't it? — I've lost your money for you but you know it was with the best of intentions. You're broke and I'm a thief. Do you know how many men I've given lectures to who committed this same kind of crime? They're all back on the street now — what a laugh they'll have when they hear about me going to jail. But you know who'll get the biggest kick out of it? — the reactionaries in the bureau with their nineteenth-century prison methods. Bet I'll be the only staff man who ever got sent up himself. But we oughtn't to go on talking about me all the time — question is, what about you? What'll you do, April sick and all? How do you think your father will take it?'

It took a half hour for Owen to marshal the details into some sort of orderly array. With sales falling off and his latest gadget meeting a cold response in wholesale circles, Blankenship had virtually abandoned production and converted the Jet company into a speculating syndicate. Unfortunately he had based all his expectations on a persuasive tip that the world would be at war again by the end of March. When this piece of inside information had regrettably proved false and there had been a decline instead of a spurt in the copper, oil and aircraft shares to which the corporation's capital was pledged, his attempted coup had turned into a disaster. The aspect of the affair that transformed it from the merely injudicious to the criminal was that he had forged Owen's name to cheques and other documents requiring both their signatures.

'I figured you wouldn't quibble about that if I made us a pile,' he explained miserably. 'And it kept looking good — so many times I'd listen to the news and think things were breaking right — Russia walking out of the Security Council — this Vogeler business in Budapest — there'd still be a chance if somebody dropped a bomb in the next few days.'

'Be quiet!' It was as sharp a tone as Owen had ever used. 'You sound much more like a candidate for an insane asylum than a jail.' He picked up the telephone and summoned Boal to rejoin them. While Blankenship sat by listlessly, the other two men computed how the situation stood as at that day and found that it fell just short of bankruptcy. By immediately liquidating the remnants of Blankenship's investments and disposing of all their remaining assets at forced prices, they could pay off their obligations and dissolve the corporation with a puny margin of solvency. Their estimate was that the residue might not even reach five figures. Owen instructed Boal to apply himself at once to the funereal details.

The partners were left together again.

'You're right,' said Blankenship after a long and, to him, unbearable silence. 'I must be crazy. There's no other explanation for a man of high character and unblemished reputation sinking so low.' He dug the fingers of both hands into his temples. 'I've had some remarkably grim headaches lately. I wonder if that . . .'

'Don't waste time with physical symptoms,' Owen said. 'Your trouble is in the spirit. Once a man starts heading toward an unworthy goal, evil methods for getting there come as a matter of course. So what you have to realize is that the particular way you went about this thing is pretty much a side issue. The basic mistake is thinking you can sustain yourself on mere material nourishment, live by bread alone.'

'That's right.' He was beginning to exhibit more animation. 'I haven't any faith in anything. I lost it somewhere on the road.'

'Find it again. Go back over your steps.'

'I'm afraid I never had it very strongly. You know, that's what appealed to me about you from the start, at Moose Head. The fact that you had values to go by.'

'I was lost,' Owen said emphatically. 'I had no relationship with God at all. I thought it was my job to figure out what was right and wrong for myself, which is moral anarchy.'

'Well,' Blankenship conceded obligingly, 'you *were* riding kind of a high horse. But what you've found now, that I envy you.'

'It's available for the asking.'

'Little late for me, wouldn't you say?' He smiled bitterly. 'Even the Catholic chaplains don't put much stock in jailhouse conversions.'

'Don't worry about that.' There was a note of excitement in Owen's voice. 'Nobody's said yet you're going to jail. Have you really ever thought about coming into the church?'

'A great deal,' Blankenship assured him. 'I think perhaps the main factor that's held me back has been my economic dependence on you: the fear people would think I was only joining your faith because I worked for you. That may seem petty to you, I know . . '

'I can understand it, even if I don't sympathize with it.'

'Now, of course, they'd say I was just doing it to stay out of prison.'

'God won't think that, if you're sincere. His opinion is the only one you should care about. And He can't be deceived.'

'You're lending me some of your strength,' Blankenship said. 'I can feel it. That's very generous of you.'

'It's not mine. There's an endless supply we can all draw on. Any new force you feel inside you comes from thinking about God for a change, instead of yourself,'

'Let's see if I have this straight in my mind,' Blankenship said. 'Supposing for some reason of your own or other, you didn't prosecute me. . . .'

'I can think of some excellent reasons.'

'You will be canonized some day. That's my first expression of faith. But what I was saying — do you really think your church would accept a depraved specimen like me?'

'The greater the sinner, the greater the glory.'

Owen spoke with understandable enthusiasm. It was his first conversion.

Not even the angry sounds coming from the library could unsettle Ruth Muir's sense of well-being. She knew that Willis was furious with Owen and that it had something to do with the boy's losing his money. But there had been strong differences between her menfolk before and they had blown over. There was no sense in letting this one interfere with the contentment she felt over the fact that her daughter was finally going to be married.

She had been guilty, she now realized, of a lack of faith in Phyllis. She had thought it a mistake for the girl to become so intimate, first with Dellie Carpenter and then with Dellie and Dennis together. And when she heard that Phyllis and Dennis were being seen places without Dellie, she had taken her daughter to task. Why re-open old wounds, she asked, especially with a married man whose church would never permit him a divorce? But Phyllis, it later developed, knew what she was about. She alone was privy to the secret kept even from Dennis: that Dellie had eloped at the age of seventeen and undergone a valid Christian ceremony with a good-looking but unstable boy whom the police had apprehended on an outstanding morals charge the first morning of their honeymoon. The marriage had been annulled by state law and the husband, unregenerate after his first prison term, was now serving a life sentence for rape. But in the eyes of the Roman Catholic Church she was still his wedded wife, as Dellie abruptly found out one afternoon in the eighth month of her pregnancy, when Dennis, enlightened by Phyllis, invoked her previous marriage to invalidate their present one. Having secured his Catholic annulment, he was now in Reno seeking a civil divorce on the grounds of mental cruelty. And Phyllis was to be his bride — his fifth as secular authority reckoned it, his first according to the ecclesiastical code.

It was odd, Mrs. Muir mused, that both her children should find their happiness with Catholics. Phyllis was not planning to join the church herself but of course her children would be born into it. Thus any and all grandchildren Mrs. Muir might acquire would be raised in a faith her own father had so frequently condemned as a putrid relic of medieval superstition and anti-democratic despotism. It only went to show, she thought, how fashions change. She had read somewhere quite recently that some of the cleverest writers, especially in England, were forsaking Hindu mysticism for Roman.

The library door opened and Owen emerged looking disconsolate.

'Isn't your father coming out?' Mrs. Muir asked. 'I thought we could have tea.'

'He's not speaking to me any more.'

'Oh. You'll have some though, won't you?'

'I'm afraid not. The fact is I'm supposed to leave the house as quickly as I can and never come back.'

'In a minute,' amended his father, appearing in the doorway. 'I just remembered one more thing I wanted to say to you first.'

'I'll ring for tea,' Mrs. Muir said.

'It's this,' Mr. Muir continued. 'You've been an incredible idiot, irresponsible toward yourself, your wife and the society you live in. But if you'll at least take the one step that's still open to you against that swindling crook partner of yours and send him to jail, then maybe there'll be a chance decent people will give you another break someday.'

'I don't see what good that would do. It would just be a pointless piece of revenge.'

'Not true. Every man whose property is stolen has an obligation to people with property everywhere to see to it the thief is punished. It's not only locking up the one criminal that counts; it's the example to others.'

'But I told you — Mr. Blankenship is on the verge of being saved. And I'm not sure his faith is strong enough to go through with it if he had to go to prison anyway.'

'That's exactly the point,' said his father triumphantly. 'Send him to jail and then see what happens to his change of heart. Then you'll know if it's on the level.'

Owen shook his head firmly. 'I can't take the risk of losing a soul. Especially one in as delicate condition as his. The surest way to sell him on Christian charity is to show him an example of it.'

'You can take your Christian charity and go to hell! Your mother and I are through with you and we hope we never see you again. Shut up, Ruth.'

Owen was gone by the time the maid entered in answer to the bell. Appraising her husband with an experienced eye, Mrs. Muir abandoned her thoughts of tea and ordered cocktails instead.

Father Boyle was a man of strong emotions and occasionally he found it hard to exercise sacerdotal restraint on his language when expressing them. Aware of this failing, he kept his eyes firmly on the crucifix of his rosary while Owen told his story, and held them there for some moments afterward before he spoke.

'I don't like to say this, my son, but I think one of your main troubles is an extremely irreverent attitude toward money. I guess you don't realize how important it is for a pastor to have a few people in the parish he can count on when things are rough. Otherwise you wouldn't come in here so blithely, without any sign of remorse that I can see, and casually drop the news that there's one less place I can turn when the school drive starts next week. It's as if you didn't feel you owed any obligation to the church at all for what it's done to your life.'

'That's not true,' Owen said. 'I'm very much aware of my debt to the church.'

'Are you? Would you say I was fulfilling my job if I turned over my main responsibilities to some curate and sat in a corner venerating the Five Wounds of Our Lord while the whole parish went to pot? Or when I was selling underwear, do you think I just dropped my samples around and went off somewhere to shoot pool while the buyers were making up their minds? No, I was in there every minute demonstrating what our special features meant, penny for penny, against the competition. And I still am.'

'I'm not trying to hide my mistakes,' Owen said humbly. 'I intend to take them up with you formally, at my next confession. But what I came to see you about today was this man Arnold Blankenship. He's going to need instruction and I want to know if you're willing to give it to him.'

'But what about your dear friend the monsignor?' There was irony in Father Boyle's voice; it was an opportunity he had long awaited. 'I thought he was the one everyone thought of automatically when there was a question of instructing a convert.'

'I don't feel it would be right to ask Monsignor Frasso to undertake this one. There are so many demands on him that he necessarily has to be selective.'

'You're very frank,' said the priest acidly. 'So I'll be frank, too. If you insist on pushing what sounds to me like a pretty suspicious case, I'll try to find some young Jesuit or Redemptorist who can take him on. But my advice to you is to forget the missionary work for now and concentrate on putting your own house in order, spiritually and economically. How is your wife, by the way?'

'Better all the time. I think I told you her pregnancy was terminated, accidentally.'

'Yes. Though you never authorized it, I took it upon myself to say several Masses for her benefit at the time. Without stipends.'

* * *

April lay in the oversize bed, exclusive occupancy of which had been hers since her illness. She was permitted to sit up for a few hours every day but as often as not she failed to take advantage of the privilege. She hated being an invalid, the more so now that she felt perfectly well, but the compromise of a measured dose of vertical inactivity had no appeal for her.

It was a hot July day and she lay naked except for a bedjacket around her shoulders, enjoying, as much as she enjoyed anything these days, the sensation of the fresh sheets against her body. Passively she let her fancy wander, and as surely as the undirected consciousness of the contemplative who has been through the dark night of the senses will turn to God, hers came back again and again to sex. No other failing of her husband's provoked her as much as his meticulous respect for her heart condition.

She heard the sound of the doorbell downstairs and presently Mrs. Armitage, the elderly housekeeper with whom they had replaced their couple as a retrenchment measure, came up to say that Mr. Couto was calling. April was so bored that almost any interruption seemed welcome but she hesitated only a moment before instructing the woman to tell him she was unable to see him.

'I won't stay long and I promise not to upset you,' said Couto, appearing in the doorway behind Mrs. Armitage.

'I didn't say it was on account of my health I didn't want to see you,' April said. 'As a matter of fact, it isn't. I feel great.'

'That's wonderful to hear.' He advanced into the room, passing Mrs. Armitage, who looked helplessly to her employer for guidance. Dismissing the ludicrous alternative of ordering the old lady to throw him out, April said 'It's all right'. She thought to herself that at least she would be able to indulge the pleasure of telling him her opinion of him.

When the housekeeper had left them, Couto inquired after Owen, and April explained that he was involved in an all-day session with his lawyers, closing the books of the corporation. Couto expressed his concern and sympathy with regard to that misfortune. 'The moment I heard about it, I figured the least I could do was take over the bail bond. Here's a cheque. I think it's the right amount.'

'No, thank you,' she said. 'Keep it.'

'It's all right, really it is. I'm giving lectures three times a week now at five hundred dollars a throw, besides everything else.'

'Have you asked Tessie's permission?'

'How could I? She won't talk to me.'

'Have you really tried? I have an idea she'd enjoy talking to you. But I don't think you would enjoy it. Anyway, it's up to her to decide who pays for her bond. She might prefer to go to jail.'

'All right,' he said, 'if you want to be difficult about it. Suppose you just take the cheque as a loan, till Owen makes new connections.'

'We're not broke yet,' she told him coldly. 'We had enough outside the company to last us a year or so. But if we were starving, do you honestly think we'd accept money that was earned the way yours was?'

'It was earned by hard work. The kind of book I'm doing doesn't write itself. And I had thirteen tough years, remember. I never got anything from the government except expenses.' He rose from his chair and began to walk about the room while he spoke. 'It's maddening how hard it is to make people understand what I did. Most of them I don't care what they think, but your opinion is terribly important to me. I've got to make you see it my way.' He came to the side of the bed and sat down on it. April edged away from the contact with him through the covers.

'Did you join the party as a spy?' she asked contemptuously.

'No, not at first. It was after about a year that I began to realize it wasn't the place for me. They were all so grim and serious and the more I thought about workers taking over the leadership of this country, the less sense it made to me.'

'Why didn't you just quit if you didn't agree with them?'

'I was going to. But then this FBI fellow came to see me and told me I could do a real service to my country if I stayed in and tried to get on the payroll as a full-time party functionary. It was only supposed to be for three or four years but then the war started and I went into the army and when I came home they said it was even more important for me to go back in and they'd see to it I got plenty to live on.'

'Did you let them know I was paying all the rent? Oh, God! I just happened to think! That time you tried so hard to recruit me. You just wanted me to get into the party so you could have somebody else to denounce.'

'Darling!' he said reproachfully. 'You know it wasn't like that. The only reason I tried to recruit you was because Ambrose and the others kept after me to. They made cracks about whether it was safe for a man with my responsibilities to be living with a non-party person.'

'You liked Ambrose a lot, didn't you? I couldn't have been wrong about that. Was it fun turning him in? I read the other day he's been indicted under the Smith Act. Will you be a witness against him?'

'I may have to.'

'What about the Lenzes and Abe Miller and Sandy and all the people who'd lose their jobs if it got out they were party members? And what's-her-name, the girl you were sleeping with when I met you — Estelle? Did you give them her name before or after you broke up?'

'I never kept anyone out of my reports, intentionally anyway. I'd promised to give complete information and I did. But you talk about these people as if they were helpless. They don't need to lose their jobs. They can get a clearance by going to the FBI or before the committee. All they have to do is agree to name names of other people. So don't think of them as innocent victims.'

'The Lenzes' children were pretty innocent the last time I saw them. They're not going to have much of a life if the Board of Education fires their father. And what about that little girl of Ambrose's you used to take for walks? Is she going to still call you Uncle Gene when Daddy's in the clink?'

'Damn it, it isn't a thing you can afford to get sentimental about,' he said.

'Naturally I'm saving Tessie for last,' she said. 'You did get pretty sentimental about her, didn't you, suggesting she run away?

'That wasn't my idea. I was told to suggest it to her. But don't worry about Tessie. She's not going to jail.'

'What do you mean? Why isn't she?'

'Because — this is very confidential — because the Supreme Court has to throw out the verdict. It's too silly to stand up. You don't really think Mom was a foreign agent, do you?'

'Of course not.' This was a twist she hadn't anticipated and it intrigued her greatly. 'But you said she was. You were the one who testified about the European tie-up.'

'There was a lot of truth in what I said. I just made it sound worse than it actually was.'

'What for? What was the idea of the trial if it's sure to be reversed?'

'To shut down the organization,' he explained. 'The State Department was finding it very embarrassing, having respectable Americans attack their policies. It did a lot of damage in Europe.'

'But that's even worse than I thought. The idea of sending innocent people to jail . . .'

'They're not going to jail. I told you. The only result of that trial was to put a crimp in a lot of dirty anti-American propaganda before this Korean thing got started. Listen, whatever you think about it, you can't blame me for it. I didn't think up the idea of the trial. I don't make policies; I take orders. A soldier isn't supposed to question what he's told to do and I happen to believe we're in a war for survival.'

'You don't have to obey orders to perjure yourself in a court.'

'Wait a minute. I didn't say anybody told me to perjure myself. They just said how important it was to get a conviction and they gave me the assurance about Mom's sentence — in case there was a foul-up in the higher courts. April dear, you've got to believe me. I don't say I was a bloody hero, but I did what I did because I thought it was right to. Look!' He took out his wallet and extracted from it a group of newspaper clippings. 'These are just some of the editorials about me. Why don't you read what the leading newspapers in the country say about what kind of a person I am?'

She started merely to glance through them; then, her interest piqued by some of the phrases that met her eye, she went back to the first one and began to read them through. It was as impressive a collection of tributes as she could recall seeing about a living man, and she was made sharply aware that there was considerable strength to the argument in his behalf. *One of the most selfless sacrifices in the proud history of American patriotism* was how one paper described his undercover work. *Our highest medals are awarded for a few seconds of bravery in battle,* said another. *Here is a record of thirteen years of daily heroism.* Nor did the great organs of orthodox opinion ignore the conflict between family and national loyalty. *This is the stuff of which classic drama is made; if there is one nobler word in the American lexicon than 'Mother', that word is 'Country'.* And *We can only imagine the pangs Eugene Couto suffered as he watched the woman who had suckled him sinking further and further into the mire of Marxist filth. How many of us could have withstood the temptation to show our hand by extending it to help her?*

'They're all newspapers except that one from *Time Magazine*,' Couto said. He stood up, turned around and bent over her pillow, resting one knee on the bed. 'Most people think it's the best of all.' He found the clipping and drew her attention to the marked paragraph. It read: *Last week in a federal courtroom in Washington, tousle-haired Gene Couto spoke the words which would send his mother to a penitentiary. Once more a lone American stood as a symbol of his nation's role in a frightened world.*

His movement had uncovered her slightly. She turned away from him to pull the blanket and sheet around her again, inadvertently revealing enough of her back for him to realize she had nothing on below the bedjacket. The discovery surprised and excited him.

'It's always pleasanter to do things in an open and above-board way,' he said. 'Unfortunately, though, that isn't always possible. The government wants to put Communists in jail. It would be simpler if they went around practising violent overthrow, or at least saying that was what they were heading for eventually. But they don't. So we have to get them for conspiring to teach and advocate violent overthrow if and when certain circumstances arise. That's an extremely hard thing to get evidence on. You can sit in on party meetings for years and never hear anybody talk about using force except with the qualification about force being used by the other side first. Then suddenly one night somebody forgets the qualification and says it in a way you can use. That takes patience and really sticking to the job. It takes what is called an informer. I don't know why that word has an unpleasant connotation for Americans. If your information is useful and you give it to the right people, informing is a very valuable function.'

'I guess I've been influenced by the unpleasant connotation,' she said. 'I don't find that easy to accept.'

'But you know me. You know me as well as anybody in the world does. I wasn't bad or mean or vicious in any of the time we were together, was I? I don't say I didn't have faults but there were enough good things to outweigh them or you couldn't have been in love with me, could you?'

'I wasn't in love with you. I was in love with what I thought you were.'

'You loved me,' he said, 'and I loved you. I still do.' Taking advantage of the fact that her arms were under the covers now, he bent over and kissed her on the lips, holding her head in place with one hand while the other crept beneath the sheet, suggesting the full extent of his intention. It only increased her rage and humiliation to find that the sensation was not entirely unpleasant, renewing her awareness of the aching void within her that clamoured to be filled.

'Get out of here, Gene,' she said. 'Get off this bed and get out of here.'

He suddenly lifted the bedclothes and threw them aside. 'You're still the loveliest girl in the world.'

She snatched up the covers and replaced them. 'I want you to get out of here right now, this second. I don't want to have anything to do with you.'

'Sure you do,' he said with a confident smile. 'What we had isn't something you can forget.'

'There's only one thing I can't forget. I don't like you.'

'You mean you like me so much you're afraid of it.' He stood up and looked down at her with his boyish grin and twinkling eyes. 'What are you going to do, call the old lady for help?' He took off his coat, laid it on a chair and started to unloosen his tie. 'I'm kind of an exhibitionist so I don't want to have anything on when she comes up.'

'You can't force me, you know,' she said. 'I'm not that weak. There's no way you can force me.'

'I wouldn't want to try,' he said disarmingly. 'Even if I could, I wouldn't want to force you.' He had removed his shirt and begun to unfasten his belt but he stopped that and returned to the bed, sitting close to where she lay with the covers pulled around her. 'Don't turn me away, April.' His voice was suddenly plaintive. 'Don't you be like everyone else.'

He swung himself over on top of her, pressing a knee between her thighs and deftly wresting the blanket and sheet from her grasp, uncovering her to the waist. Before she had time to react to the indignity, his hands were on her shoulders holding them down while his elbows immobilized her arms. As soon as he felt secure in his command of the situation, his lips began to stray over her bosom. Once, summoning her wasted strength, she tried to throw him off, but failed even to upset the steady pattern of his kisses. Then she lay silent.

Presently she spoke in an unexpectedly soft voice. 'I thought you were going to take your clothes off.'

His eyes shone with eager delight. Pausing only long enough to raise his head and kiss her on the lips, he slid back off the bed and hastily resumed his undressing. He was removing his undershorts when she suddenly sprang up, jumped from the far side of the bed and ran into the bathroom, locking the door behind her before he could reach it.

It didn't take him long to eliminate the possibility that her escape was merely a piece of tactical coyness. From the security of her refuge she told him with calm hostility that she would under no circumstances open the door until someone came to the rescue, that she was prepared to pass the rest of the day there, and that anything further he had to say would go unanswered.

He was still standing there, nude and indignant, when he heard a quick step on the stairs and Owen's voice calling 'Darling!'

It was a classic and difficult predicament. In a matter of seconds April would presumably become aware of her husband's presence and emerge to denounce him. He would be exposed to a punitive attack from a younger and bigger man while he scrambled ludicrously to dress himself. His agile mind turned quickly from this ugly prospect to a more promising alternative. He flung himself, not under the bed as a less farsighted man might have done, but on top of it with his legs sprawled across the rumpled covers, leaning on one elbow, his face directed toward the bathroom and away from the door as Owen opened it. It was a calculated risk to display one's naked back to a potentially vindictive husband, but he thought he knew his man.

He heard the sharp intake of Owen's breath and turned towards him in guilty surprise. Owen stood in the doorway, staring at him in bewildered, uncomprehending dismay. Couto sat up, clutching the sheet across his lap as if to conceal his transgression by hiding the offending instrument of it, and raised a finger to his lips. It was a curious gesture under the circumstances but Owen was too stupefied to take exception to it. Continuing his imperious demand for silence, Couto reached over for his shorts, pulled them on and gathered up the rest of his clothes, pushing Owen into the hall and closing the door behind them.

Owen was so unprepared to accept the apparent significance of what he had come upon, so anxious to hear some other explanation that would restore his world to balance, that he couldn't do anything for the moment but dazedly respond to the other man's bidding. Overwhelming as the evidence was that his wife had betrayed him, his mind would not admit such an incredible idea without further confirmation.

'Don't blame her too much,' Couto said with emotional urgency as he dressed himself. 'It was all my fault. She's a sick girl. I took advantage of her weakened resistance.'

Owen felt the foundations of his security dropping away from him. The anguish struck him most severely not in the heart, where poetry locates the seat of the emotions, nor in the brain, where science would have it, but in the depths of the abdomen.

'This is the most unfortunate thing that could have happened,' Couto continued rapidly, 'and I'd give anything to be able to undo it. But there's no point talking about that. It's April we have to think about: the shock to her of your finding out. I don't care what you do to me; it can't be worse than I deserve. This was all my doing.'

'It's never all one person's doing,' Owen said listlessly.

'Well, seventy-five per cent,' Couto conceded. 'She'll be desperate when she comes to her senses and realizes what she's done. But that's nothing compared to the blow to her if she ever finds out you know. I seriously doubt if her heart could stand it. Tell me something: do you, could you ever love her again?'

'I don't know — it's all too sudden — I can't think.'

'Because if you have any feeling left for her, there's one thing you can do that's going to be very hard, I know, but if you can see your way to make the sacrifice....'

All the sharp distaste Owen had once had for this man was returning. 'What are you talking about?' he demanded.

'I'm asking you to turn right around and go out again. I promise you I'll leave within five minutes. Go back to wherever you were and don't return here for an hour, and when you do, don't let her suspect you suspect anything.'

'You're giving a lot of orders for a guy who ought to have his face pushed in,' Owen said. 'But I'm going to do it your way for now at least, till I've had time to think about it more.'

'That's the stuff.' Couto hastened him to the stairs. 'The face-pushing you can attend to later. I can't tell you how much I admire the way you're taking this.'

When Owen was gone, Couto stationed himself at a front window to watch him leave the building. Recalling the intimation of violence, he thought it possible the younger man might decide to wait outside for him. He was relieved to see him disappear down the block.

Couto, on reaching the street himself, cautiously took the opposite direction. He felt a warm glow of satisfaction in the way he had extricated himself from a touchy situation, and his mind dwelt on the incidental advantages he might derive from his ingenuity. It was quite likely, should the process he had set in motion proceed smoothly, that he had made more progress toward regaining April's favours by his failure than if he had successfully completed the seduction.

Walking the streets did nothing to relieve Owen's misery or free his mind of the gruesome image he had seen and the even more abhorrent ones his fancy created for him. Doubting that he could subdue his emotions sufficiently to confront April without breaking down, he returned to the lawyers' office and the monotonous details which had driven him to take a recess. It was after six o'clock when these were finally resolved and he no longer had an excuse for staying away from home.

April, he found, had made a special effort for him, dressing herself up in an alluring pair of lounging pyjamas for cocktails and an intimate dinner in her bedroom. He was pleased to discover that he was able to maintain outward composure, kissing her dutifully and complimenting her on her costume, even though each sight of her aggravated the inner wound. These interior pangs were so acute it seemed unlikely that they would ever subside enough for him to be able to forgive her — were that function under his jurisdiction. Fortunately, as he had suddenly realized during the lowest part of a grim afternoon, it was not up to a layman to decide these things. It was God against whom she had sinned directly, himself only incidentally. And it was only one of God's mortal agents to whom the power of absolution had been delegated who could free her from her guilt. If and when the sacrament of penance was conferred upon her, it would be arrogant for him to question it, superfluous for him to add his own forgiveness. Of course confession was a private matter between penitent and priest, and not even the latter could know whether contrition was complete and genuine enough to make the sacrament valid. But he, Owen, would know by the infallible marks of spirituality which distinguish a state of grace from the awful extreme of mortal sin.

When they had finished their coffee and Mrs. Armitage had removed the dinner remnants, April sat herself lovingly on the floor by his chair and told him of a telephone conversation she had had that afternoon with Dr. Goldberg. She had called him to raise the issue of sexual intercourse. 'He was very detached and professional about it,' she recalled with amusement. 'Said the question of — uh — marital relations in certain types of illness was a difficult one for the physician because he was in no position to estimate the psychic values of — well, fulfilment, which so often outweighed the — uh — physical strain. But when I told him to come off it and pinned him down to a definite answer, he owned up he was pretty surprised to hear we'd abstained so long. Said he was willing to leave it up to our common sense; indeed he considered it quite likely that moderate indulgence at this point might have a — well — uh — you might term it a therapeutic effect.' She rose to her knees, joined her hands around his neck and pulled herself up on to his lap. 'How do you feel about a little moderate indulgence?'

The flagrance of her approach under the circumstances appalled him. It took all his self-restraint not to fling her from him and revile her for her perfidy. 'I don't think it's anything to be rushed,' he said.

'Rushed?' The word outraged her. 'Do you realize . . . ?'

'Not only for medical reasons,' he continued hastily. 'I think, because of the very point that it's been so long, it's like we were starting all over again. We ought to come to each other clean and fresh and pure, with the kind of grace that lifts a marriage above the flesh. I was planning to go to confession Saturday anyway. Would you like me to ask Father Boyle to come by here to see you?'

She stood up to give freer play to her emotions, which were vehement. 'Are you trying to say that you don't want to have anything to do with me till after I've been purified by confession?'

He tried haltingly to explain. She was already late in fulfilling the obligation of at least one confession annually and he felt remiss in not having pressed the issue with her before. Thus it wasn't as if he was setting up some special requirement that wasn't due in the normal course of events anyway.

'But what could I possibly have to confess to, shut up in this miserable room day and night? I've been leading such a pure life I'm getting damn sick and tired of it!'

'Inactivity is no guarantee of grace,' he pointed out. 'Some of the worst sins are in the mind.'

'Yeah, I know. "He that looketh at a woman with lust hath committed adultery with her in his heart" or whatever the quote is. But I never took that too literally. I decided long ago that if I started confessing all my sinful thoughts, I'd have to have a confessor of my own, full time. I've never done it and I'm not going to start now, so you can just abandon that whole tack. I'm at ease with myself and that's all that counts with me.'

'You are?' His voice was pregnant with hidden meaning. 'You really can't think of a single sin you've got on your conscience? An actual sin of commission, I mean, not just a thought?' Even in his agitated state, his concern for her health was still present, and he refrained from a direct accusation.

He so obviously had something in mind that she searched her memory, and quickly figured out what it must be. 'Oh, so you found out, did you? Well, in a way it's a load off my . . .'

'I didn't say I'd found out anything,' he interrupted. 'I wasn't referring to anything in particular.'

'I've got a pretty strong hunch you were. Somebody's told you, or you've guessed, that I didn't have any miscarriage. It was a deliberate, planned, sinful abortion. And I'm rather glad it's finally out in the open, because I can tell you exactly how I felt about it and why I decided to do it.'

'My God!' It was evidence of the degree of his shock that he violated the commandment listed second in the table of St. Augustine. 'You let me give daily thanks to the Virgin for listening to our prayers, when all the time you knew . . .'

'She won't hold it against you, I'm sure. No woman could resist the kind of devotion you've been giving her.' She studied his reactions curiously. 'You're not going to tell me now that wasn't what you had in mind, are you?'

'Whether it was or not, the point's the same. You've got quite a bit to answer for, not to me but to God. Part of it has probably been my fault for failing you when you needed me, and I'm certainly ready to face up to my share of the responsibility. But it's your burden we're talking about right now. I should think you'd be eager to get rid of it.'

'Well, I'm not,' she said, 'because it doesn't bother me. I don't feel I've done anything sinful and I don't want to get into an argument about it with Father Boyle, or even an intelligent priest. I have no intention of going to confession in the immediate future and the way I feel now, I may never go again. Living with you has done a whole lot to dampen my ardour for formal religion.'

'In other words you're saying the hell with our marriage.'

'No, you are. You're the one who's laying down conditions or ultimatums or what-have-you. You didn't want me tonight and you thought up this rigmarole so you could switch the blame to me. Well, I'm not going to open myself up to you that way again, and if you change your mind, you're going to find you've got quite a lot of resistance to overcome.'

'I hope and pray you'll be the one to change your mind,' he said slowly. 'I'll be waiting for you.'

'That's nice. You won't start getting impatient after about twenty or thirty years, will you?'

'We haven't any other place to go, either of us. We'll never be able to have anyone else.'

'I'm not so sure of that,' she said. 'But I'm certainly in no shape to do anything about it right now, so I guess we're stuck with each other for a while. At least, though, we won't be crowding each other quite as much as we have been. One of the things Dr. Goldberg also said today was that I could start going out a little. And I assume, though I guess it's none of my business, that one of these days you'll begin looking for a job.'

They glared at each other with the consuming resentment which only an intimate relationship can nurture.

CHAPTER V

During Holy Week of 1951, as was his annual custom, Owen added up the indulgences to his credit. No spiritual mentor had suggested this practice to him but it seemed reasonable that if the after-life were more important than this one, so an orderly accounting of one's supernatural merits was at least as desirable as mere worldly book-keeping.

It had taken him several months following his conversion to rid his mind of popular misconceptions and vulgar distortions, and to grasp fully the beauty and significance of Catholic doctrine regarding the complicated question of indulgences. They were not, as so many heretics and pagans believed, dispensations to sin freely or even pardons for sins already committed. Eternal punishment in hell, the natural consequence of sin, could be waived only by a priest in the sacrament of penance after confession. But an undefined amount of temporal punishment was still due after such penance and absolution, and this sentence had to be served either here on earth or in purgatory. In early Christian days the church had fixed the specific number of days or years in which the penitent could wipe out the penalty by fasting and mortification. If he died before completing the term, enforcement was transferred to celestial jurisdiction and the remaining time converted into its purgatorial equivalent. In a case, however, in which the sinner showed convincing signs of more than ordinary contrition during his earthly sentence, part or all of it was remitted by competent ecclesiastical authority, drawing for his benefit on the sacred treasury of merits accumulated by Jesus, His mother and subsequent saints. Those of the Saviour alone being inexhaustible, the available supply exceeded the infinite.

It was that grant to him from the treasure assigned to the church that constituted an indulgence. Having abandoned, in the effort to broaden its appeal, the rigid ritual of its early discipline, the church still retained the terminology of so many days or years of rémitted punishment, bestowed by the indulgence of a merciful Creator acting through the visible medium of the Pope.

Considering that he had been of the faithful for less than five years, Owen had amassed an impressive total for himself. He was not so picayune as to make a note of each one hundred days earned by making the sign of the cross (without the use of holy water) and he had omitted to record the exact date on which he had acquired a richly indulgenced rosary in place of his ordinary one, thus entitling himself to an extra hundred days for each Our Father and Hail Mary. Nor was he quite clear as to just which indulgences had been suspended during the Holy Year just past in order to stimulate the incentive for a pilgrimage to Rome. Even discounting this last category, however, and stacking his calculations against himself on the others, there were long columns to add up. He was fond, for instance, of the Litany of the Holy Name and recited it daily, gaining seven years on each occasion. He had secured more than fifteen hundred years from observance of the Angelus alone, and close to six hundred from visiting churches during the Forty Hours. He had a noteworthy collection of scapulars, religious medals and other objects to which indulgences were attached. And he had been generously rewarded for the endowments and other contributions he had made during his period of prosperity. All in all, the sum of remitted temporal punishment he had earned to date, without even taking his plenary indulgences into account, came to approximately eighty-four thousand years.

He realized that this by no means represented the precise amount of time that could be allotted to shortening his stay in purgatory. An indulgence of five hundred days simply meant that the present-day sinner received as much benefit as the early Christian would have gained from a canonical penance of five hundred days duration. But it was obvious, he reasoned, that the church would never have imposed penances greater than a man could perform in his natural lifetime. Therefore, and by a gratifyingly wide margin, the modern equivalent of eighty-four thousand years in penalties surely took care of any punishment still due to him, here or in purgatory, for the sins he had already committed, confessed and been forgiven.

But even if he had overlooked some glaring error in his figures, he could still find consolation in the fact that during the same period he had been granted no less than a hundred and forty-two plenary, or comprehensive, indulgences, each one by itself wiping out all accrued temporal punishment to date. Two-thirds of these had been achieved by his diligent devotion to the stations of the cross, the remainder by such pious practices as reciting the Litany of the Blessed Virgin daily for a month; making the proper prayer before a crucifix after holy communion; wearing the medal of St. Benedict to a church on All Souls' Day; and taking communion on the first Fridays or first Saturdays of the month for nine straight months. It was true that he might have failed in the right intention or disposition on some of these occasions, thus invalidating a portion of the guarantee. But this was hardly a source of worry when he considered the fact that each plenary indulgence made all the previous ones unnecessary; of the three bestowed upon him during the previous month, certainly at least one could be counted on at its full value.

Of course he was not so selfish as to retain all these superabundant benefits for himself. There were countless souls already in purgatory, waiting entry into heaven, who were not so favoured, and his church in its almost infinite wisdom had given him the right to assign his surplus to his own selection among the dead. The number of members of the Church Suffering, personally known to him or chosen from among friends of his friends, whose upward progress he had thus expedited, amounted to perhaps eighty. The figure could not be more exact than that because, in spite of his precautions against such waste, he might have chosen several souls already damned in hell and beyond the help even of Rome itself.

He had also protected himself against the possibility of his dying suddenly with his books unbalanced. If feasible, of course, he would receive the sacrament of extreme unction and the apostolic blessing which extends a plenary indulgence to the very moment of death. But there was always the hazard of dying in sin before these measures could be administered. This risk could be mitigated by regular, frequent confession at all times, and an act of contrition could serve at the very end if the sacrament was impossible. Temporal punishment, however, for sins committed since the last award of an indulgence, might still remain to be served in purgatory. To cover this exigency he had joined the Confraternity of Our Lady of Mount Carmel, equipping himself with the miraculous brown scapular, a symbol of the one with which the Holy Mother of God had personally invested St. Simon Stock on July 16th, 1251.

Considering the relatively small expense involved, this was one of the most attractive bargains ever offered. According to pious belief, the wearer was guaranteed against the eternal punishment of hell. Also attached to it was the Sabbatine privilege, endorsed by Popes Benedict XIV and Paul V. This indulgence assured that he who wore the scapular devoutly, practised abstinence on Wednesdays and Saturdays, and died in a state of grace, would be released from purgatory on the first Saturday following his arrival there. It was true that later pontiffs had declined to reaffirm these benefits directly, and some church historians felt the Carmelite Fathers were overplaying their hand in dispensing them. But Owen, probing further into the matter, found that these reservations were immaterial. There was yet another reward, granted by God through His mortal vicar and never withdrawn, to be gained from wearing the scapular; and this one precisely filled the remaining chink in his spiritual armour. It was a plenary indulgence bestowed in advance to take effect at the hour of death. That obviously took care of the question of purgatory once and for all, even for those unfortunates who died so abruptly as to exclude the last or apostolic blessing. Even if valid, the Sabbatine privilege could not match this assurance; for with it, the penitent soul which departed its earthly shell on a Monday, say, would not be obliged to await the weekend before proceeding to eternal bliss.

Against this formidable backlog of supernatural security stood the steady deterioration of his mundane life. He had failed in business and would soon be penniless, nor could he find a job which would provide the minimum requirements to which he and

April had become accustomed. His parish priest regarded him with disfavour and Monsignor Frasso had ignored him since his refusal to reconsider his defection from CACACACS. His parents had disowned him. Such friendships as he had possessed, and he had never formed any close ones, had dissolved with the change in his material circumstances.

Most crushing of all was what had happened to his marriage. April's attitude toward him ran a limited gamut between dispassionate acceptance and overt hostility. Permitted to go out now, though still restricted in her activities, she never bothered to explain her absences to him, and he was torn by the suspicion that she was continuing her adulterous relationship with Gene Couto.

He had fared badly from the world, and for it, in return, he had little affection. His brief foray into the political struggle, culminating in the shattering disillusionment of the Peekskill affair, had greatly intensified his impulse to withdraw entirely from what passed for civilization. He felt more and more that the active life was not for him, that the tranquillity he craved was to be sought in retirement and contemplation.

Yet he still had a lingering attachment to an earlier belief that men who loved God and their neighbours should contribute what they could to bettering the conditions of mortal existence, and strive in particular for world peace, upon which all progress must be founded. The campaign toward this latter end, he had observed in a detached way, was in extremely bad shape. While ready to concede that the main menace was Soviet aggression and that the cause of the American forces in Korea was a righteous one, his experience at the Robeson concert and the prosecution of Mrs. Couto had revived some of his youthful misgivings about the state of affairs in his own country. He could not see that international harmony and the onward march of freedom were enhanced by the repression of dissent at home. There were improvements and concessions to be made in both camps, he began to think, reverting to the kind of uniglobular ideal he had fancied during the era of good feeling at the end of the war.

These sentiments met a sharp challenge one evening shortly

after Easter. The occasion was a private fund-raising meeting for Tessie Couto and her fellow-defendants, whose case was on its way to the Supreme Court after losing a split decision in the District Court of Appeals. It was April who insisted that they go. Whatever her relations with Gene, she still maintained her loyalty to Tessie.

The meeting took place in the living-room of an old house in Brooklyn Heights owned by a brother of one of the convicted officers of the defunct peace council. The principal address of the evening was delivered by another of the defendants, a man Owen had never seen before, named Alfred Samish. He was a Negro, about forty, an educational director for one of the nation's most politically active trade unions, and it was what he said that shattered Owen's new-blown hopes of finding a middle path consonant with his religion and his liberal impulses.

Sketching the main outline of events since 1945, Samish laid the blame for cold and warm warfare squarely on the American imperialist drive for world domination. Coming to Korea, he said, 'You read the State Department's own White Paper on how that war began and you find something very interesting, my friends. You find our government jumped in there and pulled the United Nations along with it, in the absence of the Soviet Union, without there being a piece of evidence that would stand up in court to show which side had crossed the Thirty-eighth Parallel first. The reason we didn't wait for any proof was because we wanted a war there and we probably pushed the South Koreans into it to save their government, which had just lost an election. The whole phony act about helping the poor Korean people falls apart when you read the reports about how we use napalm bombs, the cruellest and most fiendish weapon ever thought up short of the atom bomb. We were shocked when the Nazis wiped out the one village of Lidice in Czechoslovakia. Our planes in Korea have wiped out hundreds of peaceful villages, burning every man, woman and child to a crisp without there even being a pretence of their being military targets.

'There are two scientifically proven facts so hard for the American mind to accept that we all resist them. But they're the two facts that have got to sink into our minds or we're a lost people, dragging the world down with us in a suicidal war. The first is the enormity of what happened in Germany under Hitler. We read about six million people being butchered in ovens and gas chambers, but it's too horrible to really penetrate. The other fact is that we're basically no different from the Germans, just as capable of love or hate, just as civilized and just as savage. We don't like to think we could follow a Hitler programme but we can and we're already beginning to and we're being eased into it the same way they were. Their newspapers and their radio and their government told them they were fighting a defensive war for freedom against the great Red menace, and we hear the same thing day in and day out and it works on us like a drug till we don't see the blood under our feet and we look the other way when more and more of our own citizens right here at home are being railroaded to jail by J. Edgar Hoover's Gestapo because they dare to speak their minds.'

He proceeded to relate his general analysis to the specific case they were met to consider, advancing the opinion that the government had resorted to a frame-up because of its desperate determination to keep the truth about its war-mongering programme from the American people. He cited what he characterized as the absurdly weak evidence against Ethel and Julius Rosenberg, just convicted and awaiting sentence, as another outrageous example of rampant fascism. And he concluded his remarks with a warning that only a direct and uncompromising attack against the Washington conspiracy for world conquest could prevent the subverters of democracy from launching total war against the peace-loving peoples of Asia and Eastern Europe.

Owen felt the foundations of his liberal, middle-ground approach collapsing beneath him. No one else in the room, he noticed, seemed disturbed by the speaker's words or his vehemence. They were apparently in substantial agreement with his presentation. Yet in other houses on the street, perhaps in the almost identical one next door, were people of similar background and education, equally warmhearted and unselfish, with directly contrary views.

They believed that the United States was an almost faultless realization of the ideal of human freedom, its leaders dedicated to the maintenance of peace and democracy and only thwarted in their aims by the ruthless onslaught of Soviet despotism. Both schools of thought extended throughout the human species and included among their supporters atheists, secularists and devout believers; saints and sadists; virgins, prostitutes, mothers and lesbians; sages and simpletons; workers, farmers, poets, generals and scientists; bandits, fetishists, pragmatists, humanists and psychopaths; every age, colour, nationality and temperament to be found in mankind. The evidence seemed to indicate that the confirmed anti-Americans outnumbered the confirmed anti-Kremlinites, but there was something even more disturbing than this in Owen's estimate of the situation. That was the fact that even the lesser of the two principal factions appeared to have more adherents than the dwindling third force which sought to be a balance and a buffer between them.

In order to play any significant part in the great struggle that was shaping up, he concluded, a man had to align himself with one of these main, opposing camps and apply his energies single-mindedly to the defeat of the other one; if possible before the conflict was enlivened by the hydrogen bombs now in work. But Owen knew he could never overcome his reservations about either extreme view to the extent necessary for such militant partisanship. It became clearer than ever to him that he must find a way of serving human society without participating in it.

The first measure on his agenda was to see if he could arrest the disorderly collapse of his marriage. Without consulting April, he invited Gene Couto to cocktails. Five years previously such a tripartite conference had been successful in resolving the differences among them. It was not beyond hope that a similar meeting could serve to clarify their present problems.

The two men sat facing each other before April joined them. This time it was Owen who was in nominal possession of her, but he derived no assurance from the fact. Couto was equally ill at ease; he had reacted warily to the invitation, fearing a trap, then come anyway on the slight chance he might be able to turn the situation to his advantage.

After mixing a pitcher of extra-dry Martinis and calling April to come downstairs, Owen made a halting observation about the major topic of the day: General MacArthur's farewell address to Congress. Couto responded enthusiastically. 'It was a thing of beauty and a joy for ever. The performance was in the great tradition but where it really stands out is as a piece of writing. I think every other prominent author in America will agree with me that he's the best stylist for that kind of thing there is.'

'Our allies seem to think he's a rather dangerous character,' Owen said.

'Screw them. We waste a lot of time worrying about what people think in England and France and places like that. I was explaining it to a couple of Senators last month; they came out to see me in Hollywood about an internal security bill they needed some help on. I told them this constant American sensitivity to European opinion was an anachronism, a hangover from the days when we needed Europe as much as they needed us. I'm making the same point on a television symposium Sunday night, not as baldly of course; there's no sense kicking them in the teeth just because they've always got their mouths open.'

April appeared on the stairs and the two men rose to greet her and to enjoy the physical effect of her entrance. She had been spending a good deal of time outdoors lately and her cheeks had regained their rare natural colour. Her body, a few pounds lighter than before her illness, was as youthful as ever in a simple gabardine skirt as black as the hair which fell loosely to the shoulder-line of her white silk blouse. Only the grey eyes were older, but the zest they had lost was replaced by a seasoned discernment which raised her beauty to a higher level. Unprepared for the occasion, she met it with composure, greeting Couto with neither warmth nor open antagonism and directing a curious glance toward Owen as he supplied her with a drink.

Owen accepted his obligation, as the initiator of the meeting, to open the discussion. 'In one sense, it's the same situation we met about a long time ago. What we straightened out then seems to have worked itself back into the same triangle pattern.'

'Who says it has?' April broke in, her voice expressing astonishment and indignation.

'Yes, what kind of talk is that?' Couto said. 'Are you making some sort of accusation?'

'I think we all know what I'm speaking about,' said Owen. 'April's well enough now so we don't have to worry about bringing it out into the open.'

'You don't know what you're saying,' Couto said nervously. 'If I'd realized what you had in mind, I never would have agreed to come. As a matter of fact, you know what I think? I think you and I ought to ask April to excuse us and have a little talk first between ourselves.'

'The hell with that,' April said. 'There's something damn peculiar going on and I want to know what it is.' She faced Owen challengingly. 'What's this triangle business? What makes you say a thing like that?'

'He saw me that day,' said Couto quickly. 'Last summer when I came to see you.'

'Oh.' She considered the import of this revelation, matching it with her recollections of the aftermath of the event. 'I might have figured out that something like that had gone on.'

'I guess he jumped to a conclusion about what had happened between us,' Couto continued.

'Jumped, did he?' she said. 'Or was he pushed?' She turned to her husband again. 'Is that why you froze up on me all of a sudden? You thought I went to bed with Gene?'

'I know you did. He confessed.'

'This is pointless,' Couto said, getting to his feet and plotting the route of a possible sudden escape. 'You people have things to talk out and I'm just an intruder here . . .'

'You sit down!' April commanded him. 'I'll get around to you after some other things are straight in my head.' To Owen she said, 'So that's what this session is about, is it? You've worked it out that we're in the same spot we were five years ago, only with the roles switched around between the two of you?'

'In more than one way,' Owen said with a bitter smile. 'He made a great point then about my prospects being better than his. If that's a consideration now, I'll have to admit Mr. Couto's future looks a lot brighter than mine.'

'Naturally it's a consideration,' she said. 'Especially if I'm going to be a semi-invalid all my life. I need someone to support me. Gene can do that. Gene's a man of property. Gene's a best-seller. They've made a movie about him. Gene's a national hero.'

Owen was bewildered by her sarcasm. She seemed to have even more malice toward his rival than toward him.

'I don't know why she grudges me my success,' Couto said to Owen, turning up his palms in mock despair. 'It isn't what I did she minds so much as the fact that I made money out of it.'

'That's not very reasonable,' Owen agreed. 'The money's a separate, later issue. Unless, of course, it was your original motive.'

'Motives are mixed-up things,' said Couto. 'People don't often really know exactly why they took a given step.'

'God does. There are some things it's easy for us to make moral judgments about. Like adultery. Whatever rationalizations and justifications you can think up, it's always wrong and you're both guilty on that score. But the other question is something it's hard for another person to judge. Some of the results may have been unfortunate, but that doesn't matter if your intentions were pure. And I can't possibly know. Still,' — now he was speaking to April — 'I think we should give him the benefit of the doubt.'

She got up and poured herself another helping of gin almost imperceptibly flavoured with vermouth. 'That's very generous of you, my sweet, and typical of your noble character. But I don't feel quite that humble about it. I think we can judge people like Gene and I think we have an obligation to, because his type is getting pretty common these days. But getting back to the issue, are you figuring that maybe I'm planning to leave you for Gene?'

'You can't. There's a big difference between the situation now and the way it was the other time. You're my wife and we were married by an unbreakable sacrament. Even if you decided now you loved him more than you did me, you couldn't do anything about it, at least not without giving up something a lot more important than happiness on earth.'

'I think you'd better let me take care of my soul,' she said. 'If I stay with you, you can be sure it won't be because of duty or conscience. And if I ever want to enough, I'll get myself a divorce and to hell with the consequences. You'd be surprised how much less my religion means to me now that I've seen what it's done to you. So let nobody hold anything over anyone else's head.'

'That's right,' Couto agreed. 'We ought to keep this on the highest possible plane.' He had begun to think the meeting could end only in unpleasantness for him, but now the irrepressible fount of his optimism rose to sustain him. Instead of proceeding directly to the attack on him, April was working toward some sort of crisis between Owen and herself. And such a crisis might conceivably be exploited to his own benefit.

April ignored his contribution and continued her examination of Owen. 'And now that that's clear, let's get to the next step. What would you do if I were so depraved and ungrateful as to leave you?'

He paused for only a moment before he gave her his earnest answer. 'Something I've been wanting to talk to you about anyway, I suppose. I've done a lot of thinking about it and it's taken me a long time to be sure, but I feel the place I really belong is in a monastery.'

'My God!'

'Come on, baby,' Couto said, 'let me take you out of here. Whatever you think of me, this jerk's beyond hope.'

But she was just absorbing the full implication of what Owen had said. 'What do you mean, you've been wanting to talk to me about it anyway? You said you called this session to straighten us out, didn't you? Do you mean if I said I was sorry and please forgive me and I'd be a good wife to you, you'd still go off and leave me? Or if you were wrong about me and Gene and there was nothing to forgive, you'd want to do the same thing anyway?'

'Not if you didn't agree,' he said. 'A married man can't just walk out on an innocent wife and become a monk. But what I'm really thinking about is the possibility that you might want to take vows at the same time. That way, if I ever came to feel it was my true vocation, I'd be eligible for major orders — not just be a lay-brother but a priest too.'

'You can strike that off your programme. But if all you need to go into a monastery is my permission, you've got it. Though when I think you never could have come to this if it hadn't been for me, that's something on my conscience worse than anything else I've ever done.'

'You didn't make him queer, baby,' Couto said. 'You tried to help him.'

Again she disregarded him in her effort to probe the recesses of her husband's mind. 'There's one thing I'd like explained. I'm willing to believe you're sane, Owen, in a loose sense of the word. But how could you bring yourself to think it was even remotely possible that I'd want to go into a convent? You must have gathered some idea of what I'm like in all this time, even if you don't usually act as if you had.'

Owen smiled. 'It does sound kind of far-fetched, doesn't it? But consciences are strange and wonderful things. Sometimes a sudden revelation — a facing-up to the fact of one's sins — can change a person's whole life. Like Saint Paul.'

'I see,' she said thoughtfully. 'You figured if you were big-hearted enough to let me come skulking back to you, you could work on my sense of guilt till I didn't have any will of my own left. You figured you could browbeat me and preach at me and make me so ashamed of myself I'd be willing to crawl into a corner somewhere and spend the rest of my life on my knees. Well, you can take credit for one piece of good judgment anyway. I certainly would feel ashamed of myself if I'd ever let myself become a stool-pigeon's whore. But I didn't and I don't have any particular burden on my conscience and once I've tossed you out of my life, I'll find a way to get along and make myself feel useful again, even if I do have to adjust to some kind of limitation on account of my heart.

I'm only twenty-eight years old and I feel at least that young and I'm ready to start all over again fresh and clean in all departments, including love and sex which happen to be very important to me.'

'What do you mean, you didn't?' demanded Owen. 'Are you trying to make me believe ...'

'Wait a minute,' Couto interrupted, asserting priority for his own complaint against her. 'You use a word like stool-pigeon because you think it will hurt me, but name-calling is just a cheap substitute for thinking. I've been over this same ground with you before and I thought you'd have the sense to see the point that some values have to be sacrificed to other ones or a man would just stand still, unable to move in any direction. Now mankind happens to be organized, rightly or wrongly, into nations, and it's simply a recognition of that fact that makes the intelligent individual with the courage of his convictions place the national interest ahead of his own. Provided they come into conflict. Of course when they happen to coincide, as in my case, why that's a splendid thing all round and just one more proof that a well-adjusted society distributes its highest rewards to the very people who contribute the most to it.'

'Will you be quiet!' Owen was impatient to get his chance at April. 'I'd like to know just what you claim happened that day. I came into the room and saw ...'

She interrupted him. 'I don't have any strong urge to justify myself to you. What I'd really like is if both of you cleared out of here. Or I can go upstairs; it doesn't matter. I simply want to say this first though. You' — to Owen — 'talk a lot about love of God, and you' — to Couto — 'defend yourself on the grounds of love of country. But God is an abstraction that means one thing to one person and nothing at all to somebody else, and it's only guesswork whether He gives a damn if we love Him or not. As for love of country, it always gets mixed up with love of a particular government that happens to be in power, and it can be used to justify anything from napalm bombing to making Jews into soap. The kind of love I trust is a love of people and you can't square that with informing on men and women you've given reason to think you're their friend. You had me confused for a while with your fancy argument about how the people you squealed on didn't have to go to jail or lose their jobs or whatever. They could see the light the way you did and stop being traitors to their country and all would be forgiven. But that's the same choice the people who were turned in to the Inquisition had, or the Gestapo. They were always free to recant their heresy and start turning in heretics themselves.

'I don't know whether your mother's politics are any sounder than yours. To me that doesn't matter. I just know she's good and decent and my friend and I trust her, and you aren't my friend and I don't trust you. It was completely in character for you to try to rape me and then when I got away from you, revenge yourself by making my poor simple-minded husband think I'd gone to bed with you.'

'I didn't really mean any harm . . .' Couto began, bracing himself for a quick retreat as he watched Owen's face.

'Is that true?' Owen broke in. 'Is that what really happened?'

'Ask him,' she said. 'I locked myself in the bathroom and I guess you must have come in while I was still there, and seen him. So he thought it was cuter or safer or something to make it seem like you'd caught us in the act.'

Couto put his cocktail glass down and swung a leg over the arm of his chair, sliding to his feet on the other side of it so as to keep an obstacle and a safe distance between himself and Owen, who sat transfixed in self-reproach. April also got up and headed for the stairs.

'I should have known it wasn't possible,' Owen said. 'It just never occurred to me he'd have any reason . . .' He broke off, all his emotions congealing into an outburst of rage against Couto. He stood up, his face reflecting his violent intention.

Couto moved backwards away from him, working toward the apartment door. When he reached the entrance hall, he stopped momentarily. The Muirs also stood still, watching him with hostile stares, Owen from where they had been sitting, April from the stairway. 'Can't anybody around here take a joke?' Couto inquired defensively. Then he turned quickly, opened the front door and ran out, slamming it behind him.

Owen started after him but stopped before he reached the door, looking up toward April as she ascended the stairs. Suddenly his desire to seek her forgiveness and heal the wound he had inflicted became more urgent than the impulse to vengeance against Couto.

She was sitting at her dressing-table in the gathering darkness when he came up. He stood behind her, wanting to touch her and not daring to. Only the vague outlines of their faces and the white of her blouse showed in the large mirror.

He repeated the self-indictment he had voiced downstairs, 'I should have realized it wasn't possible.'

'I'm sure Gene painted a very convincing picture for you,' she said. 'I don't really blame you for believing him. But that wasn't actually the main issue between us, was it, even though it's probably what you had in the back of your mind? The question was whether I was ready to purify myself for you by confession.'

'I was wrong on that too.'

'Were you?' There was a new note of interest in her voice.

'Yes. I should never have put it in the form I did, as a condition. I was practically blackmailing you. You've lost your faith and that's a very sad thing, but I think I can help you find it again. Only now I see that the way to do it is to first get back to what we had once and I believe we can have again. We need a foundation to build on, the foundation of our love.'

'You don't think it's too rickety after all this time?' The warmth of her smile did much to counteract the scepticism of her words. 'Full of rot and decay and little termites gnawing here and there?'

'No, I don't.' He knelt on the floor beside her stool and put his arms around her, resting his head against her breast. 'If you can forgive me, I think we'll have a more solid basis to go on than ever, now that it's weathered and tried.'

There were still too many lingering doubts in her mind for her to make an uncompromising answer. But she asserted no restraint over her physical response to him as their lips joined ardently. Nor did she indicate any reservation when he picked her up in his arms and carried her to the bed, the better to continue their embraces. And it was she who was the first to rise after a while and begin undressing.

She had removed her skirt, blouse and brassière when the barrier between them returned to her consciousness in an old, familiar form. He lay on the bed still, watching her with the unfailing delight her body always brought to him. Her own desire was so stimulated by his that she was severely tempted not to confront him yet with so direct an issue. At the same time she knew that it must be faced and that on his response rested the hope of anything more enduring between them than a fleeting moment of physical union.

'There's one thing,' she said. 'I never reported to you a point Dr. Goldberg made, because we didn't ever get far enough so I had to, but he's mentioned it a couple of times since. He doesn't want me to get pregnant till he's made definitely sure my heart has what they call "compensated" for the damage to it.'

The rapturous anticipation on his face yielded to acute dismay. He sighed as he stood up and drew her into his arms. It was an embrace of tender affection rather than the eager passion he had so recently displayed. 'Then I guess we'll just have to wait a while longer.'

'No.' She pulled away from him, her body as rigidly determined as her voice. 'No, we've waited long enough already, maybe too long. How do I know what the tests will show? It might be another year or two before it's safe for me to have a baby. But even if we only had to wait a week, I'd say the same thing. I want you to go to bed with me now, on my terms, or we're through. I mean it, Owen. That's definitely, unalterably, positively final, and if I could think of a few other words, I'd throw them in too.'

The remnants of his desire were dissolved by his horror at what she was suggesting. And along with the shock came a deep sadness, for he sensed as fully as she did the finality of the conflict. Without any real hope of persuading her, he nonetheless felt obliged to make the attempt. 'The more deliberately you put it, the worse it becomes. You want us to break a divine law in the most flagrant possible way, with cold-blooded premeditation. I know you have the ability to rationalize your way out of these things and still consider yourself a Christian, but I can't do it; I'm not made that way. If I agreed to go back now to the kind of prostituted marriage we had the first two years, I'd be abandoning the church.'

'Okay, abandon it. They won't be any worse off than they were before they got you. I'll go along with you; I know when I've had enough.'

He found it difficult to believe that she could conceive by herself of such a monstrous proposition. Perhaps she had been possessed by a devil, by one of those fallen angels who, according to Catholic doctrine, occasionally seize control of a helpless mortal's limbs and organs. If that were the case, he was powerless to rescue her; only a bishop or a properly instructed priest could pronounce the ritual of adjuration and exorcise the alien visitor.

'What you're suggesting for both of us,' he said, 'is that we deliberately choose the fires of hell in preference to eternal salvation. That's what leaving the church means.'

'Prove it.'

'I can, easily. Less than a year ago the Pope denounced those who reduce to "a meaningless formula" the doctrine that you have to belong to the true church in order to be saved. And even if there is a narrow loophole for a few people who never were Catholics, it's absolutely definite there's no possible hope for those who were once and quit being.'

'Is that all?'

'What do you mean?'

'Are you finished with your proof?'

'I don't see there's anything you'd want added to it.'

'Don't you? That's the final touch. You've cured me of a blight I've had over my life since my tiny fingers clutched my first crucifix. And now I'd like you to leave me alone if you don't mind. Forever. Get thee to a monkery, go; farewell!'

There was nothing he could think of to say, no appeal that would penetrate the shell of her corruption. He spoke her name falteringly and that was all.

'Please!' she said, her voice breaking at last. 'I want to be by myself.'

He couldn't resist taking a final look at her as he went through the door. She stood there in her stockings and panty-girdle, the incarnation of the Satanic temptation of the flesh.

CHAPTER VI

ONE more meeting between them was required to resolve the mechanics of their separation. The only question that gave them any trouble was the specific technicality which would liberate Owen for the religious life. He had not realized it would be a problem; according to canon law all April had to do beyond giving her consent was to take a vow of lifelong chastity so that his retirement would not be the occasion of another's sin. This, however, she firmly refused to do.

'I can't explain it,' she said, 'but I just have a funny kind of scruple against making a solemn promise I have no intention of keeping.'

He assured her he had not meant to propose any such deception. Rather it was his expectation that, despite what she had said, under emotional stress, about her carnal future, she would see the ugly unacceptability of taking another mate while her rightful one still lived. The vow as he conceived it would be no impediment but a source of strength and comfort to her when temptation came.

'Look,' she told him with finality, 'no vows. I'll release you from all responsibility for what happens to me, but that's as far as I'll go. Now isn't there some other way of fixing things so you can do what you want? I seem to have heard of married people going into convents or monasteries without their husband or wife making any commitments, or even being consulted.'

'That's true — where there's been misconduct. Then the injured party has the right to refuse to have anything to do with the other one, ever. He's freed of any responsibility for her and can do anything he likes, except marry again.'

'Oh.' She considered this. 'Would have been simpler for you, wouldn't it, if I really had carried on with Gene? But what about my attitude on the birth control thing? After all, I gave you a very immoral ultimatum, saying I was leaving you unless you agreed to a sin. That's misconduct, isn't it?'

'I'm not sure; I'd have to look it up. I think misconduct in that sense means adultery and nothing else.'

'Okay then,' she said with sudden resolution. 'Let's make it adultery. I won't admit to Gene, because that's going too far, but it can be almost anyone else. Six different men if you like. I had a different lover every season for the last year and a half.'

'But you didn't.'

'Who says I didn't? Who ever heard of anyone proving a wife was faithful when she confesses that she wasn't?'

'I know you were.'

'No, you don't, Owen. You don't know very much about me at all, and you certainly haven't more than the vaguest idea what I've been thinking and feeling and doing the last year or so. I'll look you in the eye and give you a list of the men I've been to bed with, and you won't be able to tell with any real assurance whether I'm telling you the truth or not.'

In the end he had to admit she was right. He didn't know and never would know the degree of evil to which she might be led by the manifest impurities of her mind and soul. What was irrefutable and decisive was that she was the one who had destroyed their marriage by refusing him his conjugal rights. That absolved him of all responsibility toward her, and the fact that he would still pray for her was simply an expression of gratuitous generosity on his part.

It was not at all hard for him to select the particular religious order in which to pass the remainder of his life. If the Carthusians had had an establishment in the United States, he probably would have settled on them because their rule was the most severe, their mortifications the most onerous. But the Cistercians, popularly known as Trappists, had almost equally appealing hardships to offer, and they were closer at hand. He made a preliminary retreat at one of the older foundations of the order; then, on the advice of the abbot there, he applied to, and was accepted as a postulant in, a new monastery housed in Quonset huts in a bleak and improbable section of the Texas Panhandle. After six months he was admitted to the novitiate, where he would remain for two years before making his simple vows. Another three years would be required until he could commit himself irrevocably by solemn vows. But even in the first months of his probation Owen knew that this was the only existence for him until that final happy hour when a merciful providence bestowed, as it did upon all deserving mortals, the blessing of death which is eternal life.

To him one of the greatest joys of the Trappist regime was the enforced silence. He had long felt that the gift of speech had never been properly appraised in terms of whether it was a function to be employed automatically and almost continuously whenever two or more persons were within voice range, or whether it was not better restricted to essential communication. Even as a layman he had begun to suspect that there was more to be gained by an hour of silent communion between one individual and another than by an hour of talk for talk's sake. Now he realized that in a well-organized community where social relations were uncomplicated and the work largely of a menial nature, a simple sign-language sufficed admirably. Words, spoken or sung, were reserved for addressing one's superiors, both local and celestial.

What misgivings he had felt about his ability to endure the rigours of monastic life were soon dispelled. His youth and physical strength won him some of the most arduous agricultural tasks but he found their very monotony a rewarding stimulus to pious meditation. His hearty appetite, at first an obstacle to ascetic fasting, withered rapidly under the subversive influence of unappealing food unimaginatively prepared. Even getting up at two o'clock in the morning to begin the observance of the Divine Office was much less of an effort when one rose from planks and straw than it would have been from a foam-rubber mattress. And his vow of obedience — the absolute surrender of responsibility for even the smallest details of his life to the authority of his superiors — freed his mind of all the besetting worries which separate the worldly man from his God.

No radio or television, no newspaper or profane reading of any kind, intruded upon his inner peace. The world as he had left it in the middle of 1951 had seemed to him an ugly place, seething with sin and discord and a frenetic drive toward self-annihilation. There was no reason to think it had improved since he had lost touch with it. But he felt no remorse over having abandoned his obligations to society. He knew that he and his fellow cenobites were actually contributing more to human welfare by apparently ignoring it than all the statesmen, scientists, artists and prelates who dwelt in the cities of men. For his church taught that while there were many acceptable variations of the truly Christian life, the noblest and holiest of them all was that of the monk or nun. A God Who demanded constant attention and praise was not apt to distribute His grace without specific and reiterated requests for it. The overwhelming majority of His creatures prayed to Him insufficiently, heretically, idolatrously or not at all. The religious in their convents and monasteries, liberated from all inordinate attachments to other individual mortals, helped to make up this lack with their unceasing prayers, both ritualistic and contemplative, on behalf of mankind as a whole.

Yet it was essential never to lose sight of the main concentration on one's own personal salvation. Passive abandonment to the adoration of God and the veneration of His mother, so long as it did not descend into the fallacy of complete quietism, was far purer than an obsession with good works, Owen learned. So many Christians, even priests, suffered from the delusion that pious activities were an end in themselves. They did not realize that mere deeds, however beneficial to others, were usually a form of self-assertion, an impulse inferior to the self-despising eminence of mystical contemplation. The first stage on the road to self-transcendence was to recognize one's own deficiencies and, like Saint Teresa of Lisieux, to glory in them — to be glad that one's immanent personality was mean, ignominious and of no conceivable consequence. From this vantage-point selfhood was clearly a condition above which a man ought to ascend.

The lives of famous monks and ascetics inspired him with their many examples of such selflessness. There was Saint Louis of Gonzaga, who was so determined to avoid impurity and preserve his virginity that at the age of twelve he gave up all contact or conversation with the female sex, specifically including his own mother, nor ever again permitted himself to touch or smell a flower lest he find pleasure in it. Such forbearance had led naturally to his selection as the patron saint of all young people. Another model was Saint Peter of Alcantara, who for forty years never exceeded his self-assigned quota of ninety minutes sleep in every twenty-four hours, reinforcing his will-power by means of a cell only four and a half feet long, making it impossible for him to lie down. And there was the Blessed Henry Suso, who showed his contempt for his corporeal person by going without a bath for twenty-five years, and equipped himself for his nightly repose with a garment lined with a hundred and fifty brass nails, pointed inward; these the holy man sharpened during his hours of daytime meditation.

The goal, he discovered in the writings of Saint John of the Cross and Saint Teresa of Avila, was to free oneself from all interest in the pleasures and paraphernalia of material existence. Then the mind and the soul, functioning in new-found unity, could abandon mere logic and the processes of reasoning, and open themselves to the awareness of God. The true contemplative did not will his intelligence to mystical thoughts; they were infused into his unresisting spirit from outside, from above. The pioneers in this field had charted the course to the heights which a divinely favoured soul might attain while still in its mortal coil. The way led upward from meditation through the dark night of the senses to contemplation; from ecstatic union through the dark night of the soul to the spiritual betrothal; and finally into the seventh mansion of the interior castle: the spiritual marriage, in which the soul is joined to the Holy Ghost in an indissoluble union, and Christ, no longer a random visitor, is in permanent residence.

It was an encouraging sign of his progress along these lines that he was able, after less than two years in the monastery, to receive the news of the death of his mother with almost none of the emotion he would have felt while still dependent on earthly relationships. The information came to him in a letter from his father, who, after a terse, formal announcement of the event, continued:

... The cancer specialist admitted to me that her decline may well have been speeded up by emotional factors, and I have no doubt that her disappointment in you played its part. The only reason your thoughtless behaviour upset her more than it did me was because I saw long ago that your sister was the only one of my children I could expect anything from. She has really settled down since Little Dennis came. For the whole last month of the campaign she wouldn't smoke anything but 'I Like Ike' cigarettes, and you know how she used to be about politics. *Vogue* had a spread on her hat collection in the February issue.

I don't imagine I will be writing you again so I will take this opportunity to say goodbye and good luck in spite of everything.

Yours truly,
Dad

P.S.: As long as you are saying so many prayers all the time, you might as well include me in some of them.

His only other link with the outside world was Arnold Blankenship, who came to the monastery for a weekend retreat and to secure Owen's signature on a release entitling him to use their former corporate name in a new venture. Owen, who felt a personal responsibility toward the man's spiritual development, was pleased to hear he was continuing to give favourable consideration to joining the church although he still felt himself insufficiently purified for the final step. It was also gratifying to listen to his enthusiasm about monastic life after observing it for almost thirty hours.

'This is big!' he told Owen when the latter finally received permission to come and visit him in the guest house. 'All those men going around thinking such profound thoughts and never opening their mouths. The silence is sensational! You get a sense of something happening on all sides of you that's larger and more important than you are, more important than all of us put together. I think it's going to catch on. Everyone is more aware of the infinity around us in these terrible days, even kids. That's why one of the projects I have a lot of faith in is this interplanetary handbook we're putting out, with maps and figures to help them really understand the action in these TV and radio programmes. I have an associate professor of astronomy at Columbia checking it to make sure everything is scientifically accurate so when they see one of these space patrol ships setting out from Mercury to Krypton, say, they'll know exactly what's involved.'

He also brought news of April. Apparently her health was progressing very nicely for she had served a strenuous term as secretary of Tessie Couto's defence committee until the case reached the Supreme Court, which found a technical error in the indictment and set aside the verdict. Blankenship had warned her of the dangers involved in such suspect activity but she insisted that she found it stimulating and was looking for more unpopular causes to embrace. She confided in him further that she was going around with a young theatrical scenic designer and would probably marry him after she secured a divorce from Owen. This revelation led Blankenship to assume that she would also be renouncing the faith of her forebears, but she assured him she had no such intention. 'I suppose they can throw me out if they want to,' she told him, 'but I don't see any reason why I should try to beat them to the draw. We had a priest on the defence committee who's still taking care of his parish even though his bishop won't talk to him. Anyway the point is it's up to me in the end to decide whether I'm a Catholic or not. How can I possibly know now what things I'll be sorry for thirty or forty years from now?'

Owen was pleased to hear that she had not damned herself irrevocably but he was distressed by her unregenerate pursuit of false gods. Blankenship, sensing how deeply affected he was, tried to soften the blow with a more cheering piece of information. The church, he understood from a dependable authority, was about to gain the adherence of Gene Couto, who was now taking instruction from Monsignor Frasso. His conversion, dramatizing the affirmative answer to the evil casuistry of Marxism, was going to be treated with appropriate fanfare, including a photographic account of the event in one of the large picture magazines.

The hour allotted to the visit came to an end before Owen had gotten around to signing the release form. Blankenship recalled the obligation to his mind by thrusting the paper in front of him and slipping a pen into his hand. The document was executed; the two men bade each other a final farewell and hurried off, the older to his waiting taxi, the younger to join the brothers in chanting *None*, the mid-afternoon division of the Divine Office.

The after-effects of the intrusion were disturbing to Owen; it was several days before he could purge himself of the unspiritual thoughts which infiltrated his meditations. He resolved to permit himself no more such unsettling contacts with secular life.

Throughout this period he had some vestigial manifestations of fleshly desire to contend with. He found his ultimate liberation from them in one of those seeming accidents by which the lives of the holy are so often guided. Some altered factor in his diet or some reduction in the sanitary refinements to which he was accustomed caused him, during his second year in the monastery, to suffer an outbreak of painful boils. At one time or another every region of his body was afflicted and he was forced to spend many hours drawing the poison outward with hot compresses or, when the location suited that technique, with sitz-baths. These treatments, at first an annoying interruption to the working and liturgical day, soon developed into a curious blend of pain and pleasure. There was something familiar and gratifying in the slow accumulation of tension as the infection rose to a focal point, and the almost exquisite relief when the noxious fluid was finally discharged.

His only form of intimate physical expression, it had the added merit of being free from any sense of guilt. There were many days when he could never have attained the composure necessary for meaningful prayer, save for the bringing to a head of a new boil.